CHAPTER 1

NOX KAGE

She's not dead.

I've been saying it over and over in my head. She's not dead. She's not dead. She's not dead.

"The arrangements for the Dark Princess's cortege need to be handled. The Dark Lord hasn't been—"

"I'm the Dark Lord." Onyx's bark cuts through the air, making one of Lord Blackwell's advisors flinch. I stare straight ahead at the cocky prick I've despised since our first introduction. "Do not speak ill of the Dark Lord Former. He's grieving the daughter he lost so soon after getting her back. There will be no cortege for the Princess. Not yet."

I study the new Dark Lord from where I stand in the throne room. The same room my Ren had her heart ripped out mere days ago. My own heart clenches at the memory of walking into the room at the exact moment The Reaper, disguised as me, shoved his hand into her back and stole her last breath.

Onyx's hands are clenched at his sides, resting on the throne's velvet fabric. While he looks angry, I can't help but feel my blood boil at the smug look on his face. He's loving this. Ruling and bossing people around. Right before Ren was ripped from us, Onyx's blood dripped into the sacred satchel. That sealed him as Dark Lord, whether Adrienne was ruling by his side or not.

"But, sir. It's disgraceful not to mourn the Dark Princess in front of our people. We need to celebrate her life and let her soul rest." Jasper, the advisor that keeps talking back to Onyx, looks at me rather than the new Dark Lord. He thinks I will agree with him. He thinks I will want to continue on with tradition.

"You will call me Dark Lord. And it's disgraceful for you to question the leader of your kingdom. We will not be mourning Dark Princess Adrienne until we have further answers." Jasper's eye twitches with the glare he still has directed at me. I haven't said a word. Mostly because I can't speak. I can barely breathe through the pain coursing through my veins. The pain of losing the love of my life. Of losing my mate.

"Yes, Dark Lord." With that, he leaves Onyx and I alone in the huge throne room, letting the quiet consume us. He turns to look at me where I'm standing. His eyes squint like he's staring at something too bright. Like the sight of me is painful.

"What?" My voice sounds foreign to my own ears. I haven't spoken since Adrienne was taken from us. I haven't told anyone about the surge of power that entered me, knocking me out, the minute Ren's heart was ripped from her. I haven't told anyone I can still feel her song dancing in my spine, faint and quiet.

"She loved you, shadvir. For some reason, she loved you."

"Loves me." I shouldn't have said it, but I can't stop it from sneaking past my lips. My mouth forms a thin line with my admission, knowing he was trying to pull something out of me.

"Ah, so you agree? You think she's still alive?" He raises a brow and a slight smirk greets me.

"Doesn't matter what I think. I'm just a shadvir. Why do you think she's still alive, Dark Lord?" While I make sure to respect him, I spit the words out like they are poison. I don't respect him.

"Well, that's exactly why, Kage. You're just a shadvir. The Dark Princess's shadvir to be exact. Tell me, what happens to a shadvir when their bond is broken by death?" My silence is answer enough. We both know the truth. "So how are you standing in front of me right now?"

"She's not dead," I whisper the words, finally saying them out loud for the first time since it happened.

"My question is how. How the fuck is our pretty little Adrienne alive if The Reaper ripped her heart out? I watched it happen right in front of me. I watched the life leave her." I clench my teeth and avoid answering, trying not to get angry. "It's a pity he did before I was able to marry her. I've imagined claiming her almost every night since meeting her. Making her forget about you while she's screaming my name."

I can't control it. I feel the anger rising inside of me and it feels like burning fire tickling every inch of my skin. I walk towards him, trying to control my breath as my eyes feel like they are going to melt from my skull. "Shut. The. Fuck. Up."

"I knew it!" The smile on his face makes me falter, the burning subsiding just barely. "I knew you two were bonded. You have her powers. I see her lilac and red shining through in your eyes. That's why you didn't die when she did. That's why you know she's still alive. Because you're her mate. You can feel her."

His voice sounds distant through the boiling rage still sizzling inside of me. "Calm down, Kage. I was just trying to rile you up so you'd get angry and show me the truth. I didn't mean any of it. Well... I mean, of course I did. Just look at the girl. But I care about the princess too. She's become a... friend of mine. I was willing to give up the throne for her. To make her happy, so you two could be together."

I take a deep breath and try to calm myself. Something inside of me whispers to think of cold things. To bring the magic back into its golden ring in my head. While it doesn't sound like an actual voice, and rather a deep-rooted feeling, I know it's her. I know Ren is telling me how to bring it back in.

"That's a good little shadvir." His mocking voice grates at my skin but I manage to cool my rage down to a slight simmer deep in my bones. "Now, let's talk about what we are going to do."

"We need to tell Lord Blackwell. We need to get the entire kingdom to start—"

"We will do no such thing. We need to be careful who knows about your little bond. That's never been seen before and it could cause an outrage. I need to control the people of this kingdom. I need to keep order and an impossible mating bond and their beloved princess being trapped somewhere unknown is only going to destroy our hopes at finding her."

I let his words sink in, realizing he's right. That's exactly what would happen. People would panic and finding her would come second to the questions of the first mating bond to ever exist.

"So, what do we do?" I try to control my glare as I look at the man before me. His blonde hair is perfectly styled on his head, most likely something a stylist spent hours doing this morning. His lilac eyes squint, the corners raised slightly with his smirk.

"We work together to find her. We put on a fake cortege to please the kingdom, and then we figure out how to get our girl back." The growl that escapes me at his words makes his hands go up in defense. "Down boy. Your girl, okay?"

"Alright, fine. We'll do it your way. I have no idea where to start." The minute I say those words, something clicks in my brain. "Actually... I do." Rather than explain myself, I simply turn and walk away, leaving the Dark Lord himself calling after me, desperate to hear my plan.

But I need to do this myself. Because she trusts me. I'm the only person who ever spent time with her. Whoever took the time to visit her. I make my way towards the stairs and descend down them, as quickly as I can. When I reach her door, I knock three times before opening it into the room that holds her. That traps her here.

"Lady Blackwell? It's me."

CHAPTER 2

ADRIENNE

I've grown to like the darkness. I can't tell how much time has passed. It could be hours or days or years even. I tried keeping track at first, but the pitch black surrounding me likes to play tricks. It sneaks into my brain and jumbles my thoughts. It consumes me until the only constant in my life is the dark.

While the darkness used to scare me, I've found comfort in it now. Comfort in the fact that it is always here. That it always listens. That it will never leave me. I've lost everyone in my life at this point. A mother who never wanted me. A sister who betrayed me. A kingdom full of my people who were ripped from me. A father. My forever... There's nothing left but the darkness.

"Oh darling, don't forget about me." His vile British accent grates against my ears. I grit my teeth through the sound, desperate for the calming silence to come back. Desperate for his voice and inner thoughts to leave me alone. I've gotten good at blocking him out, but it seems he's getting better at sneaking his way in.

I don't answer. I haven't said a word since I first realized I was stuck in his head. That seems to piss him off the most. He deserves to be pissed off. He did this to me. Him and his master or father or whatever he wants to call The Reaper.

"I've already told you that demons don't have fathers, princess. He's simply my creator." While I have managed to avoid speaking, I can't control the fact that he can occasionally invade my thoughts. He's always in my head, even when I'm stuck in his. I guess Ahri's right. He is the other constant in my life.

I feel a tickle deep in my spine and avoid thinking about *him*. I can't. If I do, Ahri will know. He'll tell The Reaper and all hope will be lost. At least, it will be for us. I'm stuck in this head until I get my powers back, but I'm desperate not to find them. Not when I know what will happen if we do.

"You don't think I already know that? And stop rambling about what ifs. We are going to get your powers, princess. I promise you of that. And then you'll stand by me in Morta. Ruling as my queen."

"I will never stand by you." I speak for the first time in what feels like a lifetime. When Ahri's deep chuckle invades my head, I hate myself for giving in. For letting him win.

"There's that sexy little voice of yours, darling. I've been missing it." I roll my eyes, clenching my fists at my sides from the irritation coursing through my body. Well, I guess it's not actually my body. More so my soul that was whisked away into the worst head that's ever existed.

"Ouch. That one stung. I know you don't mean that. Deep down you can't get enough of me. You love me, Adrienne. How could you not? I've been inside of you more than any other man ever has." I scoff at his grotesque words. He makes the hell I went through when he was trapped in my body sound sexual. It couldn't have been further from the truth. He tortured me so he could get his body back. Even though I didn't want it to begin with.

"Darling, I thought you were smarter than this. I've told you a million times now. I never tried to hurt you. If I recall, everyone else in your life has hurt you, not me. Your father giving you up. Your mother wanting you dead. Your little boyfriend and sister fucking behind your back."

"SHUT UP!" I scream into the jet-black air and hear it echo off the nonexistent walls. My chest heaves at an uncontrollable rate while Ahri's words repeat over and over in my head. "You already won, you piece of shit. We switched places. My life is over and you get the body and power you've always longed for. You get to watch me crumble into nothing while I'm stuck inside of your head. Isn't that enough? Why torture me more by reminding me of everything I desperately want to forget?"

"This is not what I want, darling."

"Could have fooled me. If I'm going to be trapped in this hell hole, the least you could do is stop talking to me and let me enjoy the quiet."

"Don't act like you hate talking to me. I can hear your thoughts, remember? I know how much I turn you on. How much you want me. How often you think of me. Dream of me... If you're a good girl, maybe I'll find someone to fuck so you can feel something. So you can satiate that need you so desperately have." His voice comes out in a deep growl, as if the thought of me feeling and seeing him fuck someone else turns him on. It probably does. The sadistic fuck.

"You're a disgusting pig. Like you could actually find someone who would ever let you touch them." When I say the words out loud, I realize he probably wouldn't need to find someone to let him. Men like him have no problem forcing themselves on women. The thought of him raping an innocent girl makes my stomach churn.

"You think so poorly of me, darling. I would never force myself on someone. I wouldn't have to."

"Just leave me alone, please." My voice sounds defeated. Like my body is slowly shutting down and the first thing to leave is my ability to speak.

"Since you begged, darling, I will. But remember, I'm always here. You know, if you get lonely up there."

How could I forget?

My eyes take in the room around me, blinking softly. The room is unfamiliar to me, filled with limestone walls and dark purple velvets. It reminds me of the castle in Ombra, but I have never seen this specific room. There is a bed to my right and a large stone patio right in front of me.

Looking down, I find myself sitting on a dark purple couch. Only, my body isn't mine. The black fabric covering my legs doesn't do well at hiding the muscles underneath. The hands resting on top of them have touched me before. Held me. Loved me.

I'm in Nox's body. I would recognize those hands anywhere. The rough callused skin from hard work. The size of them, able to completely engulf mine in a soft embrace. I itch to reach out and touch them, but I don't have hands. I'm simply a pair of eyes, looking through his.

Nox moves his head in the direction of the bed, towards a small door in the corner. The door opens at that moment, and a woman walks out of it. I've never seen her before, but I feel like I know her somehow.

She gracefully walks towards Nox, before depositing herself on the couch across the way. Nox blinks at her, letting me take in her appearance. Her dark black hair glistens like silk, pulled back in a tight low bun. The angles in her face are sharp, with deep cheek bones and an exaggerated jawline. Her eyes are dark and stormy, giving off a purple hue that sucks you in and threatens to drown you.

She's wearing a black dress with a violet cloak over her shoulders. She's thin, almost too thin, but everything about her scream's elegance. She's stunning.

Even the deep wrinkles pressing into the skin of her eyes and mouth add to her beauty.

The silence is deafening. I wait for someone to speak, for someone to say something, desperate to get some answers. When she opens her mouth, I watch it move with each word. But her voice doesn't grace my ears. I can't hear a word she says. All I can do is look through my mate's eyes and observe this silent exchange.

She laughs at something Nox says and I can't help but beg to hear the sound. This feeling of desperation, of an overwhelming necessity, to hear this woman's voice fills me to my core. I need to hear her. I need to talk to her. I can practically hear the soft timber already and so many emotions consume me. I want to cry. To curl into a ball. To be comforted by this stranger.

Nox blinks again and this time, when he opens his eyes, the room appears fuzzy. Darkness starts to creep up in the corners of the room until the view in front of me is tunneled. The woman before me slowly starts to disappear, as the black tunnel takes over, until finally, she's completely gone.

My breath comes out deep and shaky, funneling out of me into my pitch black surroundings. My eyes feel groggy and tired, as if I just woke up from a long nap. Was that a dream? Was I actually in Nox's head, seeing what he was seeing? I have so many questions, all of which I won't be able to find an answer to.

The only question I know the answer to with certainty is who that woman was.

My mother.

CHAPTER 3

NOX

It's scary how much Lady Blackwell resembles her daughter. I never acknowledged it before, but after meeting Adrienne in real life, I can't deny it now. They have the same hair, the same nose, the same mouth. The only difference is their eyes. Not only the color, but the shadows consuming them.

Lady Blackwell has a never-ending supply of darkness in her irises. She has pain and suffering shining through. She has dark memories and regret. Adrienne, while dark and mysterious, has more light than anyone I have ever seen in her unique eyes. Especially when she is with me.

"So, what's this about, Nox?" Her voice comes out shaky, contrasting against the intensity of her appearance. She's intimidating to most, but to me, she is just a friend. I visit with her as much as possible, since she can't leave this room. Lord Blackwell trapped her here after she risked Adrienne's life when she was pregnant.

She was tricked by The Reaper, manipulated into thinking he was someone else. He put a piece of himself inside of her. A demon that attached himself to Adrienne when she was a fetus, and tried to take her place. He tried to consume her. My Ren was stronger than him though. She consumed him first and gained his powers. She became the first baby made from both heaven and hell.

"It's about Adrienne." The minute I say her name, mixed emotions flash across her steely eyes. She knew about her daughter's arrival to the kingdom weeks ago. She told me she wanted to see her. To speak with her. But I haven't told her about what happened since. I haven't told her that she had her heart ripped out by The Reaper.

"What about her? Does she want to speak with me?"

"She told me she did... but, this isn't about that. Something happened. On her coronation day." I clear my throat, trying to rid the emotion from my voice. Trying to stop the sadness from seeping through, preventing me from getting the words out. "The Reaper got to her. He got through the clype and he... he ripped her heart out."

The silence that follows my admission is enough to drive someone mad. Our deep breaths and the crackle of the fire are the only sounds in the room. She blinks at me, looking as if she doesn't speak the same language. As if she has no idea what I just said. I can see the heartbreak filling her eyes. The anger. The devastation.

"I can feel her still. I think... No, I know she's still alive." A mixture of both relief and doubt takes over now and she shakes her head at me in confusion.

"How?" While she knows about my shadvir bond with Adrienne, the one given to me at her birth, in order to protect her, that's the extent of her knowledge. She has no idea about the mating bond we uncovered the night she was ripped away from me. The bond that's only known as a myth.

"We are mated, Lady Blackwell. She's my mate." Once again, the silence consumes the room. Lady Blackwell's eyes dart between mine, frantically searching for the truth in them. She thinks I'm making this up.

"That's impossible. Only pure Angels can have such a bond. And that's if the myth is even true. It's never been seen before. You must be mistaken."

"I'm just as confused as you are. But we are mated, I can assure you of that. That's why I'm not dead. Because when Adrienne's heart was ripped from her, all of her powers went into me. I'm holding onto her until we can find her. She's attached to me still, I can feel it."

"Prove it then."

I sigh, wishing she would just believe me rather than needing proof. I don't know if I can summon up her powers the way I did when Onyx was trying to get to me. It's worth a shot though.

Standing, I close my eyes and try to think of Ren. I picture her long black hair lying in soft waves down her back. I picture each intricate tattoo etched into her skin, contrasting against her tan color. The way her multi-colored eyes bore into me with such intensity every time she looked my way.

My body hums when I think about her touching my skin. Her lips grazing against mine. Her fingers threading through my hair, lightly pulling the strands. I feel her fire flaming under my skin. I feel her with me, bubbling up to the surface, begging to be unleashed.

When I open my eyes, Lady Blackwell is staring at me with a gaping mouth. Her eyes look like saucers and she's now standing with me, staring me dead on. I see a light radiating off of me, golden and bright. Looking down, I find my body glowing from the same radiant light that always shone when I was with Adrienne. When we were connected.

I can't keep the smile off of my face. She's here. She's with me. I feel her flowing through my veins. Her smile. Her laugh. Her vanilla scent. I wish I could dive into my own body with her. I wish I could find her swimming in there and pull her into my arms.

"That's impossible." Those words break me out of my trance. The flames of Adrienne coursing through my body dissipate like they were doused out by water. I instantly feel cold and desperate for her to come back. To stay with me and keep me warm. It takes a moment for me to recover, my body and mind aching for that warmth to come back. I shake my head and steel myself, trying to focus on the matter at hand

"I thought so too. But, it's real." I wait for her to answer. Instead, she shakes her head with an astonished look on her face and bolts to the bathroom. When the door slams behind her, I barely even notice it. All I can think of... all I can picture, is Adrienne.

"Princess, I miss you so much it hurts. I know you're somewhere out there, waiting for me to find you. And I promise you I will. I will do whatever it takes to get you back. I love you more than anything in all of the worlds."

Something inside of me stirs. My eyes feel like they are going to pop out of my skull. As if someone was now residing in my head with me. It feels cramped. So much so that I have to blink my eyes a few times and grab my head to rid the uncomfortable feeling. While it doesn't go away, it subsides enough for me to get it together and sit back down on the couch.

After a few minutes, the bathroom door opens back up and Lady Blackwell slowly walks back towards me. Her violet cloak glides against the cold stone floor until she places herself back on the couch across from me.

"Is she okay?" The question is quiet. So quiet that I barely hear it. Especially since I can't stop thinking about the pressure building behind my eyes.

"I don't know. All I know is she is still alive. Or a part of her is. Her body is here. And her powers are with me. But the rest of her is missing. The rest of her is calling out to me."

"And why are you here, Nox? Why are you telling me this?"

"Maybe I just wanted to come see my closest friend." I make the joke trying to lighten the mood, but it makes my stomach churn the minute I say it. This isn't a time for jokes. Not with Ren on the line. Lady Blackwell offers me a timid laugh but it doesn't make me feel any better.

"You know more about The Reaper than I do. I can't tell anyone about this because it will cause a panic. Right now, the entire kingdom is mourning their princess. If I announce that I am not only her fated mate, but that I can feel her still..."

"The entire kingdom will go into an uproar." She beats me to it and I nod my head in agreement.

"I need something. Anything to try to find her."

"Nox." My name comes out in an exasperated sigh. "I don't know how I can help you. Trust me, I wish I could. But the only thing I know about The Reaper is that he tricked me. He manipulated me into thinking he was someone else."

"Please, Layla. I know you know more. You were in love with him, even after you found out who he was. A part of me thinks you will always have an attachment to him. Or maybe, I hope you do. For Adrienne's sake."

She sighs again, looking anywhere but at me. "After Adrienne was born, I felt him. I could hear him in my head. I don't even think he knew it. It's almost like him leaving that part of him in me connected us in a way. That is, until I ended up down here. When Cole banished me to this room, the connection I had to The Reaper disappeared."

She pauses and I find myself sitting at the edge of my seat. "He would say these things. Things that confused me. I never understood what any of it meant." Confusion spreads across her face as she thinks back.

"What did he say?" I don't mean to yell the words. When she flinches, I pull myself back. I control the emotions coursing through me.

"He would call the Gods evil. He said they needed to find a way to stop them... he would talk to Lucifer and say they need to get justice. For destroying Lucifer's life and putting everyone in danger. They said Adrienne and Ahriman were the answer. They would be the ones to stop them."

"Ahriman?" The name sounds unfamiliar but the minute it graces my tongue, something rings inside of me. Something telling me I know exactly who that is.

"He's the demon that was attached to Adrienne. He's the reason The Reaper, Than, wanted her dead. So Ahriman could possess his powers again." Anger boils deep inside of me. He's the thing I was always trying to save Ren from when she would travel in her sleep. He's the monster that was constantly trying to kill her.

"Why would they call the Gods evil? Lucifer is the devil. He tried to destroy all of mankind. That's the reason we were created. So we could keep the humans safe."

"Nox... I shouldn't be saying this..." Her voice lowers and she leans in towards me. "I don't know if we have the right story. The Reaper spoke of something called imignis. Hellfire. He said the Gods are the ones that created it. That Atlas is the one to blame for the burning ball of hellfire in the human world. That he used it try to kill Lucifer when he banished him, but it backfired."

"Layla... you sound insane." I shake my head, feeling a shiver travel down my spine. "That can't be right. They are the reason we are here. Why we have food and water to drink. They have provided us with everything."

"I know. I'm not saying it's true. It's just what I heard The Reaper say in my head all of those years ago. I never told anyone about it because I knew it would make me sound crazy." We sit in silence as I contemplate her words. While it's hard to believe, right now, I can't turn any ideas away. If she really heard The Reaper say all of that, it's more insight than I had a half hour ago.

"Let's say, hypothetically, what you heard him say is right. That the Gods... that Atlas is evil—"

The ground rumbles below us and I cut my words short. Lady Blackwell gives me a stern look before leaning in even closer.

"You need to whisper if you are going to talk about any of them. They can't hear us if we whisper."

Rolling my eyes, I lean in and whisper to her, "Considering they are evil and Lucifer is trying to save everyone from the hellfire, what does Adrienne help him with? Why are Ahriman and Adrienne the answer?"

"Because Adrienne is a product of both heaven and hell. Ahriman became a part of her when she absorbed him and he always will be. No matter what she does, Ahriman will forever be connected to her." I grit my teeth at her words, hating the way they sound. I hate the idea of anyone, let alone a demon, being attached to my Ren.

"If anyone is going to be able to stop the Gods, Atlas specifically, it's going to be Adrienne. And Ahriman standing by her side will only make her stronger. At least, that's what he said."

"That means... he needs her alive. He needs her powers. And her body. He's going to use my girl as a weapon." The realization hits me hard, scaring me to my core. Only one thing can come from this. From us both wanting something the other has.

It's going to start a war.

CHAPTER 4

ONYX

If it wasn't for the fact that he was attached to the dark princess, I would have killed Nox by now. The son of a bitch is cocky and disobedient. I've been waiting for him to return from wherever the hell he ran off to for over an hour now. We agreed to do this together, and the first thing he does is keep things to himself.

Adrienne's death shook me to my core. I stood mere inches away from the woman I had grown so fond of as her heart was ripped from her body. I looked right into her eyes as her last breath bellowed out into the universe. At that moment, I could have burned the kingdom to the ground.

If I could take her place, I would. Not that anyone would ever believe that. Everyone hates me here. Everyone assumes I could care less about the princess. They all assume I was only interested in the title of Dark Lord. Especially now that I am forced to rule without my queen by my side.

Don't get me wrong, I couldn't wait to become the Dark Lord a few days ago. The thought of calling Adrienne my wife, spending every day with her as we ruled over our people, felt like a dream. The little spit fire hated my guts at first, for good reason, but we became good friends over the course of our time together. Now that the circumstances have changed, I wish this title of Dark Lord didn't sit upon my head. It's a burden to me, not a blessing.

Because as I mourn the woman who challenged me, I am being watched by thousands of eyes. As I desperately try to keep it together, I have to make decisions like when to hold her funeral and what the kingdom should do next. I have to pretend I know what I'm doing, when all I can think of is how wrong I am for this job. Adrienne would have been an amazing queen. She would have guided me through this and made me the best ruler I could be.

I think back to the first time she met her people. During the physical challenges to find her husband. When I watched her, being one of the victors, as she stood proud and tall in front of thousands of people. Her dress glistened almost as bright as her eyes as she confidently spoke to them. I swear I fell in love with her at that moment. I couldn't contain my pride, like she was already my wife. Already my most prized possession.

Fast approaching footsteps interrupt my fond memory and I turn towards the entrance of the throne room. Nox is speeding towards me, with matching looks of fear and excitement on his face.

"Nice of you to join me again. I'm already regretting our decision to work together on finding the princess." I glare daggers into him, hating him more than ever since finding out he was actually Adrienne's mate. I made the joke to her before the coronation, but I never expected it to be true. It's impossible, and yet he stands in front of me.

"I don't know if we are going to have to find her. There's a chance they are going to find us." I furrow my brows at him, confused as to what he is rambling about.

"Who are they?"

"The Reaper and Ahriman. The demon that was attached to Adrienne since birth. They need her body. Which we have. They need her magic. Which I have. They are going to eventually come find it." Ahriman. I hate him already. I squeeze my fists at my sides, trying not to let my anger show. Not to the man that is mated to my queen.

"We can't let that happen. That will destroy this kingdom. They will start a war." Nox nods his head, his dark purple irises staring at me. His brown curls are disheveled on his head and his beard looks overgrown and untidy. He looks like a wild man.

"Yes, they will. But part of me thinks the best thing for us to do is let them come to us. We don't know where they are. We don't know anything about where they are. Sometimes playing defense is the best thing to do."

"Not when Adrienne is on the line. Her body is here. You have her powers. Having either of those things next to demons is a recipe for disaster. It's too risky."

"Then what are we supposed to do, Dark Lord?" He mocks me when he says the title. I want to tell him to stop calling me that. I hate the name. The reminder of what I was given right as Adrienne was taken from us.

"We need to hide her body. Somewhere The Reaper and Ahriman can't get to it." I watch as an idea flashes through his eyes before anger takes over once more. "What is it? What are you thinking?"

"Nothing. I'm never going to let it happen so it doesn't matter." His voice is deeper than it was before. His mouth is pressed in a thin line and a spark of lilac fills his eyes.

"Relax and tell me what you were going to say. Every idea is a good one at this point. If it can bring Adrienne back to us, we need to try." I know my words get to him when he sighs and brings a hand up to the brim of his nose. Pressing lightly, as if to relieve a pounding headache, he opens his mouth to speak.

"Her body would be safe on Earth. Where The Reaper can't reach her." I consider it for a minute and then question him.

"Why does that idea piss you off so much? What's your gripe with Earth?"

"It's not Earth that pisses me off. It's who we are going get to help us. Someone I hoped I'd never have to fucking see again. Someone who knows about our world and who Adrienne really is."

"And? Who might that be?" I'm getting tired of his riddles. Of how long it is taking him to get to the point.

"Dr. Archer. The man she was seeing before she came here. The only person she ever told about me. About the demon and her nightmares. Ren told me he was married, but at this point, that doesn't even matter. I saw how much he cared about her. I saw how he treated her. He will keep her safe."

Is it wrong that I can't keep the smirk off my face? Maybe. But watching Nox feel jealous of another man, makes me happier than it should. Because that's how I feel right now, looking at him.

"I also think it's a good idea if we tell her human sister, Sophia, as well. Dr. Archer will help you tell her. She should know about this. She should be involved." He finally stops talking and I contemplate his words.

"That's not a bad idea. In fact, it's a great one. As long as you can contain your jealousy, that is. I will go there tomorrow with her body. Once that is taken care of, we will come up with a plan for the rest. Tonight, I need you to explain everything you know about Dr. Archer's residence so I can transport there in the morning."

CHAPTER 5

NOX

I walk forward into the small room. There are two beds on either side of the square space, one empty and the other occupied. I walk forward, feeling as though I'm floating, rather than walking. My body is bringing me towards the couple lying on the bed even though everything inside of me is telling me not to look.

The man on top is shirtless, grinding his half naked body against the person underneath him. I can hear the sounds of their sloppy kiss, the soft moans coming from the woman. I can't get a clear look at either of them, the only thing I can make out is the tan skin of the man's back.

"God, yes." Her soft whimper sounds familiar, but I still can't place it. I move closer, the room almost appearing in black and white around me. A gasp, which comes from behind me, makes the couple stop moving and suddenly, they turn in my direction.

Dark brown eyes look my way. The same eyes that have stared at my Ren countless times. Dr. Archer. The man that was supposed to love Adrienne. The *man that I had to watch make love to my mate over and over again. I burn with fire, terrified that when I look down at the other set of eyes, I will find hers. Her purple orbs coated with lust from another man.*

Except, what I find is almost worse. Light blue eyes stare through me. The same blue eyes I have seen throughout Adrienne's life. The same ruffled blonde hair that seemed to get even lighter through the years. The same pale skin from her childhood, except now it's flushed with a pink tint. Her sister, Sophia.

"Willow?" Sophia's voice comes out full of surprise and fear. I try to turn around, assuming Adrienne, is behind me. I never did like her human name. Willow. It wasn't powerful enough for her. Not for my Ren. Not for the power she possesses.

My body doesn't turn though. It doesn't move. I can't stop myself from looking at the scene before me. And then Dr. Archer moves. He gets off Sophia and starts to walk towards me.

"Willow..."

I gasp for air as I wake up, anger radiating off of every inch of my body. Looking around, rather than the small dorm room I was just in, I'm surrounded by the comfort of my bedroom. I stare out at the dark wood walls and take deep breaths, trying to calm myself down.

It was just a dream. A weird, horrible, upsetting dream. Except, something inside of me is screaming to tell me it wasn't. That it was a memory. It just simply wasn't mine. That feeling niggles at me, getting stronger and stronger, until it's practically screaming. What I just witnessed was real. Dr. Archer was with Sophia.

And I just told the Dark Lord to bring Ren to them. To let them watch over her body until we have the rest of her back. Shooting out of bed, I throw on a pair of pants and the shirt I wore yesterday. I need to get to Onyx before he leaves. He can't bring Ren to Dr. Archer. Not after what I just witnessed. Not after seeing such betrayal.

I run faster than I ever have. The orange glow from Morta above lights my way through the dark forest. My cabin is at the edge of the kingdom, down the sloping woods, so the trek is hard on my tired legs. It doesn't stop me as I trip over roots and push past the thick tree branches.

When I reach the castle, I don't stop running. I make my way through the open stone foyer and into the ball room where the two spiral stairs lead to the second floor. Taking two at a time, I run straight to the Dark Lord's room and throw the door open. The air feels stale when I cross the barrier.

The room is empty. I search the impressive space with cathedral ceilings and plush velvet fabrics and come up short. Onyx is gone. He already left. With my Ren's body.

ONYX

TRANSPORTING TO DIFFERENT REALMS IS NEVER FUN. I SAY THAT, acting like I've done it countless times, but I have only done it once or twice. I was interested in Earth when I was younger, along with my brother Ozul. The arrogant prick. He loved the bustling life of humans. I, on the other hand, hated it. I hated how polluted not only the air felt, but the people too.

So being here, standing on the streets of New York, I feel disgust creeping its way up. I hate this city. I hate these people. I hate this world. Luckily, I was able to put a protective clype around both Adrienne and I that conceals us both from the human eye. Once I enter Dr. Archer's home, I will take the clype off and present ourselves to Adrienne's ex-lover.

The idea of it is comical. Why would this man, married at that, ever agree to taking a dead body and holding it in his house? Saying the words dead body in my head makes my stomach churn. I refuse to think she's dead. There's no way.

I look down at her body as I walk into the high-class apartment building. Her face is so beautiful. Even after a few days, her tan skin glistens with life. Her thick lashes press together with her closed eyes. Her top and bottom lips look like pillows meshed together, providing the smallest opening at the center, where the air should be flowing in and out, but none passes.

I'd give anything to see her purple eyes again. To see her smile. Hell, I'd take her screaming at me and calling me names. Even at her angriest, I couldn't help but stare her down and picture making her scream for other reasons. The woman is absolutely infuriating in all the right ways.

I sit down in the lobby filled with twinkling lights and way too many windows and wait. Dr. Archer's description, that Kage repeated over and over, runs through my head. Cocky prick, always in an overly expensive suit, dark short hair, matching beard, brown eyes covered by glasses, glare permanently fixed on the world.

I hate to say it, but he kind of sounds like me. Besides my blonde hair and lilac eyes. I have always been an impressive dresser, but since becoming the Dark Lord, I have been forced to wear the most expensive suits and cloaks I have ever seen. Lavish materials. Rare jewels. It's all way over the top, even for me.

I watch as a few people walk past us, oblivious to the man holding a woman's body in the middle of their apartment building. I hear the glass door open one more time and look over to find the man in question sauntering across the lobby floor.

Nox was right. He looks absolutely miserable. The scowl on his face could kill and his whole body appears tense and ready to attack at any moment under the perfectly pleated black suit.

Moving from the sofa I was sitting on, I follow behind him until we are standing in the closed elevator by ourselves. The princess and I are still concealed by the clype, since I don't plan on showing ourselves until we are safely in the confinements of his house. Well, penthouse apparently.

The elevator dings and when the doors open, Dr. Archer steps out first. I hear him sigh as he places his key card on a glass table in the foyer and then walks into the expansive home. It's very similar to the lobby, full of windows that reveal the city outside. The decorations are minimal and plain, but each appliance or piece of furniture is clearly expensive and high end.

He moves to a black cabinet in the kitchen and grabs a bottle of clear liquid from the inside, placing it on his marble countertop. He grabs a crystal glass next and then places it by the bottle before pouring himself a hefty glass. I transported through the bline in the morning, but it takes hours to get through it. Especially when you bring a body with you. It's now well past five o'clock here. Once he takes the first big sip, I decide now is as good a time as ever.

Reaching inside of me, I remove the clype from us both and we slowly materialize, standing on the opposite side of the island as Dr. Archer. He doesn't notice us since he is looking out the window, so I take a second to look down at Adrienne and admire her graceful beauty again. Bringing her up higher in my arms, I place a soft kiss against her forehead and then decide it's time to talk.

"It's quite rude not to offer your guest a drink as well." I talk louder than normal, earning me a jump big enough to slosh the liquid out of his cup and onto the counter. He turns towards us and I watch as his previous glum mood turns into a territorial angry one.

"Who the fuck are you? How did you get in here?" His voice can only be described as an intimidating snarl. He reaches into a drawer and I know what he's going to grab before he even grabs it.

"A knife? Really? If I was going to hurt you, I would have already. But, if you couldn't tell, my hands are full." I gesture towards Adrienne's body, still residing in my arms. His eyes follow the movement and I watch the realization hit him.

"Willow?" It's barely audible and accompanied by worried eyes. "What happened? What the hell did you do to her?" And there's the snarl again. Rather than dropping the knife, he extends it now, walking towards us. He looks ridiculous.

"Put the knife down. I didn't hurt your precious *Willow*. That's a terrible name for the princess, by the way. Not fitting at all." Not surprisingly, he doesn't put the knife down. He advances me still, his eyes on the limp body in my arms.

"Answer my question."

"Why don't we sit down? Why don't you pour me some of that tequila? And put the fucking knife down, Dr. Archer." I don't give him time to respond. I walk myself towards his living room, to the white sectional facing the fireplace and huge windows. Placing one more kiss on the princess' forehead, I gently lay her on the couch before sitting right next to her, protecting her.

I can feel his eyes on me the entire time. He finally starts to move, bringing two glasses over and the entire bottle. He pours some into a second glass, before topping off the one he already had. And then he waits. He sits there, on the end of the sectional, staring at Adrienne's body.

"Are you... are you Nox?" I practically choke on the tequila in my mouth at his question.

"I take offense to that. No, I can assure you, I am nothing like that shadvir. If I was Nox, you would probably be dead." I snicker at my joke, but Dr. Archer definitely doesn't. His hands grip his crystal glass hard enough to break it. "My name is Onyx Asra."

"And... Willow... is she dead?" He looks down at her body, staring directly at her face with what can only be described as a mixture of fear and love.

"Well, Adrienne had her heart ripped out, so she has definitely seen better days. Her soul is still alive. And her powers are being contained. We just need to bring all of the parts back together. We need to find her heart and make her whole."

"Shit. Is she in pain?"

"I don't know. We don't know much. Nox can feel her. He knows she's out there, but that's all we know." The room goes silent for a few minutes until his eyes look into mine and squint in an accusatory way.

"Why are you here with her? Why isn't Nox? Who the fuck are you?"

"Nox can't travel through the bline to get to your world. Only a royal born from the angels has that ability. I am a Dark Lord. I was meant to marry Adrienne before this happened."

"So, Willow is into sharing now? Of course, she is." He scoffs in disgust and rage consumes me. How dare he judge her? How dare he think badly when her shell of a body is lying in front of us.

"Speak one more foul word regarding my princess and I will rip your tongue out. You have no room to judge a single hair on her head. You're the married one. You're the cheater." My voice comes out animalistic as I defend her.

"I am not married. I've been divorced for years. Willow never gave me the chance to explain that. She disappeared before I could," he says with a defeated shake of his head. "I cared for Willow. And the entire time we were together, she was in love with someone else. With Nox."

"I'm not here to discuss your love life. I'm here for Adrienne. I need your help." He finishes off the tequila in his glass and proceeds to pour himself more.

"What could you possibly need me for? My last encounter with Willow didn't exactly go well. She wants nothing to do with me."

"Again, I don't give two shits about your prior relationship. Just tell me, do you care about this woman?" I point at Adrienne for emphasis. "Would you keep her safe?"

"Of course. I have always care about her. I always tried to keep her safe." He sounds defeated, clearly reminiscing on past mistakes. Mistakes I don't care to hear about.

"Good. Because we need you to keep her body here. With you. We need you to make sure nothing and no one gets to it." I can see the confusion on his face, but it doesn't look like he's going to say no.

"Who would try to get to it? Why me?"

"Because the demon that ripped her heart out can't transport to your realm. You know about our world. You care for Adrienne. You're our best option. And if he gets her body before we get her heart, the devil is going to have exactly what he needs to destroy the world."

"And what's that?"

I look down at Adrienne, placing a hand against her soft, cold skin. "An unstoppable killing machine."

CHAPTER 6

ADRIENNE

"How's it going in there, love?" His accent almost goes unnoticed at this point. I hear it every second of the day. Even when he's not talking to me, I hear him talking to Than constantly. I refuse to call him The Reaper now that I know his real name. He uses it to try to intimidate people. I'm not intimidated at all.

"Be a lot better if you were dead." Ahri's deep laugh rattles through me..

"Darling, if I die, so do you." I can hear the smile on his lips when he speaks.

"I'm already dead. Than made sure of that. Ripped my heart out, remember?" I roll my eyes, sarcasm coating each word. I'm in my own personal hell. Stuck in the worst head I could find myself in. With the monster who tried to kill me and who wants to end the world.

"First of all, I told you that we don't want to end the world. You can't believe everything the Gods spew at you. And second, you aren't dead. As long as I'm alive, you are just sitting in limbo until we return your heart to your body. Then you will be good as new. And I'll be able to throw you up against a wall like we have both been fantasizing about."

"You're repulsive. And if you aren't planning on ending the world, why do you and Than constantly speak in your weird vague code so I can't understand what you're talking about? Clearly, it's something bad if you can't let me hear it."

"Darling, we are keeping our plans from you for your own safety. Once we have your body and we are able to keep you safe here, with us, we will tell you everything." He sounds genuine with his answer but I will never trust a word he says. He ruined my life in more ways than one.

"Safe from who? The only person who has ever put me in danger is you!" I scream into the black void, my voice echoing off the walls of his mind.

"You're going to piss me off if you don't stop saying I put you in danger. I am trying to keep you safe from the Gods. If you hold the information we are discussing in that pretty little head of yours, and the Gods get a hold of you, it won't be good. I don't want to think about the shit they will do to you, love."

"I wish you would give me more than that. How am I supposed to believe you if you don't explain anything?" I stand and start pacing around my jet-black prison cell.

"Alright. I'll give you something, okay? Sit down, I can feel you pacing around in my head. It's giving me a bloody migraine." I sigh and sit down in a dramatic huff, crossing my legs underneath me.

"I'm sitting. Now speak."

"Good girl. But I'd rather show you. Close your eyes for me, darling. Sit back and enjoy the show."

I obey, closing my eyes. The pitch blackness behind my eyelids suddenly starts to fade in and out with bright white light. Before I know it, pictures form on the back of my eyelids and it feels like I'm being thrown into another world. A bright world full of glistening white light.

I make my way towards Atlas's office, the over-the-top lights burning my corneas. The higher up you go, the brighter it is. I don't know how Atlas deals with it every single day. I'd go blind.

My dress shoes click against the blazing white tile floor, echoing off the walls and twenty-foot ceiling. I admire the intimidating portraits of Atlas's relatives. The previous towering Gods before Atlas. They all look the same. Just like Atlas himself. Stark white hair. Glowing white eyes. Pale skin that looks see through.

I've always thought the towering Gods were terrifying. Not just the way they look, but the things they do. The way they think. Everything about them. The rest of us, the lower angels, look halfway normal. At least, I like to think we do with our blonde hair and gray eyes.

I stop in front of the huge arched double doors that have a never-ending supply of white fog floating in front of it. It's supposed to look intimidating, but it just resembles cotton candy to me and makes me laugh every time I see it.

The large door knocker is shaped like angel wings, the same wings that materialize on my back every time I need them. I can feel them tingling in my shoulder blades just thinking about their iridescent sheen. They have to be my favorite part about being an angel. And the thing that we all have in common, towering or lower.

Grabbing at the heavy knocker, I let it bang against the wood door three times. The sound rings through the empty halls, echoing for all to hear. Not that will. No one's here. To be honest, I'm not supposed to be here either. I don't have an appointment with Atlas. But this can't wait. Ayla's life depends on it.

And yet, I wait.
And wait.
And wait.

But the door doesn't open and Atlas's boisterous voice doesn't call out to come in. A sane man would walk away. They would come back another time. But I've never been considered sane. And Ayla is worth the repercussions of what I'm about to do.

I can't help but picture her sparkling gray eyes, full of light and love, as I open the door. She's been my everything since we were barely two years old. Her laugh could cheer up even the saddest man. Her hair is somehow brighter than the rest of ours, appearing like golden strands of silk falling from her scalp. Her kindness is her weakness, which is why I'm here.

The door doesn't make a sound as it slowly opens inch by inch. I slip through the crack and let it quietly shut behind me. I had no plans of sneaking in, but now that I'm opening the door without being announced, it feels necessary.

I walk through the white fog that, of course, resides in his office as well. The walls match the same stark white as the hallways and there are marble statues of former towerings. Everything is overdone and exaggerated. From the hanging crystal chandelier to the fact that his desk is a full one-hundred feet from the entrance. The room is mostly empty besides the white smoke.

I slowly make my way through the fog, staying quiet when I hear voices coming from the other end of the room. It's not Atlas speaking, but one of his disciples. His voice is hushed, so I can't hear it from this distance, but the closer I get, the more I can make out.

"They are overpopulated, Atlas." Kamar's voice hisses through the air, reaching my ears. "We need to act or there's going to be chaos." I stop moving, trying to listen without being seen.

"I'm aware, Kamar. Rather than stating the obvious, why don't you start throwing out ideas of how to deal with the humans?" Atlas spits out the word humans like it's poison on his tongue.

"Imignis is the obvious answer." I think this disciple's name is Blaze. He's aggressive and full of himself. Well, most of the angels granted as disciples for our Gods are. But he takes the cake when it comes to being cocky.

"That's the problem you idiot. Imignis is obvious. It can only be created by Gods. If He gets an inkling that I sent hellfire down to humans, who knows

what will happen." The He Atlas speaks of is Aiden, the most powerful God of all. The first God. The creator of imignis, the never-ending light source that keeps heaven running. Legend speaks of him but no one has ever met him. He's supposedly an immortal being so bright, he would blind you with one glance.

"Tragedy." This voice reminds me of a snake. A viper slithering through the air, bringing dread to everything it graces. Surya. The most vile disciple of them all. He has a mind so sick and twisted, I swear he spends his free time torturing babies.

"Intriguing... Go on." I can practically hear the pleased smile in his voice. If Atlas had a favorite angel, it would be Surya.

"We cause wars among the humans. And unexplained plagues. Uncontrollable fires. Flooding the seas with waves that can't be stopped. Random things that can't be tied to us. Things that He wouldn't question as Godly acts, but rather unexplainable tragedies."

I feel my fists clench at my sides with his words. How could he think such a thing? It's our job to protect the humans. That's why we are here. That's our purpose. That's why Aiden started all of this. I wait, listening to the deadening silence for Atlas to turn the idea down.

"I'm impressed. You never cease to surprise me, Surya." I can't hold back my huff of disbelief. The minute the sound breaks through the air, the room goes silent. Fuck.

Within seconds, the fog that once hid me from Atlas and his disciples dissipates until the room is crystal clear. Four pairs of eyes glare into me, equal parts surprised and enraged at my presence.

"Lucifer. What brings you into my office without my permission?" Atlas trains his voice to sound kind, but the grin on his face makes the words sound like a promise for pain. For suffering.

I clear my throat and continue the short walk to them on unsteady feet. After what I just heard, I want to run out of this office and warn the humans. Tell them of all of our secrets and prepare them for what's to come.

"I'm sorry to interrupt, Atlas. I knocked but there was no answer. I have an urgent matter to present to you. Regarding Ayla." The grin on his face only

widens when I say her name and I can't hold back the shiver that trembles through my body.

"Your darling Ayla, yes." His white eyes glow almost too bright when they look at me, making his dark pupils look like thin slits rather than their normal circular shape. His dark veins push up against his thin skin, making it look like roots crawling across his body, trying to break through.

"I can come back later. I shouldn't have barged—"

"But since you so rudely did, you might as well explain yourself. Our meeting is over, right boys?" He looks at his disciples and nods his head, telling the three of them to leave. Each one stands at once and they start to shuffle out, staring me down the entire way. Their gray eyes appear lifeless, completely different from the sparkle in Ayla's.

"Speak, Lucifer," he barks out at me even though I'm only a few feet away from him and the room is silent.

I clear my throat and try to sound as professional as possible. As unaffected by Ayla's decisions. "As I'm sure you know, Ayla has been traveling down to Earth a lot more than usual. She's always loved it down there. She loves the humans more than any angel I have ever met. The reason she keeps going is because she met a little girl. She's barely five years old and she lost her mother when she was born. She lives in an orphanage and Ayla has been volunteering there. She has become somewhat of a mother figure to this child." I pause when I see Atlas squint his eyes at me.

"Go on. I doubt you're here to simply brag about your precious Ayla's compassion for a human child." He spits out each word at me with the flip of a hand. I hate how he calls her my Ayla. I don't want him knowing how much I care for her. I try to keep my personal life private from our God. He always uses it against us.

"No. I'm here because the other day, the little girl, Mandy, got hit by a car when she was running across a street. She's in critical condition and the doctors are saying the chances of her surviving are slim to none. So, Ayla is about to... she's going to..." I take a deep breath, trying to calm my nerves. I can't even get the words out.

"Let me guess. She's going to give up her life for this random child. She's going to give her wings to her and save her life." He speaks of it like it's a disgrace, but it is one of the most selfless acts an angel can do. Taking our life and passing our wings down to a human provides them with a protective veil that will not only save their life, but keep them safe until old age takes their life.

"Yes." It comes out squeaky, making me sound weak.

"And what exactly are you telling me this for? If she truly wants to save her, it's her prerogative. You know that."

"I need a favor. I am willing to give you whatever you want... please, can you save Mandy's life so Ayla doesn't have to sacrifice hers?" Gods have the power to save any humans life without harming themselves. He could snap his fingers and little Mandy would be safe.

I watch as his hand moves up to his chin, scratching the light white scruff covering his see-through skin. His white eyes flash even brighter with my proposition. He knows I'm desperate. He knows how I feel about Ayla, and if he didn't before, he does now.

"That's quite the offer, Lucifer. Anything I want in return for a simple human's life to be saved? Why offer me such a deal?" He is waiting for me to admit it. To admit how I feel for her. To say the words out loud. I clench my teeth and glare at the monster of a God in front of me. "Say it and I'll agree to your request."

"I am in love with Ayla." It's silent before his deep chuckle booms off the walls. I wait, not so patiently, for him to agree and give me his terms.

"Love makes us pathetic and weak. I thought you were stronger than that, Lucifer. You were always one of the most powerful of my lowers. The angel I had to keep an eye on. Your admission makes me question everything I have ever thought of you." He pauses again before standing from his seat.

"I agree to your request. I will save your Ayla so you two can be together. But, in return I will take something from you. Something that an angel weak enough to feel love shouldn't have. Something I no longer think you're worthy of."

I feel my powers surging under my skin with every word he speaks. White hot power that threatens to boil over into the air. I wait for what feels like hours *for him to say it. To tell me what he wants in return for my best friend. The love of my life.*

"*Your wings.*"

My vision goes dark as the images that consumed my brain suddenly vanish. I feel myself missing them, completely transfixed by what I witnessed and desperate to see more. To see what happened.

"Why did you stop?" My voice comes out whinier than I meant and I cringe at the sound. Ahri's deep chuckle vibrates through the dark cavern I call home and I try not to think about how much I find myself enjoying the sound.

"Jumping into a vision is exhausting, darling. I'm drained now. I will show you more at some point, I promise."

"Jumping into a vision? So that's what I did?" I lie on my back and stare into the empty abyss above me. What I wouldn't do to see stars again. Or anything for that matter.

"Well, that's what I did. Since I'm a descendent of Lucifer, I can jump into visions that he has shared with me. Since you're in my head, you come along for the ride." I nod my head, forgetting that he can't see the movement.

"Can I do that?"

"Technically, yes, you can. All descendants of Gods can, so anyone royal in your kingdom can, but never have." I squint my eyes at his words, confused by the meaning.

"Why not?"

"Think about it, darling. I can only see visions of Lucifer's past because they are visions that he showed me himself. That he wanted me to see." I realize what he's saying before he says it.

"So, the Gods don't want us to see anything? They are hiding things from us." I can tell he's nodding his head even though I can't see him.

"Precisely, love. Do you see now that not everything is at it seems?" His voice grows more gentle, bringing the British tones of his accent out even more.

"I just don't understand. So, Atlas is the God in charge of heaven? He wants to kill humans?"

"Not only did he want to, he succeeded. Because of Atlas, death has skyrocketed on Earth for the last thousand years. He is the reason that diseases and forest fires and every single war in history has occurred. He's the reason people commit murders and suicide. The world used to be a better place before he was ruling."

"Why would he do that? How has no one stopped him? How is he still alive?" I start to feel heat under my skin as anger rises. I know my powers aren't here, but that familiar feeling of magic fills my veins.

"Gods assigned as leaders of heaven can live and rule for thousands of years if a descendent isn't born. Atlas has not had any children. Because he is obsessed with power. The only angel's brave enough to stand up to him were Lucifer and Ayla. The rest support his every move."

"I want to see more. Please show me more, Ahri." I can't help but sound desperate. Ahri spoke to me when he was stuck in my head about Lucifer and the Gods. He told me how they threw Lucifer down to the darkest place imaginable. To a world of death and sadness. Now that I'm trapped in this black hole of hell, I can't help but feel bad for the devil. Feel connected to him in some way.

"Mmm." His deep moan runs through the empty space around me and brings goosebumps to my skin. "I do love hearing you beg for me, Adrienne." The sound of my name on his lips sends heat and ice through my veins. I'd prefer he call me darling. "I will show you anything you desire, but I need to rest. I won't be able to get a clear picture if I don't."

"Okay so stop talking to me and go to bed! What are you waiting for?" I throw my hands up in the darkness around me, irritated that I have to wait. His low chuckle, that comes out so often lately, grinds through my mind.

"My girl is impatient, I see."

"I'm not your girl, and I'm rotting in this miserable excuse of a head. I need something to distract me until I can get out of here and as far away from you as possible." I spit each word out at him, making them more aggressive than they need to be. I can't tell if it's to convince him or myself anymore.

"Oh, darling. Soon you will realize that it's inevitable. It's going to happen no matter what."

"What's going to happen?"

He's silent and I can practically feel the intensity of his emotions course through me. I can practically see his dark red eyes staring into me. I can feel each muscle on his tattooed body tensing with determination. With need.

"You're going to be mine."

CHAPTER 7

SAM

I picture Willow's long black hair and sleeping face and can't help but feel a knot in my stomach. Memories of everything that has happened between us shoot through my brain. The night I met her in that Mexican restaurant, only seconds after being transfixed by her sister. The many times we fucked, even though the entire time she was also with the man inside of her head. Finding out about Nox and this other world when we went to visit her bitch of a mother.

Then, my mind shoots straight to Sophia. I haven't seen her in a few days. Not since she told me she never wanted to see me again. Not since Willow walked in on us in her dorm, me grinding against her half naked body. Not since my heart cracked in two for more than one reason.

We are on our way to Sophia now. The angel with golden hair and light blue eyes. She looks like she came straight out of heaven. Which is ironic since her polar opposite sister is the one from a magical world. I have never dreaded but also wanted to see someone as bad as I want to see Sophia. She's not going to be happy when she sees me. And she's going to be heartbroken about Willow.

"She's not going to be happy about seeing me." I remind Onyx sitting in the seat next to me in the cab. We are on our way to her dorm, to explain everything going on.

"I don't quite care what she feels about seeing you. She's Willow's sister and Nox made it clear that she would take care of her. I need the princess's body to be as safe as possible. So, Sophia will be staying at your house. Whether she likes it or not."

"Excuse me?" I turn towards him with wide eyes. "You never said that. I thought we were just filling her in on the situation. Telling her where Willow was."

"We will be telling her where *Adrienne* is and making her stay at the house indefinitely. Two pairs of eyes are better than one. I refuse to take any chances." I glare at the asshole next to me and decide in this moment, I don't like him. He's cocky and arrogant and I hate being told what to do.

"She will never agree to that. I can take care of *Willow* myself." I exaggerate her name like he did and turn to look out my window. Only bad things can happen if Sophia stays at my house. Bad things that will feel so fucking good but destroy us both. Because she already decided we would never work. Not after everything with Willow.

"For a doctor, you're pretty fucking dense. How do I say this..." He pauses and puts his hand to his chin. "I don't give a shit what she agrees to. She has no choice."

"Fuck you," I growl out.

"Let me make this perfectly clear. I don't care about either one of you. You don't matter. Adrienne is the only one that matters. I refuse to let anything else happen to her. I refuse to let her die.

And if she does, I will personally destroy anyone who has a hand in it. And if you fail her, I will destroy you as well. Understood?"

As he speaks, his light purple eyes start to glow. They grow brighter and brighter, similar to the way Willow's did that day in the dorm when fire sprung from her hands. I gulp down the fear from that memory and nod my head. "Whatever you say."

The rest of the car ride is silent. The cabin of the cab is tainted with his arrogant pride, so thick I swear I can almost see it swirling around the car. I hate that I backed down, but I know my limits. He could most likely kill me in the blink of an eye before I could even get a hand in.

The tires squeak below us as we come to a stop in front of Sophia's dorm building. I look out the dirty window and watch as flashes of the last time I was here shuffle across the glass. I gulp down my uneasiness and move for the handle of the door. Stepping onto the sidewalk, I don't wait for Onyx before I continue towards the front door of her building. The glass door sparkles in the fading sunlight as if it were just freshly wiped down.

Opening the door, I hold it for the prick behind me and then make my way towards the stairs leading up.

"Excuse me? You two need visitor's passes. Who are you here for?" Shit. We stop walking as the voice from behind us calls out. I didn't even think about that. There's no way Sophia is going to agree to letting us come up if this security guard calls her.

I turn towards the man sitting behind a desk at the front and smile at him innocently. He's as fat as he is bald and his wire glasses look like they're seconds away from snapping as they squeeze his face. Sweat trickles down his temple and the brown button up he's wearing pulls tight enough that the buttons are seconds from popping off.

I'm about to answer when Onyx interrupts me. "Sorry, sir. We already have visitor's passes. We forgot them in the car. We'll be right back." Before the security guard can answer, Onyx is turning around and walking back out the door. I follow suit, confused as I speed up to match his quick pace.

"What the hell? We don't have visitor's passes." He walks past the car and moves towards an ally near the dorm building. He turns into the dark and empty passageway before coming to a stop and turning towards me.

"Whatever you do, do not take your hand off of me." He reaches for me and I pull away.

"What the fuck, man? Don't touch me," I snap at him, annoyed by his lack of explanation.

"For the love of God. I just need you to trust me, okay? I know how to get us in there without getting a visitor's pass. I'm assuming if Sophia gets warning that you are coming up, she's going to deny you, correct?" I confirm his assumption with a simple nod of my head.

"Well, then fuck off and let me get us in there." If it was any other situation, I would punch him in the face for speaking to me this way. I'm not one to take disrespect. But Willow's safety is on the line. It has nothing to do with the fact that he could probably crush me with his mind. Nope. Not at all.

Reaching out, I put my hand on him. My fingers clasp around his upper arm and I let my nails dig into his suit jacket. I can't hold back the small snicker as he just barely winces before covering it up with a cough.

"Like I said. Do not let go until we get past the security guard." I roll my eyes and wait for him to do something. Before long, I feel heat radiating off of where I'm touching him. My palm starts to burn and when I look down at it, the skin is glowing. There are small golden specks crawling up my skin as warmth travels up my arm.

"What the…" The golden bugs tickle under my skin the higher they go. There are millions of them scurrying up towards my face and through my body. Everywhere they touch heats up like a there's fire under my skin. But as soon as they come, they are gone. While the golden specks disappear, the warmth continues to radiate throughout my body.

"Let's go. Don't say a word when we get in there." I somehow get my feet to move through my shock. I stay by his side, confused as to what he just did and how it's going to get us into the building without a pass.

"He's going to stop us. What did you just do to us?" I look down at my body as we walk and find everything the same.

"We are both invisible to the naked eye. As long as you are touching me, we can't be seen." He huffs out the words like it should have been obvious to me. Once we reach the front doors, Onyx stops and waits for someone to enter. It doesn't take long, since the sidewalks are full of people and most of them are students.

Once we find our victim, we follow right behind him. The kid is tall and skinny with blonde hair and his head shoved in a book so he's pretty clueless of his surroundings. We sneak through the door once he swings it open and follow him as he waves to the security guard and moves towards the stairs. No one looks our way. No one stops us.

We continue up the stairs and the minute the kid gets off on his floor, which is two below Sophia's, I let go of Onyx's arm. The warmth engulfing me instantly vanishes and I feel cold seep through my bones. I find myself missing that feeling. The fire that was running through my veins. It felt powerful, strong, unstoppable.

"Alright, doc, lead the way." His nickname sends dread through my body. That's what Willow used to call me when we were together. She did it to piss me off, which she successfully did, but it will always remind me of her now.

"Don't call me that." The sentence is emotionless when it comes out and I don't give him time to respond before I'm taking two steps at a time up to Sophia's floor. Once we get to her door, I freeze, my hand refusing to knock. I was so excited to see her again I flew up the steps to her but I freeze now that I'm close because I know she won't feel the same.

A shoulder shoves me to the side before I hear Onyx's loud knock on the door. Great. I guess there's no backing out now. A few seconds go by before I hear the lock turn on the door and it opens slowly. Fuck.

Her golden hair is up in a messy bun with whisps hanging around her face. She has oversized clear glasses on, her ocean blue eyes and a soft smile gracing her plump lips. I drag my eyes down her body and take in the tight white crop top she's wearing and the small plaid boy shorts. She's not wearing a bra and her long legs are out on display for all to see. For Onyx and any college dick head to ogle.

The low growl that escapes can't be stopped and it makes her look up at me. The smile fades and too many emotions to name flash across her eyes. Sadness. Anger. Guilt. Want. Her hands move to fold across her chest, like she's trying to cover up, but the movement only pushes her tits up higher.

"What are you doing here, Sam?" Her voice comes out shy but I can tell she's trying to sound strong. It's the sweetest sound I've ever heard.

I open my mouth to speak, but no words come out. Never in my life have I been speechless, but staring down at this five-foot something angel glaring at me has me mute. "For fuck's sake." I hear Onyx's annoyed whisper before he speaks up for me.

"My name is Onyx. I'm a friend of your sister from her... other life. We need to talk to you. May we come in?"

"Why are you with Sam? Where is Willow? Is everything okay?" The tone in her voice changes from shy to concerned and she stands a little taller. Her eyes widen and her hands move out in front of her where she starts to pick at her nails.

"Just let us come in and I will explain everything. Please." I notice the change in Onyx's voice as well. He has been so aggressive with me but when he speaks to her, his voice gets softer. It's still rough, but the timber is more gentle, as if not to scare her.

"Okay... come in. I'm sorry it's a mess. I've been studying all day." She starts to clean up the clothes on the floor and I can't help but watch her. She frantically throws them into a hamper before moving on to cleaning up her books.

There's a small half circle of textbooks on the floor with a candle lit and a blanket crumpled up in the middle. A cup of coffee steams away next to it and the cup reads 'Life Happens, Coffee Helps.' I smile, picturing her sitting there with a pencil in her mouth, studying under the blanket.

"You guys can uh, sit on the bed I guess." She looks over at the unmade bed and then quickly turns back to me with red, flushed cheeks. I know instantly that she is picturing the last time I was in this room. When I was on top of her. Kissing her soft lips. Biting her neck. Grinding my hard length against her hot core.

I gulp down my lust, even though it has already taken over the room. The sexual tension is so thick, I don't know how any of us are able to breathe. "Um, I'm going to sit over here." She scurries away and goes to sit on her roommate's bed across from hers. Onyx and I make our way to her bed and sit down.

"So... what's this about?" Her soft voice floats across the room towards us. I realize I haven't talked since we showed up and I decide it's my time.

"It's about Willow." My voice cracks and I cringe at myself. Clearing my throat, I stare into her crystal pools and try to come up with the best words. "Something happened to her. She's..." I don't know what to call it. "She's..."

"She's dead." Onyx chimes in saying the worst possible thing he could. I hit him in the arm and he looks at me with a shoulder shrug. "You were taking too long. Figured I'd cut to the chase."

"She's... dead?" Sophia blinks at us in horror. Her eyes somehow grow wider as tears fill them. Her head starts shaking back and forth and her lower lip trembles. She stands up before we can answer and darts for the door, tears already streaming down her face.

"Sophia, wait." I run after her, catching her by the hand as she reaches the hallway. The door slams behind us and I find us standing alone under the bright fluorescents. I hear her sobs but her back is to me. She's rigid and trying to pull away. I refuse to let that happen, I'm a lot stronger than her.

Pulling her hand hard, she whips towards me and slams into my chest. Her sobbing only intensifies when my arms grab her and hold her tight. At first, she stays rigid, refusing to hug me back. But after a few seconds, with my arms squeezing her and my hand clasped behind her head, she finally puts her arms around me.

We stay like this, arm in arm, heart to heart, for what feels like hours until finally her sobbing slows enough for me to talk.

"Angel, she isn't dead, dead. That's why we're here. Her body is at my house but Onyx said that her soul is still out there and waiting to be returned. That they are going to try to save her." I know I'm explaining this horribly. I know it doesn't make any sense, but I need her to stop crying. I can't see her cry like this. My own eyes are brimmed with tears.

"What?" She pulls away enough to look up into my eyes. The minute they connect with mine, I feel a part of me get lost in them. We stand there, clutching each other, and the entire world around me disappears. All I can see is the storming waters of her eyes, glistening with tears, staring straight into my soul.

"Sam?" Her voice pulls me out of my trance and I physically have to shake my head to come back to reality.

"Sorry, I don't know how to explain it to you. Onyx can. But Willow's not completely gone. She's still somewhere out there. And Onyx needs us to keep her body safe until they get the rest of her back. Just come back inside. Let him talk to you, okay?" I rub my hands over her biceps and a shiver travels down her body.

"Us?" The word comes out quiet and I watch as her eyes dart down to my lips for a fraction of a second. My mind shouldn't be going where it is. This isn't the time. Clearing my throat and letting go of her arms, and give her a heart-felt smile.

"Yes, Sophia. Us."

"I STILL DON'T UNDERSTAND ANY OF THIS." SOPHIA'S VOICE BREAKS through the silence of the car. We spent over an hour explaining everything to her and now we are in a cab on our way back to my apartment. Where Sophia is going to live. With me. Watching over Willow.

"It doesn't matter if you don't understand. All that matters is that Willow's body is taken care of. You two are the only people who know about our world and care about Willow. So, you two have to suck it up and take care of her. Got it?" Onyx sounds more than annoyed at this point. He didn't realize what he was getting into when it came to Sophia. She doesn't hold back on the questions.

"But why do I have to stay at his house? Why can't I just come and check on her?" She's desperate to avoid staying with me. Not that I blame her. I'm both excited and nervous for this experience.

"Do you love your sister, Sophia?" Onyx's hand has moved to the bridge of his nose, where he is now pinching it.

"More than anything." I can hear the guilt in her voice. The dread of the mistakes we have made.

"Then you should understand why we aren't taking any chances and you should be willing to make any sacrifice that you have to. I don't care if you two don't get along. I need eyes on her. At all times. Understood?"

"You're right... I'm sorry." I look over and find tears threatening to fall from her eyes. I want to comfort her more than anything, but I know I can't. It's not my place and it will only push her farther from me.

"We'll take care of her. I promise." And I mean that. I owe it to her. For everything I did to hurt her. Everything we did to hurt her.

The cab pulls up to the house and Onyx quickly opens the door and gets out. Sophia and I don't move, sitting in our seats, our knees just grazing each other's. Our breath is the only sound in the car, in our own little bubble, while the loud city bustles around us.

Putting my hand on her knee, she jerks at the touch, as if it stung. "It's going to be okay. She's going to be okay." I look over at her worried face. Her eyebrows are furrowed and there is now a constant watery sheen to her blue eyes. She looks terrified. I don't blame her; I'm feeling a bit uneasy at the what ifs. At the idea of getting involved in something so much bigger than us.

"You don't know that. How am I supposed to sit there watching over my sisters' unconscious body? After everything? Everything I did to her..." I squeeze her leg softly, in a reassuring way.

"Hey, that's enough. No more putting yourself down. You are so strong, Sophia. I know you can do this. And when she's back, you two can make up. You will figure it out. She loves you so much and always will." I have a feeling she doesn't believe a word I'm saying, but that doesn't matter. I will remind her of it every day until Willow comes back if I have to.

"Can you two get the hell out of the car before I start ripping my hair out? I have a kingdom to get back to." Onyx yells through the open door and Sophia doesn't get to answer me. Not that I think she would have.

We make our way into my house in complete silence. Onyx leads the way once we are in the house, up the stairs, and into the guest bedroom. The room that Willow used to sleep in. The room that belonged to my crazy ex-wife Olivia. The wife I haven't heard from since I kicked her out when she threatened Willow.

I avoid looking at anything in the room but Willow lying under the purple comforter. I don't look at the white walls covered in floral paintings. I don't look at the dresser filled with Olivia's clothes. I don't look out the window at the city hundreds of feet below us. The only thing I see is Willow's unconscious body, looking more peaceful than I have ever seen her.

I turn to Sophia now and watch her as she takes in her sister's body. She is moving forward at a snail's pace. She seems terrified to enter the room. To look at the girl she has always known as her sister. Her face is hard to read, almost emotionless, as if she is in shock.

When she finally reaches the side of the bed, her head is positioned high, her eyes avoiding the body below her. I hear her take a deep breath before she brings her eyes down to her sister. The first tear falls within seconds. Her breathing becomes shaky and ragged.

"Willow..." The sound of her voice breaks my heart. She sounds lost. Destroyed. Completely devastated. Her hand moves towards her face and she rubs her cheek with a soft thumb. "She's so cold."

"That's because her body and soul are separated. Once we return it, she will be back to normal." Onyx sounds gentle again, which I am grateful for. His anger and annoyance towards me is fine but when he aims it towards Sophia, I want to punch him in his smug face.

"You promise you are going to bring her back?" She turns towards Onyx and the desperation in her eyes can't be hidden.

"I promise you we will do everything we can to bring her back. I promise you I will not stop fighting until the princess is standing next to me as my lady. I promise you that she is one of the strongest royals we have ever seen and she won't go down without a fight."

Sophia nods her head in response. She stares at the wall as her head continues to nod up and down over and over again.

"Alright, I have to get back to the kingdom. I'm sorry to leave so quickly, but there are matters I need to get to. And I need to come up with a plan to find the princess. You won't be able to contact me. But I will try to come back here as much as possible to check in."

He doesn't give us a chance to answer. Within seconds, he disappears out of thin air and the room becomes eerily silent. Leaving me and Sophia alone. In the silence. In my house. The air feels thick with awkward tension. The room appears even darker, offering a veil of shadows that cover every inch.

Clearing my throat, the sound makes her jump. "Sorry... Do you want some coffee?" It feels like such a pathetic question to ask during a time like this. Almost childish.

"Got anything stronger?" Her hand moves to rub the back of her neck and she offers me a wobbly smile. Even with the sadness coating her face, I can't help but stare at her beauty.

"I like the way you think, angel." The nickname slips out again and this time, she catches it. I watch her stiffen and go rigid like I slapped her in the face. Like the name assaulted her physically. Before she can say anything, I walk fast out of the room and down to my kitchen. I don't want to give her the chance to say I can't call her that.

Grabbing the tequila out of one of the cabinets holding all of my liquor, I grab some limes from my fridge and agave from my pantry. Salting two cups, I mix together a quick and simple margarita for the two of us, consisting mostly of tequila. Sophia walks up to the opposite end of the counter just as I'm stirring the cocktails and I pass it to her.

"Thanks." Her voice is clipped. I hate it. I want the Sophia from a few days ago. The Sophia that told me about her insecurities, her passions, her hopes. She was a breath of fresh air in this sick world and I found myself spilling my deepest secrets to her. Secrets I couldn't even tell Willow when I was with her.

"I figured we could order some takeout for dinner. I was thinking Chinese?" I take a sip of the tart drink and the zing from the liquor travels down into my stomach as the liquid flows down.

I watch her sip the drink, paying too close attention to the way her lips form around the rim of the glass. She closes her eyes when the first drop hits her lips and with her deep swallow, a soft, barely audible moan escapes her. So quiet, I doubt she thinks I heard it. But I did. The way my body hardens is proof that I most definitely heard it.

"What about Mexican?" The minute she says it, my mouth forms into a huge smile. I doubt she had any intention of reminding me of the first time I saw her, but I can't help it. I can't help picturing her sitting there in her light pink dress with her hair pulled up in a bun. I can't help but smell the intoxicating scent of salsa that was almost forgotten to me the minute I saw her.

"That's a great idea. I'll order. Why don't you go change into something comfy?" I look at her jeans and dark green button down tucked in and miss the tiny shorts and t-shirt she was wearing in her dorm.

"Okay, thank you. Order me whatever you get. I'm not picky when it comes to Mexican food." She takes her drink, along with her small duffle bag, and then makes her way up the stairs. We never talked about where she would be staying, but I'm assuming she is going to change in the room that Willow is sleeping in. I'm going to offer her my room tonight. I'll sleep on the couch. Hell, I'll sleep in the elevator if that makes her more comfortable.

Reaching for my cell, I call one of the best Mexican restaurants near the apartment complex and order us one of almost everything on the menu. By the time I'm done, Sophia is walking back down the stairs. I swallow hard when I see what she's wearing. Light pink Minnie Mouse pajamas lay loose over her body. The outfit she was wearing when I came to see her in Vegas. When we first officially met each other.

Fuck. This is going to be a long night.

CHAPTER 8

NOX

I'm going to kill him. Actually, I'm going to kill both him and Dr. Archer. I've been waiting for the Dark Lord's return all day and night. I can't do anything else but wait. I can't get to Earth. I can't get to Adrienne. All I can do is pace throughout the castle like a pathetic waste of oxygen.

I hear footsteps quickly approaching and by the loud clacking of dress shoes, I know it's him. I meet him halfway and take in the smug grin on his face. He speaks first. "Well, our girl is safely in Dr. Archer's home and being watched by the man himself and Sophia."

"Our girl? Our fucking girl? MY girl is not safe in Dr. Archer's home. She's with two people that betrayed her. Two people who didn't give a shit that she had disappeared and instead, started fucking each other the minute she left."

"What? You're acting like an insane person. You're the one that told me that was the safest place for her body." He rolls his eyes at me like the information I just told him is trivial nonsense. That it doesn't matter.

"I didn't know about it until last night. When I traveled to one of Adrienne's memories. She watched them practically fucking each other when she went to say goodbye to Sophia before her coronation. They were having an affair... the minute Adrienne disappeared. They don't care about her. She's not safe, Onyx."

"Kage, for fuck's sake. That doesn't change anything. Sex is just sex. It doesn't matter. They will keep her safe. I saw it on both of their faces. They care for her." I roll my eyes at his statement.

"Of course you'd say that." My fists clench at my sides.

"What's that supposed to mean, shadvir?" He spits the word at me like I should be ashamed of my status. We both move to get in each other's faces and I swear I can feel the power buzzing off of both of us floating through the air.

"It means, all you have ever cared about is getting your dick wet. You've never cared about Adrienne. You don't know what it means to love someone. You're just an asshole who fucks anything that moves."

"You better watch your mouth, Kage. You don't know anything about me." His voice is a snarl and I can't help but laugh at it. I can feel the rage heating up inside of me and I know I'm stronger than him. For once, I can actually take on someone like him.

"I know you only care about yourself. You're a selfish, pompous royal who doesn't know what it means to care about someone. To put your life in danger to save someone—"

Power hits me straight in the chest and throws me back hard. It takes my breath away and I land painfully on my back against the cold stone floor. I take a breath but air doesn't enter my lungs, it just sits stagnant in my mouth as I try to come back to.

"I told you to shut the fuck up, shadvir!" His eyes are glowing a light lilac color and his face is scrunched up with anger. He looks ravenous, like he's ready to kill something. And that something is me.

"You seem to forget, Onyx." I use his first name as a form of disrespect. "I'm not just a shadvir anymore." Standing from my spot on the floor, I stare him down as the heat inside of me burns even stronger. It's so hot now that it feels like my skin is going to blister and bubble from the inside out.

The look on his face morphs from anger to apprehension. He doesn't allow himself to show fear, but I can see him reconsidering his previous moves. Because I'm stronger now. Thanks to my Ren.

ONYX

I STEP BACK AS HE STANDS FROM WHERE I HAD JUST THROWN HIM. I barely touched him with my powers, but as he stares me down with bright red eyes, I know immediately it was a mistake. He has Adrienne's powers and he has no idea how to use them. And the fucker is aiming them right at me.

"Nox, calm down, man. You don't know what you're capable of right now." I put my hands up as he starts to move closer to me. Every step forward, I take a step back. His eyes are glowing bright red and I can see the hot embers crawling down his arms to his fingertips.

He laughs a dark and sadistic laugh and I realize with dread that Nox isn't fully with me anymore. Whatever this is, whatever powers from Adrienne he is possessing, are taking over. No matter what I say, he's not going to calm down. I don't know how I know, but I can tell there is no sign of Nox's humanity left in his eyes.

"Fucking hell." I turn towards the stairs and make a run for it. I just need to get to a room with four walls. Running as fast as I can, I hear his ragged breathing behind me. The sound of flames crackling hit my ears right before heat engulfs my right side. Bright flames take over the railing on the stairs next to me, only inches away from where I am.

I know those flames. The flames that never extinguish. The burning golden light that hurts to even look at. He's throwing hell fire at me. One of the deadliest and rarest forms of magic there is. Taking the stairs faster, I finally reach the top and make my way to the first door on my right. It's a guest bedroom that no one ever uses.

Opening the door, I run through the room and towards the huge glass door that leads to the deck. Throwing myself outside, I turn and pull on my own magic, bringing a protective layer of clype around the one room. Clype that will prevent him from exiting. Clype that will hold his powers at bay. At least, I hope it will. If he has any idea how to manipulate clype, I'm fucked and so is the rest of this kingdom.

I stand in the chilly air and watch as he runs toward me through the room. His hands are covered in flames all the way up to his elbows and his eyes are blood red, covering any white from his cornea. I brace for what's to come, fearing that the clype won't stop him. Right when he's about to pass across the threshold and out onto the deck, small sparks of gold explode like a firework as his body hits the clype full force and stops his pursuit. He's taken aback by it and the flames running up his arms start to dissipate, slowly moving back to his hands.

I think he's calm enough to bring in his powers, but once the surprise of hitting an invisible wall wears off, his anger comes back full force. No longer dazed, he bangs on the clype with his blood red eyes and screams at me. They aren't coherent screams, but I can probably guess what he is trying to say.

"Nox, calm down and I will remove the clype. Control her powers. Please. You and I both know she wouldn't be happy if she found out either one of us got hurt." I can't tell if he can even hear me over his screams and pounding on the clype. He's acting like an animal, like a monster. And I'm starting to get sick of it. This is why shadvir shouldn't have magic. They don't know how to act with such power.

"Fine. Keep throwing your tantrum and I'll treat you like a damn child. Have fun in time out." I turn my back to jump over to the next terrace, and right before I flip my legs over the balcony, I hear him call out.

"Wait! I'm calm. The powers are gone... I'm... I'm sorry. I don't know what happened." His voice sounds more like him and there is an undertone of defeat laced throughout. I can't help but smile while my back is still turned to him. I love winning. It's one of my favorite things to do.

Walking back to him, I make sure his powers are actually being contained. His skin is no longer covered in fire but rather a clammy white color. His eyes are back to being their normal violet hue and there is a hint of fear and confusion swirling through them. If I wasn't so mad at him, I might actually feel bad for the guy.

"What do you say to me, Kage?" I raise an eyebrow at him. I know I probably shouldn't mess with him after what happened a few minutes ago, but he deserves to be embarrassed. He needs to be knocked down a peg.

"Fuck off." I laugh when he spits out the words with his arms crossed in front of his body.

"You're so close. I'm looking for two words but those aren't quite them. I know you can do it." I turn so my ear is facing towards him and place a hand around it. I'm mocking him and he knows it.

"Onyx. Let me out of this goddamn room. Now."

"Poor shadvir clearly can't even count. That was way more than two words. Nine to be exact. I'm still looking for just the two. I can stand here all night. Actually, you can. I'll just leave you to it and go get some dinner. Maybe get to bed early tonight.

It's a damn shame I ran into one of the only rooms without a bathroom." I raise my hand to my forehead and salute him before slowly turning away.

"Fuck. Fine. I'm sorry, okay? I don't know what happened. I can't control it, clearly, and I didn't even feel like I was in my own body. It felt like something was taking over." I turn to face him again with a smirk.

"Or someone. A very specific someone that we both can't seem to get enough of." My mind wanders to Adrienne and I can't help but picture her chasing after me the way Nox just had. Only, the anger in her eyes would be hiding a deep seeded want for me. I would have gladly trapped us both in that room then. Where I could rip the clothes off of her perfect little body. Where I could pin her against the window and shove myself deep insid—

"Onyx?" Kage's annoying voice breaks me from my thoughts and I glare at him. I pocket the fantasy for later when I'm in the comfort of my room. "You think Adrienne took over my body?"

"I don't know. I've never seen a mating bond or a transfer of powers like this. I just can't help but picture our Adrienne getting all heated the same way you did. That girl is quite the hotheaded little spit fire and your tantrum reminded me of her." I pause before deciding to add one last jab. "Only difference is, when you get angry, I want to kill you. When she gets angry, I want to fuck her."

That one earns me a growl but before he can say anything else, I let go of the clype and set the beast free. I think I've tortured him enough and I'm a little nervous that the fire ball he threw my way is still burning on the staircase. I'm not sure how we are going to extinguish that one if it is.

"Any chance you know how to get rid of your little party trick? Hell fire doesn't just extinguish like normal fire." I walk through the room and out the door into the hallway. I can hear him tailing me as I round the corner to the stairs and see the bright light burning in a small spot on the railing of the stairs. Great.

"Yeah... I have no idea." Of course, he doesn't. He doesn't know how to summon his powers let alone how to distinguish them. I guess there's only one other option to keep anyone from getting hurt.

Walking down a few steps, I bring my powers to the surface and stare down the flickering flames. I feel my magic exiting my body and slithering its way through the air and towards the fire. Within seconds, my clype surrounds it. I push more into it, trying to use the protective clype that hides what's inside. I have never been good at that one. It takes a lot of strength and focus.

The fire flickers in and out of sight until finally, it disappears entirely. I release the last bit of magic and feel exhaustion take over my body. That took a lot out of me and still, the fire flashes back into sight every few seconds. It's good enough though. I can't use any more magic right now or I'm going to pass out.

"Now that we have managed to get entirely off topic, should we get back to the important matters at hand? Like, I don't know, saving the princess?" I make my way down the stairs, one hand on the railing for stability. My vision's a bit blurry from the exertion, so I have to take it slow.

"You don't look so good. I think you should sit down." I roll my eyes at Nox's comment.

"No shit. If you didn't create a problem I had to fix, I wouldn't be this exhausted." We walk into the throne room where I not so gently throw my body into the huge velvet chair. Taking a deep breath, I close my eyes and will my heart to slow down.

"So, are you going to go back and get Adrienne's body?" I clench my fists at his infuriating question. We just got over this argument, with minor casualties, and he has to bring it up again.

"No. I am not. I don't give two shits if her sister and ex-boyfriend fuck in the same room she's in. They will keep her safe from *real* threats and danger. And then after we get her home, she never has to see them again. And if she truly wants, I'll destroy them both."

"She wouldn't want that. That's not the kind of person she is." I can't hold back the smirk that forms on my face. Opening my eyes, I look at him with humor dancing across my features.

"Oh really? She's not that kind of person? Guess what, Nox?" I bend forward, trying to get closer to him standing in front of me. "She's not a person. She's a masterpiece created by both heaven and hell. And she's the strongest being I've ever met. You have no idea what kind of *person* she is. She's a conundrum. Something none of us will ever be able to fathom or understand. And that's what makes her so goddamn spectacular."

"I know she is..." He doesn't respond with the anger I expected from him. "I know how amazing she is. I know none of us will ever understand her magnificence. But all I was saying is I know her heart. I've been connected to her since she was born. I have seen how much she loves. And I have felt that love. And that's what makes her so spectacular. That someone as strong and powerful as her can have such a big heart."

I contemplate what he says. I think of the experiences I have had with the princess. While there were few, she left a lasting impact on me. One that no one else ever has. I could see the love she had for her people. The people she didn't even know. I could see the love she had for Nox. For her father. Hell, even the friendship we formed proved how much she could love. I was a pompous ass before I met her and she somehow changed me, dare I say, made me good.

"You're right. But it also makes her vulnerable. If Ahriman or The Reaper know how much she loves, they can use that against her. They can use you against her. Her father, her sister, the people. Hell, even me."

"Then we need to get her back before they can even think about using us against her. We need to move quick."

"Again, thank you for pointing out the obvious. We can't move until we know what the fuck we are doing and where we are going."

"I talked to Lady Blackwell. She knows The Reaper. She could hear him in her head after everything happened. I think she can help us. We need to get her out of that room."

"I can't remove someone else's clype. That room is protected by Cole. Only he can remove it." I shake my head at him, annoyed by his idiocy.

"Or someone from his direct bloodline." He gives me a cocky smirk and when I realize what he means, I can't help but smile back.

"You have her powers, which means, you can remove the clype." I pause and think for a second. "Except, you have no idea how to control your powers. You'll never be able to remove a barrier that strong."

"Right now, no. But luckily, I know the Dark Lord that trained the princess herself." I squint my eyes at him and then nod my head softly.

"Fine. I'll train you. But first, I need a drink. And then a nap."

CHAPTER 9

ONYX

We've been at this training for hours now. I hate to admit it, but he's getting the hang of this faster than I expected him to. He's smarter than he looks and when he's determined, Nox Kage gets things done. I respect that about him. One of the only things about him, actually.

He has an easier time removing the clype than he does creating it, which is exactly what we need right now. I can do the creating if we need it, but he needs to master the skill of removing clype if he ever wants to get Lady Blackwell out of her prison. The prison she has been in since Adrienne was just a baby.

"I think you're ready. And by that, I mean, I don't want to waste any more time training when we could be on our way to Adrienne." I slap him on the back and he grunts at the hit. Chuckling low, I turn away from him and walk my way back into the castle. Being out here, at the front entrance of the castle, reminds me of training Adrienne. They are bittersweet memories. Training with her was what brought us closer, but thinking about it now makes my heart clench.

"So, what do we do now?" He catches up to me, his breath shaky from the exhaustion. You wouldn't think using your powers was so draining, but it's worse than any physical exertion I have ever experienced.

"Now, we go talk to Lady Blackwell. We have to see if she is even willing to help us. I don't fully trust that she isn't a risk rather than an answer. There's a reason she has been locked up for the last twenty-five years." I make my way towards the cellar door with Nox on my tail.

"Layla was locked up because of her feelings for The Reaper. Cole wanted to make sure she didn't hurt herself or anyone else because of it. Which makes her an asset to finding Ren. We find The Reaper... we find Ren."

"I can't believe she fell in love with that fucker." We move down the stone staircase and walk through the huge hallway. There are rooms on each side of us and the hall seems to go on forever. Nox is now walking in front of me, directing me to the room that belongs to Layla.

"She was tricked. Her heart has always been so big. Just like Ren's. She thinks all of the lies The Reaper spewed her way were true. She thinks she was in love with him. She thinks he was in love with her." I snicker at the thought. The monster that ripped our princesses heart out of her body without hesitation isn't capable of love.

"She's delusional if she thinks that a demon is capable of anything other than death." We stop at a door and Nox turns towards me.

"I wouldn't be so sure about that. We can't believe everything we were told when we were younger. The only thing we know about demons are what we were taught."

"And, you know, the fact that The Reaper has maimed and murdered innocent people, tricked Lady Blackwell into fucking him so he could leave his spawn in her, and murdered our princess before our very eyes!" I whisper yell in his face, confused as to his change of heart about the very monsters that took his mate.

"I get it. I'm just saying, keep an open mind. You'll understand why I'm saying this after we speak with Lady Blackwell, okay?" Huffing in annoyance, I nod my head. I don't understand, but I'm willing to let this old kook try to convince me that she can help us.

NOX

"So, you're trying to tell me, the Gods that have given us everything are bad? The Gods that have tried to save all of mankind for centuries from Lucifer himself are monsters?" Onyx has barely let Layla get a word in and we have been in here for over half an hour. I wanted her to explain everything she explained to me before we move forward with this.

"I know it's hard to comprehend, but yes, hypothetically. Lucifer was one of the angels. And a strong one at that. He heard things he shouldn't have, fought back, and then Atlas banished him to Hell. When that wasn't enough, he tried to kill him with the deadliest imignis out there and somehow, the curse ended up suspended right between their worlds, a constant that could not be undone it was so powerful."

"So, what's the point of us? Why were we created if the Gods are the reason for the sun?" I watch as Onyx's knee bobs up and down at a fast rate. He seems overwhelmed, anxious even. I guess I would be too if I found out my ancestors were the actual monsters.

"We are the fall back. The way Atlas saved his own ass and made it look like it was Lucifer's fault. Atlas stored away his imignis and pretended the ball of fire came from down below. From hell.

Then, he created something to counteract his curse. Something that made him look like the good guy. He created us."

"You realize how crazy you sound right?"

"Yes, someone else reminded me of that yesterday," she says as she looks at me with a smile. I smile back, rubbing my neck in embarrassment. I told her she sounded insane less than twenty-four hours ago and now, I'm completely on her side.

"The Reaper ripped your daughter's heart out of her back. It happened barely a foot in front of me. You think he's one of the good ones?" I clench my teeth at the memory of her dying. I wish Onyx would stop bringing that day up.

"I realize that. And as much as I hate The Reaper for hurting her in that way, I also know that they have no intention of letting her stay dead. They want her alive just as much as you do. She's the answer to everything."

"So, what are we supposed to do? Just hand her body over to them?" His voice is raised and I've had just about enough of his attitude.

"Do not raise your voice at the former Dark Lady. She does not deserve such treatment and if you can't act like the Lord that you are—"

"You'll what?" He raises a brow at me and I clench my fists. Even after seeing how powerful I am because of Ren, he has no fear. I guess that's a good quality to have as a leader, but right now, I want to murder him.

"If you two are going to fight like children, I won't have adult conversations with you." Layla's voice comes out authoritative, like the ruler she once was. "There are times when we fight, and there are times when we put our grievances behind us and do what is right. If a fight is what you want, I can assure you, that is what you will be getting. But you're aiming your anger at the wrong side. We need to join with them so we can beat the Gods." She's whispering again, trying to prevent any eavesdroppers from hearing her. "I remember Lucifer telling The Reaper that once Ahriman and Adrienne are separated, Atlas will be coming for her too. I'm sure they are looking for her body as we speak."

Dread drops through my body. If that's true...

"Where is her body anyway?" Lady Blackwell stares between the two of us. I turn to look at Onyx and I watch his face the minute he realizes what we did.

We just left her body in the worst place we could of. We took her away from one enemy and handed her to the other.

CHAPTER 10

SOPHIA

Last night was... interesting to say the least. We barely spoke to each other. The entire time we sat in Willow's room, eating way too much food and drinking tequila. The only sound that could be heard was the quiet music playing from the Bluetooth speaker. And yet, the entire time, I felt like I was going to scream from how loud it was. From how loud my heart was beating. How fast my mind was racing.

Now, I'm lying in Sam's huge king size bed. It's six in the morning and I didn't sleep a wink. It has nothing to do with how comfortable the bed is because, I can assure you, this bed feels like I'm sleeping on a cloud. It has everything to do with the two people in this house. Willow's unconscious body and Sam's sleeping one downstairs on the couch.

Dragging myself out of the bed, I make my way through the room. It's mostly dark in here, so I have a hard time navigating through his room to the bathroom. Luckily, he has a very minimalistic style, so I have little trouble avoiding his furniture.

Once I'm in the bathroom, I turn the light on and place my hands against the black countertop, leaning my weight against it. Looking up into the mirror, I take in my appearance. I look insane. My hair is in a bun that is half up, half falling down around my shoulders. My eyes are red and puffy from lack of sleep, crying, and a minor hangover. And my skin looks dry and washed out.

"What are you doing, Sophia Taylor?" I scold myself, glaring at the person standing in front of me. I'm standing in my sister's ex boyfriend's house, thinking about him. While she's practically dead, lying in the other room. "There's something seriously wrong with you." I point at myself in the mirror, hating where my thoughts have been for the last few hours.

I spent most of the night crying, but when I was in bed, I had these visions of Sam sneaking into the room. I closed my eyes and pictured him slipping through the bedroom door and crawling into bed with me...

"I couldn't stay away, angel." His deep voice vibrates in my chest, bringing a shiver to the surface. *"I need to touch you. I've been thinking about fucking you since that night in your dorm."*

I try to push him away, but my attempt is pathetic. "It's wrong, Sam. I can't... I won't." *Even I don't convince myself of my words. My voice shakes and cracks when it leaves my body.*

"I didn't say you had a choice." He growls out as he reaches for me and rips my shirt straight off of my body.

I pull myself out of my earlier fantasy and find myself breathing heavily again. I don't know what's wrong with me but the idea of being taken... of being forced to do something my body wants but my mind refuses to do is the hottest thing I have ever thought about.

"I'm going straight to hell." I drop my head and stare down at the floor, letting out an exaggerated huff. I'm turned on again.

More than I ever have been in my life. During the worst time I ever could be. "I'm the worst sister in the world."

"Why would you say that?" His low voice makes me jump and I squeal out loud as I turn towards the door. He's standing in the doorway of the bathroom, his glasses lying lazily on his face and his long navy-blue pajama pants resting low on his hips. He isn't wearing a shirt. He's. Not. Wearing. A. Shirt.

"You scared me." I watch him with hooded eyes, partly wondering if this is just another one of my fantasies playing out a little too real. His eyes move from mine and travel down my body, making me look down with them. Fuck. I'm wearing my plain white t-shirt with no bra and a pair of black panties underneath. No pants.

He clears his throat but keeps his eyes glued to my lower half. "Sorry. Couldn't sleep. Figured you couldn't either. Came to ask if you wanted coffee and then I heard you talking to yourself." His voice sounds strained, like looking at me is physically hurting him.

I know I should speak up. I know I should say yes, I'd love a cup. But my mouth stays zippered shut. I stare at him as my eyelids flutter shut slowly. The air feels thick with tension and I know he's feeling what I'm feeling.

"Sophia, why are you the worst sister in the world?" His question sounds more like a command. I don't have a choice in answering him.

"Because..." I swallow the lust that's clogging my throat, but it doesn't go down. "Because of what I have been thinking about all night." My voice sounds like a mouse compared to his, almost embarrassingly so.

"What have you been thinking about, Sophia?" He steps closer to me, eyeing me like I'm his pray. I take a step back and hit the counter with my back, making me whimper out loud.

"I... it's... It's nothing." I lower my gaze from his and look down at the ground. He's too intimidating. Too overwhelming. If

I don't look away, I will tell him all of my deepest, darkest secrets. Including the fucked up fantasy I had earlier.

"Sophia Taylor." His voice somehow gets even lower than it already was. I hear his feet move across the floor towards me, but I refuse to look up. "Tell me what you are thinking about. Now."

Nope. Not happening. I keep my eyes down and close them, hoping that he will vanish if I keep them closed long enough. It's quiet for what feels like hours and then something brushes against my chin. At first it's a soft, warm touch, but then it turns hard. He grips my chin and forces me to look up at him. My mouth falls open and the most embarrassing sound escapes me.

I freaking moan.

"Fuck... You like that, don't you, angel?" I can't stop myself from looking into his midnight eyes. The dark brown is much darker than it normally is and the sight of it both terrifies and excites me.

He pushes me further into the counter, making it bite into my backside. I cry out and cross my legs, squeezing them tight to try to subdue the throbbing in my core.

"Tell me what has been going on in that pretty little head of yours or I'll force it out of you." Hearing him say the word force sends me back into my fantasy and my vision goes blurry with lust.

"I... I can't stop thinking about you." The words barely come out audible. I sound breathless, like I just ran a marathon. His eyes dart between mine and something dangerous flashes in them. Something feral.

"What about me?"

"It's nothing, please... just—"

His hand moves from my chin to the bun on top of my head in the blink of an eye. I yelp when he pulls it, bringing my head to the side, exposing my neck. He brings his face down until his hot breath is brushing against my sensitive skin.

"You know what I think?" He swallows hard, whispering against my skin. "I think you have been picturing me fucking you. Just like I have." His nose runs up my neck and towards my ear. His mouth hovers, inching forward and biting down on my lobe.

My knees go weak and I start to fall before his hands grip at my sides. I think he's just going to hold me there, but he lifts me up in the air and deposits me on the counter. I grip his arms, holding onto his hot skin as it flexes under my grasp.

"What did you want me to do to you, angel?" His hands are under my thighs, and he slowly brings them up my body. They run up over my ass and then he's gripping my waist, pulling me into him. I can feel his erection pressed up against me, the only thing separating us is my thin underwear and his cotton pants. God, why does it feel so good?

"I... I just..." I moan when he grinds into me and my head falls back, hitting the mirror behind me.

"Keep. Talking." He puts his hand around the back of my neck and brings my face upright again, still grinding his hips into mine. How can he expect me to talk, let alone think coherent thoughts, when he's moving like this?

"I was picturing you forcing yourself on me," I say the words quick, desperate to let them out into the world. I can't hold onto them any longer.

He groans into my ear, the gravelly sound sending goosebumps across every inch of my skin. "God damn. You want me to take you, angel? You want me to hold you down and do whatever I want to your sexy little body?"

I'm so turned on, it feels like I'm coming already. Tingles and sparks of electricity shoot through my body. I feel feverish and my vision is still blurry from earlier. My tongue sits heavy in my mouth and my blood is rushing through my body at an exasperated rate.

He grabs my neck, staring into me through my eyes, and squeezes just enough to keep the air from traveling into my body comfortably. "Say it."

"Ye-yes." I try to get the word out through his grip. I can feel myself dripping for him. I've never been this wet, it's almost embarrassing. Sam seems to notice at the same time that I do because he looks down between us, looking straight at my core, making me pulse with just his stare.

"Fucking hell. You're soaking through my pants. I can feel you all over my cock." I grit my teeth, trying to hold in the animalistic sounds that want to escape me at his dirty words. This is so inappropriate, everything about it.

"Please." I don't even mean to say it. It comes out before I can stop it and the one word makes Sam snap. His hands pull at my face and he slams his lips against mine. I cry out at the intensity of it and he takes advantage of my mouth being open, slipping his tongue inside.

He explores my mouth as his hips grind into me. Each thrust of his hips hits that sensitive spot every time and before long, I'm panting into his mouth as pressure builds up like a pot of water about to boil over. I'm right there, about to explode and find that blissful release, when he stops moving.

"You think I'm going to let you come already, Sophia?" His whisper is so low it sounds like a growl hitting my lips. "You're either coming on my fingers, my tongue, or my dick. Do you want to pick or should I?"

If he keeps talking like this, I'm going to come with just his words. Even though he stopped grinding into me, the pressure stays constant, threatening to push me over the edge at any second.

"I..."

"Too late." He moves his hands to my sides and rips my black boy shorts down my body. My legs are pushed wide on the counter, an uncomfortable stretch taking over with the position. His hand goes to my chest and he pushes me, my head and upper back colliding with the mirror behind me.

I watch him through hooded lids as he gets down on his knees in front of me. Oh my God. The anticipation of feeling his tongue on me sends a wave of pleasure down to my toes. I bite my lip, trying to hold back my moan, and wait. Barely five minutes ago I was alone in bed, thinking about him. And now? I'm living the fantasy. A fantasy I've never done with anyone before.

"So fucking pretty." I swallow my nerves and watch him stare at me. "Tell me the truth. Has any other man ever tasted you, Sophia?" He licks his lips, never removing his eyes from my naked core.

"N... no." I try not to be embarrassed. I've done things with boyfriends, but I was never comfortable with anyone doing this. It always grossed me out. Until now.

"Fuckkk." He draws out the words. "That's my good girl. Has anyone ever fucked this pretty little pussy?" His nose is right at the crease of my thigh. Every word he says sends a puff of hot air right across where I'm most sensitive. It's so distracting I don't hear his question. His hands grip my legs harder. "Answer me. Has another cock been inside of you before?"

"Only once..." I breathe out the words. This version of Sam is like nothing else I have ever experienced. Last time we kissed he was gentle. He was sweet. Right now? I can't tell if this man wants to kill me or kiss me. But then again, I asked for this. I told him about my twisted fantasy.

"Did you enjoy it?" It feels like a trick question. I can tell by the anger laced through his deep timber that he doesn't like the fact that someone else was there first.

"No." I'm being honest. I lost my virginity freshman year of college to a frat guy named Brad. I did it so I could stop feeling so insecure about my lack of experience. He didn't even know it was my first time. He was drunk, I wasn't, and it hurt like hell.

"Good. Next time there's a dick inside of you, you're going to enjoy every second of it. Understood?"

"Yes," I whisper to him, my voice lodged in my throat. The minute the word leaves my mouth, his head dips forward and he sweeps his tongue over me. I try to cry out from the sensation, but it's so overwhelming that no sound leaves me. Warmth moves from where he's licking me, throughout the rest of my body until it feels like I'm on fire.

"God, Sam." His tongue moves up and starting circling my clit, making my body convulse on the counter. I reach down and grab his head, holding him there, desperate for this to never end. When I push his head further into me, he grabs my thighs in a death grip, pulling them even wider. The pain only fuels my pleasure and I find myself grinding into him, chasing that release I know is inevitable.

He groans against me, the sound vibrating though my body and pushing me even closer. I can feel it. That same feeling I have given to myself countless times with my fingers, only this time, a hundred times better.

"I'm... I'm gonna..." I don't get to finish my sentence because suddenly, one of his thick fingers slides inside of me. He doesn't move slow. He doesn't let me adjust. He thrusts into me over and over again, curling his finger deep inside of me while his tongue does its perfectly practiced dance.

And then I'm gone. I'm lifted into the air and away from this room. My body feels like a million sparks are going off inside of it. My senses leave me, forcing me to focus solely on the intense pleasure coursing through my veins. It doesn't stop for what feels like a life time. Like I'm never going to come down from this. Like these electric waves are going to inevitably drown me in a sea of bliss.

But all good things come to an end. And before long, I'm brought back down to this moment. Sitting here on the counter, with Sam between my legs. I'm breathing heavy, my body still convulsing, as Sam continues to lick me. When I reach down and try to move his head away, my cheeks flush from both adrenaline and embarrassment, Sam finally pulls back and looks up at me. His face is glistening with my release.

I watch him lick his lips and my mouth goes dry. "You taste like fucking candy. And that pussy. Fuck. You have the tightest little pussy I've ever felt." I feel my cheeks heat up even more, now fully embarrassed. No one has ever said anything like that to me. No one has ever tasted me or made me come like that.

I don't say anything back to him. I just carefully get down from the counter and reach for my underwear. How did I let this happen? What came over me? The same thing that always seems to come over me whenever I'm around this man. My normal, collected self goes out the window and I suddenly start doing impulsive, irrational things.

"Sophia." The desire I had heard in his voice before is now replaced by a gentle tone. I look over at him as I step into my underwear and his eyes make me freeze. He looks... sad? "Please don't shut down again. Please. I know that was a lot. I know it went too far, too fast. But I could tell you needed it. I think we both did."

"That doesn't make it okay," I huff, putting my head in my hands. "I don't know what comes over me when I'm around you. All of that was not me. I'm boring. I'm inexperienced. I'm... I'm not like her." I close my eyes when I say the words out loud. His ex-girlfriend. My sister, even if not by blood. The woman lying unconscious in the other room.

"Exactly! You're not her. You're you. And that's why I can't get you out of my damn head. Do you think I want to feel like this? I feel like a piece of shit for what I did to Willow. But the way I feel about you won't go away."

"You want that!" I point to the counter, gesturing towards what we just did. "You want an experienced woman. You want someone who knows what she's doing. Someone who likes being dominated! You want someone who can actually satisfy you!" I don't know why I'm yelling, but it feels like all of the adrenaline I built up with my orgasm is now coming out in anger.

"You're the one that said you were fantasizing about me forcing myself on you. I did that for you. I don't need that. If you're not into what we just did, then we will do something else. I'll make love to you missionary style with fucking classical music playing in the background if that's what you need. And I can assure you, you more than satisfy me. My cock is so hard it hurts. When I leave this room, I'm going to fuck myself thinking about the way you taste. The look in your eyes when I touch you. Those damn sounds you make as you come."

I don't know how to respond to such a confession. Just hearing those words come from his mouth has my body tingling all over again. Picturing him standing in the shower, one hand bracing himself on the wall while he's touching himself, thinking of me. It's one of the hottest things I have ever imagined.

"Sam... I don't know what to do. This feels so right and so wrong at the same time. Willow is in the other room, and she may never come back to us, and what do I do? I spend all night fantasizing about her ex and then let him go down on me in the bathroom." I shake my head, throwing my hands up in the air.

"I know, angel. This isn't ideal. This isn't what I was planning or expecting. I was convinced I would never see you again. I was going to leave you alone and let you go on with your life. Find someone better for you. Someone younger. Someone with less baggage. And then days later we are somehow thrown back together and forced to live under the same roof for an undetermined amount of time. I'm forced to sleep in the same house as you and not talk to you. Not look at you. Not fucking touch you. I told myself I could.

I told myself this would be over and you could leave after Willow is saved. That I wouldn't stop you."

"And now?"

"Now, I've gotten a taste. I've touched you. I've heard you moaning my name. And it was the most exquisite God damn thing I've ever experienced. I can't just let that go. Not without a fight." I furrow my brows at him, trying to figure out what this is to him.

"Is this just about sex? Because if that's the case, I'm not your girl." I shake my head at him, folding my arms over my chest as my teeth clench.

"Jesus fuck, Sophia! No! Like I said. You make all of the decisions. I will never touch you again if that's what you want." He stares into my eyes as he speaks, not wavering once. "I want to learn everything there is to know about you. I want to hear about your day and help you study at night. I want to hold you when you're crying and admire you when you're laughing. Anything you are willing to give me, whether it's for five minutes, five days, or five years. I'll take what I can get." He talks so fast, I almost can't keep up. He looks frantic, less like the composed man he always is and more like someone on the brink of insanity.

"I just don't understand why. Why me?" He moves towards me, running a hand over his face before reaching for both of my hands. I go willingly, letting his huge hands engulf my small ones.

"You listen. You understand. You had me pouring my heart out to you with just one look. My secrets were no longer my secrets because I felt I could trust you to hold them too. I felt that I wouldn't be okay unless I had you there to talk to. I've never experienced that. Relationships for me have always been about me taking care of my person. And trust me, if I ever get the chance to be with you, I will make sure you are always taken care of. But, for once, I actually feel like someone will be there to take care of me. I'm not saying we are meant to be. I'm not confessing my love to you. We barely know each other. But I also won't deny this feeling I have. This connection I feel. It's something we both owe ourselves to explore."

Again, I'm left speechless after he pours his heart out to me in his bathroom. This man is like no one else I've ever met. I think back to the secrets he's talking about. The night in Vegas when we were waiting on the police to find Willow, only to find out she was in another world. Sam told me about his ex-wife. How she had terrible post-partum and she lost her mind. How she tried to suffocate their baby girl, Jane. How he was driving through a snow storm to get her to the hospital and a truck hit their car, killing Jane on impact.

I cried with him that night. That was also the night he kissed me. It was such an intense, emotional moment. I felt like I could feel all of the pain he has felt all of these years. The guilt. The self-hatred. He held onto that for so long, never talking to anyone about it, until he was able to open up to me.

"I just... I need time. I agree with you, and I want to try this. But I need to make sure Willow is okay. I can't promise you anything until then." I'm happy with my response, but I don't fully believe my own words. I can feel the pull between us, like a rope tightening and bringing us together. I don't know if I'll be strong enough to resist it. Clearly, I proved that I wasn't already.

"I wouldn't expect anything more." He pulls my hands toward him and my body is engulfed in his. It's a powerful moment and I can't control the sob that escapes me. It feels so right being in his arms. Safe. Comforting. Necessary. Like there's no point in anything else if I can't have this.

My eyes close, taking in this moment, when bright light flashes across my eyelids. It almost resembled a flash of lightening, only it was stark white. I open them and pull away, staring up at Sam.

"Did you..."

"Did I see that flash? Yeah. What the hell was that?" His brows are furrowed and he's looking around the room, clearly as confused as I am. Realization hits me and I gasp.

"Willow!" I yell out her name as I run through Sam's room and into hers. The first thing I see is Willow's body floating in the air above the bed. I look over to the side of it and find a man standing there. He has light blonde hair and stark white, almost translucent skin. He turns his head towards me and his light gray eyes bore into me. They are unnaturally light. It's terrifying and I find myself taking a step back.

My back hits a wall, except this wall has hands that grab onto my shoulders. Sam carefully moves me out of the way and positions himself in front of me. It's at that moment that I realize I am still only wearing a shirt and underwear still.

"Who the hell are you? What are you doing with Willow's body?" While I'm terrified and cowering behind him, he stands tall and demands an answer. The man with pale eyes only smiles an unnaturally wide smile. His teeth glisten as his tan lips thin out with the movement.

"Hello, humans." His voice is melodic and almost hypnotic, but I can sense doom laced deep underneath it. "I'm here to save the princess. I am the angel that goes by Kamar. I am one of your God's disciples. I'm here to collect Adrienne's body to bring her back to life." I glare at him, having a hard time believing a word he says even though my body and mind feel this pull to him. Telling me I can trust him.

"Our God?" Sam questions him but his once defensive stance has relaxed. He's no longer feeling threatened.

"Yes, Sam. Your God has sent me to retrieve her. Our sister." I smile at him, all doubt and fear that I had for this man leaving me as he sings each word our way. How could I have been scared of someone so beautiful? So kind? His skin glows bright. His golden hair appears like silken strands. His gray eyes glisten and gleam, sparkling as they stare into us both at the same time.

"So, she's going to be okay? You'll bring her back to life?" I can hear Sam's smile on his lips even though his back is to me. He's just as happy as I am. I giggle, feeling loopy from the pure joy coursing through me. I've never been this happy before in my life.

"Of course. She's one of us. We want her alive just as much as you. We love her." His smile gets wider as he stares us down and I giggle again, feeling my cheeks flush. He has such a big smile. So white and beautiful. "But I must get going, my son. God is calling. I will take care of her. You have my word."

"Thank you. Thank you so much." My body moves out from behind Sam, without me telling it to. My hands are clasped in front of me and my knees fall to the floor. I bend forward, bowing for this magnificent creature. "I am indebted to you. I love you."

He laughs at my admission and I feel myself growing sad. He doesn't approve of me. I'm not good enough for him. "Yes, child, you are. And you always will be." White flashes through the room again and then suddenly, the air is stale and empty.

I sit up, confused as to what just happened. Dread, fear, and sorrow fill my chest so fast, I suck in a sharp breath at the shock of it. I look at the bed and find Willow's body gone. No... No, no, no, no. What did we do?

"Sam? What just happened?" I turn towards him with tears streaming down my face. He looks just as confused as me. Fear sits behind his eyes when he looks down at me.

"I don't know what happened. I felt so calm, so happy. It felt like we didn't have a choice. That the only answer was for him to take Willow." I remember his hypnotizing voice and my stomach drops.

"He hypnotized us. Put us in a trance with his voice. And then he took Willow. She's gone." Fear fills me completely.

Wherever Willow is, she's in danger. And there's no way I can help her.

CHAPTER 11

NOX

I can tell something's wrong. I can't explain it, but I know something bad happened to Adrienne's body. We left her, barely protected by two humans, for the Gods to have their way with her. She's defenseless. Just a lifeless body.

I'm sitting in Lady Blackwell's room, the clype still sitting around us. I told Onyx to leave the minute we realized what we had done. We put the clype removal on the back burner in order to make sure Adrienne was still safe. In order to bring her body home.

I don't know how long he's been gone at this point. I haven't said a word to Layla since he left. I'm in my head, terrified and losing my mind. If she's gone, I will destroy every world to find her. I don't care what it takes. If I have to kill the Gods myself, I will. No questions asked.

"Nox?" Layla's voice breaks me from my murderous thoughts. "Do you think it might be smart if we try to break the clype while Onyx is away? That way we can all be ready when he gets back... with or without her body." She has a point. But right now, I'm so angry, I worry I won't be able to control myself if I summon her powers.

"Do you think that's a good idea? I don't want to cause more damage without Onyx here. He said to wait for him. He's the Dark Lord after all." I grimace at my own words, hating that I'm giving him any power over me at all.

"Nox Kage. I have known you since you were just a boy. You are my daughter's bonded mate. You have some of the strongest power in you that this world has ever seen. You do not need to take orders from anyone. Dark Lord or not." I give her a pained smile. She has no idea how much I agree with that last part. I hate that he's in charge of me. I hate that he is meant to marry my Ren. I hate him.

"I don't know if I can control my powers when I'm this angry. If I can't... I could burn this place down." That fear hasn't left me since I accidentally let a fire ball fly from my hands earlier. We are lucky it wasn't anything more than that.

"Okay, then we need to take away the anger." She pauses and thinks for a minute, her l violet eyes looking through me. "Think about her. About everything you love about Adrienne. The times you spent together. Your favorite memories. Everything. Then, focus on removing the clype. I know you can do it, Nox."

Part of me thinks that will only anger me more. Remembering everything I love about Ren, knowing that she is most likely in danger. That I have no idea where she is and can't help her. But, Layla is right. I need to try. The faster we are all able to get her out of here and, hopefully, help us get to the Reaper, the faster we can get Ren back.

Nodding my head, I stand up and walk away from her, looking out the huge glass windows. Her room is in the basement, but we are sitting on the edge of the castle mountain, so she has a terrace looking out over the huge forest below us. There are evergreens as far as the eye can see and between the trees lies our kingdom. Made up of cobblestone courtyards and small cottages covered in moss. It's not the most extravagant kingdom, but it's home. And I wouldn't change anything about it.

Ren was always transfixed by the kingdom. She loved to go out on her terrace at night and take in the twinkling lights spread among the trees. She would listen to the people as they laughed and sang, and I would just watch her as she listened. Her eyes would sparkle, her lips would curve up, the hair on her arms would stand as goosebumps covered her skin.

I think about the night she begged me to fly. I can never say no to her. She could ask me to throw myself off the castle roof and I wouldn't blink an eye. When I saw her taking off, gliding through the air with her magnificent wings, the breath left my lungs. I was so in awe by her, more than I already was. I had never seen anything like it.

And then, she brought me up there with her. Not physically. But she managed to bring me up there in her mind, where I could look out over the kingdom with her, through her eyes. I was mesmerized. Not only by the view, but by her. By her beauty, her power, her strength. I knew I had loved her long before, but that night, I had fallen even harder. I felt that last piece of my heart crack and she consumed every corner of it.

I don't realize I'm smiling until I feel Layla's hand touch my shoulder. "That doesn't look like an angry face to me. Do you think you're ready?"

"We can give it a try. But I can't make any promises." She nods her head in understanding, rubbing my shoulder one more time for good measure. Then, she's walking back over to where the couches reside. I turn towards the room and take a deep breath. It was easier for me to remove the clype with Onyx than it was to make it. I'm hoping that's the case with Lord Blackwell's clype as well.

I close my eyes and take a deep breath. Reaching deep inside of me, I pull at the ring of magic I can feel in my chest. I picture the golden specks floating around in a tight ball, perfectly contained inside of me. Then, I push on the ring with my mind and force some of them out. Each fleck that floats through leaves a tingling path in its trail, until eventually, my entire body is tingling. The ring is now empty, and there are millions of small flecks floating through my body.

I focus on the buzz of the clype, once nonexistent to me and now a constant sound since having her powers. Reaching out for it with my magic, I feel the tiny bug like flecks leave my body through my fingertips. They reach out like long arms, moving towards the walls where the clype holds strong.

Once every drop is out of my body and attached to the clype, I picture the barrier being broken. I picture the glistening clype cracking and fading. I hear a gasp from Lady Blackwell but don't open my eyes, unable to with the amount of energy being sucked out of me.

What feels like a gust of wind strong enough to blow a tree over hits my body, practically pushing me back, and then all at once, my magic comes flowing back into me. It moves so fast, being sucked back into my body at an uncontrollable rate. It takes my breath away, my body is no longer big enough to contain everything seeping back into me.

Layla blinks back at me once I open my eyes. Once the power sits dormant inside of me. There's a smile gracing her lips that reminds me so much of Adrienne. A soft, sweet smile that makes you take a second look just to make sure something so beautiful could actually exist.

"You did it, Nox. You broke the barrier." She sounds just as surprised as I feel. I didn't expect it to happen. I didn't think I was strong enough. I didn't think I could control her powers. Clearly, Layla didn't either.

"She's... she's so strong. Her power is... it's..."

"It's like nothing any of us have ever experienced." She finishes for me and I nod my head in agreeance. Before I can get another word out, Layla turns away from me and carefully steps toward the door. She hasn't left this room in twenty-five years. She has been trapped here for a quarter of a century, and now, she's free. I can't imagine what that must feel like.

I move with her, making my way towards the door and watching when her fingers clasp the metal handle. She takes a shaky breath and then she pulls it open. My eyes stay on her face, taking in the emotion flowing from her eyes. She's both scared and excited as she takes a step forward and her foot lands on the other side.

And then she's laughing. She's smiling and laughing and crying all at the same time. I don't have time to react when she pulls me across the threshold, into the hallway, and hugs me tighter than she ever has. I hug her back, part of me picturing her as Ren. They are so similar in so many ways and it brings tears to my eyes just picturing it being her in my arms instead.

"She's gone. They fucking took her!" Onyx's loud shouting breaks us apart and I turn towards him barreling down the hallway towards us. His hair is stands on all ends and his eyes are glazed over with rage. He looks manic.

"What?" Fear lodges in my throat. There's no way. There's no way the Gods could have taken her already.

"They let Atlas take her. Kamar collected her body and left. He put a trance on Sophia and Dr. Archer and took her right in front of them. Weak fucking humans." The name Kamar sounds familiar from my time back in school. We all know about Atlas, the longest ruling God since Aiden. But I remember that name belonging to one of his disciples. Kamar, along with Blaze and Surya, is one of the three that rule under Atlas.

"Fuck!" I can't hold back my scream as my hands run through my hair, pulling at the ends of it. I can feel her power bubbling up inside of me. I can feel it trying to be released. Like it wants to escape me and try to find the body it belongs in.

"Calm down, Nox. Take a deep breath." Layla puts her hand on my shoulder and it does nothing to calm me down.

I feel my body pulling at me to move. Like I'm not in control of it anymore. "I... I think her power is trying to take over. I think it is trying to get her body back. I think it can sense that it's in danger."

"Shit, I was worried that would happen if her body was taken. Her power is connected to her body. She was safe here and when she was with Dr. Archer, so her power stayed calm. But now that she's in danger, her powers are going to force you to find her. They are going to make it nearly impossible to resist that pull."

I furrow my brows, confused as to why Lady Blackwell sounds worried about her powers bringing me to her body. "That's a good thing. Her power can lead me to her and I can get her back."

"You don't get it. If what Than said is true, then that's what they want, Nox. If you make it to heaven, they could try to kill you and then place her powers in a vis lock. It's something that was supposedly forged by Aiden himself and only the Gods have access to. It's a locket that can hold onto someone's powers. And according to the legend, the only beings that can absorb the power is Aiden, the original holder of the power, or a fated mate."

"So why not just take Nox and leave her body alone? If all they want is her power, they have a being that possesses it right here." Onyx speaks up and I glare at him, trying to ignore the way her power screams inside of me.

"As powerful as Nox is with Adrienne's power, he can't reach her full potential. No one can but the original being. And they need both Adrienne and Ahriman for whatever they have planned. The two of them together is a force that could destroy... well, everything."

"I don't understand what they want with all of that power." Onyx says with a shake of his head.

"They want what everyone wants. Power. Wealth. World domination." The last one makes a shiver run through me. "Well, I guess not everyone wants world domination, but they definitely do."

"Alright, well Nox can't go to heaven, but what's stopping Atlas from coming here? I thought Aiden gave the leading God the power to travel to all of the worlds?" I try to remember everything I learned in school about the worlds and their bline. How royals are the only ones able to travel across it. How no one, but the leading God, can travel across more than one bline in either direction.

"Atlas wouldn't do that. He's not going to risk anyone finding out what he's doing. And I have a hunch Aiden doesn't know the extent of what Atlas is doing. Atlas isn't going to want to draw attention. So, he's going to wait for you to go to him. He knows about the mating bond. He knows you won't be able to resist it."

"No offense, Layla, but there's no way you know all of this for sure. And if you did, you should have told us sooner." Onyx says it with at least some fake respect which keeps me from ripping his head off.

"I spent a lot of time stuck in The Reaper's head. Having this attachment to him and hearing things he said and thought. Things Lucifer himself said. I'm not going to say I'm one hundred percent positive but these are all educated guesses. And I know how people in power act. I know what they will do to protect it." I cringe knowing she is talking about how Cole locked his wife away for twenty-five years. How The Reaper tricked her to gain power.

"If I had known you were going to bring my daughter right into Atlas's hands, I would have specifically told you not to. But you two decided to do that without keeping me in the loop." Her voice is laced with disappointment and it makes me feel like a little boy again.

"So, what do we do? How do we get to heaven if Atlas is the only being that can move across more than one world? How would they expect us to go to them anyway?" Onyx asks the obvious question while I lean against the wall with one arm, trying to rid some of the pain and pressure building inside of me.

"I have a few theories. But I want to get to Ahriman and The Reaper first. We need to try to work together. They know a lot more than we do. With Lucifer on their side, we can figure out the full truth."

"And how are we supposed to get to them? We can't just travel through the bline into Morta and start screaming their names. We'll be dead in seconds." I grit my teeth where I stand, my skin feeling like it's being ripped apart from the inside out. Like her power is trying to tear at the barrier and zoom off to save Ren's body.

"That's the easy part. Once we leave the clype of the kingdom, they will find us. Lucifer is always watching. We just have to wait until they find us."

CHAPTER 12

ADRIENNE

"Ugh, Ahri! Can you wake the fuck up yet?" I scream through his head, pounding on the black walls of his mind. He's been sleeping for what feels like days. I haven't been able to focus on anything but the vision he showed me. I want to see more. I want to know everything there is to know in order to destroy them.

I hear him groan, low and husky, and the hair on the back of my neck stands up. I feel a random, unwanted spark low in my stomach. I can't control the way my body reacts to the sound. I can't control the want deep down that confuses me.

I clear my throat and take a deep breath before his groan from waking up turns into an even lower chuckle. It vibrates through my body and I have to bite my lip to keep from making a sound. What is wrong with me?

"Something wrong up there, darling? You seem a bit... flustered." My teeth grit and I clench my nonexistent legs tight, trying to rid the desire that is coursing through my body. Who knew a fake body could feel such intense feelings? I've felt so numb for the last few days that I almost forgot what it feels like to feel anything good.

"I..." I swallow hard and try to catch my breath. "I feel things. Things I wasn't able to before... Ever since I got stuck in your head, I felt so... numb. And now I feel... I feel..." He groans again and I fall to the floor, the vibrations from his gravelly voice rubbing against my sensitive spots. The moan that escapes me can't be contained.

"Bloody hell, love. That might be the sexiest god damn noise I've ever heard." Every word he speaks sends another shooting spark straight down to my pussy. This doesn't make any sense. I hate Ahri... don't I? I'm just a soul stuck in his head. How can I feel so aroused? How can I feel my clit throbbing?

"You don't hate me, Adrienne. You are meant for me. We are one in the same. And I can assure you, from years of experience, it's more than possible to feel so aroused. I got off more times than I can count stuck in that sexy little head of yours."

I cry out and throw my head back, the pleasure feeling so intense, so powerful. I'm panting where I'm sitting, not even touching myself and close to something... some unknown release that might damn near kill me.

"Open your eyes, darling. Look at what you do to me." A small twinge of doubt niggles in the back of my mind but I ignore it and peel my eyelids apart. The once black room is now filled with bright colors and images like a private movie theater. And the scene before me steals my breath.

Ahri's hand is stroking his huge cock, moving up and down over and over again. The tattoos that travel across every rippling muscle on his tan skin continue lower... and lower... and lower.

They cover every inch of him. The black swirls and symbols even cover the perfect, soft flesh of his thick, rock hard dick. The dick that is being pulled at an erratic speed, glistening at the tip and making my mouth water.

"Do you have any idea how bad I wish my hand was your pouting little mouth, darling? How much I want to fuck your lips until tears are streaming down your face?" I whimper and arch my back, feeling each one of his words deep in my core.

"Yes. Fuck... yes." I don't mean to talk. I don't even know what I'm saying. I feel animalistic. Desperate. Completely raw and ripped apart for this man. The man I've hated for years. The man that I thought was the death of me. In the end, he might just be.

"That's it, darling. Tell me how wet you are." I reach down and find myself naked, my pussy on display. I touch my skin and the wetness engulfs my fingers. I moan when my hand moves and it feels like someone else is touching me. Like my hand isn't attached to me and instead, attached to Ahri.

"Tell me, Adrienne. If you were here right now, could I shove this dick deep inside of you in one thrust?" Pure ecstasy fills me and makes me dizzy. The room spins around me and the words and images of him touching himself tumble through my brain on repeat.

"I'm... I'm soaked, Ahri. I'm so fucking wet for you." My voice doesn't sound like it belongs to me. My hand moves without me telling it to and the other joins in. One circles my clit while the other shoves two fingers deep inside of me.

"Mmm, darling. Picture my cock pounding into you. Picture me fucking you right there, between those delectable little legs of yours. Picture me making you come all over my length and then shoving myself deep inside of you and filling you up."

I scream out, thrashing against the floor as the beginning of my orgasm hits me. "I'm gonna... I'm... Oh, Ahri!" I cry out his name and then feel the vibrations from his guttural groans swim through my veins.

I try to keep my eyes open as the first spurts of Ahri's cum leave the head of his cock. As he jerks and spasms with sloppy movements, grunting out my name with each thick release he shoots. It's one of the sexiest things I've ever seen. And every inch of me screams and burns for him. Begs for him. Strains to feel his hands on me.

Breathing heavy, I let my head fall against the jet-black abyss below me. I'm exhausted. I'm completely satisfied. I'm utterly confused. I open my eyes and find Ahri's view still staring back at me. He's lying on his back, staring up at the ceiling of his room. Each blink of his eyes makes the space go black for a split second.

"That was..."

"Absolutely marvelous, my darling. You're perfection." He responds before I can finish my sentence.

"I was going to say unexpected. I'll admit... I can't deny how good it felt. I still hate you though." He chuckles and I find myself smiling a half smile.

"As I have said before and as I will continue to remind you, sweet Adrienne. Hate and love are dangerously similar."

"I'm confused, Ahri. For the entire time I have been trapped in your head, I haven't felt anything like that. I felt... numb. I knew I was here, I knew I was sad, but I never actually felt like I had a real body in here. I never felt... this." I sound like a child trying to explain herself, stumbling on her words.

"I don't know. But I do remember that every time you were under that clype of your kingdom, I felt close to numb too when I was in your head. Like it cut off the signal of our connection and I almost felt like a piece of me was missing."

I sit up with his words, realization hitting me. My heart starts to pound and burst with love. It has to be the reason. It has to be why I feel so much right now.

"What are you thinking, my darling?" Ahri listens to my thoughts and I grit my teeth at the invasion of privacy.

"It means, asshole, that my mate is no longer under the clype. It means that I felt all of that, because I could feel Nox. Because our connection is back. It's the only explanation as to why... that would happen. Especially with you." I laugh to myself, clapping my hands over my mouth. "My body was reacting to the signal being restored with Nox."

Silence takes over the room and then Ahri cuts me from his vision and leaves me in the suspending darkness. My eyes try to adjust, like they always do, but there is no way to adjust to darkness this thick. It's what I imagine death will feel like.

"Glad it all makes sense then." His normal cocky voice sounds different now. Almost resembling disappointment or sadness... as if someone like him could ever feel that. "Guess that means your little mate is waiting for us to come to him."

I furrow my brows at his statement, forgetting about his sad undertone. "What does that mean?"

"It means, he is coming out of hiding so we can talk. There's no other reason he would make himself vulnerable with your powers on the line. He's finally smartening up." I think about what Ahri is saying and a huge grin takes over my face. My boys are going to work together to try to save me.

I regret thinking it the minute I do. Ahri's not one of my boys. He's the enemy... isn't he? Why would I ever consider him one of my boys? Nox is. I'd even consider Onyx in that category. But Ahri? He's the reason I'm here. The reason I'm stuck in this nothingness.

I feel him listening to my thoughts. Hearing everything I'm thinking, and then suddenly, he's gone. He leaves my mind completely. He puts a barrier between the two of us and I feel no connection to him. Nothing at all. Like I'm no longer in his head.

And sitting here, completely alone, letting the darkness take over everything and pull me down with it, I realize something.

I miss his sarcastic voice.

I miss feeling him here with me.

I miss Ahriman Reaper.

IT FEELS LIKE DAYS SINCE I FELT HIM WITH ME. HE'S COMPLETELY SHUT me out. I can't see anything. I can't hear anything. I can't feel him prying inside of my mind. He's just left me here, alone. Stupid prick.

"Ahriman, where are you?" I call out in the darkness and it sounds small and pathetic. I roll my eyes and try again. "Ahriman?"

Still nothing. He ignores me completely and pretends I don't exist. Screw that. Standing from my spot on the floor, I walk over to the thick black walls and I start pounding on them as hard as I can.

"Ahriman Reaper! Answer me now! This is bullshit! You can't shut me out!" I scream each word and continue to bang, not hearing the sound as my hands make contact with the walls but hoping he can. I hope it makes his head pound and his damn ears bleed.

"I swear on Lucifer. When I get out of here, I'm going to rip your stupid smug head right off of your shoulders!" I bang harder and harder and scream at the top of my lungs.

"I'd be careful what you say, darling. Swearing on Lucifer when he's right in front of you is never a good idea." He finally acknowledges me and I can feel him everywhere. My breath hitches and I am finally able to breathe fully. I relax where I'm standing and my heart rate slows down.

"Wait... what did you say?" Instead of answering, Ahri lets me see out of his eyes. The room lights up with the scene before me. The woods I know all too well. Dark and foreboding but somehow comforting now that I know what it hides. The kingdom it holds. My kingdom.

The trees surround us and standing among the dark branches, I see two figures. One is very clearly Than, covered by his dark cloak that hides his features. The drama that man possesses is like nothing I've ever experienced.

The second man is someone I've never met but know without a doubt in my mind. Lucifer. He stands in front of Ahri, staring into his eyes. Staring into mine it seems. His light blonde hair is cut short on his head. It spikes up at the ends. The pale tint of his skin is hidden behind a black suit. It's black as night and fits his muscular body perfectly.

And then there are his eyes. So gray, they appear white. But the fascinating, transfixing part about them are the small orange and red lines snaking their way through the gray hue. They look like thin tree branches arching in different directions and the sight is completely mesmerizing. I never would have thought the devil would be so handsome.

"I'll be honest, dear, I wouldn't mind watching you rip his head off. He's only been alive a few days and I already want to rain hellfire down on him myself." His voice sounds like a dark and dangerous melody. Something that pulls you in and steals your entire attention.

"He... he can hear me?" My question is aimed at Ahri, since he's the only person I've been able to talk to since getting stuck in here.

"He can not only hear you, but he can see you as well." Ahri's response makes me shiver as I remember feeling my naked body earlier today. I look down but can't see my own body to make sure it's covered.

"Don't worry, dear. You are not exposed. It's a pleasure to meet the woman who has all of the worlds in an uproar. I'm sure you are more of a pleasure than your familiar here." Ahri growls low at Lucifer as if what he said was an insult.

"I'm sorry, what do you mean my familiar?" I have heard the word before, but only in human fantasy books and movies.

"Ah, has Ahriman not explained his connection to you yet?" Lucifer shakes his head with a soft smile on his face.

"I was waiting for the right time. I wanted her to be out of my head when I explained it." I can feel the glare Ahri is aiming at his God.

"Well, now is as good a time as any. Dear Adrienne, a familiar is a demon created with an attachment to one of power. He protects, enhances, and loves his... how should I say this? His master?" I almost laugh at the word. Did he just call me Ahriman's master?

"I thought familiars were supposed to be cats or something?" This earns another growl from Ahri and I laugh. "Judging by all of that growling, I'd peg you for more of the dog type, actually."

Lucifer laughs and I find myself smiling at him. "Oh, Ahriman, I'm going to get along very well with this one. To be honest, a familiar is even less common than a mated bond among angels. We don't know much about them or what they consist of. But, a familiar is something that can't be unbroken. Something that will follow you both into the afterlife.

"Ahriman is yours and yours fully. Without you, he is not him. And without him, your powers are weakened. Your safety is questioned. Everything you know in life will not be as it was. He's part of your soul."

"I don't understand. I thought Ahri was created to rule Morta? To take over for Than?" My throat starts to close with the words Lucifer is saying.

"If that were the case, my dear, Than would have simply created a demon on his own. Demons aren't created like you are. We don't have parents and children. We can simply create life, something unattached to us by blood, but attached to us by mind."

"Then why did he attach Ahriman to me?" I feel like I'm losing my mind. There's too much information floating through my head right now.

"I had a... vision over twenty-five years ago. A vision of a girl with red and purple eyes. Of a girl who had the first bonded mate for thousands of centuries. A girl who was going to help destroy the hierarchy of the angels and save the human world." My eyes widen with his words.

"And I knew, at that moment, that you needed to be on my side. That without me, you wouldn't get there. Because I am the only one that knows the truth. And seeing that red in your eyes, seeing how bright it shown, I knew what I had to do. I knew we had to give you a part of hell. You needed our powers.

"The familiar was a bit unexpected, but everything happens for a reason. And now I see that Ahriman is here to make you even stronger. Without him, you would not win against Atlas. Now I see that from the start, Ahriman would have found a way to get to you, even if he wasn't attached to you from birth."

I let what he's saying sit in my brain for a few seconds. He's saying that Ahri and I are meant to be together? That if he wasn't attached to me, I would have ended up with him in my life anyway?

"What do you mean when you say a familiar bond is stronger than my mating bond?" My heart squeezes at the thought of something getting between my bond with Nox. He's my everything. My other half. The man I would die for.

Ahriman speaks before Lucifer can. "He means, I would die for you, darling. In fact, if you left me, I would wither away and eventually die. You're my power source. You're my life. And if you weren't to sit by my side in Morta, I would eventually turn to dust. I would do anything for you. Do anything to keep you safe."

I laugh and shake my head. "So, you're using me? For my power? And the whole 'keep me safe' thing is bullshit. You tried to kill me! You did kill me! That fucking asshole ripped my heart out! How is that keeping me safe?"

"Enough, Adrienne!" Lucifer speaks up and his voice booms through the forest. "Ahriman has no choice in the matter. He was created and this bond was forged into his blood. And as for trying to kill you, I know he has told you the truth countless times. Ahriman was desperate to get out of your head, he couldn't protect you in your head. Any injury you sustained when you transported to Ombra at night was self-inflicted. And I will not say this again, so listen closely. Than needed to kill you. We knew how to do it so your body would stay preserved. We knew Ahriman needed to leave your head so he could help you. You were going to die either way. It was just a matter of if it was us or Atlas. And Atlas wouldn't care about what happened to you after he used you."

"And you do?" I glare at him and hope he can see it. He's speaking to me like I'm a child.

"Yes, Adrienne. Believe it or not, I do. We all do." He stares into me and a flash of admiration fills his eyes. Or maybe it's pride? I can't tell. Either way, it makes me believe his words even if I don't want to. "No more talking. We need to find your mate and bring everyone back to Morta where we are safe. Atlas can see and hear us here."

"Wait... how are you here anyway? I thought only the leading Gods could travel more than one world from their own?" That's what Nox and my father always said at least. That's why Aiden created the extra worlds, so Lucifer couldn't get to the humans. Clearly, their history lessons aren't as accurate as they thought.

The serious look on Lucifer's face scares me and makes me want to bow to him at the same time. It's a look of leadership and poise. "Forget everything you once knew. And, as much as Atlas wants to deny it, I am a leading God."

CHAPTER 13

ADRIENNE

I hear him before I get to see him. His voice hits my ears and I swear they perk up like a dog hearing its owner's voice. Because Nox Kage owns me. "Stay the fuck back." Are the first four words I hear him say since I last saw him the night of my coronation. His voice sounds pained and drawn out.

"Ahri, let me see him. Please," I beg into the darkness, desperate to have my sight back. I hear him huff, but then Nox's perfect face graces my eyes. Tears fall when I take in his curly brown hair and dark purple eyes. His soft lips that I haven't been able to kiss nearly enough. His dark beard that has only scratched my face a few times.

"Nox." The string in my spine tugs and pulls, singing our song and making my heart feel like it's going to burst. The minute I say his name, Nox's violet globes stare straight into Ahri. He looks like he's in pain. Like he is trying to hold himself together.

"Ren..." His voice is low and full of emotion. "She's in your head. I can feel her." He starts to walk up to us and then falls to the floor. I scream out in fear and bang on the walls confining me to this hell. I just want to touch him. To feel him.

"Kage," Onyx says with warning in his voice. I turn my attention to him and my eyes tear up more. I've missed him too, with his cocky smile, lilac eyes, and perfectly placed blonde hair. And then I see the last person I expect to see. The woman from my vision days ago. Someone I've never met, who made me the person I am. My real mother.

She's staring straight at Ahri, straight into me. Her hair is the same color as mine but her eyes are dark and full of shadows. Shadows, I'm sure, from the horrible life she has had to live. Deep seeded pain covers her features, making her dark brows furrow and her thick lips purse.

Her eyes dart to the side for a split second and then I realize why. Than is standing right there. The man that tricked her. The man she fell for, only to be used and thrown away. My heart cracks for her. I know the feeling of being tricked and hurt by someone you care about. And what Sam Archer did to me doesn't even compare to what Than Reaper did to her.

"I'm glad everyone finally realized what needs to happen here," Lucifer says, his voice booming over all of ours. "But we can't talk here. Truthfully, we are putting Adrienne's soul and power in danger just being here together to begin with. We can have this conversation in Morta."

Before anyone can react, Lucifer snaps his fingers and, in an instant, the world goes black before we are thrown into Morta. How the hell did he do that?

"How the fuck did you just do that?" Onyx asks my question for me, confused as to how he transported all of us at the same time with just a snap of a finger.

"I am the devil. I can do anything I want... well, almost anything." I watch him wink at someone with a smirk and wish I could turn to see who he was looking at.

Lucifer hasn't stopped staring at your mother, darling. Ahri's thoughts ring through my head and I can't help but snort at what he says.

"He does realize that my mother is in love with Than, right? That little devil." The pun doesn't go unnoticed by Ahri and he chuckles out loud, making everyone look at him. Onyx and Nox glare while Lucifer gives him a raised brow in warning.

Your mother was tricked by Than. I doubt she will ever forgive him. And I don't think Than truly loves anyone. He likes to be alone. He's a miserable prick who doesn't believe in love. One of the things I love most about the bastard.

"I've never met my mother," I admit it out loud and let my nerves fill me up. I wanted to meet her before everything happened but I was anxious about how I would feel when I saw her. Because I blame her for a lot of what happened. But now that I see her, I just want to reach out and hug her.

I know, Adrienne. You'll be reunited soon. We are going to bring you back and then the two of you can talk. I promise you, my darling. I smile at no one, appreciating his promises. I felt the air between us shift when Lucifer told me the truth about him. I felt my fear for him dissipate and my respect increase.

"Ahri, why didn't you tell me about the familiar bond?"

I wanted to tell you when you were able to look into my eyes. When you were able to touch me. And... and when you had decided, on your own, that you wanted to be mine. I didn't want you to feel forced to have me in your life because you were worried I would die.

His honesty is overwhelming in the best way. "Thank you for telling me the truth. I'm happy I know about it. I'm sorry for being so horrible to you. For blaming you for everything." I pause and then try to lighten the mood. "And what makes you think I'm not going to let your grumpy ass die anyway?"

Oh, darling. After hearing that sexy little mouth of yours moan my name today, I promise you, I'm not going down without a fight. You're going to have a hard time getting rid of me now. I can't control the quiet gasp from his words and then shake my head with a smirk.

"You're going to be the death of me, aren't you?" He just laughs low in response. The room goes silent again besides a growl coming from Nox.

"Ahriman, would you like to share what's so funny to the rest of the group? Or should I?" Lucifer threatens to reveal our internal conversation, and I wonder if he can actually hear it or if he's bluffing.

"Sorry. Continue. We won't interrupt again." Ahri clears his throat and both of us start to listen to the conversation. I want to reprimand him for saying we, since that gives us away, but there's no point. Everyone already knows I'm in his head.

I stare through Ahri's eyes at the thick black and gray rock surrounding us. There are rivers of orange lava flowing around in winding trails, but the majority of the world appears to be flat stone.

"Is this what all of Morta looks like? It's pretty... depressing." I know I should stop talking, but I can't help it.

Lucifer answers me, proving that he can hear me in Ahri's head still. "This is the same as your overgrown forest. It hides our true world, or kingdom as you would call it." He stares at me, or more so Ahri, with a raised brow and then just like before, he simply snaps his fingers and our surroundings change.

I gasp at the sight before me. The only place I have seen is Ahri's room, and that is full of dark reds and black accents. This world that Lucifer envelopes us in is nothing like that. The world I pictured to be dark and terrifying is the complete opposite. In fact, it reminds me of the home I've known for the last five years.

Tall glass buildings that reach into a night sky stare back at us. The sky, while dark, is filled with golden stars that shine bright enough to light the world below and leave a calming cast around us. Between each tall sky scraper there are winding cobblestone roads and lanterned street lights showing the way around. It's magical. A perfect city. Something I never expected.

So, she likes it, I see? Ahri's words echo through his head and I try not to smile.

"Why didn't you show me this before? This is... this is beautiful." I've been stuck in his head for days and he's kept all of this a secret.

I, once again, had this bloody stupid idea that you should see it for yourself once you're out of my head. I thought it would be romantic and more meaningful for you to see it in person. It was wrong of me, darling.

The smile I tried to hide comes out full force as I stare through Ahri's eyes at the city, or kingdom, that he wants me to rule alongside him. "That's abnormally sweet of you, Ahri. Thank you."

I hope one day you will see the truth about who I am. About what I want and what my heart looks like, darling. I think about his words. He's right. I don't know much about him even though he's been trapped in me for my entire life and I've been stuck in his.

"I know you're extremely sexual." I say it as a joke but I do mean that. The things he has said to me both turn me on and terrify me at the same time.

I've been trapped in that head of yours all of my life. Cut me some slack. But also know that I only think like that for one person. One hot headed, stubborn, pain in the ass princess that sends my heart on a bloody marathon every time I hear her voice.

I don't answer, mostly because I'm too scared of what will come out of my mouth if I do. Nox comes into view and I see him staring at Ahri rather than the city. He's glaring but I can see the love and despair behind his eyes. God, I missed him so much. I want to touch him, hold him, reassure him that I'm okay.

We all follow Lucifer as he walks to the tallest glass building in the city. It's right in the center of everything and it's surrounded by bright red and orange flowers that resemble a mote full of lava. It's gorgeous. Something straight out of a dream.

We walk over the small bridge above the flowers and then we enter the sparkling glass building. And holy shit. What I assumed would be hundreds of floors is simply one huge open space with stairs crawling up along the perimeter. The room is full of golden accents that almost look like fire.

There's a huge sitting area in one corner, with fire booming in a golden fire pit in the center, a table big enough to seat twenty in another corner, and then a huge bar area filling the rest of the space. When we walk forward, Ahri looks up at the ceiling. The air is filled with small golden specks floating around us and all the way at the top, hundreds of feet up, there is a huge chandelier made of flames that dance together in unison.

"This is... magnificent," I whisper the words as Ahri continues to look up at the ceiling for my benefit. I'm curious about the stairs and where they lead. They go so high up but there doesn't appear to be anything attached to them.

"Your kingdom is, um, not what I expected." Onyx speaks up first and then everyone joins in with their praise of the castle.

"We don't use the word kingdom. A kingdom is run by one ruler with citizens underneath them. While we have rulers, to make sure everything runs smooth, each demon in this city is deemed equal. They are welcome in this castle at all times. They have the freedom to do and say what they want, as long as it doesn't pose a threat to the wellbeing of others."

"That's quite admirable, Lucifer." My mother is the first one to speak and I try to get used to her voice. It sounds so familiar yet so unnatural at the same time.

"Thank you, my lady. My name gets a bad rap, but I can assure you, I care for my people more than anything else." Another wink is aimed her way and Ahri turns toward my mother to see her reaction. She's blushing but her eyes turn towards Than and the light in them dims. He's not even paying attention. He's moving over to the bar and pouring himself a drink. His stupid cloak is still on and if I could, I'd rip it off of him and scream at him.

We all take a seat around the fire, Nox on one side of Ahri and Onyx on the other. My mother sits next to Lucifer and Than sits on his other side, across from us. It's awkward and uncomfortable and I wish I could have a drink to calm my nerves.

You know, darling, if I get drunk, you will too. He whispers the thought to me and I get a little too excited. Feeling drunk sounds better than feeling nothing.

"Alright. I'm going to get straight to it. Atlas is planning on destroying all of our worlds. And he needs Adrienne and Ahriman's joint powers to do it." Silence takes over the room while everyone grasps what Lucifer just said.

"Why should we believe you?" Nox asks the question and his voice sounds strained. Ahri looks over at him and I notice the way his hands and teeth are clenched.

"Because I was one of them once. And Atlas threw me out for trying to stop their plans of destroying the humans. I know firsthand what he is capable of."

"Is Aiden a part of this too?" Onyx interrupts him.

Lucifer glares his way before answering. "Aiden doesn't normally interfere with anything the Gods do. No one in heaven even knows if He is actually real. And Atlas knows how to make it look like everything that happens is the fault of others. He turned imignis into hellfire and convinced the worlds that I am the cause of it. That I cursed the humans with the fireball in the sky. The truth is, he created that fire to destroy me. I tried to counteract it and when I fought back, with imignis to both of our surprise, the fire ball turned massive. Big enough to destroy the entire universe. And now it's trapped, suspended in the sky, where I had to place clype around it to keep it from blowing up all of our worlds."

"We were told the Gods are the ones that put clype around it. That they are the only ones that can create clype and they protected the humans by creating us."

"It's easy to convince the world of something when the one person who knows the truth isn't talking. I created Morta to save the human world. I had the idea to create beings that held clype for each human on Earth. When Atlas caught wind of my plan, he murdered most of my demons and then created a world of his own right above this one. And he created the Shadvir and took my idea." I want to murder Atlas. He sounds slimy and despicable.

"Why not tell everyone? Why keep it to yourself?" My mother asks the next question.

"First off, who would believe the devil? I tried to get into your kingdoms, but Atlas put a spell on all clype that his descendants created. I, nor my magic, can get through it or manipulate it. I convinced a few people though. A few shadvir from your kingdom."

"What are you talking about?" Nox sounds even more pained and he's fidgeting where he sits.

"The stories you heard about shadvir needing to be protected from the hellfire raining down on your world? They aren't true. Not all hellfire burns. I created a hellfire that told a story. It sang to you and spoke to you about the truth. And any shadvir that experienced it was convinced to come to Morta and witness the truth for themselves. Now, those shadvir have become demons who still protect their humans from this world."

"Prove it." This comes from both Onyx and Nox at the same time. Lucifer simply huffs and then nods at Than sitting next to him. We all turn our attention to the cloaked man and our eyes widen as he starts to remove his hood.

His face is nothing like I expected. He has dark, spiked hair, violet eyes, and a kind smile that contrasts against the vile one I once saw. His beard matches his hair and lays messy on his chin. I've never seen this man before but he resembles a shadvir.

"Nathaniel?" Nox speaks up as his eyes widen. Ahri keeps his attention on Than and watches as he nods his head.

"Hello, Nox," he says in a voice that sounds a lot less sinister than it did the night he killed me.

"Who is Nathaniel?" Onyx asks the question I'm wondering.

"I am a former shadvir. One of Nox's old school teachers to be exact. I went across the clype many moons ago and Lucifer showed me the truth. I came to Morta, changed my name, and became his second hand man. I became a demon with more power than you can ever imagine. I am forever grateful for my God."

"You have the power of deception. How do we know you aren't just pretending to be someone?" My mother glares at him as she speaks. She wants to kill him, I can tell.

"I wouldn't lie to you, my lady." Lucifer answers for Than. "But, if you all need more proof, here." He snaps his fingers and suddenly, the glowing orbs above us start to fall. They plummet towards our heads and I duck, forgetting that I'm not actually here.

But the orbs don't burn anyone. They just fall towards us as a soft, sweet melody rings through the room. It speaks of Atlas. Of Lucifer. Of their story. It's absolutely magical. Something I have never heard before but pray to hear again.

"Did you know all of this?" I ask Ahri as we both stare up into the air.

Yes, darling. But I couldn't tell you. It was too dangerous. I still wish you didn't know in fear of what will happen if Atlas gets ahold of you.

"What will happen?" I swallow hard and continue to look up, admiring the song and the glowing fire balls careening towards us.

"He will end you."

CHAPTER 14

NOX

The pain is getting worse the farther from her body I get. I'm trying so hard to keep it together but it's nearly impossible at this point. I wait for the fire to stop falling and then look at Nathaniel. He disappeared from Ombra when I was barely ten years old. This whole time, he's been here? He's the one that ripped my Ren's heart from her body?

"How could you kill her?" I glare his way and try to control the anger coursing through me.

"She isn't dead, Nox. And we had to do it or Atlas would first. Her full powers came in the night of the coronation and they would have not only killed her, but taken both her and Ahriman away from us for good. And the worlds we know would be destroyed."

I feel Ren's magic pull in my chest and the pull is so strong, I stumble forward with a grunt, falling to the floor.

"Nox!" This comes from Ahri but the sound of it reminds me more of Adrienne. I look over and find him kneeling next to me, his hand coming out to touch me. I start to pull away but the minute his fingers touch my arm, I stop. It's not his fingers I feel. It's hers. Goosebumps cover my skin and the string in my spine starts to pluck. All of the pain inside of me disappears as I stare at where we are connected.

"Ren? Is that you?" I look into Ahri's eyes and only see hers. He nods his head slowly and then I'm up off the ground and throwing myself into her arms. I know I'm actually hugging him, but I don't care. I feel her everywhere. I feel her touch, hear her voice, smell her vanilla scent. All of it is my Ren.

"I missed you, princess. God, I missed you so much." My eyes are closed, tears falling from them, when I hear a throat clear behind us. I turn my head and find everyone staring at us. And then I realize that Ahri and I are embracing like our lives depend on it. Or more so, I'm embracing Ahri like my life depends on it.

I let go and take a step back, looking at his face again and finding my Ren gone. All I see are red eyes staring back at me with confusion on his face. "Um, I'm sorry. That was uncalled for."

"She took over my body. I... I don't know how she did that. When you fell to the ground, she pushed my body forward and I had no control." Ahri turns toward Lucifer and questions him.

"She's stronger than we thought. But, on a more important note, why are you in pain, Nox?" I turn my attention to the devil and blink at him, wondering if I should tell him the truth.

"Um, it's her magic." I sit down and don't explain any farther.

"Why is her magic hurting you? The only reason it would hurt you is if her body was in..." Lucifer cuts off and then stands up, glaring at all of us as his gray eyes glow. "Where is her body? What did you do?" He's talking to no one in particular and his voice booms through the room.

No one answers at first. We all look at each other, not sure what to say. Ahriman growls next to me and I turn my attention to him, noticing his glare is directed solely on me. "We were trying to keep her safe from you. We knew you were planning on taking her body."

"Where. Is. Her. Body?"

"We brought her body to Earth. And... the angels. Kamar took it. Her body is in heaven right now." I look down with my answer, ashamed, like I'm a child getting scolded.

"Fuck!" Lucifer screams and the fire in the golden bowl between us blazes to terrifying heights. I back up and my eyes widen with the raging fire. "How could you let them have her?"

"We didn't mean it! We didn't know the truth about the heavens. We didn't want to believe it, okay? We thought she was safer there where you couldn't get her!" Onyx yells at Lucifer and I cringe. I don't think anyone should yell at the devil.

"I could have gotten her on Earth if I wanted to you fucking idiot! You handed her over to Atlas on a silver platter! He's one step closer to getting what he wants!" The fire rages even higher and the heat it lets off burns at my skin. It's hotter than any fire I have ever experienced.

"They made a mistake, Lucifer. Surely, there is something we can do to get her back." Layla speaks up and grabs Lucifer's attention. The fire instantly calms when he looks at her and I sigh a breath of relief.

The devil huffs and then places his fingers against the bridge of his nose. "There is something we can do. But it will cost us someone else's life and it's risky. Plus, there's a chance we won't be able to get her back in her real body if we do it."

"What do you mean cost us someone's life?" I squint my eyes at him in question, still not fully trusting him.

"I mean, one of my demons is going to have to give up their lives in order for us to put Adrienne's soul into theirs." I blink at him, confused and intrigued by what he means.

"How is that possible? Her magic won't go into someone else's body. It barely wants to be in mine and I'm her mate." I feel it pulling at my chest as I speak. Begging me to bring it to Adrienne's body. To bring her to safety.

"We can trick her magic if her soul is in someone else's body. It requires us removing the demon's heart and replacing it with hers. And then Ahriman has to kiss her. The familiar bond will transfer her soul into the body with her heart." I blink at him, confused as to if I heard him right.

"Familiar bond?" I turn towards Ahriman and he has a cocky grin on his face.

"You heard me right, Nox. Ahriman is Adrienne's familiar. There's no denying it. They need each other, and always will." That's not possible. She's my mate. My everything. My one and only. She can't have another bond with someone. Something even less heard of than a mating bond. Something that can't be broken unless through death.

"Sorry, mate. Looks like we are going to have to get used to each other." I glare at him, trying not to lose my temper. She can't be connected to this monster. This demon.

"How do you know? You have to be wrong. There's no way." I won't accept it. I can't accept it.

"It's written all over his body, Nox. The story of their connection. Of his love for her. Of the power that they possess together. He will protect her until the day that he dies." Her power sizzles inside of me, almost as if it's agreeing with Lucifer's words. As if it's trying to tell me to listen.

"I've always been a good sharer, mate." Ahri winks at me and I all but jump at him.

"That's enough, Ahriman. Don't antagonize the man. This can't be easy on him. Now, if we can all move on from this for a minute, I'd love to bring our Adrienne back to us."

My stomach churns with excitement. The thought of seeing Ren again, even if she looks like someone else, is almost too much to bear. I nod my head, ready to do whatever he needs.

"Let's do this."

AHRIMAN

I DON'T KNOW IF I CAN DO THIS. I'M TERRIFIED OF NOT HAVING HER IN my head. I selfishly want to keep her in here with me, where I can hear her thoughts and keep her beautiful soul safe. But I can't be selfish, not with her.

Even though I'm almost positive she's going to leave me once she's out of my head. Once she's not trapped by the prison of my thoughts. I can still feel her hatred for me and her disbelief of the things she has been told. Even if there is some love shining through, it's not going to be strong enough to keep her here. Not in the end.

"I'm scared, Ahri." Her voice breaks me from my private thoughts and tingles spread under my skin at just the sound of her voice. My mouth falls open to answer her, but given my current company, I opt out of it and answer her in my head.

Why are you scared, my darling? I watch as a young demon walks into the room. My eyes dissect her and I glare, wishing it wasn't her body I was looking at, but my Adrienne's instead. She has long blonde hair, and red eyes that contrast against her porcelain skin. She looks about the same age as Adrienne. Her body is slim and tall, covered in a pair of black cargo pants and a matching black shirt.

"What if it doesn't work? What if we make a mistake? And instead of being in your head... my soul is just gone." It's a valid fear and I'd be lying if I said I hadn't thought the same thing. It scares me to my core thinking about this woman not being in my life.

Lucifer would never let that happen, love. He knows what he's doing. You're safe in his hands, I promise. I look at the man in question and watch as he brings the demon girl over to the bed in the middle of the room. We moved upstairs into one of the spare rooms on the second floor. It's large and empty, with a king size bed sitting against one of the walls.

"I'm safe in the devil's hands? Yeah, said no one ever." I chuckle at her sarcasm and find Nox's glare aimed at me. He knows I'm talking to her. And it pisses him off more than anything that I'm able to and he isn't.

I would never put you in harm, Adrienne. Trust that. If this was dangerous, I'd burn this city down before letting him do it.

"I... I believe you. I believe that you would." The genuine truth in her voice brings a smile to my face as warmth spreads through my heart. I'm losing my bloody mind over this woman. I don't know who I am without her. In fact, I never have. Because I'm no one without the little spitfire in my head. And I thought I only cared for her because of our familiar bond but, now, I know it's more than that.

Thank you, love. That means more to me than you know. Even if we weren't bound together, I'd walk through hellfire for her. I'd spend my entire life trying to show her how incredible she is. How unworthy all of us are to even breathe the same air as her.

"Guess your wish is coming true. You'll finally get to kiss me for real. Or, the fake me. That's her, right? That's who I'll be residing inside of for who knows how long?" She sounds unsure. I don't blame her. I feel doubt niggle at my mind when I look at the blonde positioning herself on top of the bed.

Yes, darling. That's your girl. She has nothing on you, but she will do for the time being. Until we get your body back and I can properly kiss the lips I have wanted to kiss my entire life. I have dreamed about those lips of hers. Kissing them until our lips morph together into one.

"You're cheesier than I expected, Ahri. You have to work on your pick-up lines." I laugh again and shake my head. Then, I decide to fuck with her one last time before she's out in the open and no longer in my head.

Alright, darling. How about this? I can't wait to run my tongue down your body and then make you come with my head between your legs. I can't wait to see your mouth wrapped around my cock as I fuck your tight little throat and make you swallow all of me down. Is that better, love?

I can hear her heavy breathing pick up and grin to myself. She's flustered, whether she wants to admit it or not. I know I have an effect on her. I know how much she wants me, even if she doesn't know it herself.

"I'm not going to swallow you down..." she says a little breathlessly. I furrow my brows, not understanding why she would say that. "I would make you bend me over and fuck me after I sucked you off until we both came."

Bloody fucking hell. I feel my knees buckle slightly at her dirty words spinning through my head and try to keep myself from getting hard in a room full of people I should not be hard in front of. God, she makes it nearly impossible to keep it together.

You're absolutely ravishing, darling. I'm going to make sure you get exactly what you want when you're finally free. I'll spend days locked in my bedroom with you. Where no one can interrupt us... well, except maybe your mate. I'm assuming he won't let you out of his sight once your back.

She gasps and then whimpers low, so low I almost don't hear it. "Is it... is it wrong that the idea of both of you... of all of us..." She can't get the words out and I can't suppress my groan at how turned on she is. I can feel it pulsing through my veins.

No. It's not wrong. And if you want us both at the same time, I will make sure you get it. I'll make sure you get everything you want.

"Ahriman!" Lucifer's bark makes me jump. "How about you and Adrienne stop fucking each other in your mind and pay attention? We need to get on with this." Awkward and angry tension sits in the room and I feel the anger coming from not only Nox, but from the Dark Lord as well. Hm. So Onyx is a bit more involved with my princess than I originally thought. Good to know.

"Sorry, Lucifer. What do you need me to do?" I walk over to the side of the bed next to the demon, where Lucifer is sitting. I give her a half smile, but she doesn't return it. She's putting on a tough front but I can see and feel her nerves coursing through the room.

"I'm going to put Sabrina in a trance so she doesn't feel any pain when we remove her heart. Once I remove her heart, we will place Adrienne's into her body. Than, do you have her heart ready?" I look over at Than and he nods his head, reaching into his cloak and pulling out the chamber that has been keeping her heart from deteriorating.

The red organ levitates in the clear glass box. It pumps softly, dull and strained beats, as blood swirls around it in flying ribbons. The blood circulates in and out of the heart, a never ending cycle. It's quite the sight.

"Perfect. Once her heart is safely contained in Sabrina's chest, that's when you come in and kiss her. It's going to feel weird, but you need to keep the connection until every ounce of Adrienne's soul has left your body and moved into hers. You need to picture her leaving you. And Adrienne needs to think about leaving. You got that, princess?" Lucifer speaks to Adrienne through my mind and she responds to him with a simple, shaky yes.

"Good. Once the soul has transferred over, her magic should pull to her. Nox, you have to let go of it. Let it do what it wants. It's going to hurt, but it's going to be over within a few seconds." We all nod, understanding our jobs and trying to hold it together. I can tell everyone is just as nervous as I am.

"Can we do anything to help?" Lady Blackwell speaks up, referring to her and Onyx. I almost forgot hey were here. They are standing at the edge of the room, keeping their distance and letting us do what we need to.

"Right now, no. But thank you, my lady. Once your services are necessary, I will let you know." He winks again and I want to roll my eyes at the devil. He's like a love sick puppy with this woman.

"Alright, Sabrina. I want to thank you again for your sacrifice. It will not go unrewarded. Your willingness to provide us with your body is going to save all of our worlds and because of your selflessness, you will be rewarded in the highest regard in Posvita. I will make sure of it."

"What's Posvita?" Adrienne whispers the question to me, as if that would keep the devil from hearing, and I see Lucifer's jaw clench at her interruption again.

It's where we go when we are finished here. Those stars you can see above heaven? That's it. Where we get to rest and be rewarded for our hard work. An afterlife of sorts, if you must. I can feel her nodding her head and then my attention is brought back to Lucifer.

He places his hands over Sabrina's face as two tears fall from her closed eyes. Within seconds, her face changes from worry to peace and she's clearly knocked out. Without any warning, Lucifer slams his hand against her chest and his hand moves through the black clothing and past her thick skin until it's thrust deep into her chest.

There's no blood, there's no screaming or any inkling of discomfort. And then his hand is retreating from her body and in its grasp is a bloody organ that slowly stops beating, fading until it's completely limp in his hand.

"Go ahead, Than. Put hers in." Lucifer instructs him to move quickly and before I know it, Adrienne's heart is out of the box and safely secured inside of this stranger's body. Her clothes aren't torn, there's no blood anywhere, and a relaxed expression still sits on her lifeless face.

"Ready, Ahri?" Lucifer turns toward me and I nod my head, even though I can feel the panic filling up both me and Adrienne. I don't want her out of my head. I love having her with me all the time. Feeling her there. Knowing she's mine.

I walk up to the edge of the bed and sit down, looking over the face of the dead demon that will soon be my everything. She has a kind face once you get past her roughness, but she's nothing compared to my darling.

Ready for this, princess? I whisper to her as I lean down to claim this stranger's lips.

"As I'll ever be, I guess." She pauses and then her voice graces my ears again. "If anything happens... just know that I don't blame you anymore. And I'm so grateful for everything you have done for me. I'm going to miss being in your arrogant head." She sniffles and it all but breaks me in half.

I won't be whole without your incessant voice ringing through my ears, darling. But I'll try to make due having you standing in front of me. No matter what, I'm going to protect you.

"I know you will, Ahri. I'll see you on the other side." I bend the rest of the way down, my lips hovering over the cold, limp ones in front of me. Right before my lips collide with hers, I whisper something, so quick, so quiet, that I doubt she can catch it before we are engulfed in a strong wind like pull moving through my brain.

I love you, my darling.

CHAPTER 15

ADRIENNE

The blackness surrounding me starts to feel like a wind tunnel. I hear the strong gusts careening through the empty space and threatening to pull me with it. And then it does. I'm swept up and spinning faster than I've ever spun. Dizziness takes over and I have to squeeze my eyes shut.

I want to fight the wind. I want to try to get away from this storm, but I know I can't. Fighting it won't help anyone. It will just prevent me from leaving Ahri's head. A small voice in my head tells me I don't want to. The same voice that whimpered and swelled when I thought I heard Ahri whisper those three words just seconds ago. I can't tell if it was real or my imagination.

The wind tunnel pulls me around the room, moving faster and faster. It feels like I'm stuck in a whirlpool, and pretty soon, I'm going to be engulfed into the thick black water. The circles around the space get smaller and tighter until I'm seconds away from falling down the hole. The hole that will bring me back to life or suspend me into nothingness for the rest of time.

I scream out when it feels like I'm being ripped to shreds. Like someone is taking a knife and slicing it through my brain, across my face and nonexistent body. It's excruciating and never ending. I see no solitude in sight. Fear consumes me at the thought that this is it. That this is what the end looks like.

And then everything stops. The wind is no longer there. I no longer feel pain. No. This is the opposite of pain. Tingles and sparks tickle my face, radiating from my lips. Everything inside of me relaxes, as if this is where I'm meant to be... how I'm meant to feel for the rest of time.

I move my lips and the warmth that engulfs them feels like home. Like everything is right where it should be in the world. I feel the warmth spread down to my toes and back again. It makes me feel alive. It makes me feel free. It makes me feel strong.

A deep groan vibrates against my lips and a shiver travels down my spine. I reach farther into this feeling, pulling at the warmth that engulfs my lips. My hands move up to grab at it and hold it there, preventing it from leaving. Long hair slips through my fingers until my hands land on someone's head.

And then I realize, the warmth is coming from someone specific. This feeling is from a kiss. One of the best I've ever had. Something that not only sparks fire deep inside of me, but makes me feel calmer and safer than I ever have. It feels like I belong here. With his lips on mine. My hands in his hair. His huge body covering me up and hiding me from the world.

But then he's pulling away. I hear my own whimper grace my ears as I reach for him, but the sound doesn't register as my voice. And then I remember. It's not my voice. It's the voice of the random demon I have been forced into. The demon that died, sacrificed herself, to bring me back.

"Adrienne?" I recognize his accent, but it sounds clear and louder than it ever has. I feel the corners of my lips turn up at their own accord and then beg my eyes to open. They don't respond, as if my mind and this body aren't fully connected yet. They feel heavy and weighed down.

"Come on, darling. Open those eyes of yours for me. Show me you're here with me." His voice brings life to me. Every word he says makes my blood flow faster, my heart beat harder. His warm hand caresses my cheek and tickles every nerve it touches. I want to call out to him. To tell him to keep talking. To help me wake up.

I open my mouth to say his name. To hear the word leave my lips and bring me back to life. "N- Nox."

Silence surrounds me and my mind screams, banging on my skull and asking why I said Nox's name. I was supposed to say Ahri. I can feel the disappointment radiating off of him where his hand touches me. And then he's pulling away.

"Ren?" Another voice fills my ears and my heart speeds up again. My spine tingles with the song of our love. And when his hand falls onto my chest, my eyes snap open. I feel the body I'm in suddenly fill up, like a balloon being blown up until it's ready to pop. And then I feel sparks of golden light swim through my veins and explode inside of me. My magic.

I spring up on the bed and take a deep breath, my body feeling energized and exhausted at the same time. I blink my eyes and take in the space around me... all of the faces. I see Nox first. His dark curly hair unruly on his head. There are tears glistening in his dark violet eyes and his lip is wobbling.

Then I see Ahri. He stands at the side of the bed, a wall of muscle and mass. He's huge. His long hair falls around his head as he looks down and the black clothes he's wearing do a terrible job at hiding the tattoos underneath. The tattoos that represent our connection. His thick black beard surrounds the slight frown on his lips. The lips I was just kissing. The lips that felt like home.

Lucifer, Than, my mother, and Onyx all stand behind them around the bed. Everyone's eyes are on me, taking me in and waiting for something to happen. What am I supposed to do? Crack a joke? Do a dance?

"Um... Hi." The voice is foreign to my ears but it makes everyone around me move at once. Everyone but Lucifer and Than. They just stand back and stare ahead, with an approving smile on their faces.

"Princess, are you okay?" Onyx speaks up and I turn towards him. His lilac eyes dart between my own and his always perfect blonde hair is falling into his eyes.

"Worried about me, huh? So, the Dark Lord does have a heart." I joke but the timber of my voice comes out weird and I sound less sarcastic than I normally do.

"There's that humor I missed so much. Glad to see you didn't lose it." He smirks at me and I can see the relief covering his face. His handsome face that I truly did miss after all of this time.

I turn my face towards my mate and my heart squeezes when I take him in. "Hi, Nox." The minute I say the two words, he attacks me with a hug and I'm being squeezed tight. My spine plucks out our lullaby and my heart thumps in my chest, cherishing the feel of his arms around me.

"God, Ren. I missed you so much. I don't know what I'd do without you. I love you so much." Each word comes out frantic and rushed, like he's terrified I'm going to disappear into thin air and he won't be able to tell me everything he wants to.

"I love you too. I'm right here. I'm not going anywhere." He pulls away and looks over my body, taking in my new appearance. "What do you think? You into blondes?" I laugh awkwardly and Nox just smiles and shakes his head at me.

"I'm into *you*. I much prefer your dark hair, but I'd love any body your soul was in. At least you still have your eyes. I missed your eyes." Hm. Good to know. I didn't think my eyes would be the same but I guess people do always say the eyes are the windows to the soul. It would make sense that my eyes would come with my soul.

I turn towards Ahri now and rather than my spine tingling and plucking like it does for Nox, my skin prickles with small needle like zaps and my mind feels like it's on an axis, going round and round until I'm drunk and dizzy from endorphins.

"Ahri," I say his name and his red eyes blink back at me. His frown turns into a soft smile and he brings himself closer to me, standing at the edge of the bed. I look into his eyes, letting everything else fall away. "Thank you for keeping me safe."

"Of course, darling. It's quite lonely not having you invading my every thought though." He winks at me and I bring my hand out to run against the black swirls on his arm. The tattoos are so beautiful. So intricate. So entrancing.

"I rather like being able to look at you instead of just listening to your irritating accent." I smile at him and the skin my hand graces forms small goosebumps. He gives me one of the most beautiful smiles I've ever seen and the rough, scary exterior he sports fades away into this graceful creature I can't stop looking at.

"I hate to break up this moment, but we have work to do. It's a pleasure to finally meet you, Adrienne Blackwell. I am looking forward to saving the worlds with you by my side." I nod my head at Lucifer, still staring into Ahri's eyes. The red color is contrasted by swirling black branches that I swear move across his irises.

"We need to get you some food. Get you up and walking. And then we can start discussing our plans." I look over at Lucifer now and sit up straight.

"I need more answers before we discuss any plans further. I expect no secrets to remain between the two of us if we are to work together. Everything that has happened between you and Atlas to get you to this point must be divulged. Understood?" My voice floats through the room with a twinge of authority.

"As you wish, princess. I will show you the rest of my story once you have some food in your stomach."

"L*uc, I don't feel good about this.*" A*yla's voice sounds worried as* she puts her hands on my face, staring into my eyes. Her gray orbs shine so bright, they are almost blinding. And while fear rings through me, I don't let it show. I just smile back at her.

"I already made the deal, my love. Mandy will be saved and then you and I can stay together. I can't lose you. I won't." I didn't tell her about the conversation that I walked in on. The one about Atlas exterminating half of the population. I will figure that out once I know my Ayla is safe.

"But your wings. You can't give up your wings. It will destroy you." I breathe out a shaky breath and give her another smile. I won't let my fear show.

"Sweetheart, I would give up anything for you. My wings are not who I am. They are simply a small part of me. Nothing more." It's a lie. My wings shake in my core, terrified of what's to come. They know what's about to happen. They are a huge part of me, no matter how much I deny it. They are like a best friend, a family member, that I am giving up to save the love of my life.

I whisper my apologies to the wings that have been a part of me since birth and then place a gentle kiss against Ayla's lips. "It will be over before we know it and then Mandy will be safe."

"Atlas is a bastard for this. For abusing his power. He's threatened by you. That's why he wants your wings. To knock you down a peg. To prove that he will always be above you." Ayla is one of the only other angels that sees right through Atlas's façade. We hold no loyalty or respect for him. Or for what he stands for."

"He's not threatened by me, my love. He is simply power hungry and loves to show how much he has. I am nothing to be threatened by. Just an angel in love. An angel who would do anything for his other half." I kiss her nose and she nuzzle her head against mine, before resting her forehead against my own.

"How did I get so lucky, Luc? I don't deserve your love. No one does. You have the kindest soul I have ever known. I love you dearly."

"And I love you to the end of all of our universes."

"Lucifer." Surya's serpentine voice breaks us from our moment. "It's time." I turn towards the vile man and glare. He has a smile on his iridescent skin and his gray eyes hold no remorse. Only giddy excitement for the pain and suffering I'm about to endure.

"It will be over soon, my love. I'll be back before you know it. Go home and wait for me. We will dance the night away and celebrate Mandy." My heart rate picks up with my nerves. With the fear of what I'm about to endure. My throat feels clogged with emotion. Emotion for the wings I have cherished all of my life. The wings that were exact replicas of my late father. A part of both of us that will no longer be a part of me.

I walk with Surya into the huge arena. Of course, it had to be done in here. For dramatic affect. The room is cold and musty. There is a single marble stage in the center and the normally full stadium is completely empty, minus the two other disciples and Atlas himself. They sit front and center, each boasting a nauseatingly big grin.

I step up onto the stage and wait for instruction. I've never seen an angel get his wings removed before. I don't know what it entails. I can't imagine it's going to feel good. Our wings are a part of us. Like one of our limbs. Only, they are connected to our heart and spines. Our magic. So, it's going to be so much worse.

"Kneel, Lucifer," Surya barks out the orders. "Summon your wings." I do as he's told, but when I pull for my wings to appear, they shake and cower inside of me. They refuse to show themselves. Refuse to come out, knowing what will happen if they do.

"I said, summon your fucking wings!" He screams at me and I glare back at him.

"I'm trying. They know what's about to happen. Give them a minute." I spit the words out and try again, begging them to come out. Apologizing over and over and trying to get them to understand. This has to happen. It's not personal and I'm just as scared as they are.

After a few more seconds, they begrudgingly unfold from my shoulder blades. I look back at their iridescent hue and watch as they shake and cower. My heart breaks with each tremble. I feel a tear fall from my eye and turn my head away, looking down at the ground in shame.

"I'm so sorry. I will forever miss you," I whisper the words and then feel my wings wrap around me in a soft, warm cocoon. Their way of saying goodbye. Of telling me they understand.

"Unwrap yourself. It's time." Atlas's voice booms through the room and my wings squeeze me one last time before pulling away and standing tall behind me. I close my eyes, terrified of what this is going to do to me.

Surya places his hand at the base of my wing, where it connects with my back and without any warning, he brings an axe down on the hilt. I scream out at the fire burning across my skin. I scream when the pain only intensifies with each messy chop. I can feel it scorching my heart, burning my skin, breaking my spine.

It's so excruciating, I swear I'm going to die. There's no way this kind of pain can exist without death following it. It's not just the physical pain, but the heart break that squeezes my heart and threatens to make it explode. A piece of me, something that has been there for me for my entire life, is gone.

After what feels like hours of chopping, I'm left a bloody, tear ridden mess. But then, the worst part comes. I watch as Atlas laughs and stands from his seat. He looks at Surya, who is holding my discarded wings, and with one blink, he lights them on fire. I cry out, tears falling from my eyes, as the memories attached to my life burn in front of me. The patterns that match my fathers. The strength they held when they kept me from falling.

Gone in the blink of an eye. As if they never existed. I fall to the ground and let the sounds of the crackling fire burning away their last remnants drown out the booming laughter from the men watching. Watching as I break right in front of them.

"Your Ayla's human friend is no longer suffering from her accident. I gave you my word and I meant it. It was a pleasure doing business with you,

Lucifer." Atlas comes up to me and then pulls at my hair harshly, making me look up at him.

"And if you ever tell anyone about what you heard in my office that day, I will make this pain look like a god damn walk in the park compared to the pain you'll feel then. Got it?" I nod my head, too weak and exhausted to answer. And then he throws me back down to the ground and all four of them walk out of the room.

I don't move. I don't try to stop the thick black blood pouring from the nubs on my back. I don't try to stop the tears from falling from my eyes. I simply give in and let them win. Just for a few more minutes. Because sometimes, fighting is too hard. Sometimes, we all need to surrender to the pain and let it drag us down. At least for a moment.

I COME TO FROM THE VISION LUCIFER SHARED WITH ME AND FEEL tears falling from my eyes. The pain he went through. The heartbreak. I felt it as if it was my own. I lived through every excruciating slice of his wings as if they were my own. I lived through every vile word Atlas threw his way. Every trembling beat of his heart as he lost a part of himself.

Lucifer avoids looking me in the eye. He had to live through it again in order to show me. Without thinking, I wobbly get up from my seat and walk towards him. I put my arms around him and feel his body go rigid from the embrace. And then he's hugging me back, as if this small act of kindness is the most meaningful thing that has ever happened to him.

"I'm so sorry for what he did to you. No one deserves that. No one. That deal was bullshit." I am still trying to get used to my unfamiliar voice.

"Well, you're right about that part, princess. Atlas tricked me. He took my wings and promised to rid Mandy of her injuries from the accident. Well, while he did that, he decided to grace Mandy with something just as bad. If not worse. He gave her cancer. Terminal cancer."

"No..." My voice gets lost in my throat and I shake my head in disgust. "So, after all of that, Mandy died anyway? You lost your wings for nothing?"

"Actually, Mandy lived to be ninety-eight before she passed away of old age." I furrow my brows at Lucifer's admission.

"But... you said—

Realization hits me like a mac truck. "Ayla... she sacrificed herself and gave Mandy her wings." Lucifer nods his head, dropping his eyes down to the ground.

"My Ayla's best and worst quality was the size of her heart. She would do anything to save an innocent. She adored the humans. She believed they were the superior race. So, when she went to visit Mandy and found out about the cancer, she sacrificed herself. She left in the middle of the night, leaving me with a measly apology note. By the time I woke up, she was gone."

Fresh tears fall from my eyes. I swear, if Lucifer doesn't kill Atlas himself, I will for him. He's a monster. Someone who shouldn't be ruling anyone. "I'm so sorry, Lucifer. So, what happened after? How did you end up here?"

Lucifer clears his throat and then looks up from the floor. We are all seated at the huge table on the first floor. The table is almost as long as the one in our castle in Ombra, but we are all sitting at one end.

"I had nothing left to live for. I made a plan, refusing to let them destroy the world my Ayla loved so much. I spoke to Aiden every night. I looked up into the abyss. The black night above us full of all of our fallen ones. Humans, angels, everyone together as equals up in the dark sky. And I told him of Atlas's doings. I told him of Atlas's plans. I begged him for help. I begged him to be real. To listen."

"And did he?" I'm so invested in this story I almost forget there are others in this room with us.

"I believe he did... but I was impatient and he decided to help me after I tried to stop Atlas myself. There was no way I could win against him and his disciples. I was weak without my wings. Weak without my love in this world anymore. But I was determined to stop them or die trying. One night, when Atlas was asleep, I snuck into his chambers and tried to kill him. It wasn't smart. But I was a man in mourning and I wasn't thinking straight. I stabbed him but it missed his heart. He woke up and the wrath I felt was like nothing else. I tried to use my magic to fight him, but he won. He banished me from heaven. He sent me to the deepest depths of darkness. Cursed me to never return and to die alone, terrified and surrounded by darkness forever."

He stops and swallows hard, still having a hard time with his story. "I gave up for a while. Let the darkness take over. The monsters that I created from my own fear and depression. But, one day, I heard a whisper. It was soft and barely audible. But after a while, I was able to make out the words.

"It told me of Atlas's plans. It told me Atlas was going to send imignis down to destroy me. That he decided a lifetime of solitude wasn't enough. He wanted me, and the rest of the world, to burn into ash. But this voice told me I was strong. It told me I could defeat him. I could destroy this curse."

"That voice... you think that was Aiden?" Lucifer nods his head, answering my question.

"Yes. It's the only explanation. He gave me the power to leave the darkness. I escaped and when I saw the fireball flying through the atmosphere, I used all of my strength. All of the power I had left. And I was somehow able to stop it. I stopped it from moving and put a shield around the fire. I created the sun. A constant threat that sits above the world. Something that both Atlas and I are not strong enough to destroy."

"And you think I'm strong enough to destroy it?" I raise my brows at him, unsure of his confidence in me.

"You and Ahriman together? Yes. And you're strong enough to overthrow the dictatorship that Atlas holds over the angels. I know of it." I look at him, trying, and failing, to hide my puzzled expression.

"How do you know that?"

"Because. I still hear Aiden's whispers. He told me about you. About what the girl with purple and red eyes was capable of. We have all been waiting for you, princess." I blink at him as he gives me a soft smile. He's nothing like I expected him to be. He's kind, with a big heart. He's been burned and scorned more than any man ever should.

"That's a lot of pressure... I was barely able to learn how to control my powers before someone decided to rip my heart out." I glare at Than and he winks at me with a lopsided grin.

"Had to do it, princess. No hard feelings." I snort and shake my head at him.

"Hard feelings because you were a scary mother fucker who threatened my mate."

"I never would have hurt Nox. He was my favorite student. Sometimes fear gets things done. In that specific instant, I knew I needed to scare you."

"Well, I hold grudges. So, you better watch your back, Nathaniel." I give him a smirk that shows my threat is fake. I'm grateful for how hard they have tried to save the human world. I think back to the fact that Morta was the original Ombra, like Lucifer said, before Atlas created a duplicate and stole the idea. It makes me sick how conniving and horrible that man is.

"So, what happens when the curse is broken and Atlas is taken down? What happens to our worlds? We have no point then." I don't want to destroy my kingdom. I care about the people there, even if I barely know them at this point.

"We do what the humans are doing. Live our lives. Rather than having to stress about the world blowing up every second of the day, we can focus on being happy and living our lives. That's exactly what I've been trying to do for my demons in Morta. Since they are no longer obligated to protect the humans, I try to let them live as relaxed as possible while still preparing them for the potential war."

"Humans are the opposite of relaxed." I scoff and think back to the miserable humans I had to deal with back in New York. Then again, I was one of those stressed out, miserable people.

"No matter what, people are going to have their own issues. But imagine how the human population would act if they knew the sun they loved so much was actually a deadly curse that could, potentially, at any minute, destroy the world. How would they act then?"

"Alright, you got me there. They would lose their shit. They would end up destroying the world themselves with their panic." The world burning from a magical curse is far worse than the pandemics and wars we have delt with on Earth... and look how we reacted during those.

"Exactly, dear. So, once Atlas is gone and the curse is broken, the humans, and our people, will all be able to exist happily. Well, as happy as we allow ourselves to be." I snicker and then nod my head. I like the sound of that. We all need a little peace and quiet in our lives. My life was turned upside down in the last month and I don't even remember what relaxation feels like anymore.

"Alright. Well, what's the plan?" I'm ready to destroy every single person that gets in our way of saving the world.

CHAPTER 16

ADRIENNE

"I still don't understand why we have to wait. Waiting never works." I'm being led to a room upstairs, Lucifer in front of me and the three men that are going to be the death of me tailing us.

"Trust me, princess, I don't want to wait either. I'm ready to raid their shit hole of a world right now. But you're exhausted. And you and Ahriman need to practice using your magic together. On top of that, I have some finishing touches to my plan on getting into heaven. It will be a piece of cake for you two. But I've been banned for eternity, if you remember correctly."

"I figured you had that part covered. Since, you know, you've been plotting this attack for the last like thousands of years." I smirk at him and the devil gives me a conniving smile.

"Undoing an irreversible curse isn't easy, dear. But yes, I do have the logistics of it figured out. Just a few loose ends I want to tie up."

"Loose ends?" I raise a brow at him as we reach a door that he stops in front of.

"Yes, princess. Loose ends. Don't you worry yourself about my hardships. You have enough of your own you are going to endure." He opens the door to the room and before I can look inside, he speaks again. "Rest. We will see how you feel in the morning and then discuss more plans then. Training will commence midday. Good night, Adrienne. I'm happy you're here. Ahri, I trust you will bring make sure everyone gets settled accordingly?"

Ahri nods before I answer. "Thank you for helping me... for helping everyone. I'm sorry. I'm sorry for everything I thought about you. For everything the entire universe thinks about you. You're an admirable leader, Lucifer. And I am forever indebted to you for your kindness." I bow my head slightly, needing to show my gratitude to him.

"Oh, my dear Adrienne. We are the ones who will be forever indebted to you. You're our miracle." He puts his finger under my chin and raises my head so I am no longer bowing to him. And then the devil does something that I never expected the devil to do. He bows his head to me before turning and walking down the long balcony towards another set of stairs.

"Lucifer just bowed to you, blondie. You're like a celebrity now." Onyx's sarcastic voice breaks me from my amazement and I turn towards him and glare at his handsomely smug face.

"Blondie?" I cringe at the name and flip him off.

"Well, if you haven't looked in the mirror recently, you have about three feet of platinum blonde hair coming out of your head." I look down at my hair and remember, once again, that I am not in my own body.

"Damn, I keep forgetting I'm blonde. I miss my dark hair." I realize how insensitive I sound so I silently say a prayer for the woman who sacrificed herself for me. I will never forget what she did to try to save humanity.

"Same." I get this response from all three boys and my eyebrows skyrocket into my hairline. They are all staring at me, each one a walking contradiction from the other. Ahri's long hair and huge body covered in tattoos. Nox's curls and soft violet eyes that match his perfect smile. Onyx's thick blonde hair and lilac eyes that sport more confidence than most.

I ignore all of them and look into the dark room. My stomach flutters at the thought of our sleeping arrangements. Surely Lucifer didn't expect us to share a room... right?

"Who's sleeping where tonight?" I beat around the bush, not caring about making anyone uncomfortable. Two of them are bonded to me magically and the other is supposed to be my husband.

"I'm assuming that Lucifer assumed that we assumed we would all assumingly sleep in the same room... Am I assuming right?" Onyx, of course, manages to make me laugh and forget about any discomfort I felt before. Not that I felt any... No... I'm not uncomfortable with sleeping in the same room as three men... Three men that all send my body into overdrive.

We all look at Ahri, waiting for him to give us instructions. "I'm sleeping wherever she sleeps. I don't care where you two sleep. There are lots of rooms available down the hall." He nods his head in the direction of the long hall and Nox glares him down.

"Just get in the room. I already know that Ahri and Nox don't snore... Onyx, if you do... I fucking swear. I will behead you myself." I point a finger in his face and then look at all three of them as my finger directs them into the room. Like the children they are, they all walk into the room in a single file line until Onyx passes me with a smirk.

"Good news for you, blondie..." Onyx brings his mouth close to my ear and I hold my breath. "I snore like a fucking bear." Before I can react and punch him like I want to, he slips into the room and leaves me standing in the hallway by myself. Fucking dick.

I take a deep breath, looking up at the ceiling and wanting to pray to someone... but not knowing who. Then, it hits me and I smile to myself. "Aiden, I hope you can hear me. First off... please give me the strength to overcome the hierarchy that is taking over the world. And second... Please, please help me overcome the hierarchy of these three men that are taking over my body. In Aiden's name, Amen."

Happy with my prayer, I walk into the room and shut the door behind me. None of them turned the light on, so I flip it on myself and illuminate the room around us. And damn, it's quite the room.

The California king on steroids has a sheer, glistening canopy surrounding it. The walls are black and the floor is a dark tile with marbled white throughout. One of the walls is made of windows that looks over the city and there is a black couch facing a bright fire. It flickers red, orange, and blue colors and I swear I can hear it singing a soft lullaby to me.

I turn to the opposite wall of the bed and find all three men standing there next to two open doors. One of which clearly opens into a bathroom that looks bigger than the room and the other is a walk-in closet. Both are more extravagant than anything I have ever experienced.

"Damn. The devil doesn't fuck around, huh?" I crack the joke and annoyingly, no one else laughs.

"Do you want to take a shower, darling?" Ahri speaks first and I watch as Nox's jaw clenches in anger. I feel equal parts irritated and turned on by his anger. What the hell is wrong with me?

"I guess I probably should. I can't shake this feeling like she's still here and I'm just borrowing her body. Like I'm dirty and doing the wrong thing." I shiver in her skin and look down at her pale, thin arms.

"No, darling, that's not the case. She gave herself up for the greater good. She knew what Atlas had planned and she wanted to better the future of those after her. She's gone and it has nothing to do with you. No matter who it was, she would have done it." His accent flows through the air and I feel conflicted by it.

"Th... thank you for saying that, Ahri," I answer, deciding that there's no reason to feel conflicted. As much as I hated him for my entire life, I believe everything they have told me. That Ahri never hurt me. That this was all a part of their plan to save the world. A small, quiet voice whispers to me that I always knew it, but I shove it down and give Ahri a comforting smile.

"Do you need help, princess?" This comes from Nox. My love. My life. My mate. My everything... *besides Ahri. He's part of your everything.* I shake my head and rid my brain of the involuntary voice ringing through my head.

"Yes, please." I try to answer as nonchalant as possible, but on the inside, I am screaming for him to please help me shower. To please touch my body. Kiss my lips. Put his co—

"Are you sure I can't help, darling? I know my way around this place. The hot water can be hard to navigate sometimes." Ahri's deep voice rumbles through the room and I feel the vibrations deep in my core. My eyes shift to his and they promise pleasure and pain at the same time. Holy shit. I'm done for.

"Um... Ye... N... No. It's okay, Ahri. I'm sure Nox can help me figure it out." I ignore every single nerve that is screaming Ahri's name and reject him. It hurts a deep seeded part of me, but most of me doesn't care. I just want Nox. He's my world. He's all I want. Isn't he?

I walk towards the room that has no door and feel like I'm wading through thick honey. Both of Ahri's and Nox's eyes are plastered to me as I move and I can feel exactly what they are thinking. Exactly what they are imagining.

She's never going to pick you, you bloody beast. I pause when I hear a distant voice ring through my brain. When my head turns in Ahri's direction, he stares blankly at me and then turns away and pretends to be busy. Does he know I just heard his thoughts?

I chance it, walking into the huge black, marble bathroom and letting my eyes roam around. *Ahri? Can you hear me?* I speak into my own head and look into the huge, wall length mirror sitting in the corner of the room. My body is both muscular and slim. I'm barely five and a half feet and my platinum blonde hair is lying limp down my shoulders. I hate to admit it, but Sabrina's appearance reminds me so much of my sister and it makes my heart clench.

Darling? Is that you? His thick husky voice barrels through my brain and I almost moan from the sound. God, how do I miss his voice this much already? I have no idea what changed, but suddenly, I can't get him out of my mind... literally.

"Ren? The water is warm now." Nox invades my thoughts and I turn towards him. He's standing, still fully clothed, by the massive shower.

The black marble continues throughout the open shower that showcases three different spouts spraying thick rivets of steaming water. There's a huge light illuminating the whole space and a marble bench taking up one of the walls. It's massive. It's like nothing I've ever seen.

I don't answer as I walk towards Nox. I feel awkward in my own body and can't convince myself to remove my clothes. What if he likes her body better? What if I'm not good enough compared to her?

"Ren?" His voice breaks me from my thoughts and I look into his amethyst eyes. "Don't ever think that anyone can compare to the real you. My Ren is remarkable. Sensational. Extraordinary.

And while any body that contains your soul is perfect, nothing and no one will ever compare to you. So don't you dare second guess yourself. Never with me, my love."

I don't realize I'm crying until his hand is caressing my cheek and wiping away a tear. "Shit. I'm sorry. I don't know why I'm so emotional." I try to pull away but his hands hold my face still.

"Ren, you have nothing to apologize for. You've gone through more in the last few weeks than anyone should in a thousand lifetimes. You're allowed to be emotional. Sometimes we need to let it out and I want you to be comfortable doing that in front of me." I dart my eyes between his dark purple ones and notice the lilac swirling through them. A part of me, always attached to him.

I can't stop myself as I lean forward and press my lips against his. My whole body feels like it's floating as our lips mold together. My lips are smaller than normal and I have a hard time getting used to them, but his are perfect and exactly how I remembered them. They are soft and supple. They are gentle yet rough.

He moves my head with his hands and then deepens the kiss, pulling a low groan from me. That only feeds his hunger more because suddenly, he's picking me up, placing his hands under my ass and turning us so my back hits the cold marble wall.

"Fuck." The word vibrates against my lips and I whimper at the feel of it. "I missed you so much, Ren." And then his tongue is invading my mouth, preventing me from answering. Not that I would have been able to anyway. I'm too consumed by everything Nox. The way his lips feel. The way he tastes. The way he smells. The way our song flows through the air around us, each soft note plucking away at the same rhythm our lips are moving.

I can hear your thoughts, darling. I'm going to lose my bloody mind. I gasp at Ahri's voice in my head and Nox pulls away with furrowed brows. "What's wrong, Ren?"

Shaking my head, I smile at him and bite my lip. "Nothing at all. I just... well, Ahri and I are still able to hear each other's thoughts." Nox grits his teeth for a second but then grins at me.

"This is karma for me talking to you when Dr. Archer was fucking you, isn't it?" I laugh, throwing my head back, while Nox just groans in fake annoyance and stares at me with sparkling eyes. Back before I was thrown into this world, Nox was the one in my head. And he loved to show his presence whenever Dr. Archer had me bent over.

"Might be. How does it feel being on the other end of it?" I bite my lip and raise a brow at him, bringing my hands around his neck.

"Not great, I'll be honest. Especially if you pick the voice in your damn head over me like you did to that dip shit." I shake my head at him and roll my eyes. There was no question on who was the one for me back then. I always felt a connection to Nox that I didn't feel with Sam. I wasn't totally honest with him and he wasn't honest with me. We never gave each other our full selves. Not like I did with Nox.

But now there's Ahri. Someone I have hated all of my life that now, I can't seem to shake. We are bonded just as Nox and I are, but in a different way. While Nox is my mate, the man that loves me whole heartedly and makes my heart skip a beat, Ahri is my familiar. My protector who makes my skin prickle and my brain swirl a million miles a minute. He is a pain in my ass but he's managed to embed himself under my skin and now I can't satisfy the itch.

"Nox Kage. You're not getting rid of me that easy. But... he's also not going anywhere. I can't leave him behind. He'll... he'll die without our connection." The fact that Ahri's sole purpose is to protect me and if I leave him, he will fade away into ash, scares me to my core.

"Don't lie, princess. I know you better than that. That's not the only reason you want him around." He raises a brow at me and I squint my eyes at him.

"Alright, fine. I... I kind of like having him around. I can't explain it. I hated him so much and somehow all of that hate turned into... into something else." I think back to Ahri's favorite saying. 'Hate and love are dangerously similar. But, is it love I feel for him or something created by our familiar bond that I can't control?

"I understand, Ren. And I'm not going to make you choose. Just like I wouldn't have made you choose when you were supposed to marry Onyx. And as much as I can't stand Ahri, I think I hated Onyx even more." Nox places a soft kiss against the tip of my nose and then gently places me back down on the ground.

"Yeah, no kidding. Somehow these assholes keep sneaking there way over to the good side though." I think of Onyx and a smile graces my lips. He's become such a good friend. Someone that can brighten my day with a joke or an inappropriate remark.

"Alright, Ren. Let's get you cleaned up." We undress before stepping under the burning hot stream and I close my eyes. In most instances, I would take advantage of the naked man with me, but the water beating down on me hypnotizes me and makes my eyes close. It feels so good as it burns into my skin at the same time that Nox's hands lather the soap all over my body. I let my head fall back when he shampoos my hair and let myself drift away in this moment.

I open my eyes and find myself being deposited in bed. Confusion takes over until I look up into Nox's eyes and he smiles down at me. "You were half asleep in the shower. I wrapped you up in a towel and carried you to bed."

I look around the room and find Ahri and Onyx both facing the opposite direction, giving me privacy since I'm practically naked. "Thank you." I curl up into the warm, soft sheets and let them pull me back under.

"You take the bed with her, Nox. We'll take the couches." I just barely hear the sound of Onyx's voice and part of me wants to yell out and say no, they can all sleep in the bed. But I'm too tired. So, I let sleep take over as Nox's body slides into bed and holds me from behind.

Sweet dreams, my darling.

"*You need to move. There's not much time left.*" *I spin around where I'm standing and find myself suspended in darkness. Am I in Ahri's head again? No... That voice didn't sound like him. This voice is new. Someone I've never hear before.*

"*What? Who are you?*"

"*You know who I am. You need to hurry. Before it's too late.*"

I startle awake, shooting up in bed and breathing heavy. My mind wanders back to my dream. Or my vision. Or whatever the hell it was. Who was that? *Aiden.* A voice so far in the back of my head whispers the name. Was it really? Did Aiden reach out to me?

"Adrienne? Are you okay?" His hushed British accent flows through the room and I turn my head in the direction, unable to see anything in the dark room. Nox is still sleeping next to me, his heavy breath even as it leaves his body.

"Ahri... I had... I don't know what I had." I talk into the dark and wish my eyes would adjust so I could see him.

"May I come up there, darling?" He asks from somewhere in the room. I'm assuming he is on one of the couches, which is comical to me since we are in this huge skyscraper of a castle that has to have over three hundred rooms in it.

"Yes," I whisper the word and it comes out breathless. My skin prickles at the thought of him being closer to me. Of both of my bonds being within reaching distance. Faint movement catches my eye in front of me before the edge of the bed dips with his weight. My stomach flips and butterflies burst when I see him.

He crawls, so slowly, up the gigantic bed towards me. His hair falls around his head and his massive body flexes with each movement he makes. But what makes me gulp down nerves is the naked chest he sports. He's only wearing a pair of boxers, leaving the rest of his body exposed. I can practically feel the heat radiating off of him.

When he reaches me, he lies down on his side, his head only a few inches from mine. I can feel his breath and just make out the crimson of his eyes staring into mine. "Alright, darling. Tell me what happened."

"I think Aiden was trying to warn me. It wasn't really a dream. It felt more like it does when you were in my head." His eyebrows furrow but besides that, he doesn't react.

"And what did Aiden say?" I can't tell if he's mocking me or not but I squint my eyes at him in annoyance.

"What? You don't believe me?" He smiles, his lips spreading to reveal two rows of white teeth.

"I'd believe anything you told me, darling." I feel one of his hands snake between us and land on my hip underneath the blanket. When his hot hand makes contact with my bare skin, I suck in a breath. I can tell we both realize at the same time that I'm naked.

The air shifts and I forget what I was going to say. All I can focus on is the feel of his hand on my hip. I feel each of his fingers flex and close my eyes as fire glitters across my skin.

"Do you know how long I've wanted to touch you?" His deep voice flows through my brain and a soft whimper escapes me.

"He's sleeping right next to me... this isn't right." My brain speaks before my body can stop it. And while I'm panting, desperately seeking his touch, a part of me is still scared of him. Still mad at him and confused by my feelings.

"Darling, nothing we do is going to be right. Hating me isn't right. Loving me isn't right." He whispers it as the bed dips when his body gets closer to mine. "So, let's be wrong."

Somehow everything he is saying makes sense to me. "I've hated you for so long... I'm so confused by my feelings for you now." I open my eyes and look into his. He's now only an inch away from me. His nose close enough to brush against my own. His breath fans across my lips and makes them tingle.

"It's okay to be confused. But let me clear something up for you." He gets even closer to me and his lips brush against mine for barely a second. Enough to have me begging for more. "I know what I want and I'm going to keep fighting until I get it. You can hate me if you need to. But one day, you're going to realize the truth."

"Wh... what's the truth?" I'm drunk on Ahri. I'm completely flustered and the room is spinning around me.

"That hate creates the strongest love." His eyes stare into mine with genuine admiration. His hand brushes up and down against my waist, comforting me and turning me on at the same time.

"I'm scared." I don't mean to say it, but I do anyway. I feel hypnotized by the swirling world in his eyes.

"Of?"

My breath shakes as it leaves my body. "You."

His eyes spark with fire and I swear I feel heat grace my face. "Good."

And then his lips are on mine. He presses himself against me fully and the room around us falls away. They feel like fire and ice as they burn into me. As his lips glide across mine in a graceful punishment. He feels like sin. Like danger. Like everything bad. And it hurts in the best way possible.

His hand pulls my body into him even more until my naked body is flush against his barely clothed one. His hands are harsh and controlling, but every move he makes, everywhere he touches, relaxes me.

When our chests are completely pressed together, I feel this strange tickle across my skin. It feels like small snakes slithering between us and rather than scaring me, it only makes me want to get closer. To become one with him. Always.

"You're everything I ever dreamed you would be, darling." His words tickle my lips and I smile against his. The bed moves and I feel a hand touch my shoulder from behind me. I instantly stiffen, knowing that hand doesn't belong to Ahri.

"Ren? Are you okay?" His groggy voice breaks through the silence and I can tell the instant he realizes we aren't alone in bed. His body stiffens and he removes his hand from my back.

Ahri nods his head at me, placing a small peck against my lips and then lets me turn towards Nox. I can just make out his handsome face in the darkness and his expression confuses me. While he looks jealous, he also looks intrigued. Like part of him wants to sit there and watch.

"He... he just came up here because he heard me wake up. I had a weird dream." I try to make the situation better, completely unsure as to what his reaction means. Or, what his reaction is at all.

I feel Ahri place a hand against my back and his finger rubs against my skin in slow circles. It makes me shiver under the sheets. Nox gulps and then looks me in the eyes, smiling at me as desire shines in his purple orbs.

"Keep going," he says it as if it's a question. As if he's fighting himself on the inside. Half of him wanting to stop this and the other half desperately wanting to join in. I blink back at him and don't move, unsure if I'm physically able to anymore.

"Wh... what?" I stumble on the word and wait for him to save me. Instead, Ahri's hand slowly moves down my back until it stops, hovering right above the crest of my butt, making small, torturous circles.

My eyes stay on Nox's and through the darkness, I can see the lust pouring out of them. I can feel the desire thick in the air. He moves his eyes to my open mouth, which is currently gasping from the feel of Ahri's hand squeezing my ass and pressing his rock hard body into my back.

"Go ahead, Ahriman. Touch her." His voice is a deep whisper and it sends a zap of electricity through my body. My spine tingles and my whole body hums from our connection. From how intensely their attention affects me.

Nox slides in closer, both of us under the sheets, and presses his front against my naked chest. I'm now sandwiched between the two of them, both of their breath tickling my sensitive skin.

"Do you want that, Ren? Do you want his hands where only my hands belong?" The protectiveness in his voice is raw and dominating. My Nox is both sweet and rough in the best ways. The perfect combination.

"I... I." Arhi's hand moves lower at that moment and his thick finger slips through my folds, making me hiss at the feel of it. I'm so sensitive that I have to reach out and grab at Nox's arms for stability.

Nox brings his lips down to mine and I close my eyes in anticipation of the contact. His lips are so soft. They feel like velvet pressing against mine. He takes control and deepens the kiss, knowing exactly what to do. Every kiss with him is better than the last and I feel my power coursing through me, begging to be unleashed.

A soft glow hits the back of my eyelids and when I open my eyes, I see the glittering, golden light seeping out of both me and Nox. Our bond. Enhanced when we are connected. When we are one.

Ahri growls behind me and then grabs at my hips with his hand and pulls my body into his. His erection presses against my ass and I moan into Nox's mouth. He's massive. Scary big. Big enough to rip someone apart. The thought makes my mouth water and I deepen the kiss with Nox even more, tasting him with my tongue.

"I want to finger her pretty little pussy." Ahri says it as if he's asking for permission. Not from me though. No, he's making sure Nox gives him the okay. Because he knows my body belongs to him.

Nox smiles against my lips, his ego skyrocketing in this moment. "Make her come, Ahriman. Or I will." I whimper into Nox's mouth when his teeth nip at my lip. He sucks the pain away and then dives back into my mouth as his hand grabs at my nipple. He pinches it between two fingers and then massages the soft flesh, eliciting more sparks throughout my body.

At this point, our bodies are glowing bright enough to light up the entire room. And when I feel Ahri's hand reach back towards my core, it shines even brighter. I wait in anticipation for his finger to fill me. To bring me to my breaking point. To send me into bliss.

And that's exactly what he does. He isn't gentle. He's rough, just like I expected him to be. He shoves one of his thick fingers inside of me with one punishing thrust and I cry out, my moans being muffled by Nox's mouth.

His finger moves inside of me, rubbing against my walls and stretching me. It's both painful and full of pleasure. It's perfect. He groans behind me and at the same time, I feel both Nox and him start grinding against my body. Their erections press against my ass and my stomach and their hardness sends zaps of ecstasy through my veins. It's too much to handle. The most exquisite thing I've ever experienced.

"Fuck, darling. Ride my fingers. Just like that." Ahri's rumbling whisper hits my ear and I feel myself crawling up that cliff. The cliff that could very likely destroy me. Because a body, human or magical, can't withstand this much pleasure. This much tension and pressure filling it to the brim. Can it?

I squeeze Nox's arms as his head dips down. He puts my nipple in his mouth and that's all it takes. The feel of his hot tongue circling the sensitive pebble sends me crashing hard and fast.

"I'm..." I get the one word out before Ahri rips my head to the side and engulfs my lips with his. Where Nox's were soft and controlled, Ahri attacks my lips and I scream into his mouth as tears fall from my closed eyes.

The light around us is blinding as my body pulses against Ahri's fingers, squeezing them like a vice. It lasts for what feels like hours, days, it could be years for all I know. And then, I'm back down to reality and my body feels like it's filled with pins and needles, being dragged down by heavy weights.

The glowing light still blares through the room against my eyelids. The air sits silent besides my heavy breaths. Both of them are still kissing my body, touching me as much as they can.

"Ahem." A throat clearing stops both of them in their tracks, Nox stopping on my chest and Ahri on my shoulder blade. "Hate to break up the party I wasn't invited to, but you guys need to see this."

I peel my eyes open and sit up quick, taking the sheet with me to cover my naked chest. The minute I pull away from them, the twinkling golden light fades away and submerges us back into darkness.

"Bloody hell. We were just getting started, you cock. This better be important." Ahri groans as he sits up in bed too. We all stare into the darkness, waiting for our eyes to adjust.

"Just turn on the damn light, Nox." Onyx ignores Ahri's comment and within seconds, the lights are blaring through the room and burning my pupils that were just starting to adjust. I blink a few times until Onyx comes into view in front of us.

He's leaning against the door frame of the bathroom right in front of us. One of his arms rests above his head on the frame as his blonde hair falls into his purple eyes. He's shirtless, showing off his sculpted abs and he's wearing dark purple pajama pants. My eyes go wide on closer inspection, noticing the very obvious bulge in the front of them.

Onyx was... watching? And he was very clearly aroused by the entire thing. I gulp down my nerves, and unwelcome excitement, before bringing my eyes back to his. He has one brow raised with a cocky lopsided smirk covering his lips.

"Like what you see, princess?" His eyes dazzle with humor and I bite my lip to try to hide my own smile.

"Shut up, Onyx. What did you want to show us?" I mock glare at him and earn myself a snort before he shakes his head and walks towards us. Damn... I was enjoying the way he looked leaning up against that door...

He points his finger at us and I furrow my brows at him. "I wanted to show you, you." I turn toward Ahri first, who is still glaring at Onyx and then look over at Nox. That's when I notice something strange on him. Something that doesn't belong.

Black swirls and designs crawl up one of his wrists. They match Ahri's tattoos exactly, but on a much smaller scale. They only cover a few inches up his one hand and that's it. Nox stares at me while I stare at him and his eyes are just as big as mine.

"You... you have... why are those on your wrist?" I grab at his arm and hold it in my hand, rubbing my fingers over the soft skin.

"Ren..." Nox sounds concerned and when I turn my attention back to his eyes, I notice he is staring at my body, not my face. I look down at myself and gasp at what I see. My one arm is covered in swirling black patterns. They look nothing like the art work I have on my real body. These branch off like limbs on a tree and crawl across my shoulder, to my collarbone and chest, and all the way down my wrist on to my hand.

"What the fuck?" The words come out before I can stop them. I wait for the fear to settle, for the anger and annoyance to fill me up, but it doesn't come. I'm just surprised and confused. Each beautiful design tingles with a whisper of Ahri's name. They make me feel closer to him. Nox and I share a song deep in our spine that shines bright with golden light, and now Ahri and I share these tattoos. At least... we do in this body.

"Did you know this would happen?" I look at Ahri and I can tell by the look on his face that he didn't. He stares at the intricate drawings that match his with wide eyes and then finally, a small smile sneaks through the thick beard on his gruff face.

"No, but damn. I want to do that again so I can cover you even more. Actually..." He stops talking and then grabs the sheet covering me, whipping it off my naked body before I have time to react. I squeal and then attempt to cover myself, before deciding that it doesn't matter. They have all already seen enough.

"Oh, darling. That's sexy as hell." I look down at where he's looking and there are more dark black shapes snaking down my stomach, across my hip and bare ass, and between my legs. Everywhere Ahri touched me. Everywhere our bodies collided while I was floating off into oblivion.

"I guess the familiar bond transferred your marks over to me during... that. But why is it on Nox's hand too?" I look between the two of them and while Nox looks concerned and a bit annoyed, Ahri has a shit eating grin on his face. I turn to Onyx and after a few seconds, he too has the same grin. He starts chuckling, throwing his head back.

"Oh, this is good," Onyx says as he claps his hands together.

"It appears to me, Nox and Ahri are becoming bonded together as well. The happy couple will be inseparable before we know it!" A snort slips through my lips and when I hear a growl from Nox, I slap my hand over my mouth. Giving him a shy smile, I try to comfort him with my hand on his shoulder.

"It's okay, babe... the good news is, if we save the world, everyone will be able to tell you two are together just by looking at you." Onyx bursts out into a fit of hysterics and I can't stop my own from bubbling out too. I watch, my laugh making the bed shake below me, as Nox glares at me with a scowl on his face.

And then the smallest glimpse of a smile slips through. That one small smile turns into a full blown grin as he shakes his head at me with a low chuckle. "I'll be connected to this fucker if it means you're safe and right by my side for the rest of time."

"Always and forever." I wink at him and he offers one right back.

"Don't you dare get any ideas with me man. I don't swing the other way. I like pussy, got it?" I slap Ahri on his shoulder and he gives me a wicked smile along with a low laugh. "Just clearing the air before things get awkward, darling."

"Yeah, because this isn't already awkward," Nox says as his hand reaches out and grabs mine. "Onyx just got done watching us make Ren come, I now have your mating marks on my skin, and not only is Ren still sitting here naked in front of the three of us, but it's not even her real body. What's awkward about this?"

"Don't remind her that she's naked, man. I've been enjoying the view for the past few minutes." Onyx winks at me and I flip him off, pulling the sheet back up over my chest.

"Jokes on you. That just means you find another woman's body attractive which makes you lose points with me. Dumb ass." I spit my tongue out at him and then lean my head on Nox's shoulder, suddenly feeling exhausted. Ahri puts a hand on my back and I feel safe and sound in my bubble of bulking men.

"As long as your sweet, bubbly personality is in said body, it's going to be hot." I glare at Onyx, knowing he's being sarcastic about my personality.

A frantic knock at the door stops me from answering him and both Nox and Ahri grab the sheet that's around me and try to cover me up at the same time. I try to hide my smile as the door is thrown open and none other than Lucifer's fuming face stares back at us, moving from me to Ahri and back.

"Fuck!" he screams the word so loud, it makes me jump on the bed. No one says anything, as all of us stare at him, both terrified and confused by the outburst this late at night. Before anyone can respond, he storms out of the room.

"Um... anyone else know why the devil just got mad at seeing us naked in bed?" I ask the question, half joking, half scared. He looked angry. I don't think you want to piss off the devil.

"I think we should get dressed and go find out. Whatever it is, it can't be good." Onyx grabs a pair of pants and a shirt before throwing them at me on the bed. Ahri catches them for me and then places them on my lap. Everyone moves silently, before we exit the room and make our way down stairs.

Something bad happened, and I'm scared to find out what it is.

CHAPTER 17

ADRIENNE

We've been waiting for Lucifer to say something for the last few minutes. It feels more like a lifetime. We are all sitting around the fire downstairs, me in the middle, with Ahri and Nox on either side of me, and Onyx next to Ahri. The two of them seem to be getting along a lot better than Onyx and Nox do. Probably has something to do with their matching cocky personalities.

We are squished together, all staring at Lucifer's fuming face as he stares at the tattoos on my arm. I look down at them and can't help but smile. They are so beautiful. And the fact that they came from Ahri himself, that they represent our bond, makes them even better.

"You couldn't keep your fucking hands to yourself for one night? One fucking night? Told you to get everyone situated, Ahriman! As in, separate rooms! Damnit!" Lucifer finally speaks up and I find myself glaring at him. He's starting to get on my nerves.

I answer before Ahri can, annoyed that Lucifer is yelling at him. "Excuse me? I just got my body back after being stuck inside of my familiar's head. I haven't been with my mate in a long time. What did you expect was going to happen? Here's an idea... warn us if we aren't supposed to do anything!" I cross my hands in front of my body and feel my magic spurring to life inside of me. "What's the big deal anyway? It's just a few markings on a body that isn't even mine."

I swear I see fire raging inside of his red eyes. They look like deadly flames that threaten to leave their confinement and burn the whole world to the ground. "Atlas knows. He sent me a message just a few minutes ago."

Everyone is silent and I try to understand what he means. "Sent you a message?"

"Yes, Adrienne. A vision. Of him looking at your body. Your body that had slowly growing black markings. Markings that only show up when a familiar and their master connect. It's all a part of the legend... it slipped my mind. I wasn't thinking. I should have thought of this." I hear the self-hatred in his voice and for a second, I feel bad for him.

"We all make mistakes, it's okay. There's a lot going on. For all of us." I feel weird trying to reassure the devil, but I understand the anger that can come with making a mistake. That feeling of wanting to blame everyone around you because you don't want to admit that you messed up.

"This mistake could end with your body being destroyed if we don't get you up there. If you don't surrender." I blink at him, speechless as fear shoots through me.

"Say that again?" Nox speaks for me, clearly just as scared and confused by what we just heard.

"Atlas spoke in the vision. He said he knows I have you. He knows you're in someone else's body. And if we don't deliver you to him, he's going to destroy your body... he said each day you're not there he's going to remove a limb. And in the end, he's going to burn the parts. So, your real body will be gone."

"Okay... um. Give me a minute to digest this." I take a deep breath and then pick at my lip, trying to think of what to say. "Okay, I'm confused. Why would it matter if he destroyed my body? Obviously, it would really suck to be stuck in a completely different body forever, but it's not the end of the world."

"I may have left something else out before. I didn't want to risk you saying no. We needed to start this process... We needed your power to be strong with Nox and Ahri by your side. I was desperate..."

"Get on with it!" This comes from Ahri, his loud voice making me jump where I'm sitting. His hand falls softly onto my knee, where he gently squeezes, apologizing for scaring me.

"Your powers and soul are going to reject this body eventually... they are going to realize that this isn't their original host, and they are going to fight to get out of it. Fight to find their real body."

"So, if my real body is gone, I will spend the rest of my life body hopping from one person to the next?" While that sounds like a horrible way to live, it's not something that can't be managed.

"No, princess, it's not that easy. There's a limit to everything. Every time you transfer to a new body... your heart weakens. It's not meant to be restarted over and over again. No magic can keep it from eventually deteriorating."

"So... you're telling me that what we just did weakened my heart? By how much? How many times can I transfer before my heart gives up?" I feel sick. I feel like I'm going to throw up. How could he keep this from me? How could he trick me into this?

"I'd say, you would be able to transfer three, maybe four more times, until your heart stops. Unless your heart is returned to your original body."

"Holy shit. And how long does she have in this body before she rejects it?" Nox's voice sounds deadly.

"A few weeks... a month, tops." We all absorb the facts. If Atlas destroys my body, I have at most, four months to live. And then I'm gone. Every part of me. I cease to exist.

Standing up, I start to pace the room. I feel my heart racing in my chest and then start to freak out more. Pretty soon, it won't be able to beat. Pretty soon, it's going to stop completely and then I'm going to disappear. I'll never see Nox again. Never see Ahri or Onyx. Suddenly, everyone I want to see again flashes through my mind.

I want to get to know my mom. I want to hear stories from her life. I want to tell her everything about mine. I want to see my dad again. I want to hug him and reassure him that I'm okay. I want to see Sophia. I want to tell her that I forgive her. That she's allowed to love who she wants. That she will always be my sister.

I feel my body falling and can't stop it. I careen towards the ground, my panic making me feel numb as my heart beats away in my chest, reminding me of the inevitable. Before my knees make contact with the ground, hands grab me and pick me up, holding me close to a hard chest.

I don't have to look to know it's Nox. He's always there to pick me up. He's always there to steal the pain from me and replace it with comfort. He's my rock. My lifeline. My everything.

I cuddle up into his chest and let the first tear fall. The fat bead is full of sadness, fear, and regret. Because I have so many things I want to do. So many people I want to see again, that I will never get to.

"Shhh, it's okay, Ren. We're going to figure this out. It's going to be okay. I won't let anything happen to you. I promise. Never again," he whispers into my ear and the sound of his voice makes another tear fall. I can't leave him. Not after I just got him. He can't be ripped from me so quickly before our life together even gets to start.

Nox holds me until the tears stop, and when I finally feel my heart beat slow to a normal pace, I pick my head up. I look into his violet eyes and then place a kiss against his stubbly cheek. "Thank you, Nox."

He gives me an unsure look, fear flowing through his eyes, and then he bends down and places a soft kiss on my forehead, resting his nose against it until he decides it's time to place me back down on my feet.

I clear my throat and turn towards everyone. Onyx and Ahri both have matching worried looks and Lucifer avoids my eyes, clearly regretting his decision to hide things from me. "I'm not going down without a fight. I have too much to live for." I reach for Nox's hand and then make eye contact with Ahri, followed by Onyx. Ahri nods his head at me once, his hands clenching into fists at his side. Onyx simply gives me an apprehensive smile.

"Giving up is not an option. But we need to come up with a plan. Everything is different now that he knows. We no longer have the upper ha—"

"I don't care what we have and don't have. He wants me there? Fine. I'm going there." It's what needs to be done. Fear set aside, I know it's the only option.

"Princess... he will try to control you. He will turn you into his zombie. His slave. He's stronger than you think when he has his disciples." Lucifer scratches the back of his neck and finally looks me in the eyes.

"And I'm stronger than he thinks. Plus, I have something he doesn't have. Something that will always trump strength." I pause, mostly for dramatic effect, before finishing my sentence. "I have something, and someone, to live for."

"Blondie, I don't know if this is a good idea." Onyx's voice surprises me as I pack a bag full of clothes. I don't know why I found this a priority, but here I am. I turn towards him, seeing that he walked into the room and is now standing behind me, leaning against the wall.

"Do you have a better one?" I raise a brow at him and wait for an answer. He sighs and rubs a hand over his face, clearly stressed out. "Exactly. That's what I thought." I turn back towards what I'm doing. Everyone, except Onyx apparently, went to fill my mother and Than in on what happened. Lucifer thinks he can come up with some sort of alternative to my plan, but I know it's not going to happen. We've run out of time.

Hands grab at my forearm and stop me from what I'm doing. I look at where Onyx's hands hold me and then up into his lilac eyes. He's now kneeling right next to me in front of the dresser, face to face with me.

"It's too dangerous, Adrienne... We can't... I can't lose you. Not again." The emotion swirling around in his eyes makes my stomach flip. All of this time, I've been thinking about how hard it has been for Nox to lose me. How hard it was for me to lose him. But this whole time, Onyx has been hurting too. I had my heart ripped out of my chest right in front of him.

I put my hand on his cheek and give him a soft smile. "Onyx, if I don't do this, you'll definitely lose me. Whether it's now or in a few months, it's inevitable. If I go, and I fight, at least I have the chance to win."

He presses his cheek into my hand and closes his eyes, a pained expression on his face. "I know our marriage, before everything happened, was arranged. I know it was forced on you. I know in the end, you will always choose someone else. And I can't compete with either of them. But... just know that I'm here. I'm always here. I would die for you, Adrienne. I truly mean that."

My heart squeezes in my chest with his confession. My relationship with Onyx has been confusing to say the least. He's an arrogant asshole one minute and a sweetheart the next. I hated him at first and grew to respect him through our time together. Our marriage was forced, but I had accepted it. A part of me had even wanted it.

"You don't have to say anything. I just needed you to know that. That I haven't been whole since losing you that day. That being Dark Lord wasn't the end game. That without you standing by my side, I've hated every second of ruling your kingdom. I would trade places with you in a heartbeat if I could."

He opens his eyes when he finishes talking and the love that resides in them surprises me. Part of me is unsure about it while the other part, the more prominent part, is so happy to see it there.

"Oh, Onyx," I say as I rub his cheek with my thumb. Tears are threatening to fall and I can't tell if they are from his admission or the stress of our situation. "I..." I try to come up with the words to describe how I feel. But then I realize that no words would be able to. Because I don't know what this feeling is.

"It's okay. I don't need you to say anything. I just needed you to know before anything happened... in case... in case. Never mind." The fear in his eyes cracks my heart even more than it already is. I want to make him feel better, to reassure him. But I don't know how. Especially since I'm just as scared as he is. Just as unsure of what is going to happen.

I open my mouth to talk but, again, no words come out. Onyx's eyes fall down to my open lips and stare at them like they are an artfully crafted painting. I watch, unable to move, as his tongue darts out to lick his own, and before I can respond, his face moves towards mine.

His lips press against my own and I'm taken aback by the gentle softness they possess. I find my eyes falling closed, involuntarily, and my mouth relaxes against his, letting him take control. The kiss both confuses and entices me. It feels comfortable and safe.

Rather than the tingles I get from Ahri or the burning fire I get for Nox, I feel this sense of calm when Onyx moves his lips over mine. Like I've been thrown into a still sea and I'm floating there, with no worries on my mind.

He tastes like mint and smells of burning wood. He grabs the back of my head and threads his hands through my hair as my hands move to the back of his neck, holding each other exactly where we are. Cherishing this moment that makes the world around us disappear.

Somehow, the unsureness I felt about Onyx makes this kiss even more meaningful. I can tell my body wants him, but this kiss is intimate in a different way than just sex. This kiss is like a warm embrace from your best friend. A reassurance that they have been here for you the entire time. That no matter what, you will never be alone.

"Ahem." We pull apart with a jump as someone interrupts us. I turn to find Lucifer standing at the door, staring at us with a concerned expression. I can't tell if it's from what he walked in on or from the situation at hand. "It's time to go."

I turn back to Onyx and he's staring straight at me. His mouth wobbles slightly as his eyes take me in with a sparkle. He looks both transfixed and terrified. Because this kiss was laced with the possibilities of a future that may not come for us. A future that may be cut short if one mistake is made.

"I'm coming with you." Onyx says it matter of factly at the same time I open my mouth to say goodbye. I furrow my brows at him and then shake my head.

"No. You aren't. There's no point in putting anyone else in danger. You need to go back to the kingdom with my mo... I mean,

Lady Blackwell. Go make sure my dad is okay. Tell him I love him... Take care of our people." I feel bad that I haven't spoken to Lady Blackwell, but to be fair, she hasn't put in the effort either. I was so nervous and excited to finally meet her that I almost forgot how angry I was for the danger she put me in years ago.

"You want me to sit there and wait? Nox and Ahri get to go keep you safe and I have to sit back and hold my breath until I see you again? *If* I see you again?" His voice is raised and he's visibly shaking. I know this is hard for him. I can't imagine someone telling me to do what I'm telling him to. I, truthfully, wouldn't listen.

"I need them with me to make me stronger... power wise. If it wasn't for that, trust me. I would be making them stay behind too. I don't want to put any of you in danger. This is my battle to fight. Not yours."

"This isn't your battle! You didn't ask for this! It's not fair, Adrienne. You don't deserve this shit." His anger weirdly warms my heart. Before these wonderful men, I always felt like I had to fight for myself. Because no one else would. Because in the end, I was blamed for most of the shit I was dealt in life.

I reach for him one last time, placing a soft kiss against his lips before my brain can stop me. "I will come back, Onyx. After I save us. After I save the humans. And we will all get our happily ever after. We will all get what we want in the end, okay?"

"All I want is you, Adrienne," he whispers as his forehead falls to mine. We sit like this, our breath mingling, for as long as possible. And then I hear a huff coming from the door and I know it's time to go. Before I piss the devil off even more. The rumors about him may not be true, but he's definitely one impatient man.

"I'll see you soon. Take care of our kingdom." I let my fingers drag across his cheek before their pads fall from his skin and I stand up. I take one last look at him, with a sad smile on my face, and then I grab my bag and I walk out of the room.

Please... Please let me see Onyx again.

CHAPTER 18

ADRIENNE

"Wait!" I stop in my tracks when her voice echoes through the room. The four of us, consisting of me, Nox, Ahri, and Than, are just about to reach the exit of Lucifer's castle. According to Lucifer, all of us will have the ability to travel to heaven. Apparently we always have. Another the God's lied to us about. But Lucifer refused to come with us. I don't blame him... If we all die, including him, there's no hope left.

I turn towards my mother's voice and watch as she runs up to me, concern covering her features. When she reaches me, I expect her to stop and say something, but she doesn't. She plows into me and pulls me into a tight hug. A hug I don't expect. A hug I don't know how I feel about.

My first instinct is to push her off. She is a stranger to me after all. But, something about this embrace, about her hugging me, makes that instinct fade into the distance. And suddenly, all I want to do is squeeze her back and cry into my mom's arms. My real mom. The woman who gave birth to me. The woman that I resemble so much.

I let my arms circle her waist and I hold onto her like my life depends on it. Like it's the last time I'll ever see her. Which, it may be. This could be the first and last hug I have ever had with my biological mother. The only memory of our relationship I will ever have.

"I wish I could have done this for the last twenty-five years, sweetheart. I'm so sorry for not being your mother." Her words are whispered into my ear but they ring so loudly in my head. They are the words, the apology, I have always longed for.

"Hopefully, after this is over, that can change." I try to hide the thick emotion in my voice but it's nearly impossible. My voice quivers and shakes with my hopeful sadness. With my desperation to be close to this woman.

She pulls away and I find myself wishing she wouldn't. I find myself needing her touch. Her dark eyes stare into mine as her hands come up to cup my cheeks, an embrace I wanted from my mom for all of my life.

"If it's any consolation, I am so proud of the woman you have become. You are so strong, so beautiful, so full of love. Our kingdom couldn't ask for a better leader. And this world couldn't be luckier to have you fighting for it."

Damn you, tears. I didn't expect to cry. But each word she says makes them build up in my eyes more and more until the dam finally breaks and one huge droplet falls down my cheek. She wipes it with the pad of her thumb before it can get too far and then her hands fall from my face.

"I'll see you back at home," I say matter of factly. Because I will. I refuse to let there be any other alternative. I will destroy Atlas. I will save the world. And I will return to my people.

"Time to go." Nox's voice grabs my attention and I turn towards him, confused as to why he's rushing me. He knows how long I've wanted to connect with my mom. I walk towards all of them and stand between Nox and Ahri. Than stands on the other side of Nox with his cloak on, hiding himself from everyone. He hasn't said a word since we all came down here.

I feel fingers tangle with my own and look down to find Ahri's hand slipping into mine. My skin prickles and my heart rate picks up when he holds it tight and doesn't let go. Somehow, this monster of a man has figured out exactly what I need, when I need it. Somehow, he has snuck his way into my heart and soul in a way I didn't think anyone could. Besides Nox.

We're going to make it through this, darling. And then you will be reunited with your mother once again, he whispers into the darkest depths of my mind and I have to hold back a sob.

I'm scared, Ahri... I'm scared I won't get to see any of them again. I'm scared you guys are going to get hurt... I don't know what I would do if Nox... if you, got hurt. I need to be honest with him. We may not make it out of this and he should know that he was right. That somehow, he's already crawled his way into my heart.

It sounds to me like you care about me, darling. I told you I'd convince you. I'm very convincing... especially with my fingers. Wouldn't you say? I snort out loud and instantly regret it when I see Nox turn towards me out of the corner of my eye.

I know they were both able to... share me earlier, but I can still feel the jealousy tickling my spine. I know Nox can tell that I'm talking to Ahri in my mind and he's jealous that he isn't able to.

I chance a look at Nox and when I see his eyes looking at me, I furrow my brows. Rather than jealousy, like the intense feeling coursing through my spine at the moment, he just stares at me blankly. Almost unattached.

"Hey," I say with concern in my voice. "Are you okay?" The minute I speak, Nox seems to come out of his weird trance and he gives me an awkward smile. It doesn't quite reach his eyes like it normally does when he looks at me.

"Yes, Ren. Just nervous and want to makes sure you are safe." He sounds weird, but I can feel his jealousy change to love as it skitters across my spine. If it wasn't for our magic bond shining bright, I'd be concerned.

Instead, I reach for his hand and put it in mine. I'm now holding both his and Ahri's hands and I feel stronger. Except, while Ahri holds mine tight and rubs his thumb over my skin, eliciting tingles across the surface, Nox just holds it limp in his. Like he's holding the hand of a stranger, rather than the love of his life.

I shake it off, trying not to worry about that when there is so much more to worry about. Like how I'm going to destroy Atlas. And how I'm going to save the world.

WE TRAVEL THROUGH THE BLINE UNTIL WE CROSS BACK INTO OMBRA. Once we are there, we do what Lucifer told us to do. We make our way to the sparkling body of water that showcases the sparkling night sky. The water that delivers food to the people of our kingdom. The water I was told not to swim in.

Apparently, this whole time, this has been one of the ways we can get into heaven. Without a leading God, any ruler, shadvir, demon, or human for that matter, can travel through the shimmering water and make it to heaven.

I stare up at the castle that I know and love, my body wishing I could walk in there and hug my dad. Wishing I could reassure him that I'm okay. Reassure the people. But right now, I'm not me. And right now, there's more important matters at hand.

Taking one last deep breath, we jump into the water. The minute my body is engulfed by the wetness, bright white light flashes across my eye lids. I let the tingling warmth of the water caress my body for what feels like hours. It feels like I'm drowning, but instead of scaring me, it calms me. Like the water is reassuring me that even if it fills me up, I'll still be okay.

And then, I feel it spit me out, throwing me onto a hard, cold floor. I take a deep breath and cough, ridding the water from my throat. "Adrienne? Where are you?" Ahri's voice graces my ears first and I open my eyes against the harsh brightness assaulting my eyelids. I wince at how white it is. My pupils burn at the invading light. But I manage to keep them open and take in my surroundings.

I gasp at the sight before me. Above us is a sky full of never-ending stars. The sky is both bright and pitch black at the same time and it's mesmerizing. Surrounding us, there are clouds of stark white floating around, glowing a bright white light that is almost blinding. While they obscure our view, they don't completely hide the world before us.

The huge homes are on either side of us, made up of white stone. There are columns so high, they could touch the stars, on all of the front porches. The arches look like they were made by the most talented Greek architects. And then my eyes land on something else I've never seen.

Each home has rows and rows of what look like weeping willows, but instead of the normal brown bark and green leaves, these are made of what looks like crystal. I'd assume they were glass statues if it wasn't for the fact that their branches are moving and the crystal leaves are glistening in the light.

"Adrienne?" Ahri calls my name and I look through the thick clouds to find them.

"I'm here, just follow my voice." The minute my voice floats through the atmosphere, every single cloud surrounding us glides out of the way and leaves us out in the open, exposed. I find Ahri and Nox standing close to each other, with Than standing a few feet away. They are all facing me, still lying on the hard ground.

I turn my body around, so I can get on my knees to stand up, and a small scream leaves my lips. The ground below me is completely see through, showing off Earth thousands and thousands of miles below. It shouldn't be possible to see anything from this height, but I can just barely make out the landscape of the place I called home for most of my life.

I feel a hand wrap around my arm, the grip soft and gentle, before I'm lifted to standing position. I turn to find Ahri holding me, his head nodding as my eyes take him in. To my surprise, all of us are completely dry, like we weren't just engulfed in deep waters.

"This place... it's amazing." I do a complete 360, taking in everything around us. It's like something out of a dream. A place where everything is perfectly pristine. A place that makes happiness bubble up inside of you... where nothing can go wrong...

"Wh-where is everyone?" I question even though I don't expect an answer. We are standing in what looks to be a courtyard in the middle of the city, and at the end, I see a huge building, one resembling the white house back on Earth, but a hundred times bigger and more extravagant. There's not a single soul but us. It's eerily quiet... unsettlingly so.

"I don't know. Something doesn't feel right, though. We need to move." Nox walks up to us and places a hand against my back, pushing me forward. Than stands right next to him, too close in my opinion. I feel Nox's comforting pull at my spine and our song glitters through it, reminding me that everything is going to be okay. I take a shaky breath, trying to calm down my racing brain.

"What do we do? Just walk in there and start a war? Bargain with him?" It just hit me how unprepared I am. I was so confident, desperate to get here so I could save everyone, that I didn't realize how screwed I was. I have no plan.

"We try to go unnoticed. That's what Lucifer told us to do. He put a spell on us that should keep us off Atlas's radar. That makes up invisible to everyone but each other. We take out his disciples and once we have his foundation weak, we go for him."

"And how are we supposed to take out his disciples exactly?"

"You're forgetting how powerful you are, darling." Ahri walks next to me as we make our way to God knows where. "With Nox and I by your side, you will burn these fuckers to the ground. Use your mind control. Use your hellfire. Use all of the anger you feel inside of you that you've been holding deep down since your powers arose. It's time to unleash the wrath."

Each word of encouragement makes my power bubble up inside of me. It gives me strength. Sends a wave of confidence through each cell, each vein, in my body. He's right. I can do this. I'm stronger than them. And with my men by my side, we will burn this place to the fucking ground.

CHAPTER 19

SOPHIA

I don't know how many days it's been. It could be three days, three months, three years since I let them take Willow, for the second time. Since I betrayed my sister, for the second time. Since I let my emotions control me, for the second time.

I haven't gotten out of bed since then. I didn't say a word to Sam as I left his house that day and haven't since. His calls go to voicemail. His messages go unopened. My classes go unattended. My shower goes unused. My food is most likely spoiling in my mini fridge.

I don't care. Why should I? I don't deserve to eat. I don't deserve the hot water cleaning the scum off my body. No matter how many times it did, I'd be left just as dirty and vile. Because showering can't cleanse a soul. It can't wash away your regrets. Your sins.

I check the clock on my dresser and it practically screams at me in red numbers telling me it's seven at night. Not that it matters. I don't sleep either. I just lie in bed staring up at the ceiling, morning and night. I see her face every time I close my eyes. And then I see his. And then I cry.

Knock, knock, knock.

I don't react to the sound. Unless Willow is on the other side of that door, I don't care who's there. I hear another round of knocks but again, I don't say a word. The room stays silent around me and I assume whoever is on the other side of the door got the message. Until the door creaks open. Huh, I probably should have locked my door.

"Sophia?" A feminine voice assaults my ears and I move my eyeballs only in her direction. It's Carly, one of the only girls I would consider a friend in this school. She's been in almost every one of my classes since we started and she's just as focused on her school work as I am. Or, as I was before stupid Dr. Archer.

"Sophia, are you okay?" She comes closer but I notice her keeping her distance and breathing weird, like there's something rotten in the air is invading her nose. That rotten thing is me. My soul. My heart.

I don't respond to her and drag my eyes off of her petite frame and perfectly styled curly brown hair. While I am a smelly, rats' nest of a mess, she is perfectly done up in her high waisted jeans, t-shirt, and mascara lining her brown eyes.

"Sophia Taylor. Answer me before I call 911. Is this about your sister? Have you heard from her since you found out she left town?" That's the story. The story we all told the cops. The story we all have to believe. It's not wrong. But I'd much rather her just choose to move out of New York than be in the danger she is now.

"Mhm," I respond, not wanting to say anything else but knowing she won't leave unless I do.

"I know I don't understand because I don't have a sister... but I promise you it's going to be okay. She's not gone. She's just living her life. You can still go see her and text or call her whenever you want. She will always be your sister."

She has no idea how wrong she is. I can't go see her. She is gone. She's not living her life. And she isn't my sister... not in her eyes anymore. No matter how she feels, I will always love her like a sister. I will always call her my true sister. Even if I've made some horrible, betraying, life choices.

"Soph... I need you to get up. You need to shower. You need to leave this room so we can send in a cleaning team in here to get rid of this smell." I almost laugh but stop myself. She chances her own health by sitting down on my bed and putting a hand on my arm.

"Please? Let me take you to my apartment and we can eat something and then cry together and get drunk on wine. You can sleep there for a few days so you aren't alone." I groan and turn around, facing the wall so my back is to her.

"Sophie. I'm not taking no for an answer. So, either you get up and come with me now, or I get Brady to come pick your smelly ass up out of bed and carry you to my apartment himself." Brady is her boyfriend. And someone she knows I'm not a huge fan of.

He's your typical frat boy. I support their relationship because she loves him, but I think he's just using her for her money. Or, more so, her parents' money. Hence why she has a huge apartment all to herself.

"Fine. I'll come. But I'm going to be a downer the entire time. So don't expect anything more than that."

Two hours later and I'm sitting in Carly's apartment on her huge white couch, freshly showered and wearing her expensive silk pajamas. I'm staring out at the city lights below, since her apartment has an entire wall of windows.

"Here. Drink this." She walks up to me and hands me a goblet of red wine. I just stare at it for a few seconds before shaking my head no. "For the love of God. Take the damn wine, before I force feed it down your throat and ruin my white couch."

I glare at her and then take the crystal glass from her hand, holding it in front of me. She has the lights on in her modern apartment and on the wall opposite the couch, there is a huge flat screen TV with *The Vampire Diaries* playing on full blast. I look into her massive, stainless-steel kitchen as the smell of frozen pizza and chicken tenders fills the room.

"Drink." She stands in front of me, her arms crossed and her brows raised. She's not going to leave me alone until I do as I'm told, so I bring the glass up to my lips. The dry aroma is strong and fruity. When the crisp liquid hits my tongue, it coats it completely and makes my mouth dry, forcing me to swallow down more.

"How is it?" she asks as I gulp down the bitter liquid and let it calm me down with each inch it travels farther down my throat. I nod my head with a fake smile and then hold the glass in both of my hands.

"It's great. Thank you." It's not great. And it's not because it tastes bad. It's delicious. But it reminds me of Willow. And Sam. Because the last two times I drank red wine were with both of them. So, I do the thing that makes me remember and forget them at the same time. I chug my wine down.

I instantly feel buzzed. And luckily, the wine offers a barrier between my brain and the self-hatred and depression I've been feeling. I suddenly feel lighter. Able to breathe. Able to smile when I watch a scene on the TV unfold.

"So, are you going to tell me the truth? Or are we going to pretend this only has to do with your sister leaving?" Carly sits down on the ouch next to me, raising a brow as she fills my glass with wine again.

"What are you talking about?" I play dumb, praying that it's enough to convince her to drip it.

"Sophia. Don't act like I don't know you. And even if I didn't, I know a girl suffering from a broken heart. A broken heart resulting from some class act dick, baby." I can't help but snort at her comment as she laughs next to me, clearly tipsy from the wine as well.

"There's no class act dick in my life. Just a piece of shit I kind of like a lot." I don't know why I say it, but the minute it leaves my lips, I regret it.

"Piece of shit, huh? And why's that?" She squints her eyes, clearly questioning every word I say back to her. If only she knew. And then I realize... why shouldn't she? What's keeping me from telling her the truth? At least, some of it?

"Well, he was my sister's therapist who she started dating while she was his patient. I told her how unethical it was and she ignored me. Then she goes missing during her birthday party in Vegas, and I have to call him. He shows up and I can't breathe every time I fucking see him. I fight it, barely, until we can't anymore and we completely betray my sister who was, you know... MISSING! And when she decides to let me know she's okay, she finds us making out in my bed and she disowns me as a sister. So now I'm obsessed with a man I can't be with, I've lost my only sister, and I'm completely confused as to what is wrong and what is right."

Her silence concerns me more than anything. I've barely seen Carly silent. She always has something to say. Her eyes dart around the room before she clears her throat and looks back at me.

"Okay... that's a lot. Is Willow in love with him?" She should be judging me. I'm judging me. And yet, I don't hear a lick of judgment in her voice. Just concern.

"The night we left for Vegas she thought she found something out about him and she was done with him. She's seeing someone else now." Not just someone else. The man she is supposedly bonded with. The man she was meant to be with.

"So they broke up? I mean, it's a shitty situation, but it's not like you stole her boyfriend. You just, handled it wrong."

"They didn't technically break up... she just left and ignored his calls and messages." I watch her carefully for her reaction. For her to change her mind and tell me I'm the shittiest person in the world.

She sighs deep and then grabs my hand. "Look, we all make mistakes. That's how we learn from them. She's going to be upset, but she's your sister. She will forgive you. It's not like you killed someone."

"But... I didn't learn from them. I still want him. And I let him touch me the other day... I let him..." Her eyes go wide and a smirk forms on her lips.

"Sophia Taylor! What did you let him do?" She slaps my arm playfully and her smile widens with excitement. She knows I never do anything with guys.

I cover my face with my hands and shake my head in embarrassment. The wine has hit me hard and now I suddenly can't stop smiling. "I let him go down on me... on top of a bathroom counter."

"Oh my God! You're fucking with me, right?" She shouts the words and makes me jump before she starts bouncing on the couch next to me. "This is huge. I want all of the details! Now!"

"Carly! Don't make this sound like a good thing! I am a horrible person. I'm the worst. And now I'm avoiding him completely. I've ignored every damn call and text because I'm a coward." I chug down my second goblet of wine and feel my head go loopy.

"You are not a horrible person! You are a horny person! Because you've withheld your body from a basic human need for the last twenty-two years! It's your time to shine! Let that man screw your brains out!" She's clearly drunk too, judging by the glossed over look in her eyes.

I shake my head at her, my cheeks blazing red and my heart racing from the wine. She's not wrong there. I have never experienced anything like I did with Sam that night. I didn't know my body could feel that way. I didn't know that kind of pleasure existed.

"I can't let him screw my brains out. I can't ever see him again. It's not fair to Willow." I watch as something in Carly's eyes shifts and before I can blink, she grabs my phone off the table and jumps over the couch like a maniac, into the kitchen.

"What are you doing?" I scream after her, getting up and wobbly running after her. The room spins around me so I'm not as fast as her.

"Hello? Is this the therapist? I am in desperate need of some help!" She speaks into my phone and my heart drops to the floor. No. She didn't call him. There's no way.

"Carly. Stop! Please!" I chase her around the island as she runs faster than me, my phone still plastered to her ear.

"Yes, she's right here and she needs to get fucked. The situation needs immediate attention. It's an emergency. Her wellbeing depends on it!" Oh my God. I'm going to throw up. This can't be happening. I'm going to kill her. And then I'm going to kill myself.

I finally reach her and rip the phone out of her hands. I run, as fast as I can, into her bathroom and somehow manage to lock the door behind me before the can get in. And now, I'm alone, breathing heavy, with the seconds on the phone call slowly ticking away. I have to say something. I have to apologize. Right?

Clearing my throat, I put the phone up against my ear. Silence greats me besides the sound of his low, steady breathing. "Um, h-hi." The words come out as almost a whisper and I roll my eyes at myself.

"Sophia?" His voice sounds demanding... controlling... authoritative.

"Yeah. I'm sorry. That was..." I trail off and end up going silent, unsure of what exactly I was going to say. Sorry my friend just bothered you to tell you that I'm horny? That I'm talking about you?

"Where are you? Do you need me to pick you up?" His voice is a mixture of tired, concerned, and angry. The combination sending chills down my spine.

"No. I'm at my friend's house. I'm sorry. That was immature and uncalled for. I didn't know she was going to do that." I'm so embarrassed I could throw up. I want to crawl into my own skin and disappear forever.

"Were you talking about me, angel?" Amused interest flows through the phone and I find myself speechless for a few seconds.

"Psh. No. Of course not." I am pacing around Carly's bathroom, biting my fingers through my words.

"Are you lying to me, Sophia?" His tone turns serious and every inch of me tells me not to lie to him again.

"Yes." It comes out breathy, proving how much his voice affects me.

"What were you talking about?" This can't be happening. Why does this have to happen to me? I was fine with never talking to him again. With sulking and drowning in my own depression.

"Nothing. It was nothing." I plop down on the toilet and squeeze my eyes shut, wishing I was sober enough to talk my way out of this conversation. Should I just hang up? Should I throw my phone against the wall or drop it in the toilet?

"Sophia Taylor. Tell me what you were talking about." The command echoes through my ear and I can feel the deep vibrations of his voice all the way down to my toes. "Please?" he adds in a softer tone and that's all it takes for me to crack.

"She asked me why I was in a slump the past few days... why I haven't gotten out of bed. I told her about Willow... kind of. And then I told her about you. What we did. How I feel."

"And how do you feel, angel?" His question holds all of the answers he seeks. He already knows how I feel. He just wants to hear me say it out loud... again.

"Scared. Confused. Sad."

"You know that's not what I meant." The commanding tone comes back out, his impatient personality taking over.

"Jesus, Sam. I want you and can't have you. Is that what you want me to say? I'm desperate to forget every moment we had together and obsessed with memorizing every last detail. I hate myself because of you and hate you because of how much I want you!" I'm screaming the words into the phone by the time I'm done.

"Want me or want to be with me?" He ignores everything else I just screamed at him and I roll my eyes.

"Seriously? What's the difference?"

"If I recall, from that night in the bathroom, there's a big difference. You asked me if all I wanted was sex. I told you my feelings. Do you want me to fuck you? Or do you want me to love you?" The questions hit hard. Especially since I'm drunk.

"I... I..." I take a deep breath and then form a coherent sentence... barely. "I... I want It all."

"Then we will figure it out. Whether it's now or in five years. We will figure it out." He sounds so sure. So confident.

"How? How can you say that? Because of us, Willow is gone. Because of us, Willow hates me. Because of us—"

"There's so much wrong that came from what we have done," he interrupts my rambling and I'm internally thankful. "But there is also so much good. And we can't take back what we have done. The mistakes we have made. The heartache we have caused. But we can move forward and try to make the right decisions from now on."

"And us being together is the right decision? How can you say that after what we have done?" I feel tears brimming the corner of my eyes with the memory of Willow taking over my thoughts.

"Maybe not right now. But, yes. I believe in the end, we will be together. I will give you your time. Your space. I will let you mend your relationship with Willow. I will stay out of your way to create a life that you want. That you need. But I will always be here, waiting. And when you're ready to be all in. When you're ready to give me your heart, I will hold onto it with all of my might. And I will never let it go." I sniffle, trying to hold back the flowing tears that won't stop. Where is this coming from? Why is he being so understanding? So sweet?

"What if she never comes back, Sam? What if I don't get the chance to mend it? What if..."

"No. That's not happening. Your sister is a lot of things, but weak is not one of them. She's a fighter. She's going to come back from this. She's stronger than any of those fuckers that took her. She'll be back. I know it. And it's going to be hard when you see her again... She's going to be mad... She's going to hate us both. But in the end, she will forgive you. Because you're her sister. And she wants you to find what she found... True love." I can't help but snort through my sob at his words.

"That was all believable until the true love part. You don't peg me as the fairy tale, happily ever after type." I wipe the tears from my cheeks and wait for him to answer.

"Just because I've never experienced something, doesn't mean I don't believe it's out there. Or that I can't hope that it's out there." My heart swells at his words. I feel the same way. Call me a hopeless romantic, but I have always craved that heart stopping, soul aching love that you see in movies.

"Okay." I want to say more, but nothing comes out. I want to blame it on the alcohol, but I know it's because of him. Because of his words and what he does to me.

"Angel, I want you to do something for me, okay?" I nod my head in response and then feel my cheeks blaze in embarrassment when I realize he can't see me.

"Mhm," I say back to him and wait for him to say something else.

He chuckles low and the sound digs itself into my brain so I will never forget it. "If anyone else said 'mhm' to me, it would annoy the hell out of me. But you?" He stops and I desperately want to hear what he was going to say.

"But me, what?"

"But you're the exception, angel. Only you." I try to come up with a response to that, but for some reason it leaves me speechless. No one has ever said something like that to me. No one has ever made me feel special enough to be incomparable to anyone else.

"As I was saying, I need you to focus on you right now. Sleep. Eat. Study. Work hard. Be the best you can be. Take care of yourself until the time is right and I can take care of you. Until you and Willow mend things. Until we can have our time. No matter what, I'm right here. When you need me, call me. When you want me… come get me."

My stomach twists in knots at the way his voice lowers with the last three words. Like it's a dare. A threat. A promise. "Sophia? Can you do all of that for me?" He speaks after I go radio silent for almost a minute, too lost in my own thoughts.

"Yes. I'll try."

"No. There's no trying. You take care of yourself or I will do it for you. I will not let you hurt yourself. I will not let you throw away the bright future you are going to have. Do you understand?" That commanding voice comes back out and I swallow down my nerves, or maybe it's excitement, so I can answer.

"Yes, Sam. I understand."

"Good. Now go to sleep. If you need me, I'm a text or call away. But until then, just know you'll be on my mind until I see you again. Every day... Good night, angel." My lower lip wobbles with his words but I manage to keep the tears at bay.

"Good night, Sam."

CHAPTER 20

ADRIENNE

"The problem is going to be getting to the disciples without alerting Atlas. They are all going to be in the main estate. The downstairs is the main headquarters, where Atlas's office is. The floors above are where they reside. They should be up there." Ahri speaks up as we make our way through the courtyard towards the main house.

"And if they aren't there?" We still haven't seen a single person, not that it would matter, since we are invisible. But the fact that it's completely silent and void of all life doesn't sit well. Something's off.

"Then we burn the place to the fucking ground." Nox answers for him and I turn to look at my mate.

"Why don't we just do that to begin with?" It seems a lot easier than trying to sneak around and kill these fuckers behind Atlas's back. Part of me doubts he doesn't already know we are here. He's a God. You can't deceive a God, can you?

"Because your body is in there. Burning the place down is last resort. And we try to get your body out of there before it burns to the ground." I nod my head, embarrassed that I already forgot about the body issue.

"What if we walk in there and my body is already destroyed?" I already know the answer. If that's the case, I'm a lost cause. I'm dead already.

"No more what ifs. That's not happening." Ahri sounds like he's ready to murder someone, his breath labored and his hands flexed at his sides. I reach for his hand and he relaxes slightly, letting his fingers lace with mine.

"Once we get in there, you're going to need to pull power from me and Nox, okay? The power will be the strongest if we covet it into one body rather than the three of us separately. We will watch your back, we will protect you. But you need to be the one to do the damage. And Than will hold a shield over us all to keep us safe."

"Sounds like a solid enough plan, I guess." I pause and stop walking as something hits me. "Wait a second… Lucifer said Atlas put a spell around all of the kingdoms to keep Lucifer and his magic out of the other worlds. How is any of this possible? How are we here?"

Ahri and Nox look between each other before Nox sighs and rubs the back of his neck. "Before we left, Lucifer offered Aiden something in return for the spells to be broken. He wasn't positive if Aiden would respond, but he did."

"What did he give up?" I stare at Nox, his eyes not meeting mine.

"His immortality," Ahri answers and I can't help it when my eyes widen.

"What? But… How? Why would Aiden make him do that?" Why would Lucifer give that up?

"No one knows how or why Aiden works the way he does, darling. We don't even know what he is necessarily. And besides Lucifer, no one has ever actually been in contact with him. The fact that Lucifer has been granted anything from the higher being is more than anyone could ask for."

"Well, that's fucking stupid. He should be helping people. If he's as powerful as everyone says, he should be down here taking care of Atlas himself! This is bullshit." I think back to him talking to me in my dream. His voice is a distant memory that I can barely remember at this point even though it was just last night.

"Well, take that up with the big man if you ever meet him. Right now, we need to get your body back and destroy Atlas. It's time to focus." Nox sounds annoyed when he talks and I blink at him, confused as to where the attitude is coming from.

"Jeez. Sorry. I'm just focused." I glare at him and watch as his eyes soften. But even when they soften, they don't reflect the love they normally hold. They look irritated. Unattached. Which makes my stomach drop. Is he upset about Ahri? Is he falling out of love with me?

He loves you, darling. I promise you that. Don't ever doubt his love for you. Ahri must have heard my thoughts and he whispers his reassurance into my mind. It's hard to believe it with the distance I feel from him. Even though I feel him in our bond, I can't feel him in this moment, physically. He seems like a different person.

He's acting weird. I don't know what to do... it seems like he wants nothing to do with me. I don't know why I'm being so honest, but I can't hold it back. Ahri has been the voice of reason I have needed lately.

He's stressed, my darling. Once we save your body, everything will be back to normal. I promise. Somehow his promise makes me feel better. I look over at the hulking man with tattoos peeking out of his black armor and stare into his red eyes. His hair is pulled up into a messy bun and his mouth is set in a hard line, but he winks at me and the corner of his lips lift up.

I wink back and mouth the words thank you before we continue walking. I chance a look at Nox and his mouth is in stuck in a permanent frown as his body remains rigid. He looks straight ahead, pretending I'm not walking right next to him.

The closer we get to the main estate, the larger it looks. I let my eyes drag up the two-hundred-foot building with columns the size of giant sequoias. It's intimidating yet beautiful at the same time. I think back to Nox's comment to me when I first arrived in Ombra. When he told me the most beautiful things are usually the most dangerous.

"Keep your eyes and ears open. I know where to go since Lucifer shared his visions with me, so stay behind me and I'll lead us to where we need to go." Ahri takes control and I nod my head, happy that I'm not going to be in the lead right now.

We walk through the front entrance, taking small, quiet steps even though we are invisible. The foyer is huge with marble everywhere and a ceiling over a hundred feet high. There are two white, winding stairs on opposite walls leading up to the second floor. Where we need to go.

There's not a soul in sight, but there are three long white hallways surrounding the large room that seem to go on forever and don't have an end in sight. It's eerie, to say the least. We make our way up one of the sets of stairs and then Ahri stops in front of the first door.

"This is Kamar's room. He... he's the one that took your body from Dr. Archer and Sophia." I have a feeling the only reason Ahri tells me this is because he wants me to get angrier. He wants me to torture him. Trust me, I'm way ahead of him.

As the door opens and a spotless white apartment comes into view, my power bubbles up inside of me. I can feel it desperate to unleash itself and kill this angel even though I haven't even seen him yet.

We walk through the apartment, bypassing the elaborate kitchen and living room. When we pass through another door, we find him. He's asleep. Lying on top of a king size bed. His skin is sickly thin and translucent, showcasing veins that remind me of what lightening looks like slashing across a dark sky. His hair is long and blonde and his face is sharp and intimidating.

"Stay back. I've got this," I command everyone else to stop as I move forward. I feel the shield from Than surrounding me as Nox and Ahri's connection flows with power. Part of me wants to cover his entire body with hellfire right away. Burn him to a crisp. Turn him to ash. But that would be too kind. For everything he has done to the humans. Everything he plans to do with his master.

Instead, I reach for my power. I reach for that sizzling fire inside of me and I feel it flicker and spark to life, as if I just clicked a lighter. My body heats up and my eyes and hands burn to an almost unbearable temperature.

"I hope this hurts, you piece of shit," I whisper the words through clenched teeth and then imagine the fire tickling his hands and climbing up. I watch as the brighter than life fire engulfs both of his hands.

"Aghhh!" I scream, the guttural sound ringing through my ears as the sharpest, most intense pain I have ever experienced fills both of my hands. I scream louder, unable to control it, as it grows with each tendril that covers Kamar's arms.

"Adrienne! Stop! Shut it off! You're burning yourself!" I hear Ahri's distant screams through the haze of pain and somehow muster enough strength to turn off my magic and take the hellfire with it. And then I fall to the ground, my lids closing and everything going black as arms catch me.

"Wake her up." A voice I don't recognize assaults my ears, stealing me from the darkness surrounding me.

"Darling?" I know that voice. The voice that kept me company in darkness much similar to this one. "You have to wake up, love. It's... it's time to wake up." He sounds desperate yet defeated at the same time. Sad and angry. Anything but the normal sarcastic Ahri I grew to love.

I try to peel my eyes open but the space around me is too bright. I squeeze them tight, wincing from the pain before new pain suddenly takes over. Pain throbbing in both of my hands. Pain that feels like knives and fire and glass tearing through my skin.

"Adrienne, please, open your eyes for me." He's begging me. And somehow, that sound takes away most of the pain and gives me enough strength to open my eyes. To do whatever he asks of me as long as it keeps him from using that voice again. That horribly sad, gut-wrenching voice.

When I open my eyes, I wish I had kept them closed. The bright room around me looks like a stadium made of the whitest marble I've ever seen. I'm lying in the center, with thousands of people sitting in seats hundreds of feet away, staring at me with waiting eyes.

I try to use my hands to push myself up off the ground and instantly regret it when pain shoots up my arms. I can feel it in my bones and try to pull my hands away, making me plummet back down to the ground and hit my face against the hard tile floor.

Laughter echoes off the walls around me, too many different voices to count. They are all laughing at my pain. Laughing at how weak I am. Laughing at the injuries I somehow gave myself.

I look down at my hands and find bloody handprints on the ground where I once touched. My hands and forearms are raw. There's a rainbow of black flesh and red meat showing underneath. Some spots are completely charred and others are bright red and oozing bloody puss. The pale skin and tattoos underneath are completely gone. Leaving me open and exposed to all of the elements.

I turn my head and the gasp that leaves my mouth can't be stopped. There I am. Mere feet away from me is my old body. My black hair. My sharp jaw. My tan skin. My old tattoos, covered in a stark white shirt and matching cotton shorts. My eyes then take in the black designs now etched in my skin from Ahri's touch.

But, when I look lower, I notice the same charred, bleeding skin on my old hands. Perfectly matching my own. Confusion takes over but it doesn't stop me from trying to reach for myself. To grab onto my body. Could it be that easy?

Do—Don't. To—touch. I— it. Ahri's voice breaks and cracks in my mind as if the signal is fuzzy and before I can comprehend what he says, my bloody hands collide with something. It warps and glows around my old body, blocking me from it.

And then the pain comes. I scream out as it courses through my entire body. It feels like my organs are being squeezed. It feels like my bones are being grinded up into dust. It feels like my eyes are being plucked out from my skull.

I cry out, trying to hold in my guttural sounds, as I curl into a ball on the floor and beg for the pain to stop. Beg for salvation from this torture. Laughter fills my ears again, but above all of the distant chaos, one deep, menacing laugh rises above the rest. And as the pain slowly dissipates, leaving me breathless, I realize exactly whose laugh that is.

My head just barely turns in the direction of it and I find him standing there. Atlas. Surrounded by three other men. One of which is Kamar. The same angel I had just seen sleeping in his bed. The same angel I tried to torture with my hellfire. Except, he's standing there, unharmed, and smirking an evil smirk at me.

They all stand there, ten feet away on the white stage I am lying on. Atlas resides in the middle, his hair white as snow and his skin completely translucent, revealing black tar veins underneath. His eyes resemble snakes, his irises undetectable from the white of his scleras, leaving only a slit of black pupil in each beady eye.

"Glad you finally decided to join the party, Adrienne. I was just starting to get bored." His voice booms through the room and I try not to wince at the way it assaults my ears. Every part of me hurts now, the aftermath of whatever coursed through me when I tried to touch my body still sitting dormant inside of me.

I hear a low growl coming from the other side of me and turn my head that way for a second. Kneeling at the other side of the stage, their hands trapped in futuristic looking handcuffs, are my men. Ahri, Nox, and Than reside there, staring back at me. Than has his hood up still, but I can feel his eyes staring at me through the darkness.

Nox looks angry. He looks at me for a split second longer and then his eyes turn towards Atlas. The hatred in them is like nothing I've ever seen. Hatred that could kill. Hatred that only comes from unforgivable pain.

And then there's Ahri. He looks nowhere but at me. His eyes travel down my body, taking in all of my injuries, and then back up to my eyes, only to do it again. There's concern, anger, and desperation swimming through both of his red orbs, so thick I swear each emotion is about to explode out of him.

What happened? I try to push the words out and into Ahri's mind, but I don't hear any response back and Ahri gives no indication of receiving the message. I try to grab at Nox's melody in my spine, but the song doesn't play. The strings remain tight and unplucked, as if there is no longer a connection.

I look down at the handcuffs, each one of them glowing bright with white light, and can only assume those are the culprit for the loss of connection. Somehow, Ahri reached through for a second, but even that was cut out and hard to understand.

"Angels of heaven!" Atlas's voice grows loud again, echoing through the room. Everyone around us goes silent, waiting for their master to continue. I can practically feel their desperation to hear each word that comes out of Atlas's mouth. Feel the loyalty each and every one of them has for their God.

"We finally have our traitor! A sister! A fallen angel that has turned her back on us all and sided with the devil! She has come to destroy everything we know! She has come to kill me and my disciples! And once she's done with us, she plans to destroy all of mankind! Every last human that we work so hard to protect!"

I furrow my brows at his lies and then open my mouth to speak. "That's not true!" I scream out the words but they seem so quiet compared to his. Muffled and mouse like.

"Silence, traitor! After everything we have done for you? After giving you power and then protecting your body from Lucifer himself? After giving you wings and magic that no other descendent of the angels has ever been given? This is how you repay us?"

The crowd erupts into a chorus of boos and profanities. Each angel throws their insults and hatred at me, supporting their conniving God and believing every lie he spews out of his wretched mouth.

"You're the liar! You're trying to kill the humans! I love them! I was one of them for most of my life!" I don't know why I continue to try, but I yell each word out to Atlas as if it will make a difference. As if it will resonate with any of the angels in this room.

"Why would I ever try to kill the humans, you stupid girl? I spent my entire existence trying to save them! Trying to save them from Lucifer, one of our own, from destroying them!" The crowd goes wild again, cursing out Lucifer's name.

"You're the monster here, little girl. Look what you tried to do to our dear Kamar! You would have turned him to ash in seconds! That kind of power should not be bestowed upon someone so dangerous and careless." The word 'tried' repeats in my head before I realize what happened.

"You tricked me..." I picture Kamar lying peacefully on that bed, ready for the taking, and curse myself for being so stupid. It was too easy. I should have seen it.

"Lucifer may have his own powers that somehow snuck by me, but so do I. I knew you were coming, even if I couldn't see you. I knew you'd go for my disciples first. I had to keep them safe. Any good leader would do the same for his people."

I look over at my body and stare at the burns scarring my skin. He disguised my body as Kamar's. I burnt myself and that's why each flame that hit my old body scarred my new one. Because it's a part of me, no matter what. And whatever happens to it.... will happen to me.

"Risky game knowing I could have just turned my body to ash and killed myself in the process." I glare at him, knowing he doesn't want me dead.

"Dear girl, I couldn't care less if you killed yourself. That's the end game. To kill you and all of your little followers. But, I also knew you would torture him first. I could feel it in you. That deep seeded need for revenge. That anger and love of destruction. That high from being in control."

"Because that's how you feel?" I ignore his other words, desperate to come up with a plan. Lucifer said he would want me alive. So, is Atlas bluffing? Or is Lucifer wrong?

"I am not in control, right, angels?" His voice echoes through the room and the cheering that commences makes me roll my eyes on my spot on the floor. "We are a kingdom of equality and serendipity! I simply make sure everything runs smoothly. I have no desire for control. No desire for revenge or destruction! Simply peace and protection over my people. Over all people."

"That's why you deceived Lucifer? Why you ripped his wings from him? Why you created a fireball that would have destroy not only Lucifer in the hell you banished him to, but all of mankind? If it wasn't for Lucifer, every human alive would be gone! Earth would be nothing but a burning pile of ash! He is the one searching for peace! You simply want power! You're a monster!"

"Shut up, you lying bitch!" The room goes silent besides Atlas's screams. He's breathing heavily and inching closer. But then, his demeanor changes. He smirks at me, his breath going even, and he turns his head slightly, to look at Surya, his favorite disciple, before nodding just barely.

Surya's sharp, menacing face turns even more vile. His smile becoming sinister before he turns his eyes towards me. A flash of something resembling pleasure takes over his gray irises and then I'm groaning and screaming in pain again.

I can feel it coming from Surya. The punishing grating on my bones and brain. His gaze alone makes my blood feel like it's boiling in my veins and I swear I can feel them each bursting inside of me. I try to hold in my scream, but it's uncontrollable at this point. My back arches off the floor and I squeeze my eyes, begging for the pain to stop.

"Please!" His scream is so distant. "Stop hurting her!" There's that voice again. The gut-wrenching sound of Ahri begging. A man on his knees, pleading as if he feels the pain more than I do.

"Enough! You need her alive and you know it!" This comes from Nox. He sounds both angry and calm at the same time. And the minute he says it, the pain falls away. My body collapses to the ground as I gasp for breath. My vision is blurry and everything inside of me is crying out for some sort of relief.

Silence fills the room besides my low whimpers and Ahri's heavy breaths. "And what makes you think that, Nox Kage?" I can hear the evil smile in Atlas's voice.

"You need her to rid Lucifer's curse, remember? To rid the world of the hellfire suspended over the humans that Lucifer created. Isn't that right, Atlas?" I turn my head, using as much strength as I have, until I'm looking at my men. Ahri looks defeated, his shoulders sagging as his ferocious gaze is aimed at me. But Nox kneels with his posture perfect and his brows raised at the God before us.

"Smart little shadvir you are. I do, in fact, need Ahriman and Adrienne alive for at least a little while longer. Until they can prove to me that they are strong enough to complete such a task. That requires a lot of power. More power than any of us have seen."

"You mean more power than you have? As in Lucifer is stronger than you?" I cough through my sentences but smirk to myself when I see the fury in Atlas's eyes aimed at me.

"We don't possess such power. Hellfire is something angels can't alter. It's an evil curse from hell that only devils like Lucifer can bend or destroy. Which is why we need you two. To see if you possess enough of Lucifer's power to destroy what he created."

"And how are they supposed to prove that they are strong enough?" Nox glares at Atlas as he asks the question.

"They will find out soon enough. And while we prepare for that, I think it's time we place our dear traitorous sister back into her old body. It's only fair, right?" My heart speeds up as both fear and excitement course through me. "Surya? Would you do the honors?"

"It would be my pleasure." His voice is laced with humorous death. I watch as he walks toward me, his hair cut short and spikey. His face is an angular square and his lifeless gray eyes match the distaste on his lips. The way his huge body moves reminds me of a snake slithering towards its prey.

He kneels before me and I try not to cower in fear. I'm stronger than him. I can take him. I know I can. "I've been wanting to do this for a long time." Excitement flows with each word and when his hand reaches toward my chest, I hear someone shouting behind me. I can tell its Ahri, but I'm too focused on my own fear as his hand reaches closer and closer to my skin.

The minute he touches me, I feel ice cold death enter my veins. It's not like the boiling pain I felt earlier. This hurts in a way that I've never experienced. The sort of pain that you get when you're empty... alone... nothing at all.

His hand rips the thick armored shirt I'm wearing as if it was simply paper and suddenly, I'm exposed for all to see. Cold air hits my bare chest and I hear whistles and cat calls in the distance at my nakedness. Surya's eyes land on my pebbling nipples from the chill of the air and he smirks even wider, clearly enjoying this.

I would try to cover up, but my body feels frozen in place with Surya's hand on my skin. Like he's paralyzed me, leaving me a helpless bag of flesh and bones. "I'll fucking kill you!" I hear Ahri scream behind me and I feel my lip wobble from his protectiveness. I can practically feel his anger radiating off of him and towards me.

"Blaze, take care of the other body." Atlas's voice cuts through Ahri's screams, no one but me paying him any attention. Out of my peripheral vision, I watch as the third disciple walks over to my old body, his eyes glued to my naked chest as he walks. When he reaches for my body, he isn't stopped by the invisible barrier I so luckily endured minutes ago.

I watch him rip the shirt from my chest and suddenly, I'm even more exposed than I was before. The crowd erupts even louder and somehow, them exposing that body feels so much worse. Because that's my real body. That's the body I've lived in all of my life. Those are my breasts everyone is staring at. My stomach.

My skin. All of it is mine. And I didn't give any of these asshole's permission to see it.

"Mmmm." Surya groans low in his throat as he looks over at my other body. "Hiding all of that under those clothes, little one? I'll make sure to get a taste before Atlas makes me rip you to pieces," he whispers low and each word he says feels like a knife slicing me open. I feel a tear well at the corner of my eye before it falls and hate myself for being so scared. So weak.

"But first, this is going to hurt, little one. A lot." His hand moves toward my breast, where he squeezes and fondles it, making bile rise in my throat. Then, he moves it towards the center of my chest and his fingernails dig into my skin. I bite my teeth hard at the excruciating pain of them slowly entering my flesh, ripping through layers of muscle and fat so slowly, it almost seems like he's not moving.

But he is. I can feel each millimeter his fingers move into my body. They push at my skin and when the blood bubbles around each of his fingers, they slip in faster. He pushes all five of his bony fingers into my chest and when he's almost three knuckles deep, he pulls back out almost all of the way before shoving them deep inside of me again.

I look completely unfazed on the outside. I don't move. I don't make a sound. Because I can't. But on the inside, I'm screaming. I'm crying. I'm thrashing my body uncontrollably from the pain.

"Surya, let everyone see her true reaction." I hear Atlas speak next to us. And then, like the flip of a switch, my internal screams turn external. My animalistic sounds echo off the walls and my tears fall from my eyes. My legs kick and flail and my arms try to reach for Surya's hand but fail.

Surya moves his hand in and out of my chest again, toying with me, shoving his fingers deep into the searing holes before pulling them back out again. Each insert hurts worse than the last and I can feel his fingernails scraping against my heart.

"You like that, little one?" Surya whispers close to my face, his eyes staring at where his fingers are embedded inside of me. If I could pass out right now, I'd already be gone. No body, human or magic, should be able to live through this type of pain. "This is what I'm going to do to that little pussy of yours soon."

"Surya! Get on with it!" Atlas screams again and I see Surya's jaw tick for a split second before he growls out a 'yes sir.' And then he shoves his hand completely into my chest. My voice is almost gone at this point. But I manage to get more screams out.

I can feel each one of his fingers close around my beating heart and when they squeeze, I feel it flutter and spurt, trying to fight against the intruder. But it's no match for this monster. He smirks at me, shutting off my ability to move again and then he pulls.

I feel my arteries and veins tug and stretch, trying to hold the necessary organ inside of its protective cavity. But Surya just pulls harder. They stretch against the pressure until finally, I not only feel, but hear, each nauseating snap. And then my heart is ripped from my body.

The crowd erupts into applause and cheers. I watch as Surya raises my still beating heart into the air, blood dripping down his arm, for one, two, three seconds, before death crawls across my eyelids and leaves me empty and alone.

CHAPTER 21

AHRIMAN

I'm going to rip each and every one of them to shreds. I swear, when I saw all of the angels staring at her exposed body, I felt pure rage like never before. They don't deserve to see something so perfect. Something so beautiful and precious and one of a kind. And yet, they all took without asking. The greedy fucks bore their wide eyes at what's mine.

And then there's Surya. The piece of shit looked at her like she was his last meal. And the pain he caused her, I felt my heart crumbling as I screamed along with her. As I begged and pleaded to nothing and no one for her salvation. For me to take her place. I felt something crawling deep inside of me. Something ripping and shredding me from the inside out, desperate to be released. But these cuffs prevented any of my magic from coming out.

When I watched her eyes flutter closed, I was so grateful for death. Because finally, after she had to endure the worst pain anyone should ever have to endure, she can feel some semblance of peace. She can be free of the dread we all feel with what's to come. Because we failed. And now our Adrienne is paying the cost.

I watch, my glare sported at the disgusting viper holding Adrienne's beating heart, as he walks towards Adrienne's old body and stops in front of it. The way his eyes stare at her naked chest sickens me. He wants to touch her. He wants to feel her. But I will burn him to the ground before he gets the chance.

His eyes meet mine when he kneels down to place Adrienne's heart back into her body. He stares right into me and then winks, and I push against my restraints as a growl escapes my throat. I feel like a wild animal. I don't feel like myself. And every single cell in my body is ready to rip Surya's head straight off of his neck.

"Contain yourself, Ahriman. Don't let them see how much this is getting to you." Nox's voice whisper yells to me and I glare his way.

"Fuck you. You don't know what this feels like," I answer him through clenched teeth. My whole body feels like it's on fire. Like it's filling with pressure that needs to be released or I'm going to explode. Like something needs to be let out but can't because of their fucking restraints.

I turn my attention back to Adrienne's body and watch as Surya bends forward, his eyes flicking up to mine for a second before he inches his face back down to hers. "No! You mother fucker!" I pull at the cuffs and rip my skin to shreds, desperate to get free. Our legs are bolted down the ground where we kneel and I can't move an inch.

"What the fuck are you doing? Don't you fucking dare! Get your disgusting lips away from her! I'm going to kill you! You son of a— Mhh! Mhhhh! Mhhh!" I try to finish my sentence but suddenly, my mouth refuses to open. I murmur the words out, but my lips remain sealed. I turn towards Blaze, and he's smiling at me with a knowing look. He did this. The piece of shit.

"I told you to shut the fuck up," Nox's whisper fills my ears again as I watch Surya's lips touch my Adrianne's perfect ones. "Surya needs to kiss Adrienne, you idiot. Atlas transferred her soul to Surya's mind when he ripped her heart out. Just like how you had to kiss her, he does too."

I roll my eyes at him, hating that he's right and thinking rationally right now. I feel like a beast and it only gets worse when I see Surya deepening the kiss more than necessary. He's kissing a fucking corpse right now. She's lifeless underneath him.

And then she's moving. Her hands whip up before he can react and she pushes him off of her, making him stumble back onto his ass. Her first breath echoes through the stadium, deep and desperate, trying to fill her lungs back up.

Finally.

There's my girl.

ADRIENNE

I GASP FOR BREATH AND SIT UP, TRYING TO RID MY BRAIN OF THE horrid thoughts I just had to endure. Even though it was pitch black while I was dead, I could feel Surya around me. I could hear his disgusting thoughts. Hear the things he wants to do to me.

He wants to fuck me while he rips my body open. He wants to cover us both in my blood as he forces himself on me while my last breath leaves my body for good. He wants to rip me limb from limb and lick each wound. He's the most vile creature I've ever met.

So, when I wake up to his face above me, his lips touching mine, I do the first thing that I can think of. I push the pig away from me and back myself up. I get as far away as I can from the monster. The pain in my burnt hands barely registers from the nausea filling me up.

"You sick fuck." The words escape before I can stop them and I hear the faintest snort behind me. I can't tell if it comes from Ahri or Nox, but I know it was one of them.

"You'll enjoy it. I promise, little one." His eyes stare at my chest rather than my eyes and I quickly cover my breasts with my crisp hands. They've had enough of a show already. I'm done being their play thing.

"Adrienne Blackwell. How nice to finally have the real you in our presence." Atlas speaks up and walks towards me, his white hair is piled neatly on his head. He looks so evil and intimidating even though he's put together perfectly in his crisp white suit and porcelain skin.

"Nice isn't the word I would use," I spit back at him and he only chuckles at me.

"Little spit fire when you're all confident in your own body I see. That will change soon." He kneels next to me and his white eyes squint as they take me in. "Here's the deal. You try to use the bline out of here, you die. I cursed this body. And now that you're in it, you're stuck here until I say otherwise. Same as your little pets. If they try to leave, it kills you dead."

He stands up again and looks at the three of them. "Understand? If anyone wants to test if I'm bluffing, be my guest." He raises both of his arms in waiting, knowing none of them are going to risk it.

"Alright, well now that that's out of the way. It's time for my guests to go get some rest before the big show. You and Ahri are going to need your strength, dear Adrienne. This is life or death. If you die, I know you would never be capable of destroying the curse. If you live, well, congratulations. You get to destroy the curse before I kill you both."

"What about Nox and Than? Do they get to fight?" I speak up and judging by the look on Atlas's face, I asked the exact question he was looking for.

"Good question, Adrienne. No. Since Than proved to be Lucifer's favorite little pet, I have decided to keep him as my own. He will make a fantastic addition to my team once this is over." He pauses before looking me directly in the eyes. "And as for Nox? Well, I suppose there's no point in keeping him around any longer, is there?"

"Wh—

"Go ahead," he interrupts me before I can finish and I whip my head in the direction of my men. Blaze is standing behind Nox with a wicked smile on his face. I try to stand, but my body is now stuck. I try to scream, but the screams are again trapped inside of me. I reach for our bond, but it's still disconnected.

My eyes lock onto his violet ones for a half a second. And in that half a second, everything falls away but him. All there is, is us. And every moment we have spent together.

From the nights when his shadow would protect me on Earth. To when he comforted me in Ombra with a simple touch of his pinky. To his boyish grin when I brought him up in the sky with me to stare down at our kingdom. To the first time he told me how much he loved me...

"I exist for you. I breathe and bleed and burn for you.

My life would be meaningless without your heart beating because you are my life. You swim through my veins. You eat up all of the space in my brain. You have

carved yourself into my heart to the point that there is no room for anyone else.

My heart beats to your name. Forever and always, my princess."

Tears fill my eyes as I watch him, helplessly. I try to tell him I love him. I try to fight the hold Surya has on me, but I'm too weak. And when Blaze puts his hands on Nox's head, I can't do anything but watch. Because Surya won't even let me look away.

He forces me to watch as Blaze pulls up on his head and disconnects it from his body like it was never even attached. He forces me to watch as my mates blood spurts from his open neck, where his perfect head used to reside. He forces me to watch as Nox's body falls forward onto the ground and his blood explodes on impact, splattering against my face.

And when Blaze kicks Nox's head, his lifeless eyes still staring straight into mine, and it lands right in front of me on the ground with a thud, then, and only then, Surya releases me from his hold.

And yet, no sound escapes me. I can't breathe. I can't move besides letting my head fall to the ground below me, now staring straight into the eyes of my mate. The man who saved me. Who was with me since birth. My Nox.

I can't hear anything. I can't see anything but his dead eyes. I can't feel anything but pure heart break. All of the pain I endured today is nothing compared to this. This pain is something indescribable. Something I didn't know could exist. Surya didn't rip my heart out when he tried to before. No. My heart was fine until this moment.

Because half of me is gone.

There's nothing I can do now.

There's no power I can unleash to fix this.

Because this time, it's real.

This time. I don't feel him.

Nox. Is. Dead.

CHAPTER 22

ADRIENNE

I haven't spoken, I haven't moved, I don't even think I've taken a real breath. They tried to get me to walk. They screamed at me. Surya used his power to make my insides cry out in pain again. But nothing worked. Nothing they did to me would be enough to bring me out of this.

Because all I can see, all I can think of, all I can feel, is Nox. Or more so, Nox's absence. He ceases to exist. And the last conversation we had was full of hostility and annoyance. I should have stopped and said I love you when I had the chance. I should have pulled him into my arms for a hug. Kissed his soft lips. Made him laugh one more time.

I can't even remember what it sounds like now. I can't remember what his hands felt like on my skin. I can't remember what his lips felt like as they pressed against mine. It's all a distant memory, floating away with his soul and leaving me forever.

Tears drip to the floor from my position on someone's shoulder. Since I refused to move, they resorted to picking me up and taking me to where I would be kept prisoner. I have no idea which vile disciple is carrying me. I have no idea if Ahri and Than are with us. They could be in another realm right now and I wouldn't know.

I barely notice when the person holding me throws me onto the hard ground. I barely notice when hands move around my neck and something cold and sharp gets locked onto my skin. I barely notice the words coming from the person who brought me here. And I barely notice him placing Nox's severed head on the floor next to me before leaving the room.

I squeeze my eyes shut, refusing to look at his face again. I can't see the lifeless look in his eyes. I can't see his mouth, gaped open in a silent scream. So instead, I curl up into a ball and I cry. Because there's nothing else I can do. I don't want to fight anymore. I don't want to walk out of here with my head held high and perform whatever show Atlas has planned for me. I don't want to do anything but see my Nox again. Smiling back at me with love in his eyes.

Hands scoop my body up and hold me into a hard chest. Even in my lucid state, I can tell it's Ahri holding me. So, I curl into his warmth and let the sobs escape. I let him take them for me and hold onto them tight, because the pain of Nox's death shouldn't be contained in one body. It should be felt by all. Mourned by all.

"Darling, it's okay. Please, calm down and look at me." I hear him speak but I don't do as I'm told. I feel him move us across the space until he sits down on something. His hands caress the naked skin of my arms and back. "Jesus, just come over here and calm her down."

His comment makes my sobs halt for a split second as I try to understand what he means. Who is he talking to? Than? Why would he calm me down? I hear a whisper in response to Ahri's comment but I can't make out what he says. It's too quiet and my sobs are too loud.

"I don't give a shit if they're watching. Talk to her at least. So she can calm down. We'll never make it out of here if she is like this the whole time." I sniffle away my sob and pull my head away from Ahri's warm chest a few inches. My tears blur my vision but I can just make out Than's dark cloak in front of us.

"Wh... what's going on?" I barely get the words out. Ahri's hand comes down to my face where he gently wipes my tears away.

"Darling, you can't react, okay? They could be watching us. I have a feeling they put the three of us in here to see what we would say to each other. What we would reveal to them. And if they find out... it's going to be really bad." Ahri's soft whisper tickles my ear and hurt my brain. I'm so confused. What could Than have to tell me that's so important?

"Say you understand, Adrienne." Ahri speaks one more time and I nod my head, desperate to know what's going on. What could be so big that they would interrupt my mourning?

Than kneels before us and his cloak remains intact on his head, hiding his features from all. "Ren?"

That one word.

That name.

That voice.

My heart stops as my breath hitches. I shake my head as disgust and anger fill my stomach. "That's not fucking funny. How dare you?" I try to pull the cloak off of Than's head, ready to slap his rotten face, but the cloak refuses to budge.

"Princess, Lucifer charmed the cloak so it wouldn't come off. You won't be able to remove it." That voice again. His voice. How is he doing that? Why is he doing that?

"Why? How is that still working? Our invisibility is gone, so how is this charm still working?" I don't know why I'm humoring this, but something deep inside of me is telling me to.

"The invisibility spell is a power that comes from the angels. It wore off when we were captured. But this charm, the locking charm that Lucifer used is one he created himself while he was in hell. One that Atlas has no control over. One he doesn't know about."

"And would you care to explain to me why the fuck you sound like Nox? Is this some sick joke? Something to make me feel even worse? Fuck you, Than. I knew I hated you for a reason."

Ahri's lips brush against my ear as he whispers his next sentence. "Darling, that's not Than. I'm sorry we lied to you, but we had to. Let him speak, please." I furrow my brows with each word he says and blink at the cloaked man before me. And then Than does something that brings tears to my eyes.

He reaches toward me, revealing his fingers from his sleeve, and his pinky hooks onto my burnt, raw one. Just like Nox used to do. I don't even notice the pain. Instead, I take a deep, shaky breath as a tear slips from my eye. Ahri's dark markings crawl up the hand that is just barely exposed. The markings that were etched into Nox's skin when we were all in bed together.

"N... Nox?" His name comes out as a breathy whisper that barely sounds like a word. Could it really be him? How? When? Why?

"Yes, Ren. It's me. I'm okay. I'm right here. I told you I would never leave you. My heart beats to your name. Forever and always." I can't stop the tears now and when I try to reach for him, to hold him, to feel him wrapped around me, Ahri holds me back.

"Let go of me!" I try to fight him off, but can't, too emotionally overwhelmed by the fact that the love of my life isn't gone. That he's right here in front of me. That I don't have to live without him.

"Ren, remember what we told you. They can't find out that I'm alive. If they see you hugging Than, they are going to get suspicious. I want to hold you so bad but I can't. I love you so much, princess. I promise when this is over, I won't let you go again."

I huff, still in awe and desperate to feel him. But I know I can't risk it. Not after everything I just witnessed. I look over at the head still sitting on the ground and my stomach flips.

"If you're still here, then... that..." Realization hits me and I cry for a different reason. This whole time, the person I thought was Nox, was actually Than. He was disguising himself as Nox. That's why he was acting so weird since we got up to heaven.

"When we went to tell Than and your mother of the plan, Lucifer tried to get Nox to stay back. He said that since Atlas doesn't need the magic that is shared between you and Nox, he would be more of a threat to you than anything else. That even though he would make you stronger, that's not the magic that would get us out of there alive. They would use your love for him against you." Ahri's sad voice whispers from behind me, his arms still circled around my waist.

"But... I refused not to go. I couldn't let you go without me. And then Nathaniel offered up this idea. To trade places. To keep me disguised as him but close enough to provide you the comfort and power to make you stronger. I denied it at first... but it was the only way. And Nathaniel wouldn't take no for an answer. He sacrificed himself for us. For the greater good." Nox squeezes my finger and I can feel his sadness with the small movement.

Taking a shaky breath, I look over at the head on the ground. "We must make sure his death does not go in vain. We need to destroy Atlas and everything that he stands for. We need to save the world. And we will. Together. For Nathaniel." Even though I'm whispering, my voice sounds more confident than it has in the last few hours. While I'm still weak and sore, I feel strong having both of my men by my side.

"How? What are we going to do?" Ahri says it behind me, resting his head against the back of my shoulder. It's weird seeing such a huge, hulking man act so scared and vulnerable. The fact that this long haired, tatted beast takes comfort in me never ceases to amaze me.

"We fight. We survive. And then we fucking burn this place to the ground." Ahri snorts behind me as his hands squeeze my sides.

"That's my tough girl." He places a soft kiss against my back again and I smile, so thankful that I have them both with me.

"What about all of the other angels? The children? The innocent?" Nox whispers the questions from underneath his hood and a flashback of everyone laughing as I was being tortured and groped flashes through my mind.

"What innocent? They all watched with smiles on their faces and laughter bubbling from their chest as I was humiliated and beaten down. As someone was murdered in front of them. They are all monsters. Every last one of them." I feel my anger boiling under the surface, but my magic feels far away. The anger isn't accompanied by the usual fire that comes when my magic starts to activate. I'm assuming it has to do with the collar bolted to my neck.

"He's right, darling. They're under Atlas's rule. They are being manipulated into thinking you are the enemy. They don't know what they're doing. They don't know the truth."

"I don't care if they don't know the truth. I would never take pleasure in someone else's humiliation. I would never sit there and watch someone be tortured and beaten for fun. It's complete bullshit." I'm so angry at every single one of them. Each smiling face I saw. Each pair of waiting eyes staring down at me.

"Ren, traditions like this are normal in our worlds. Think back to the competition for your hand in marriage... everyone got together and watched as the eligible suitors fought for your hand. The entire kingdom watched them beat each other to a pulp. And they cheered and applauded. It's the way things are."

"Well, I didn't agree with it then and I definitely don't agree with it now. All I can say is if it's the only way we can get out, I will burn everything down. Without a blink of an eye." I know I sound heartless. I know any person with a conscious wouldn't think that. But here's the thing. I grew up resentful and bitter. I grew up on my own and only caring about Sophia and myself. While that list has grown by many, I am still the same woman I was, deep down.

"Well, until then, it's time to rest. Atlas isn't going to heal you and I have a feeling that magic restrictor is going to prevent your body from healing properly too, so rest is your best bet right now. We need your mind and body sharp." A shirt is placed over my head as Ahri covers me up with his own black long sleeve. He then pulls me back onto the bed with him as Nox stands up, poised and proper.

"Are you guys wearing these collars too?" I turn to look at Ahri and find his neck bare. I realize then that his handcuffs have been removed as well.

"The room itself prevents any new magic from being cast, both angel or demon. They have no control over any spells that have already been cast though. And, apparently, they found it necessary for an extra precaution with you." I can't help but smile to myself at his words. As much as they don't want to admit it, these fuckers are terrified of me. As they should be.

I look around the small white room we are in and search for any sign of a camera. The room is bare besides the bed we are lying on, a bolted table with four chairs, and a toilet and sink in the opposite corner. It's then that I realize that the white walls are completely bare. There's no door. A prison with no escape.

I turn my attention back to Nox and watch as he makes his way towards the bolted down chairs at the table. He sits down and shifts his weight, trying to make himself comfortable. Screw that. He needs his strength just as much as we do. Putting on my best acting voice, I glare his way for Atlas's benefit.

"Than, don't be so fucking dramatic." I roll my eyes with my words. "There's enough room on the bed for the three of us. Just don't get any ideas or I'll cut your dick off." Ahri snorts behind me before pulling my body into his and even though I can't see it, I can feel Nox's proud smile staring my way underneath that dark cloak. I internally apologize to Than's spirit for my words.

Rather than answering, he just stands from his chair and makes his way over to me and Ahri on the bed. There's a thin sheet on it that does a terrible job at warming us, but being between my two men is all I need to heat me to an inferno.

"I'll keep watch while you two sleep and then we can trade off," Nox says to Ahri and gets a nod and a grunt in response. I turn on my side, facing Nox, with Ahri pressed between my body and the wall. I stare at the cloaked man in front of me and my smile sits steady on my face.

Nox remains on top of the sheet but his hand sits at the hem of it, his fingers hidden from sight. I move my hand towards his and grab his pinky in mine, holding onto it like my life depends on it. And as I touch both of my men, the two people I have come to realize I may not be able to live without, I drift off to sleep.

CHAPTER 23

ADRIENNE

"Mmmm," I moan as sparks travel down to my toes. I can feel him pushing into my backside, his hard length pressing against my ass. I grind my hips against him and his deep groan vibrates against my ear. "Ahri..."

"Fuck, darling. I love when you say my name like that." He grabs onto my hips and thrusts against me harder, making my mind go crazy thinking about him thrusting deep inside of me instead.

His body molds to my back as a hand reaches for my neck. I look through the darkness surrounding us and find Nox in front of me, his face finally visible through the cloak. His dark violet eyes stare into mine as he squeezes my neck, just enough to elicit a moan from my throat.

Nox steals the sound before it can pass my lips by pressing his own against my mouth and consuming me completely. I get lost in his mouth. In his touch. In the way his tongue caresses mine with a gentle pressure.

Ahri moves behind me, ripping my pants off of my body and letting the cold air crawl over my naked skin, leaving goosebumps in its wake. He flips me harshly so I'm on my back rather than my side, and somehow Nox's lips never leave mine.

I gasp as I feel Ahri lower himself until his lips are at my thighs, kissing their way up as his hands clasp around each leg, spreading me wide open for him. I'm dizzy with lust. Overwhelmed by both of their hands and mouths on me.

"Do you want him to taste you, Ren?" Nox whispers the words against my lips, his hand moving down to squeeze my pebbled nipple. I whimper from the sharp pain but nod my head yes. He then moves his hand towards mine and wraps his fingers around it, pulling it towards him.

"I want you to taste me while he tastes you. Can you do that for me?" I gasp as my fingers brush against Nox's rock-hard dick. There's nothing covering the impressive length, and my fingers wrap around his warm, soft skin.

Ahri moves up, his beard rubbing against the sensitive skin of my upper thighs and making my entire body clench with anticipation. I need his lips on me. I need his tongue in me. I need him everywhere.

"Answer the question, princess." His breath tickles my lips and I breathe out a shaky exhale. Question? Did he ask me a question? I whimper as I try to remember, all the while Nox moves my hand up and down against his huge erection. He groans with each pump of my hand and the sound vibrates against my lips.

"Wh—what?" I barely get the word out, too consumed by the feelings coursing through me. Ahri's tongue licks its way up my thigh until he reaches the crease, mere centimeters from my sensitive core. I hear his deep inhale and then a throaty growl follows after.

"I want to fuck your mouth while Ahri fucks you with his tongue. Do you want that, Ren? Do you want to feel my cock slip down that tight little throat of yours?" Oh. My. God. My body hums as tingles shoot through every nerve ending under my skin. My mouth waters with the thought and I desperately try to respond.

"Ye— Oh, God, yesssss!" At the exact moment I try to speak, Ahri's hot, wet tongue glides against my pussy from bottom to top. His lips circle around my clit and he flicks his tongue, sending my body into overdrive.

"Fuck, yes." Nox groans as his hands grab at my body. He repositions me, pulling Ahri's lips from my core for a less than a second. Then, I'm deposited effortlessly on top of Ahri's face, my legs straddling his thick beard and plush lips. He goes right back to it, as if he never missed a beat, and his tongue finds its way to my entrance, circling the sensitive wetness.

I watch with blurry vision as Nox gets off the bed, standing just at the edge, in front of me. His cloak falls open, revealing his naked body underneath. The darkness isn't enough to hide the deep ridges of each one of his mouth watering muscles. And when I bring my eyes lower, I find his hand pumping himself mere inches in front of my face.

"Mmmmm. Keep looking at it like that and I'm going to cum all over that pretty little face rather than deep down your throat, princess." I moan again, my eyes threatening to fall closed as they get heavier. I feel Ahri's fingers find my clit as his tongue slips inside of me, tasting how desperate I am for him.

"No. Eyes open. I want you looking right at me when I'm deep throating you, got it?" I whimper and look up at Nox. He moves closer to me and I feel the hot skin of his cock brush against my lips. He moves it around, circling my closed lips with the head.

"Open." One word. One command. But it's the sexiest damn thing I've ever heard. I open my lips, just barely, and Nox positions himself at the small opening. He pushes against the resistance and thrusts his huge length into my mouth. He stretches me completely, making me gag from the size of him as I try to adjust.

"Oh, fuck. So damn perfect." I barely register Nox's words of approval. They sound so distant. I can't focus on anything but the feel of Ahri savoring me while Nox stretches me. I can feel my body pulsing, begging for the release to come. Begging for this intoxicating, torturous pressure to dissipate as I fall.

"You don't come until I do. Understood?" Nox's hand wraps around my throat, where he lightly squeezes. He hasn't even moved yet, and I already have tears falling from my eyes. It's so raw, so primal, so sexy, I don't think I can hold on until he's ready. He squeezes a bit tighter in warning, waiting for me to agree. I nod my head, his cock shifting in my mouth with the movement and making him groan out.

"Good," he pulls out slightly before finishing the sentence, "girl." The deep thrust into my open lips that accompanies the word makes saliva fill my mouth. I cry out at the stretch but it comes out muffled and inaudible. Nox holds onto my neck still as his hips thrust forward into my opening, taking me the way he wants.

I feel his head press against the back of my mouth before he slips into my throat. He's so big, my lips are still inches from the base when he deep throats me. His hand squeezes my neck again as he stays in my throat, thrusting shallow so he doesn't slip out of it.

"God, I can feel my cock pressing against your throat with my hand." He squeezes his hand again as he moves in and out, stealing any source of oxygen from my lungs. Right as my vision dots with black and my lungs start to burn, he pulls back out enough for me to breathe.

I take a deep, desperate breath and then he's back at it. His groans fill the room along with the sound of Ahri's tongue flicking against my wetness. He moves his fingers towards my entrance and replaces his tongue with two of his thick digits, thrusting into me at the same rhythm as Nox.

"Ride his face, Ren. Ride his face while I fuck yours." I do as I'm told but Nox's dirty words are too much. I can't hold on any longer. I feel it rising, threatening to boil over. "Almost there, baby. Fuck, I'm close."

He continues to thrust into me and I look up at him with my tear filled eyes. I moan against his dick and that's when I feel him pulse in my mouth. "Aghhhh, that's it. Come with me, Ren." He growls out each word and then shoves himself deep into my throat with his release.

My entire body trembles and I feel myself squeezing Ahri's fingers as—

MY EYES SHOOT OPEN AS A SOMEONE SHAKES MY BODY AWAKE. My heart races in my chest and my pussy throbs as if it's seconds away from climaxing. Just like in my dream. I turn to look at Ahri and he's staring straight at me with desire bubbling up in his dark red eyes.

"You were moaning. I wasn't sure if it was from a nightmare or..." He cuts his sentence short and swallows hard. I turn to look at Nox and find him sleeping soundly, his body rigid and avoiding my touch.

Shifting where I'm lying in bed, I get closer to Ahri and my breath hitches when I feel his hardness press against my hip. I turn to look into his eyes, the lights still on and blindingly bright.

"What were you dreaming about, Adrienne?" His voice is deep and dangerous. It's threatening and terrifying in the most glorious way. I swallow down my lust and open my mouth to answer, his eyes darting to my lips.

"It... it wasn't a nightmare." My voice shakes as it leaves my body. My heart pounds and I can feel it deep down in my sensitive core.

"What was it then?" He asks the question as if he already knows the answer. His body molds to mine and his cock twitches against my hip, the thickness of it grinding into me.

"It... it was... a, um... a really good dream." I sound like a child as I whisper the words. Ahri doesn't seem to notice because instead of making fun of me, his eyes only darken. His hands reach for my waist and he turns me on my side, so we are face to face.

"And what happened in this really good dream, my darling?" His accent sounds thicker with his lust. His eyes dart between my own and the tension in the air is so thick, I swear it's going to suffocate me.

"We were... we were all in this bed." His fingers find their way under the hem of his shirt I'm wearing and touch my hot skin.

"Tell me what we were doing to you." The command sends shivers down my spine. He trails two fingers up and down the skin of my stomach, teasing me without actually touching me where it matters.

"Um..." I can't focus with Ahri's fingers grazing the underside of my boob and then moving down to the band of my shorts. "Your head was between my legs and Nox was..." I gasp when his warm fingers squeeze my breast and my sentence cuts short.

"Keep talking, Adrienne. What was Nox doing?" He smirks an evil, handsome smirk at me and I find myself desperate to kiss the smug look off of his face.

"He was fucking my mouth." As I say it, I reach my hand towards his hardness and press my palm against it before wrapping my fingers around the thick rod. He hisses through his gritted teeth and his eyes squeeze shut.

"Bloody hell." The two words come out throaty, and when he opens his eyes back up, his irises look like a raging inferno threatening to burn me to the ground. "And did you come on my tongue in this dream?" I squeeze him in my hands, appreciating how big he feels.

"I was about to... and then someone woke me up." I smirk at him and his deep chuckle vibrates against my chest. He brings his fingers down my stomach again and when he reaches the hem of my shorts, his fingers make their way under the fabric.

"Looks like I owe you now, darling. We don't want you all distracted and pent up later, do we?" I shiver when his fingers brush against the sensitive flesh right above my clit. He stays there, circling my skin with the pad of his rough thumb and pulling a soft moan from my lips.

"Those moans are enough to bring a man to his bloody knees, my darling," he whispers into my ear before placing a soft peck against my lobe. "Do you want me to touch you? Hmm? Do you want to feel my fingers deep inside of you?"

If I'm being honest, his fingers don't seem like enough right now. There's this beast deep inside of me that is begging for all of him. Begging to feel his thickness buried inside of me. But this isn't the place. Not when someone could be watching. Not when Nox can't touch me too.

"Yes. Please, Ahri. I want you." I unzip his pants and he helps me pull them down so I can get my hand around his length. He's so intimidating and hot, yet so soft and supple at the same time.

When my hands move up and down on his hardness, he groans into my ear and brings his fingers lower. He slips them into my wetness and I watch as his eyes flash with danger. "You're fucking soaked."

I raise a brow it him with a smirk and then remove my hand from his cock. "That so?" I say before bringing my own hand down to my sensitive core. I find his fingers there and move with his, letting them glide through my wetness and slip deep inside myself. I gasp quietly, my body tensing at the tight fit of both his and my fingers inside of me.

We move as one, in and out, for a few seconds before I remove my hand and return it back to his dick. I use my arousal to slip up and down his length with ease and he bucks into my hand, squeezing his eyes shut as he moans out my name.

"Fuck me," he growls out as my hand continues to pump him, the sound of my arousal slipping against his skin being muffled by the sheet covering us. "I want to shove myself deep inside of you so I can feel how warm and wet your perfect pussy really feels on my cock."

His dirty words send a spark of pleasure through my body and I clench around his fingers still thrusting into me. I'm so close to coming undone, I'm right there at that crest.

We move as one, our hands matching the same rhythm as our breath hits each other's faces in hot puffs. And then I feel the faintest touch against my back. A graze of a hand before it disappears. And I turn my head slightly, looking at the cloaked man that was just sleeping.

He's no longer sleeping. I can feel his eyes on me even though I can't see them. "I want to watch you come, Ren. Can you do that for me?" he whispers the words so quietly that I almost miss it.

I close my eyes and let out my moan, feeling myself reaching that cliff. Knowing, in seconds, I will be free falling into the abyss. "That's it, princess. Come to my voice as Ahri fucks you with his fingers."

And I do exactly that. My body arches off that bed as Ahri's fingers dive in and out of me in punishing thrusts. I loosen my grip on Ahri, unable to jerk him off while I'm flying through bliss, but his other hand wraps around mine and he continues to work himself.

I cry out, trying to be quiet, but it's impossible. My veins feel like their swimming with pleasure. My pussy clenches and tightens so hard I swear I'm going to cut the circulation off of Ahri's fingers. My brain turns to mush and I forget, for at least a few seconds, where we are and what we are doing.

And then, after what feels like hours of blacked out ecstasy, I fall back down onto the bed and try to take deep even breaths. I notice sticky wetness coating my hand and stomach and look down, finding Ahri's glistening release covering my skin.

"That was the sexiest bloody thing I've ever experienced." His words come out breathy and I puff out a laugh. He's telling me. Having the two of them at the same time is going to be the death of me. I don't think a body is meant to go through that kind of pleasure more than once.

I place a soft kiss on Ahri's lips as he uses his corner of the sheet to clean me up. Unfortunately, we don't have much to clean ourselves off in this pathetic excuse of a room. I turn my head towards Nox and look into the dark cavern where I know his beautiful eyes are taking me in.

"I promise I'll make it up to you," I whisper as quietly as I can as my pinky reaches for his under the covers.

"Oh, I know you will. Over and over again. I still haven't showed you what it truly means to be fucked, if you remember correctly." I shiver at his words, remembering what he told me back on Earth when I was with Dr. Archer.

"How could I forget?" I squeeze his pinky and then yawn a huge, uncontrollable yawn.

"Go back to sleep, Ren. I love you." I smile, my eyes falling from the heavy weight pressing on them. I cuddle up into the warm sheets as my body melts into the mattress, completely relaxed.

"Mmm," I moan from how comfortable and safe I feel as I drift off to sleep. "I love you both so much."

AHRIMAN

She fell asleep hours ago. Nox fell asleep shortly after. And I'm still lying here with my heart beating out of my chest.

"I love you both so much."

Her sleepy words repeat on overdrive in my head. She was half asleep when she said it, but I heard it. Did she mean it? Does she love me? And if she does, is it because of the bond? Because I'm her familiar? Or because she loves me for who I am? Because she truly cares about the person I am on the inside?

It's not the time to ask her. It's not the time to pressure her into admitting her true feelings. But I can't deny my feelings for this woman. The woman who I was trapped inside of for the last twenty-five years of my life. The woman who beat me down, hated me, and wished me dead every second of the day.

The woman I am in love with. It doesn't matter how much I deny it. It doesn't matter if it's wrong. It doesn't matter if she doesn't feel the same way. I would and will die for her. If she asked me to leave right now, I would leave. Even though it would turn me to dust and ash, I would leave her side in a heartbeat just to make her smile again.

And after what just happened. After the way she touched me, the way she looked at me, the way she came undone at my touch, I'm even more lost than I was before. She owns me. Heart, body, and soul.

I look over at Nox and while jealousy tries to rear its ugly head, there's a level of respect and understanding I feel for him. He's just as much a part of Adrienne as I am and I know he would risk his own life for her, just as I would.

I pull Adrienne's body into me and rest her head in the crook of my arm. Placing a kiss against her forehead, my eyes drift over to the severed head still sitting on the ground. Nox's face stares at us, reminding me of who actually sacrificed himself so we could survive.

My creator. My master. My friend, even though he drove me crazy. I squeeze my eyes shut and will the tears to leave. I need to be strong. I can mourn Than once we are safe. Once I can tell him that his sacrifice did not go in vain.

I will forever remember the loyalty you had to keeping everyone safe. I will spend the rest of my existence convincing the worlds that you were a hero. Your name will not be forgotten, nor will your selfless acts. I know you're somewhere better, mate. Rest in peace.

I let the prayer spin around in my brain and hope, somewhere out there, Than can hear it. I think back to Lucifer sitting by himself in hell and wonder if Than's spirit already reached him. If Lucifer is aware of his passing.

It upset me that Lucifer stayed behind. He told us he was planning on sneaking into heaven. He told us he's been devising a plan for years. And yet, when push came to shove, he stayed back to watch the destruction. To watch others fight a battle that began with him and Atlas.

I understand that if we all die, including Lucifer, all of our worlds will be destroyed, but still... I would never send others in my place to fight my battle. I would make sure to be at the front of the line, standing tall and fighting for what I know is right. Fighting for my darling. Fighting for the people and the world she so dearly wants to protect.

And that's what I'm going to do. She will walk out of this world, whether I'm with her or not. And she will rule better than any ruler ever has. Because she's the change we all needed. And she's stronger than us all.

CHAPTER 24

LUCIFER

I pour one for Nathaniel, clinking my glass of amber against his as my chest aches. He was my closest friend, a brother that I will never forget. I felt it the minute he passed. Deep in my bones. And when I heard his voice, a passing whisper telling me he's okay, I knew he was on his way to the afterlife up in that star filled sky. To Posvita. To a better place.

I didn't want to stay back. I hated the idea of letting them fight my battles. Letting them risk their lives with the monster that already took so much from this world. But Aiden told me what I had to do. The voice in my head that only seems to show up in dire situations.

And yet, he's never shown himself. He's never done anything to the monsters he so desperately wants me to stop. He watched as death and despair were dispersed around every world. But now, I know the reason why. I know everything.

Aiden spoke to me about using Adrienne and Ahriman as a distraction. Keeping Atlas busy so I could do what needs to be done. It puts my demons in danger. My people who have done nothing but sacrifice since the beginning of their existence. They never question me. Never second guess me. And I know, in this case, they won't either.

They will do exactly as they are told. They will risk their lives just as I will, since Aiden now holds my immortality. Just as Adrienne, Ahriman, and Nox are. Just as Than did. The hard part is going to be getting everyone else to agree. But hopefully, with Onyx and Lady Blackwell's help, we can convince them all.

Hopefully, we can form our army.

ADRIENNE

I don't know how long it's been. It could have been four hours since we were thrown in here or four days. Every minute blends into the next and I am worried we are running out of time to come up with a plan. Not that we can necessarily devise a proper plan with eyes on us at all times.

The only thing I can think to do is unleash hell the minute we finish whatever battle Atlas has for us. Since we will both have our powers available, it seems like the only option. To take him by surprise before he can trap us again or remove our powers.

I have this theory that could end up getting me killed. Getting all of us killed. But it's something I need to try. I've had more powers, both angel and demon, than any other royal ever has. So, my theory is, I have each one of the different powers the angels and Gods possess. And I'm going to use it against them whenever they try to use it against me. Maybe.

It's a shot in the dark, and something that will potentially destroy us. But, if it fails, I'll just rain hellfire down on them. If I can... again, I've never done something like that at that magnitude.

"Do we have any idea what's in store for us? What Atlas plans on making us do?" I turn towards Ahri where he lies on the ground and ask him. I've been avoiding speaking to Nox, since I don't want to give away that he isn't who he says he is. The fact that they haven't figured it out already makes me think the Atlas is a fucking moron. He's too focused on power to see what's right in front of him.

"No, but whatever is the worst-case scenario in your head, I'd picture worse. He's going to make this close to impossible. And he's most likely going to play at our weaknesses." Ahri throws the small ball of toilet paper he crumpled up into the air and catches it again.

My weaknesses? I look down at my quickly healing hands and try to think. What could Atlas use against me? My bonds? He already thinks Nox is dead. Onyx is safe in Ombra and Ahri will be with me during this shit show.

"Hey, don't think too much about it, Adrienne." Ahri stops throwing his paper ball and looks over at me with concern in his eyes. "There's nothing we can do until we get there. There's no point in killing ourselves with stress."

I glare at him before answering. "What is up with you? We are most likely about to die and you can't stop smiling." He's been all smiles since what we did. I can't imagine getting off made him this happy. Then again, he's been in my head for his entire life and probably never experienced that with anyone. I smirk to myself when I realize the big tough Ahriman Reaper is most likely a virgin.

"No, we aren't, darling. And I'm just in a good mood for some reason." He winks at me and I watch as love flows through his irises. He looks like a love sick puppy. And it's one of the most adorable things I've ever seen. I look down to prevent him from seeing the blush covering my cheeks.

I stare at the clean skin on my legs and my lips push out in a dramatic pout. I was hopeful that what we did together would bring more markings to my body. I want to be covered in them. I want everyone to know who I belong to and who belongs to me. I'm assuming the magic blocker has something to do with the lack of new ones.

"Stop thinking about things in that lovely little head of yours." I can't help but snort at him. Sometimes it boggles my mind how British he sounds.

"Why do you have a British accent?" I question it for the first time ever and it seems to take him off guard. He blinks at me and then furrows his brows while he clears his throat.

"Do you enjoy British accents?" He asks a question rather than answering mine and I want to roll my eyes at him.

"I mean, doesn't everyone? Accents are sexy. I just don't understand why you have one."

"Think about it. Maybe it will come to you, darling." He goes right back to throwing his little ball up and down in the air and this time, I can't resist the urge to roll my eyes.

That is, until what he says hits me. *Do you enjoy British accents?* I stare at his bulking tatted body. I stare at his long dark hair that looks so fucking sexy when it's up in a bun. I stare at the beard that I always want to grab and hold onto while he kisses me.

"You... you're the way you are because of me?" I always denied having a type, but if I'm being honest, Ahri is the closest anyone or anything has ever gotten to it.

"Darling, you created me. I'm your familiar. I am a part of you. Whatever you were looking for, deep down... whatever you craved and wanted... I became that. Right down to my huge d—"

"Alright, shut up now while I process this!" I try to hide my smirk at what he was about to say but fail. And then I look over at Nox. I can't see him, of course, but I know that admission can't feel good. And the worst part is I can't comfort or reassure him the way I want to. Not while we're here.

"Darling, Nox was created for you as well. And he didn't even have to be derived from your brain to be perfect for you. He just was. Your other half. Your best friend. Your mate." I feel my heart squeeze as Ahri says what I wanted to say out loud. He must have known what I was thinking. Felt what I was feeling.

Thank you, I mouth to him, not saying the words out loud. He gives me a nod accompanied by a soft smile and then turns back to his ball. At that moment, the sound of a lock clicking fills the room and all three of us stand at attention, moving to the center of the floor.

Right in the middle of the wall, where there was previously nothing, a door appears and opens up, revealing Surya's wicked smile. "Well, if it isn't my three favorite prisoners. You enjoy your time in here?"

No one answers, simply glaring back at him, as he inches his way towards us. He stops right in front of me, his eyes dragging up and down my body. "It looked like you enjoyed yourself quite a bit before, little one."

Ahri growls next to me, trying to position himself between us, but I put a hand on his shoulder to stop him. I'm not scared of Surya. Not anymore. I refuse to be. Instead, I give him a cocky smirk and bat my eyes at him.

"Did you get a good look, Surya? Did you watch Ahri touch me? Did you sit there like the creepy fuck you are and wish, just once, a woman would come all over your fingers? I bet you've never made a woman come, have you?" His previous smirk turns into a murderous snarl, but he doesn't move for me. He just stares into my eyes with a mixture of hatred and arousal.

"You better shut that whore of a mouth of yours before I shut it for you. Every snarky word you speak will only make your punishments from me that much worse."

"If you hadn't noticed, I'm not scared of you. You can try to hurt me all you want." This makes him laugh and I watch as the snake of a man shakes his head.

"Clearly murdering your mate right in front of you wasn't enough to teach you a lesson. Moved right on to the next cock in sight. Well, once Ahriman is dead, mine will be next in line. And I'm going to enjoy ripping you to shreds from the inside out."

This time, a chill runs through my body but I don't let my fear show. My fear for Ahriman and Nox. They can do whatever they want to me, but the thought of Ahri or Nox being hurt is too much. It's too much to bear.

"That's what I thought, little one." He throws white clothes at both me and Ahri before continuing. "Get dressed. It's time for your final act."

CHAPTER 25

ONYX

"I can't believe it." I look at the crowd of people, the crowd of all of the rulers, standing before us. Somehow, Lucifer, Lady Blackwell, and I managed to gain the support of every ruling family and hundreds of their people. Every kingdom, both small and large, is standing before us, waiting for our instruction.

"And you're sure this is going to work?" I look over at Lucifer, who is standing near me in my kingdom. The clype was removed, allowing Lucifer in, and after explaining everything, we managed to convince everyone to trust us. It wasn't as hard as I expected. Everyone seems to have their own doubts about the Gods and their sincerity.

"No. But I trust Aiden. And he says it will work." I hate that answer, but it's the only thing we have. And if this is going to bring Adrienne back to me, I will do whatever it takes.

"Why didn't you do this before? Why not try to create an alliance among all of the people years ago?" It's been bothering me since Lucifer told me of his plan.

"I always tried to gain the trust of the people, but fighting against the lies of Atlas made it impossible to get through to anyone. And on top of that, I needed a distraction like Adrienne. Nothing, besides her, would draw Atlas's attention away from Earth long enough for us to complete this."

"Let me remind you how much I hate you for using my Dark Lady as your distraction. She's so much more than that." I glare at him but it isn't completely serious.

"She's as much my Dark Lady as she is yours, Onyx. But you're right, she is so much more than that." His answer eases my anger and I turn my attention to Lord Blackwell. He didn't handle any of this well. He was angry that we let Lady Blackwell out. He was angry that we lost Adrienne's body. And he was terribly depressed. To the point where I had to drag him out of bed to get him here.

I don't think he fully believes us still, but he's not strong enough to fight this. All he can do is join the cause or be left behind. And I know if there's even a chance that this will bring Adrienne back, he will do it.

"Alright, Lucifer. It's your time to shine. Don't fuck it up." He rolls his eyes at my sarcasm and then stands tall, clearing his throat.

"I know this is confusing for most of you. I know I am the last person any of you ever believed you would follow. But I want you all to know how grateful I am to be given a chance. I have been made the enemy, but all I want to be is your neighbor. Your friend. Your ally. And after today, I believe we will be. Because today... Today is the day we overthrow a dictator!"

Every demon that Lucifer brought from his world cheers, while the rest of us stay silent. "We have already told you of the many lies Atlas has sprung your way. But, one of the most important lies is that only royals can travel to Earth, or any of the other worlds for that matter. That is far from the truth. With the help of your ruler's every last shadvir and demon here can travel to any of the worlds they wish. The way it should be! Equal and fair for all."

This time, more people cheer. I see smiles and excited expressions on some of the shadvir in the crowd and I can't help but smile myself. I was under the same impression as the rest of them. That they were unable to travel. It was something we were told from birth. That only royals had such a privilege.

"And today is the day that every last one of you will be able to experience not only Earth, but Heaven! With the help of all of our powerful rulers, we will be able to destroy the curse Atlas placed on Earth! And with the help of everyone else, we will have an army larger than Atlas's followers! We will be able to overthrow his throne. Take what is rightfully ours and create peace between all of the worlds!"

Another round of cheers commences and finally, almost every person in the crowd is clapping. "Our dear Adrienne, the strongest ruler any of our kingdoms have ever seen, is currently fighting for our freedom right now. She is fighting to save not only her own kingdom, but all of the worlds. And we will not let her do this alone!"

"Princess Adrienne! Dark Lady Blackwell!" I hear her name being shouted through the crowd and my chest hurts. My dark lady. The woman I should be standing beside right now. The woman I accidentally gave my heart to.

"What do we have to do?" I turn my attention towards the voice that booms from the crowd after it settles down. My brother. Ozul, the cockiest prick I've ever met. I've never liked him. But, when I went to him with my concerns, when I asked him for his help, he didn't bat an eye. And he brought at least a hundred men from his kingdom here without a word.

"Every shadvir needs to be armed, just in case. And every ruler needs to be ready to use a fuck ton of clype." I speak up this time and everyone laughs at my vulgar vocabulary. "It's going to be risky. It's going to be painful and exhausting. But it's going to work."

The entire crowd nods their head and cheers again, the sound ringing in my ears. Am I as positive as I sound? No. Am I worried that we are going to kill every human and shadvir that will be on Earth? A little. But, it's our best option.

So, it has to work... right?

ADRIENNE

My eyes scan the crowd above me and my stomach drops to the floor. We are in the same area we were before, but rather than a stage, Ahri and I stand in an arena. The crowd is cheering and booing at the same time as we walk into the white arena below them, filled with nothing but our small bodies and three trap doors on the walls surrounding us.

I turn towards Ahri and he nods his head at me, grabbing my hand in his. They removed the metal ring bolted to my neck but Surya made sure to tell me that the arena is charmed. We can't touch anyone outside of the huge sparkling space we are currently standing in.

"Channel your anger and your love, darling. Use me. Do whatever it takes to get out of here. No matter what they throw our way." I nod my head, already feeling my magic flicker inside of me. I haven't used it in a long time. And I've never used it to actually fight anyone. Or anything.

"People of Heaven. Fellow Angels and friends. Today, we gather to watch a very special show! Our traitor deserves a fighting chance, correct? We are willing to give anyone a second chance if they can prove themselves! So, today, our sister will prove herself or die trying!"

I roll my eyes, hating this act he puts on for his people. They think he's a fair ruler. They think he's kind and smart. Little do they know, he's corrupt and maniacal. He's a horrible leader and he will pay for what he has done.

"Adrienne Blackwell and Ahriman Reaper. You will now fight to prove yourselves! You will have three separate rounds. And, if you manage to complete each round, we will set you free. You have my word." I scan the crowd above, glaring at each face I see. I'm searching for his face as I curse his name and his word. It means shit to me.

"Now, it's time to begin! May the strongest beast survive!" The sound of a bell ringing along with loud cheers fills my ears and makes me wince. Then, deafening silence consumes me and the only thing I can hear is my rapid beating heart and my Ahri's shallow breaths.

And then, the door to our right opens up. The hinges squeak and groan as the huge gate rises up and leaves a dark gaping hole in its wake. We wait, holding our breaths in anticipation of what's about to exit from the space. What beast could possibly walk out of the opening.

Footsteps echo from the darkness and after what feels like a lifetime, movement catches my eye. From this distance, the person looks small and fragile. She steps out, shaking from fear, squinting her eyes at the bright lights surrounding us. Her hair is as brittle and dry as the last time I saw her. Her skin sagging and wrinkly. Her frame thin and weak.

And when Catherine's eyes find mine, they hold the same hatred that they did back when she told me she wasn't my real mother. The same anger and disgust. The only difference is, when she takes me in, her smile grows. It grows unnaturally big and reaches the corners of her eyes, revealing razor sharp teeth.

"Hello, Adrienne." Her voice comes out thick and deep, scraping against the edges of my brain like gravel. I gulp down my immediate fear and then glare at the woman before me.

"Pull your magic from me. Don't let the emotion get to you. Do it now. Before she can strike." Ahri squeezes my hand and then lets go of it, letting me do what I need to do.

Gulping down my fear, I smile at her. "Catherine. I'd love to catch up, but I think it's time for you to go." And then, without a second thought, I reach into the golden ring inside of me, feeling Ahri's presence inside of it, and I grab at my fire. I grab at the burning inferno deep sweltering underneath, before aiming it straight at her.

A fireball, the size of a car, flies out of my hands and careens straight for the woman who tried to kill me years ago. It's so quick, if you blinked, you'd miss it. And then it hits her, exploding into a million sparks of bright orange light.

Her screams echo through the arena, cutting off the sound of the crackling fire engulfing her. And then, her flaming body falls to the ground and her screams cut out, leaving the never-ending flames in her wake.

I turn towards Ahri, confused as to why that was the first round. Did Atlas think seeing her again would make me freeze? Would bring back horrible memories and throw me off? It doesn't make sense.

Until it does. Until the sound of her loud cackling fills the arena, so loud, so vicious, I wince and find myself involuntarily reaching towards Ahri for comfort. I turn my attention back to the flames and watch as what was just an unmoving, charring body turns into something more.

She twitches and contorts, before her flaming body rises from the ground again. Only this time, she's not her normal five-foot, five-inch self. She rises and rises, my eyes dragging up the flames as she reaches inhuman heights.

"Fuck," Ahri hisses out the word as he tries to get in front of me, protecting me from the now twenty-foot flaming beast that resembles my monster of a fake mother. "The fire ball made her stronger!"

"No shit, sherlock," I scream back at him since the sound of her deep laugh is too loud to simply talk over.

"Hit her with something else. Something she can't use against you." I fight the urge to roll my eyes and bite my tongue. I don't have time to be sarcastic. "I'll distract her. You hit her where it hurts." Finally, he says something that actually helps.

"Got it!" I scream back as we run to opposite ends of the arena. She stands, or rather towers, in the middle of the floor, darting her fire filled gaze between the two of us. Her eyes are dark holes in the middle of the orange flames and her smile, still unnaturally large and sinister, is filled with sharp ten inch teeth. She's something out of nightmares. My nightmares.

"Oh, Adrienne. You poor, stupid girl. You know that no one has ever loved you. You know how much of a waste of oxygen your existence is. So why do you continue to fight? Why do you set yourself up for failure over and over again?"

I try to ignore her words. I focus on the powers inside of me and siphon through the different ones. I'm so inexperienced with this, I can't tell which feeling belongs to which power. But I can feel how strong each one is. I can feel the pressure radiating behind them.

And then suddenly, I feel something pull towards Ahri, and I realize, somehow, he made us both invisible. I search for him, for a split second, and the only thing I see is a small red string that travels from me, towards his invisible body.

I smile to myself, so fucking in love with him at this moment, and then glare at the mom-ster in front of me. She whips her head around, trying to find both of us, as she screams out in annoyance.

It's so loud, so deafening, that I almost fall to the ground from the pain in my ears.

You can do this, darling. I'll keep her looking for me. Ahri's voice takes over the loud screaming in my head and I nod my head in response, too focused to say anything else. And then I run to a corner, as far away from her as possible, and I kneel down, trying to focus.

I pull on my angel power, reaching for the small branches that I have not yet touched. I remember what it felt like when Surya made my blood boil. When he made my bones grate against each other. And then, like a lock being picked, I feel something deep inside of me unlock. It clicks into place and I know I have it at my fingertips.

I stare into the spinning giant of flames, watching her scream as Ahri runs around her, shouting her name and zapping her with random flames. It's not hurting her or making her grow, but it's distracting her. It's giving me the chance to do what I need to.

I imagine that feeling again. That searing pain that took my breath away, and then I picture it shooting through my fingertips. I picture it hitting her hard and bringing her down to her knees. I picture her blood boiling in her body. I picture her flames being drowned by water. I picture her bones breaking one by one inside of her body.

And right on que, her body goes from an inferno, to sopping wet. She's left a charred, burnt giant with barely any flesh left on her thin body. And then her bones start to snap, the noise deafeningly loud. Her limbs twist and turn at unnatural angles. She screams and howls, completely consumed by the pain, but it only fuels me further. It fuels my need to destroy her. To watch her cry and beg for salvation. Just as she made me. As she cut my arm and let me bleed out.

I walk up to her, still invisible thanks to Ahri, and I raise my voice to a booming shout. "You will not bully me into submission!

You will not belittle me and make me second guess my worth! I am stronger than you! I always was and I always will be!"

I reach my hand out and imagine it crashing through her chest. I picture my fingers wrapping around her cold, black heart. I can actually feel it in my grasp, even though there's nothing in my hand as it clasps around the thin air in front of me.

"This is for the years of pain you have caused me. For the years of hardship you put me through! This is for every person that ever felt less than! For every last person that felt alone and worthless! Go fuck yourself, Catherine."

I close my hand into a tight fist as hard as I can and feel the invisible organ explode in my hand. I watch as Catherine's disfigured, beast of a body goes still. I watch as the black holes for eyes finally find me in the arena and stare blankly, lifeless, at the last thing she will ever see. And then, I watch the woman who made me feel inferior, breathe her last breath.

Silence sits dormant around us as Catherine's body disappears from the floor, taking every charred patch of skin and drop of blood along with it. My knees feel weak and my head pounds from the toll using new magic had on me. The exertion is worse than I expected and I have to hold myself up against the wall to keep from falling.

That was bloody amazing, darling. I'm so proud of you. Ahri's voice sounds distant as it rings through my head, making me feel dizzy. I blink my eyes over and over again, trying to stop the room from spinning. Trying to keep the nausea down and hold myself up at the same time.

I take deep breaths, closing my eyes for a few seconds, and then feel Ahri's arm slip under mine, helping me stay vertical. *It's okay, take deep breaths. You're stronger than you know. Just let this pass. I'm right here.*

Luckily, his presence gives me more strength and after a few seconds, the dizzy spell fades away and I can stand straight on my own again. *That's my girl.*

"Well, I have to say, Adrienne, I'm a bit impressed." Atlas's voice booms through the arena and I grit my teeth in annoyance. "You have the power of dolorian, I see. Something I passed down to Surya, and Surya only. I wonder... what else are you keeping from us? Perhaps this next test will reveal more of your secrets."

I can hear the anger in his voice. He sounds like he's ready to murder me, which, is accurate given the situation. *I'm assuming the power of dolorian is the power to inflict pain on someone?* I push my question through our bond and Ahri shrugs his shoulders next to me.

I've never seen anything like what you just did to her. Even when Surya was hurting you, it was nothing like that. I don't think Atlas or Surya would be able to do what you just did.

I can't help but smile at the astonishment in Ahri's voice. I could barely control what I just did to Catherine. My anger, my resentment, and my need for justice took over and sent me into an uncontrollable frenzy of destroying every last part of her. And while that scares me, it also felt fucking amazing.

Before I can respond to Ahri, the lights around us cut out, leaving us suspended in pitch blackness. I reach for Ahri's hand, my racing heart beating even faster than it already was.

It's okay, darling. You have the ability to see in the dark. Lucifer had to create something to help him see when he was sent to hell. When it was too dark to see. Reach deep down and search for it. You can do it.

I listen to Ahri's voice and find comfort in the way his fingers brush against mine. Then, just like he said, I reach into myself and search for anything that resembles night vision. I picture Lucifer trying to see down in hell. I picture his eyes glowing and the dark space lighting up before him.

And then, right on que, I feel power unlock behind my eyes and the room around me starts to appear. I turn my head and take in the dark space, outlined in squiggly white lines, and fine Ahri's silhouette next to me. I smile at him before sending a message through the line.

I can see! Can you? I watch as Ahri's white teeth shine back at me with his smile and then see his head shake.

I need to supply you with as much of my power as possible. I don't want to take away from yours by trying to see too. You need to be my eyes—

He cuts off when a loud roar vibrates the entire arena, making my insides jostle and my ear drums scream out in pain. I see movement in the corner of my eye and turn my head, wishing I hadn't when I see what moved.

It's like nothing I've ever seen. It runs around the arena like a bull, only it's the size of a semi-truck. In the darkness, I can see inside of its massive body, each huge organ illuminating as it jumps around and flails it's huge, horned head. Its four legs are thick, resembling a bear rather than a bull, and each foot has long razor-sharp talons that glisten in the darkness.

"You want to tell me what's making that bloody noise?" Ahri screams over the mind-numbing roars of the beast in front of me. How do I describe this thing to him? I'm at a loss for words and judging by the way it just stopped, turned directly toward me, and is staring me down with beaty eyes, I'm not the only one that can see in the dark.

"Umm it's huge and it has horns and talons and razor-sharp teeth! Oh, and it's massive and staring me down as we speak!" I shout, starting to back both of us up towards the opposite wall. His eyes stay on me, not once looking at Ahri. "Do you trust me?" I shout one last time, an idea popping in my head.

"Always!"

The beast roars loudly again and then barrels toward me.

"Start running along the wall! Now!" I let go of his hand as he darts away from me at lightning speed and right before the monster reaches me, his teeth on display as its horns aim straight for my heart, I reach for my wings and jump up into the air.

My foot just grazes the beasts head as I launch into the air. I hear the crack of its skull as it collides with the hard wall and smile to myself as it wails in pain. Turning my head from up above, I spot the beast struggling to remove his two long horns from the white stone and take that opportunity to reach into my body and grab at the same power I used to destroy Catherine.

Only, when I do, it stays dormant inside of me, feeling like a heavy weight carrying me down. I'm too weak. I can't use that power again, especially while I'm flying. I turn my attention to Ahri and find him still running, making his way straight for the monster.

"Ahri! Stop! It's right in front of you!" I scream out from my spot high in the air but it doesn't stop him.

"I know! I can see him right now! He lit up when he hit the wall! I'm going to distract him while you gain strength!" Everything inside of me tells me that's a terrible idea. I try to fly to him, desperate to stop him, but he's so much closer to the monster than I am.

Ahri hits him over and over again with his fire, making the monster scream out in anger. He flails and whips his head, trying to get his horns out of the wall. I fly faster, ready to grab Ahri and bring him up in the air with me, and right before I reach him, the beasts head comes loose.

It all happens so fast. He whips his head in our direction and from my height in the air, his horn hits me perfectly, catching me straight in the stomach and throwing me hard through the air. I cry out from the pain as my wings lose control and I go careening towards the opposite wall.

My back makes contact, my head cracking against the stone and my wings snapping behind me. I feel my body slide down the wall with no control. I try to grab at something. I try to will my wings to work. Instead, I hit the ground, and everything goes black.

CHAPTER 26

ADRIENNE

My eyes shoot open to the sound of multiple roars echoing through my head at once. I wince from the pain as I open my eyes and remember where I am. I try to pull myself up and scream out Ahri's name, terrified that he's dead. That the beast destroyed him after I passed out. That this is over for good.

My eyes dart to the movement at the opposite end of the arena and I find the beast, but it's not alone. Equally as big, I watch as what looks like a giant black panther pounces on the monster, its long claws embedding into its skin and tearing it open. I blink at it, trying to figure out if I'm hallucinating or not, and then search for Ahri again.

He's nowhere in sight. The only things in this arena with me are these two feral beasts, attacking each other and screeching loudly for all to hear. I watch as the huge cat aims its razor-sharp teeth at the beast's neck and right before it makes contact, the beast hits the panther with one of his horns, throwing it down to the ground.

The minute the cat gets hit, patterns of bright light illuminate all over its black fur. But they aren't just any patterns. They are the same markings that Ahri has. The black tattoos I love so much. The tattoos I carry too, shining bright all over this giant cat's skin.

Ahri? I reach through our line and feel it stop right at the cat. The cat that is now back to fighting the beast that hurt me. The cat that looks back at me for a split second and stares into my soul the same way Ahri does.

I smile through my pain and watch the scene unfold before me. Ahri hits the beast from the side and digs his teeth into his flesh. The sound of its screams are painfully loud and I can see spurts of blood flying out from where Ahri's mouth is clamped down.

Ahri flails his head back and forth, refusing to let go, and then he digs his paws into the monster. One paw goes straight for its heart and somehow, he manages to stick each six-inch claw deep into the creature's beating organ, killing it instantly.

When its body hits the ground, the entire arena shakes. Within seconds, the beast disappears and the lights turn back on. I stare straight ahead, at the huge panther like cat that stares right back at me. His muscles ripple under his silken, black hair and his red eyes, now appearing feline, still carry the same swirls as Ahri's normal ones.

He stalks toward me, at least four of me high, and a chill runs through my body. A chill filled with admiration, power, and a bit of fear. He's so powerful, so beautiful, that I can barely stand to look at him.

When he reaches me, the entire world around us falls away. His massive body bows to me and he waits, his head inches away, for me to pet him. I reach forward and my fingers thread into his soft hair, engulfing each digit in his warmth. The minute my hand touches him, he starts to purr, vibrating against my skin and into my bones.

I guess I was wrong. I reach through our bond and talk to him. *I always pegged you as the canine type. I much prefer this feline version of you. You're so adorable.* He lifts his head and squints his eyes at me in a glare, but I can see the smile in his glimmering irises.

And then, right before my eyes, he transforms back to the Ahri I know and love. I let my eyes drag down his body, noticing that his white clothes are still intact. I can't stop the pout that forms, wishing desperately that his clothes were ruined in the process.

My dirty girl. He must see the look in my eyes. The lust. The uncontrollable pull I feel to him. *I'll take my clothes off for you once we beat this last round, okay, darling?*

Oh, shut it. I was simply wondering how you turned into a huge fucking jaguar. Did you know you could do that? I glare at him with a smirk on my face, my injuries in the back of my mind now.

No, I had no clue. When you hit the wall and passed out, something inside of me cracked and I felt this overwhelming surge of power fill me. Next thing I knew, I was twenty feet tall with four legs.

I smile at him, reaching for him so he can help me up. And when he does, he pulls me into his arms in a warm embrace and I inhale everything Ahri. My body aches less and my powers vibrate and hum inside of me, getting stronger again.

"Hate to break this beautiful encounter up, but we aren't finished!" Atlas's voice booms through the arena. He sounds angry. Angrier than I've ever heard him. I'm assuming he didn't expect us to make it this far.

"Why do you sound so angry, Atlas?" I yell back to him, spinning in a circle as I stare up into the crowd of eyes. "I thought you were rooting for us? So you could destroy the curse that Lucifer put on the humans? Unless... it wasn't Lucifer's curse after all. And you want to keep us from helping the humans if we win!"

The crowd gasps before going silent, waiting for their fearless leader to respond. I can feel a shift in the air. After the past two rounds, I can feel an attitude change from the people around us. As if they are starting to see the truth. That Ahri and I are not evil. That we aren't the bad guys.

"Shut up, you little brat!" he screams so loud that his voice cracks. He's not just angry, he's fuming. Uncontrollably so. And the angels around us react by whispering among each other. By keeping their voices hushed, but questioning the real motives of their God.

"Ahem... anyway, there's one round left. If you are able to complete this one, you win." I glare at no one as I listen to him try to recover.

"And just to clear things up one more time. What happens when we win?"

"*If* you win, you will help me destroy the curse that Lucifer created and most importantly to you, neither of you will die. Your fate after that is undecided and unclear. But I can assure you, it will be better than being dead."

"Doubtful," I say the word under my breath as Ahri squeezes my hand in comfort.

"Let the last round begin!" Atlas booms one last time before silence takes over and we wait for the next monster to show itself. The next beast or nightmare that will inevitably try to murder us.

The door across from us creaks and groans as it opens, giving us a peak into the pitch-black room it was once concealing. I hear it before I see it. The sound of a body dragging against the cold hard ground. The sound of someone whimpering. It's a feminine sound. A familiar one that makes me search through the dark depths of my mind to figure out who it is.

And right when it clicks, her face crosses the threshold and is illuminated by the bright white light. Her blonde hair is matted with blood. Her hands reach in front of her, completely crimson, as they leave handprints on the ground wherever she tries to drag herself.

Everything around me fades away as my heart stops and my breath hitches. No. This can't be happening. It can't really be her. It can't really be her disheveled body. It can't really be her blood pouring out of unseen cuts and holes sitting in her once perfectly porcelain skin.

I run, or stumble, my way to her as tears fill my eyes and blur my vision. I try to call out her name, but I can't make out any sound through the dull ringing in my ears. When her eyes meet mine, death circulating in her irises, I know she must hear me.

I finally reach Sophia and throw myself to the ground, pulling her into my arms. I don't care that her blood is now completely covering me. I don't care that the entire arena is watching me shake and cry uncontrollably, showing one of my many weaknesses. Because all that matters is making sure she's okay. Making sure I can make her better. Take care of her.

My eyes scan her body and I find where the blood is coming from. She has slices through her satin pajamas that puncture her stomach, deep and oozing. A deep stab wound through her shoulder pours blood onto the marble floor. All injuries that will eventually kill her, from the blood loss. Which, she has clearly lost a lot of already, judging by the thick drag marks behind her.

"Ph... Phia.," I sob out her name as my hands hover over her wounds, shaking violently, trying to figure out what to do. How to fix this. I turn my head to look into her eyes and find her staring up at me, tears streaming down her red cheeks, leaving small rivers of her unnaturally pale skin underneath.

"Willow." She says my old name with a soft smile on her face and another sob escapes my lips. I missed her voice. I missed that name. I missed her. "I... I'm sorry. I'm sorry for hurting you. For..." She swallows hard, clearly trying to fight through the pain. "For betraying you."

"Shhh." I shake my head at her and bring one of my hands up to her cheek, wiping a thumb over the warm liquid covering it. "No, Phia. I'm sorry. For everything. None of that matters. I love you so much. You're my sister, always. And I'm going to get you out of here, okay? You're going to be okay."

I reach for my power and then push as much as I can into her. I try to reverse the pain I so easily threw into Catherine, and instead try to heal her. I put my all into it, but it barely fizzles inside of me. It cries out in exhaustion, like I no longer have as much power as I used to.

"It... it's okay. I just wanted to make this better. I love you, Willow. You're my sister no matter what." She talks cryptically and I can see the light in her eyes fading.

"NO!" I scream out, pushing all of the power I have into her, desperate to heal her. Desperate to take away her pain. "Please! You can't do this! This can't be happening!" My body shakes uncontrollably as I stare at her body with wide, unblinking eyes. I reach for the power from Ahri's connection, but find it missing. The only power I have available is my own and it's weak and depleted from my exhaustion.

Turning my head to find him, to beg him and scream at him to help me, I find him standing close to us, but unmoving. He looks stuck in a running stance, like he was trying to make his way to us before being frozen in time. His eyes stare at me, pain and fear coursing through their red depths.

And then the sound of their footsteps approaching sends a bolt of fear through me. Three sets of feet, each clacking loudly against the marble floor. I turn to find two of them smiling their vile grins at me, while the third focuses solely on Ahri. Their thin skin glimmers in the light, showing off their veins underneath.

They're here to end this. Because no matter how much Atlas needed me to help him, he sees the threat I am. He sees that if I survive this without being completely destroyed, he won't.

So, he sent his disciples to break me. For good this time.

CHAPTER 27

LUCIFER

We stand as an army, strong and united, among an empty field full of tall green grass. At least a thousand members of Ombra stare at me, waiting for my command. Something I never thought I'd witness. The descendants of the angels backing the one man that has been deemed the literal devil for centuries.

I watch as a gust of wind brings the grass to life around us, each tendril dancing in the cool breeze. It's peaceful here. And as my eyes turn up to the golden orb above us, heat tickles my skin. The hum of imignis that could destroy us all vibrates through my veins with each ray of sun that sneaks through my clype.

"Alright, Lucifer, what's the plan?" I look over at Onyx as he speaks and my eyes shift over to Lady Blackwell. Something about her. About the way her eyes sparkle yet dim with darkness at the same time. The way she smiles yet frowns all at once. The demons and shadows hiding behind such a beautiful cover. She intrigues me. Almost as much as my Ayla once did.

Clearing my throat, I look away from her and turn my attention to the hundreds of eyes staring at me. "I know you've all existed assuming that the only powerful beings are your leaders. That you hold no power, besides the power they bestow in you to protect your humans. Well, I'm here to tell you that that's complete bullshit!"

Everyone stares at me, utterly silent and questioning my words. "A ruler is only as powerful as his people. And I can assure you, my demons are what give me my strength. They are what make my magic thrive. I need them, just as I need all of you now. There is a protective layer of my clype sitting around that ball of fire up there." I point up at the deadly imignis suspended above us. "I need each one of you rulers to put your all into creating the strongest clype you've ever made. You're going to use your shadvir to give you more power. And then, I need you to make a protective barrier around the imignis. But, here's the tricky part."

I pause and swallow hard, nervous that this is going to end in each one of us getting blown up. "I am going to remove my clype at the exact same moment that you all create yours. Once my clype is removed, that imignis is going to explode. And as long as you all have your barrier surrounding the explosion, everything should work out just fine."

"Should? Real convincing there, Lucifer," Onyx huffs out a sarcastic comment. I raise a brow at him, needing his support more than anyone's. He's the one that convinced the rest of the realm to follow us.

"Look, is it risky? Yes. But if we don't try this, we are all going to die anyway. Atlas is either going to use Adrienne to remove my clype, destroying all of us, or he is going to kill her and eventually figure out another way. Trust me when I say, we are not safe. And this is the only chance in centuries that we have had to do something like this. Because nothing, besides that girl, would distract Atlas enough to completely forget about his curse sitting up there."

"Okay, you have our support. Whatever it takes to make sure Adrienne is safe and the world doesn't explode." I turn toward Cole, Adrienne's father, and nod my head at him, grateful that he has finally spoken up and come to his senses. He stands on the opposite side of Onyx that Lady Blackwell stands, avoiding her completely.

"How do we pull more power from our shadvir?" Onyx asks this question next.

"We need to form circles. A circle with everyone from your specific kingdom holding hands." I get a few eye rolls and snorts. "I know, I know. It sounds cliché. But I need every ruler's power to be attached to their people. And as long as no one breaks the connection, each of our power will be stronger than ever."

"Alright, you heard him! Everyone get together. Form a circle with your kingdom. Now!" Onyx yells out and everyone shuffles quickly in the field until suddenly, there are huge circles all formed right next to each other. Hundreds, if not thousands, of people hold hands, ready to fight for good. Fight for the humans. For Adrienne. My demons form a circle with me, staring at me with pride and love in their red eyes.

"Everyone pull deep inside of yourself. Picture your loyalty to your leaders. Picture your love for you people and the humans! Picture pulling that out of yourself and giving it to your ruler. Letting it flow through you and into them! And as for the rulers, picture your magic like a magnet! Pulling at each one of their support and clinging to it! Making it stronger!"

I feel that hum of my magic growing deep inside of me as my demons do exactly as they're told. I feel it bubbling up, bigger and stronger, the way it always does when I reach for them. When I reach for that pull that makes my heart swell and my body heat up.

"I... I feel it!" One of the rulers yells out and all of the others join in, laughing and smiling in awe of the beautiful connection they have been withheld from for centuries.

"Alright. It's going to happen quick. And it's going to feel like your power is being ripped from you! But we can do this! I believe in every last one of you! On the count of three..." I take a deep breath and find Lady Blackwell's eyes in the crowd of people. She holds Onyx's hand and her eyes are locked on mine in worry.

Nodding my head once, I wink at her and then look up into the sky. "Three... Two... One!"

And then, in the blink of an eye, an explosion so loud erupts through the world, sending gusts of burning heat whipping down on us before darkness invades each and every one of my senses.

CHAPTER 28

ADRIENNE

"I was never meant to leave here alive, was I?" I let my tears fall down my cheeks as Surya, Kamar, and Blaze stand before me. Sophia's breath is so shallow, I can barely see her chest rise as her eyelids rest over her blue irises. Ahri still remains frozen next to me, clearly suffering through internal pain I can't see or feel.

"Alive? Yes. But whole? No. We knew that you could help us simply because of the fact that you possess even an ounce of both Lucifer and our power. But you were too strong. You were more of a risk than anything else."

"So, your plan this entire time was to break me down? Make me weak before taking away the only things left that I truly love?" I can hear whispering around us and realize that all of the angels can hear. That all of them are questioning what's going on.

"Sometimes breaking someone down until they have nothing left to live for is more effective than getting rid of them completely. Because then, we will own you." I shake my head at him, holding onto my sister with all of my might before looking over at Ahri again.

"You won't own me. If you do this... If you take away the two people I love most in this world, like you already took away my mate... I will never succumb to you. To Atlas. You can torture me every day. You can beat me and break me. But I will never do as you ask. I promise you of that."

Surya, since he seems to be the only disciple who ever has anything to say, kneels down in front of me, mere inches away from my face. His eyes drag down to Sophia before one of his snake-like fingers reaches out to touch her bloody face. I pull her towards me, trying to prevent his disgusting skin from corrupting her innocence.

"You say that now, little one. But... I think that will change once we start bringing in the rest. Every day, we will bring in innocent shadvir... innocent humans... and we will murder them. Right in front of you. One by one. In the most gruesome ways possible. Until you finally agree. Until you become mine."

"You're a monster. You think that Atlas is going to give you what you want? You think he's going to ever let you be anything more than his pet? You're wrong. And you're a fool. A naïve fucking bully who will never be anything more than that."

The slap that lands on my face is expected. And when I watch blood shoot out from my mouth, where one of his sharp rings cut my lip, I only laugh. "Like I said. Bully." I spit the blood at his face and his anger bubbles up even more inside of him.

"You're going to regret ever talking to me that way. Once we kill your little familiar and rip your pathetic human sister limb from limb, I'm going to make sure you never speak again." Surya grabs for Sophia and pulls her to him, ripping her from my arms.

"No! Don't fucking touch her!" I grab onto her foot and pull her back to me, but the minute I try to bring her back to me, pain erupts inside of my body. I try to fight it, pulling at my own magic, but find it absent. As if someone is draining the rest of it out of me. My eyes turn to Kamar and I find his hand reaching out as his eyes turn to the back of his head. He's doing this. He's blocking me from using my magic.

"Poor, weak Adrienne. Not as strong as we all thought now that her mate is dead, her familiar is being tortured to the point of being brain dead, and her pathetic little sister is dying in front of her. You're just a useless child who was given a God complex. That's it."

I grit my teeth as my bones feel like they are breaking inside of me. I try to look over at Ahri, but I can't. Surya won't let me. Instead, I have to watch as Surya brings Sophia to Blaze and drops her body in front of him. No. Not again. Please, don't do this again.

I try to close my eyes, desperate not to see this. Not to watch Blaze destroy another one of the people I love. But of course, Surya prevents me. I am left in the same position as I was before. Helpless and in pain.

"Say goodbye." Blaze speaks for the first time and the two simple words send a chill down my paralyzed spine. I stare at Sophia's blank, sleeping face, and do exactly as he instructs. I say goodbye.

I'm so sorry for everything. For failing. For putting you in danger. For letting something come between us. I forgive you and I pray you forgive me. Until we meet again, baby sister. I love you forever.

And then I watch as Blaze smiles wickedly at me before his hands reach for Sophia's head. They clamp around her bloody neck, ready to rip it straight from her body.

Suddenly, the arena rumbles and shakes around us. The disciples stumble in their spots, falling to the floor, and finally, I'm let out of my trance. I take advantage of it, standing up and feeling Ahri run up behind me, where he places a hand on my shoulder.

With Ahri by my side, I feel my magic bubbling back and push all of it forward. I throw the power of pain and mind control into the air and hit all three of them at the same time, freezing them in their spots and pushing as much pain and suffering into them as possible.

The ground continues to shake around us but I don't stumble as I make my way to them. I don't falter or cower in fear of what could be happening. The screams of all of the terrified, confused angels, assault my ears but go unnoticed.

"I should burn you three to ash!" I scream out the words, feeling my hellfire pulsing inside of me. I know my eyes are glowing red, I can feel the heat behind my irises. "I should torture and break you down until you are begging me for salvation!" I can see the fear in their eyes hidden behind the pain.

We make it to Sophia and Ahri reaches down to pick her up without me having to ask. He holds her carefully in his arms, trying not to touch any of her bad wounds. I keep my attention on the disciples. The three men who now look like children below me.

"I should make you hurt, the way you've made so many hurt before. I should take pleasure in giving you such pain, the way you three have done with me. With Sophia. With all of the people I love!"

I let the fire tickle my fingers before it engulfs my hands completely, begging me to let it loose. To let it find something, or rather someone, to eat up. And part of me desperately wants to. To destroy this entire world. To kill every last one of the monsters that took part in these games. That watched and laughed as we fought for our lives.

"But, I won't. Because I'm nothing like you. I will not use my powers for evil. I will not determine the fate of thousands of people's lives. I will not stoop to your level." I let the fire dissipate and extinguish from my fingers, but keep the three of them frozen on the ground.

The minute my fire disappears, the arena stops shaking. Hushed whispers fill the room as Atlas's loud shouting replaces mine. "You fucking bitch! All of the work I put into this! The years I spent trying to finish what I started! How fucking dare you?" It's so loud I have to cover my ears with my hands. His voice booms off of every wall and invades every inch of my soul. He's everywhere yet nowhere at the same time and I can feel the anger and hatred radiating off of him.

I have no idea what he's talking about but I can tell he's about to attack. I can feel the palpable danger floating through the air. "Ahri, get her out of here! Please!" I scream at him and wave a hand for him to leave. I can see he wants to argue, he wants to stay by me, but in the end, he trusts me. And he runs toward one of the open doors with Sophia in his arms.

The minute Ahri disappears, Atlas comes running out of one of the other doors, straight for me. His muscles ripple with each step and I can see the fire burning under his skin. He's so angry that he's letting his imignis shine through. The power he kept dormant for centuries so Lucifer would take the blame.

I smile to myself as he comes to a stop in front of me, his breathing shallow and jagged. "I have no idea what you're talking about but I'm enjoying this little show of yours, Atlas." I try to instigate him. Anger him more. So he finally lets his imignis loose. So all of the angels will see the liar he is.

"You destroyed it! I don't know how you did. I don't know what the fuck you're playing at here. But you're not walking out of this arena alive." His uncontrollable anger makes him weak. Vulnerable.

"I have been fighting in this little game of yours. I have been trying to keep myself and the ones I love alive! I don't know what you're talking about." I feel myself getting weaker as I talk to him and hold the three disciples in their place at the same time. My magic is faltering and crying out inside of me.

"Stop fucking lying! You're a disgrace, Adrienne Blackwell. You will never be good enough to be one of us. You are no angel! You are a creature straight from hell! Something unworthy. Something that needs to be exterminated."

He moves quick, throwing a flaming ball of bright fire straight for me. In order to dodge it, I have to let go of my hold on the disciples. I just barely dodge the fire ball as my body rolls across the hard floor. I right myself just in time for the next to come spiraling towards me. I try to dodge this one but it hits my foot and searing pain engulfs my skin.

I feel the fire eating away at my flesh, refusing to stop until there's nothing left, but I can't focus on that. I need to stay alive. I need to get out of this. Somehow. I put clype around my body but my clype goes in and out, fading as my magic pulses inside of me. I'm too weak without Ahri or Nox by my side.

Blazes hand reaches through the clype when it goes out again and clamps around my neck. At the same time, Surya hits me with a wave of pain and my body freezes, unable to move against the pull Blaze has on me. He drags me to my feet until I'm suspended in the air.

The grip he has on my neck steals the oxygen from my lungs. I'm helpless now. Unable to fight. Unable to breathe. Unable to think of a way out of this. In the distance, I swear I hear people screaming my name in the crowd. So close, yet so far.

"The fact that you, this pathetic little whore, managed to destroy my curse right underneath my nose... And yet, you can't even fight off these three imbeciles! It's a disgrace! You don't deserve to breathe the same air as us."

I watch, since that's all I can do, as Atlas creates a huge ball of fire in his hands, letting it grow bigger and bigger, ready to throw it straight at me. I try to close my eyes, not wanting to look at

Atlas as he burns me to a crisp, but I can't look away. They make me watch, the last few seconds of my life being poisoned by his sickening face.

"If you throw that, you're going to regret it, Atlas." His voice seems to surprise Atlas as much as it surprises me. Suddenly, the pain from Surya stops, as if I have been shielded. As if someone put clype around my body.

"Put her down, Blaze." Lucifer's voice is commanding and without question, Blaze listens, clearly under a mind control trance from the devil himself. I take a deep breath as my body falls to the floor and the oxygen burns my throat and lungs.

Hands grab at me and at first, I try to pull away, until I see the face they belong to. A face I was worried I'd never see again. Onyx's brows are furrowed, but it doesn't take away from his beautiful features. The features I didn't realize I missed so much until this moment.

"Onyx?" The minute his name leaves my lips, he pulls me into his arms and squeezes me so tight, I find myself unable to breathe again. I hold onto him as tight as I can, desperate to be as close to him as possible. His heart beats against mine, just as fast and pounding as my own.

"It... it was you! You destroyed the curse. But... how? You're not strong enough!" Atlas sounds stunned, his voice booming through the arena and making me pull away from Onyx to see the interaction between him and Lucifer.

Lucifer stands confident and tall, his hands reaching out in two different directions. One is aimed at the disciples, and the other at Atlas, where all four of them stand, motionless. "You're right, Atlas. I, myself, was not strong enough to destroy it on my own. Not without killing everyone in its wake. But, with the help and support of all of them, we got rid of it for good."

He turns his attention to the doors leading into the arena and suddenly, all of the leaders of Ombra, and what looks like thousands of shadvir and demons come piling in. They stand together, strong and united, glaring Atlas down. I spot my mother and father, along with Ahri and Nox, no longer disguised, standing beside them.

Both of my men are staring right at me, pride shining through their contradicting irises. The irises that make up my own swirling ones. Two parts of me that I wouldn't be whole without.

When I look at Ahri, he must see the worry in my gaze and knows exactly what I'm thinking. *She's safe, my darling. She's being protected by Onyx's brother and his father. They have expertise in healing. She's okay.*

I sigh a breath of relief and send my thanks through our line before reaching for Nox's next. The minute I do, our song tickles my spine and from this distance, I see Nox's skin glowing. I look down at my own and see that same golden hue. The light of our love.

"You're all fools! You think you can take me down? Take the angels down? Even with all of you, we are stronger! I made you! And I can destroy you just as fast!" He's spiraling. I can hear the panic in his voice, see the fear in his eyes.

"You may have created them, Atlas. But I liberated them. I educated them. Strength comes from knowledge. Power comes from honesty. You have neither. Which makes you the weakest of us all." Lucifer speaks so eloquently. So calmly. If I were him, after what he did to Ayla and Than, I'd have ripped his throat out already.

"Angels! Attack these imposters! Before they destroy everything we have created! Before the destroy us!" Atlas tries to look up at the crowd of angels, but Lucifer still has a hold on him, preventing him from moving. "Do what Aiden would want! Save heaven!"

None of the angels move. They all glare down at Atlas, unwilling to help him. To take orders from him again. "Aiden, huh?" Lucifer speaks again. "Do you even know who Aiden is, Atlas?"

"What are you talking about? No one knows who Aiden is! He's an all-powerful being. He doesn't exist or walk in any of our worlds." He spits each word out in disgust.

"While you're not wrong, dear friend, you're also not right. Aiden is here with us. He always has been, but now more than ever. You see, when Aiden died over one thousand centuries ago, he made sure that there would always be a part of him in heaven. He put a spell on his soul so every angel born had a small piece of Aiden. All of the good and the pureness that he possessed. But there's more than just that. And I didn't know about it until just the other day. When He spoke to me for the last time. He told me, that upon his death, He made a promise. A promise to the Earth and heavens that He cared for so much. An eternal promise that can never be unbroken." We all wait, me especially, to hear what this promise is. To hear what Aiden did.

"That promise was that every one thousand centuries, He would walk the earth again. Not as himself, but as someone else. And if any of you recall, this year is the one thousandth century plus twenty-five years." Lucifer's gaze turns to me and I furrow my brows at him. What is he trying to say here? He's talking in riddles.

"Our beautiful Adrienne Blackwell. Aiden Ren, if you mix up the letters of her name." Everyone in the room gasps and whispers among themselves, but I'm too shocked and confused to do anything but stare at Lucifer with my mouth gaped open.

"Her? That pathetic, weak girl? You think I'm going to believe that? You're a liar! You always were! And a traitor! Why would Aiden ever choose to speak to you over me? He wouldn't!" Atlas's screaming again, and while I don't agree with what he's saying, I also don't understand what Lucifer is getting at.

"Lucifer... I'm not. There's no way I can be... I'm sorry, but I think you're wrong." I sound like a child when I speak, which only helps my case. The all-powerful God wouldn't sound like me. This weak and timid child that can't even hold her own against the people in this arena.

"My dear, you are so much stronger than you know. Stronger than any of us know. But without the throne, you won't be able to access any of it. Right now, you are at one of your weakest, power wise. You think this is all you are capable of, but there's so much more. More than any of us can comprehend."

Lucifer offers me a soft smile and it makes me feel calm. "What do you mean, without the throne? As in being Dark Lady of Morta and Ombra?"

"That's what I originally thought, but Aiden spoke to me in my dream. He told me everything. That you are meant to rule all of the worlds. That you are the all-powerful God and the minute you take the throne in heaven, you'll remember everything. That you will regain all of your powers."

"He... I heard a voice the other night. Telling me there wasn't time left. That we had to hurry. To save the world." I look down at the ground as I speak, trying to grasp all of this.

"Adrienne, that was your voice. You are of Aiden's spirit and deep down, that spirit must have been able to shine through for just a second." I think back to that night and remember not being able to place the voice. That it was neither male nor female and seemed more like an internal thought than anything else.

"This is absurd! Prove it! You can't, can you? I'm tired of this! Angels, attack these traitors! You're letting the devil hold your God powerless! Do something!" Atlas again tries to interact with his people, but no one speaks. That is, until one male voice squeaks out from the crowd. If... if what you say is true... take the crown and place it on her head. Maybe that would be enough to prove it? The crown belongs to the throne." He sounds so meek and small in the crowd but his words pack a punch.

"What a splendid idea, fellow angel. Thank you for offering up your theory." Lucifer looks right into his eyes and loyalty and respect flow through his pupils and into the singular angel. He has to feel it, since I can and I'm not even at the receiving end.

"You'll be punished for that, Felix!" Atlas screams out as Lucifer calmly walks toward him. Each step clacks against the cold floor and the closer he gets, the more fear permeates off of the pathetic God in front of us. He's terrified of Lucifer.

"His name's not Felix," I say it without thinking and suddenly, all eyes are on me. "His... his name is Dion." I don't know how I know that, but it sits in the back of my brain as a fact I can't forget. A fact that one would know as well as they would know how to count to ten. Engraved in your brain for the rest of your life.

"Would you like to explain how she knows that?" Lucifer speaks to Atlas directly, but the rest of us listen intently. "She seems just as surprised as you, don't you think?" He reaches the God and stops in front of him.

My eyes move up to the golden crown sitting on Atlas's head. If I'm being honest, I never really noticed it before. It sits there, falling to one side a bit. There are small diamonds strown throughout that remind me of constellations along with branches and leaves that dance across his forehead.

"If you don't mind, I'm going to borrow this for just a second." I can hear the smirk in Lucifer's voice as he carefully removes the fragile, golden crown from Atlas's head. Atlas looks like he's ready to murder him, and I wonder how he's still being controlled to stay still. Lucifer no longer looks like he's casting any spells.

I look at the rulers standing around us, and realize that all of them are staring intently at the God and his disciples. They are all using their powers on them too. Every last ruler is helping alongside Lucifer to make sure none of them can move. I turn back to Onyx but his eyes are only on me. He's using his clype. Protecting me.

Lucifer walks the distance to us and stops in front of me. His eyes shine with love and admiration, and I can't tell if it's actually for me or for the God he thinks I am. "May I?" he asks with a smile on his face.

I stand up, my legs shaky from both nerves and exhaustion, and lower my head with a nod. Slowly, so slowly in fact that I actually question if he's doing it, Lucifer places the cold gold crown on my head. I expect it to be big, but somehow, it fits like a glove.

I raise my head to look into his eyes, waiting for something to happen. Within a few seconds, the crown starts to heat up and squeeze my head. I reach up to pull it off, but no matter how many times I try to, it doesn't budge. Like it has already molded itself to my brain.

I start to hyperventilate, feeling the crown burning into my skull and making my brain feel like it's going to explode, when suddenly, my feet start to rise off the ground. I have no control and when I turn around, my wings aren't out.

Something strong and powerful radiates through me, leaving a nonstop pressure in my veins and bones until finally, it pops. My arms fly out and my back arches as the most intense pleasure courses through my body. Every ache and burn I had leaves. Every weak thought dissipates. Every morsel of self-doubt fades into oblivion.

The only thing left is power. Power so strong, so clear and abundant, my body doesn't feel like it can contain it. Like I'm too small for the amount of power coursing through me. But, when my feet hit the ground again, that power curls into itself and lets me breathe. It lets me think clearly and lets my heart beat at a normal pace.

I'm glad you finally know the truth. That voice, the same one I heard in my dream, floats through my mind and I know now that it belongs to Aiden's spirit. The spirit that now sits inside of me, strong and powerful.

I turn towards Lucifer and find his face pale and blank. He stares at me, completely in awe, before suddenly, he falls to the ground on his knees. And the minute he does, everyone else in the room follows suit. Besides Atlas and his disciples. While they are no longer being held captive, they simply stand there, staring at me in awe.

"It... it can't be. It's not possible." I turn my attention to Atlas and glare at him as a smile takes over my face. Suddenly, an array of images flash through my mind. All of the bad, evil, and corrupt things he has done as a ruler.

"You have created this illusion that has divided our worlds forever. You fought against every pure thought instilled in your brain until there were none left. And then you sent one of the most kind hearted angels to a world that never should have existed."

Atlas's eyes are huge, staring straight at me and unmoving. I walk toward him, feeling strong and confident. Feeling more like myself than I ever have in my life. Feeling alive.

"He tried to kill me. He deserved to be banished," he says it breathlessly, still staring at me, unblinking, like I don't exist. Like I'm just a figment of his imagination.

"Rightfully so. You tricked him. You took his wings. The love of his life died because of your deceit. He was trying to avenge her death and save the humans from what you had planned. And for that, you banished him to a place no man should ever have to endure. A place of death and darkness and pain. And yet... what did he do? He created a world of equality. He turned a world of darkness into a world filled with light that will never go out. He thrived and survived with what he had." I now stand inches away from Atlas, his height much taller than mine and somehow, he seems so much smaller.

"He's the devil. A traitor who needed to be punished. I don't regret what I did. And I'm not scared of y-you." His voice shakes with the last word, contradicting his statement.

"He's the devil because you made him that. The devil had no standing until you created the word and reputation. And I don't want you to be scared of me. I want you to respect me. To respect everyone in this room. You aren't better than any other angel here. I want heaven to go back to the pure world it once was. To a place we can all be proud of."

He shakes his head with a smirk. "I'm done with this conversation." Without hesitation, he sends a flaming ball of fire directly at me. My first instinct is to dodge it, but I'm too late. The burning magic engulfs me in seconds and I flinch, squeezing my eyes shut as I wait for the pain to hit me. For the never-ending searing to take over my skin and burn away every layer of flesh and muscle until there's only bone left.

Except, it never comes. Instead, a warm, comforting heat takes over like a blanket being wrapped around me. I open my eyes and look down at my body, gasping when I see it. The golden flames are now a glowing white as they flicker and wave against my skin. They don't burn me, they simply become a part of me. Caressing every inch of skin on my body.

"What the…" Atlas's mouth is gaped in fear and now, everyone that was bowing to me is staring at the flames engulfing my body. It's the most beautiful thing I've ever seen. And with each flicker of the flames, my power feels stronger. Like the fire is feeding me. Replenishing me. Creating me.

I stare into Atlas's eyes, wordless, until he falls to the floor and bows down to me., finally surrendering. Finally giving up the fight. Finally ending this war. And the minute he does, the flames absorb into my skin.

I hear someone walking towards me and turn to find not only Lucifer coming up to me, but my three men following behind him. Lucifer smiles at me as Ahri, Nox, and Onyx stand at my backside, surrounding and protecting me.

"May I?" Lucifer asks with a hand suspended in the air, waiting for mine. I nod my head and place my hand in his. And then, he brings both of our hands high up into the air, his eyes looking around at the room of sparkling angels surrounding us.

"I give you, Adrienne Lilithia Blackwell! Our savior! Our friend! And our Goddess! All hail Goddess Ren!" My heart races in my chest with each word he says. His voice booms through the room, so loud that not a single soul could miss a word.

And after a moment of silence, thousands of voices ring out in unison, making chills run down my arms. Making my heart swell with love and pride. Making my eyes water with unshed tears of gratitude. Because this is how it was always meant to be. This is what we were all waiting for.

"All hail Goddess Ren!"

CHAPTER 29

ADRIENNE

It's been three weeks since everything. Since Lucifer destroyed the curse. Since I was made the ruler of all of our worlds. Since I created a prison full of only darkness for Atlas and his disciples. I felt it was necessary, just like I felt it necessary to take away their powers. I didn't absorb them, I am simply holding them in a vis lock until further notice.

While they deserve so much worse, I didn't want to kill them. I refuse to stoop to their level. But, they needed to be punished. And I knew no one would be safe unless they were contained.

This has definitely all been an adjustment. Something I wasn't ready for. I've been living in heaven for the last few weeks, along with Nox and Ahri. Onyx is planning on coming back, but he's currently trying to make sure his kingdom runs smoothly without his presence. Thanks to my dad, it shouldn't be a problem.

Against his wishes, my dad knew he had to return home. He begrudgingly left after only one day of time with me, which involved him crying and hugging me for the majority of it. He completely avoided my mother, which wasn't hard given she seemed to be avoiding him too.

"Ren? Lucifer's about to head out." Nox interrupts my thoughts as I sit, staring at myself in the mirror. I took over Atlas's old room, which is about the size of a football field and has barely anything in it besides a lot of white sitting areas. The vanity I'm at somehow has all of the makeup and hair products I could ever want, which I've been taking advantage of thoroughly.

He walks up behind me and places both of his hands on my shoulder, looking at my face in the mirror. "You look absolutely beautiful, Ren." His hands massage my shoulders as he speaks and I find myself closing my eyes, loving the way he kneads my tired skin. Being a Goddess is hard work and moments like these are what help me get through it.

"I'm scared for Lucifer to leave. He's been such a big help. What if I disappoint all of the angels? What if I mess something up? What if—"

"Adrienne Blackwell, no more what ifs. You were born to do this... literally. You're not going to mess up." He bends down and places a kiss against my head, letting me lean back and rest on his hard chest. The past few weeks have been so busy, we've barely had any time alone together. Which means, we still haven't had sex. I feel like I might explode if we don't soon.

His fingers continue to massage my shoulders and I can't control the soft moan that leaves my lips from how amazing it feels. He groans in answer and then brings his lips down to my ear.

"Keep moaning like that and we aren't going to make it to see him off, baby." His voice is gruff and thick, vibrating against my lobe and sending shivers down my spine.

"I'm sure we'll see him again soon, right?" He shakes his head with a soft laugh and the sound of it makes the hair on my neck stand at attention. Instead of responding, he spins me around in my chair so fast, the room blurs and I grab at him for dear life.

Within seconds, I'm suspended in his arms and my back presses up against the cold wall. I gasp at the feel of it, but he cuts it short with his lips slamming into me. His tongue caresses mine and it tastes of sugar, making him even more intoxicating than he already was.

"Fuck, I want to finish this so bad." He groans against my lips and presses his body against mine, squishing me between the wall and his hard ridges. He perfectly aligns himself against my sensitive core and pleasure courses through me as his huge length presses against me, teasing me.

"Then finish it," I say, breathlessly, grabbing at the buttons on his white shirt so I can take it off. My fingers fumble with the first few before he stops me, holding my hands with one of his while the other holds me up still.

"We will, Ren. I promise. But right now, we need to go say goodbye to Lucifer. Trust me, you aren't going to want to miss it." I look into his dark purple eyes, darting between the two and looking for even a semblance of a crack that will let this keep going.

But his eyes show his seriousness and I know I won't win this battle. Sighing, I nod my head and place a soft peck on his lips before he places me to the ground.

"Do I look okay in this?" I ask as I look down at my outfit. I opted out of a gown, instead going for a pair of wide leg white dress pants and a matching white blazer. It shows off the small white tank underneath and a sliver of my stomach.

"You look ethereal. Like nothing these worlds has ever seen." He was always the best at giving me compliments. Saying things no one else would. Most guys called me hot or sexy back on Earth. But not my Nox. He has a way with words.

We make our way through the large marble hallways, my eyes avoiding the dozens of pictures of previous Gods. Their stares freak me out. I feel like they are actually watching me, dissecting me and laughing at the joke of a God I am.

When we reach the foyer, I spot Lucifer descending one of the winding stairs in the room. He's wearing a black robe, and the minute I see it, I recognize it as Than's. My heart constricts at the thought. Than was like a brother to Lucifer. I know the thought of returning to hell without him by his side is painful.

Movement at the top of the stairs catches my eye and I look up to find my mother following behind Lucifer a few paces back. I asked her to stay for a while, rather than returning back home with my father and Onyx. She happily obliged, wanting to get to know me more and help me with adjusting.

She has successfully managed to do both. Every night she ends up in my room where she brushes my hair while we talk about the past. And every time I feel overwhelmed, she's one of the first people to grab my hand and help me through it. While our relationship isn't perfect, it's the best mother daughter dynamic I have ever had.

"Well, my dear, it seems it's time for us to leave now. How time flies when everything is right in the worlds." I turn my attention back to Lucifer when he speaks and smile at him. The destruction of the sun was one of the best things that could have happened to not only the magical worlds, but the human world as well.

While the humans felt the shake from the explosion, it was believed to be an earthquake. And as for the missing sun, we created an illusion using the heavenly light, so the humans never suspected a thing.

"Wait... what do you mean us?" I furrow my brows at him, confused by what he means. My mind instantly goes to Ahri, and I feel my heart clench in my chest. He can't be taking Ahri. That's not what we talked about. I can't be away from him. I'm not me without—

"My darling, I can hear you worrying in that bloody little head of yours from the other room. I'm not going anywhere. Not unless you're right by my side." Ahri makes my jump when he sneaks up behind me, placing one of his huge tatted arms across my shoulders.

"Then who?" I say as I lean into his touch.

"Me." My mother says the one word and I look at her in confusion. Her? She's going with Lucifer?

"I don't understand. Why would you go to hell? I thought you would go back to Ombra. To your home." She walks up to me and her hands reach for mine. I let her take them, staring into her eyes which are glossy from unshed tears.

"Sweetheart, that's not my home. It hasn't been for a long time. Your father isn't a bad man for what he did to me. He did what he needed to do, what he thought was best. But, I can't go back and live in that world. Not with him there, always watching me."

One single tear rolls down her smooth skin and my heart breaks for her. After talking the past few weeks, I sympathize with her. She's a hopeless romantic. She never loved my father and it was hard for her to accept the pregnancy, especially after she was tricked into loving someone else. I can't imagine how hard it was to live through every day alone after my father locked her up.

"Then stay here with me. You don't have to leave. You are welcome here forever if that's what you want." I don't ever want her to feel unwelcome. Not after she did for twenty-five years. My home is her home.

"I know, sweet girl. And as much as I want to be by your side every day, I need to follow my heart. Just as you have. I've been so lonely for too long. I desperately want to make up for it and try to live." Her eyes dart between Ahri and Nox as she speaks and then it all hits me at once.

"Your heart... you and Lucifer?" I look up at Lucifer who is slowly walking towards us. He has a relaxed smile on his face and when he reaches my mother, one of his hands moves to her back in a comforting yet protective manner.

"I haven't felt this way in a long time, Adrienne. And your mother agrees. We don't know what the future will hold, and we don't know if this will work, but we are too old not to try. We are too old to wait and let time continue on without taking a risk. Especially now that my immortality is gone."

I bite my lip, feeling like that part is somehow my fault. Aiden took Lucifer's immortality in return for breaking the curse of Lucifer's powers in heaven and the other worlds. Now that I know Aiden is a part of me, I feel responsible. "Yeah... I'm sorry about that one."

"My dear, it was the best thing I could have asked for. No one wants to live forever, watching their loved ones pass before them. Taking my immortality is a blessing I will never forget." His eyes turn to look at my mother and they sparkle with admiration.

I smile at his words, nodding my head in understanding. "Well... I'm going to miss you both." I try to conceal my emotions but my lip wobbles as my voice shakes. My mom pulls me in to her arms and squeezes me in a tight hug, which only makes a tear form in my eye.

"Oh, Adrienne. I love you and I'll be back to visit soon. I promise you. Now that I have you, I will never ever let you go, you hear me? I'm so proud to call you my daughter." I sniffle, taking in every soft whisper she presses to my ear. And then I say something I haven't said to her yet. Something I never thought I would say to my mom.

"I love you too."

After saying my goodbyes to Lucifer and my mom, I make my way upstairs to one of the guest rooms, where Sophia has been staying. She's completely healed, thanks to my magic and the help of some extremely attentive and motherly angels.

Unfortunately, because she was so exhausted from healing, I haven't been able to talk to her much. She tends to sleep most of the day, and when she's awake, I'm usually up to my eyeballs in work. I didn't realize how much work being a God was. Every issue with the angels and humans is directed straight to me.

Knocking on the door, I let myself in when I hear her soft voice on the other side. I expect her to by lying in the huge white bed that resides in the middle of the room, but instead, she's folding up a blanket and cleaning up the room.

"What are you doing? Shouldn't you be in bed?" I make my way to my petite blonde-haired sister and find myself jealous of the comfy white sweats and matching hoodie she's able to wear. I haven't worn anything like that since getting here and I'm starting to miss the luxury of a good pair of sweats.

"I'm all healed up. Full recovery, thanks to you." She smiles at me quickly before focusing her attention back on the plush throw she's folding into squares. I walk up to her and grab the blanket, removing it from her grasp. Placing it on the bed, I then lead her to sit down on it with me.

She sighs and I can feel her nerves radiating off of her. "What's wrong?" I question her as she fidgets with her fingers.

"I have to go home, Willo... I mean Adrienne." I grit my teeth at how she uses my new name. I don't like it. Not with her.

"Phia, please don't stop calling me Willow. I'm still the sister you grew up with. That hasn't changed, so my name shouldn't either when it comes to us. And what are you talking about? Why do you have to go home so soon?"

"Soon? Low, I've been missing from school for the last three weeks now. I'm most likely expelled. Plus, when the angels came and took me from Earth, I was sleeping at my friend Carly's house. She is probably losing her mind. She probably called the cops. And if she didn't, Sam..." She cuts off with the name and then looks up at me with wide eyes.

I wait for the jealousy, for the anger at the mention of Dr. Archer, but it doesn't come. "You can say his name, Sophia. I promise you, I am supportive of whatever happens between the two of you. I've moved on, and then some. I have enough testosterone to last me three lifetimes, I don't need to worry about anyone else." She laughs at my honesty and I join in with a chuckle.

"Yeah, you do have your handfuls with those two. Or... is it three?" She raises a brow at me and I smirk back.

"I can't believe I'm saying this, but it's three. I couldn't let any of them go if I wanted to. They've seared themselves into my heart."

"Just your heart, huh?" She nudges me and wiggles her brows suggestively. She knows who I used to be. The girl that screwed guys on the first date and then threw them to the curb.

"Actually? Yeah... I haven't had sex with any of them yet..." Her eyes go wide again and I roll my own at her astonishment. "Oh, stop. It's not *that* surprising. I can behave myself, you know."

"I just wasn't expecting that answer, that's all. I mean, with the way they look at you and of course, the way they look in general, I figured you guys have been jumping each other's bones for weeks."

"Trust me, I desperately want to. But life hasn't exactly been... calm?" I breathe out a laugh before continuing. "There's just no time in the day and when we go to sleep, I'm so exhausted that I fall asleep the minute my head hits the pillow."

"Do they both sleep with you?" I knew that question was coming next.

"They both refuse to leave my side, so yeah. I'm surprised they aren't here right now. But they've been respectful about how tired I am. How busy I am. They never push me to do anything and I think they are both exhausted themselves as well."

I bite my lip, realizing how sad that sounds. We are finally able to be together, no longer fighting for our lives, and rather than screwing like bunnies like I wanted to, we are too tired to do anything but barely cuddle. Something needs to change. And I'm going to change it.

"Stay tonight. We'll have one last celebration and drink wine all night like we used to and then you can leave in the morning. Please?" I have no idea what day it is at this point, but I'm hoping it's a weekend so she won't miss more. And if she does, I'll just compel her dean to forget about this little leave of absence.

"Fine. One more night. But no work, okay? Just fun. We both need a little fun."

Oh, trust me... I'll be having fun tonight.

CHAPTER 30

ADRIENNE

I managed to run from the rest of my duties before dinner. Then I locked myself away in my room, along with Sophia, Nox, and Ahri. We opened up the huge marble patio doors, letting the soft breeze flow through the room, and popped the corks on multiple bottles of wine.

"So, how'd you manage to get the workaholic to take a break?" Ahri is sitting on one of the white plush sofas out on the patio, where the rest of us are headed now. He directs his question to Sophia, who already has a glassy look in her eyes.

"Just had to threaten her with my leaving, and boom. She begs me to stay and get wine drunk with her. You're welcome." She smirks back at my hulking, long haired familiar and he shakes his head back at her.

"I knew I'd like you, Sophia. Thanks for giving us our girl back." I glare at him and rather than sitting at the edge of the sectional like I was planning, I make my way to him and plop down on his lap.

"I haven't left and you've been just as busy as me, ass." I wrap an arm around his thick neck and he circles my waist with his arms, holding me hostage. His warmth seeps into me and if we were alone right now, or at least, lacking Sophia, this would be a lot less innocent.

"Sure, my darling. Whatever you say." He places a kiss against my shoulder at the same time that Nox comes and sits down right next to us. He grabs my feet and places my legs up on his lap.

"Do you agree with him, Nox?" I squint my eyes in the direction of my curly haired mate, his violet eyes finding mine as his smirk widens between his dark stubble.

"Do I normally agree with Ahriman Reaper, Ren?" I smile, thankful that he's on my side, even if it's just a joke. "That being said, you could definitely use a break from your workaholism." He winks at me before returning the high five Ahri has aimed at him and I roll my eyes.

"I think I prefer when the two of you aren't getting along." I chug the rest of my wine and enjoy the tiny buzz circulating through my brain. I know they're right. I've been spreading myself thin the last few weeks. We desperately needed a night like this.

"So, what does everyone think of heaven? Is it everything you ever dreamed of and more?" I look out over the city as I ask my question. The courtyard in front of us is lit by a soft white glow, the ground showing the clouds and sky below. All of the homes surrounding the yard are marble and match each other perfectly, with their Greek architecture.

I look up at the sky and find the stars staring straight at us, so close I feel like I could touch them. All of the souls of those who have passed. The ones we have lost, watching down on us. I picture Nox's dad up there along with Than.

"It's something, that's for sure. But I can't quite get the bad taste out of my mouth after how I arrived here." Sophia is the first to respond. She stands from her seat on the opposite side of the sectional, pouring me some more of the orange, glittering wine.

"Oh, being tortured almost to death isn't your cup of tea?" Ahri jokes with her and Sophia shakes her head at him with a smile.

"You're a funny little kitty cat, aren't you?" I choke on my wine with her come back and practically spit it all over both of my men. Nox laughs along with me as Ahri glares at Sophia, no real malice behind the stare.

"I thought you said your sister was nice." Ahri directs his question at me.

"Almost dying changes a person. I mean look at me. I went from hating your guts to loving—"

I stop myself before I finish, not meaning for the words to slip out here, in front of everyone. Ahri's hands grip my hips tighter and everyone else remains silent. Nox clears his throat and moves my legs off of him.

"Hey, Sophia? Would you mind helping me pick out our next bottle? There's a wine cellar just down the hall." Nerves fill me instantly, worried that Nox is upset with my admission. But within seconds, I feel him dancing along our magical string, telling me he loves me and he's not mad at all. He's just giving us space.

They walk out of the room and the minute my bedroom door shuts behind them, Ahri spins me around on his lap. He forces me to straddle him, his red eyes searing into mine, leaving a burning hole that will definitely leave a scar.

"Finish that sentence, Adrienne." His voice is breathless as his pupils dart between my eyes and lips.

I swallow hard, overcome with the intensity of so many emotions coursing from his body into mine. "I love you, Ahriman Reaper." The minute I say it, I watch his circular pupils flash into the feline slits I have only seen once, before going back to normal.

And then his lips are on mine. His hands are holding onto my hips so tight, I swear I will forever have his fingertips marking my skin. Not that it bothers me. The more of Ahri on me, the better. I'm desperate to get more of his markings on my body. Desperate to be marked by him for all to see.

He pulls away from me for a second, breathing heavy against my lips. "I have loved you since the moment I heard your first cry. Twenty-five years ago. At that moment, all I wanted was to rid myself from your brain so I could protect you. I knew then I would burn the world to keep you safe. I would sacrifice myself if it meant seeing you smile again.

"I love your pure heart. I love your bloody anger that is usually directed at me." I laugh through the tears forming in my eyes. "I love your humor. I love your confidence. I love each and every one of your insecurities. Simply because each one of them makes you, you. And I will only ever love you for the rest of my pathetic existence. With every cell in my body. I have no purpose in life besides loving you, Adrienne Blackwell."

He wipes the tears from my eyes and then rests his forehead against mine, our breath mingling together as one. "Damnit, Ahri." I sniffle once and then continue. "Why do you always have to one up me?"

This earns me a laugh before his lips form to mine again. The perfect match. The lips of a man I have hated for most of my life, that perfectly mold to mine. I place my hands on his thick beard and pull him away again, needing to say something else.

"You already know I love Nox, too... and I think..." I cut off, not knowing if I should say it out loud.

"Bloody hell, darling. I already know you love that sarcastic prick." He's referring to Onyx and I can't help but snort. "I've known how you have felt about all of us for a long time now. I just needed you to say it when you were ready. I'm here for it all. I promise."

"I love you, Ahriman Reaper."

"I love you to hell and back, my darling."

A KNOCK ON THE DOOR PULLS US APART AFTER WHAT FEELS LIKE hours of pouring our souls into each other through our lips. "Guess who we ran into." Nox rolls his eyes when he walks back into the room, holding two more bottles of wine. Sophia follows behind him carrying another one and I wait for someone else to enter.

His blonde hair is the first thing I see and then his lilac eyes land on me. When they do, his smile broadens across his face and I swear I can feel his relief flow through the room. I stand, removing myself from Ahri's lap, and run over to Onyx.

He catches me in his arms, twirling me around the room without hesitation. "I wasn't expecting this kind of welcome, but I'm definitely not complaining." He sets me back down on the ground and I place a kiss against his lips. It's a simple peck, but I see the surprise and pure happiness bloom behind his purple irises.

"I missed you," I say, the wine coursing through my veins and making me both confident and a bit over the top.

"I missed you too, Adrienne. I always do." His eyes scan the room and then stop on the many empty bottles of wine. "Is our Goddess a little drunk?" He raises a brow at me but his lips form a soft smile.

"The wine here literally sparkles, dude. What do you expect? For me *not* to drink it?" he chuckles low before placing another soft kiss against my forehead this time.

"First off, you're so damn adorable. And second off, never call me dude again." We pull apart as Nox hands him a glass of wine and Ahri comes over and shakes his hand.

I watch the scene play out before me. The light glow from the heavenly light permeating through the room and casting an iridescent sheen on everything. The laughter bubbling out of all three of my men's chests as Onyx makes a lighthearted joke. Their eyes all turning to me at random moments, love and pure adoration beaming from each one of them.

And then, Sophia hooks her arm through mine, placing her head against my shoulder. And I realize, this moment, right here, right now, is all I've ever wanted. To be happy and surrounded by the people I love. To love, and be loved unconditionally. To feel at home and at peace, not because of where I am, but because of who I'm with.

This right here, was the end game all along. And finally, after a lifetime of searching for it, I found where I belong.

And who I belong with.

The End

EPILOGUE

(DON'T WORRY, IT'S DIRTY)

That same night
NOX

After hours of drinking wine, we are all tipsy and full of uncontrollable laughter. I haven't been able to take my eyes off of her. She glows with this addicting light that practically spills from her soft skin.

Our eyes meet for the millionth time tonight, and behind her glassy ones, I see promises of something more. Promises of something that we haven't done yet. Something I've desperately wanted to do for years.

"Well, I'm getting pretty tired." Adrienne puts her arms up in the air, faking a yawn and an overexaggerated stretch. "Do you all mind if I sleep alone tonight? I'm exhausted and kind of feel like hogging the bed."

While a bit of disappointment fills me, I oblige, along with Ahri and Onyx. Not that Onyx expected to share a bed with her in the first place. He hasn't been doing it like Ahri and I have the past few weeks.

Everyone says their goodbyes, Sophia going first as she hugs her sister tight and promises to have breakfast with her in the morning. Then, Onyx and Ahri go next, both placing a kiss against my mate's perfect lips. I catch the quiet *I love you's* that are exchanged between Ahri and Ren and search for jealousy, but come back empty handed. Instead, my heart squeezes at the thought of another person caring for her so much.

Finally, it's my turn to say goodnight to her. I walk up to her and cup her face with my hands, staring into her glimmering rainbow eyes of purples, reds, and whites. She's the most beautiful creature I have ever laid my eyes on. From her dark flowing hair down to her tan little toes, every morsel of this woman is addictive and downright sinful.

"Good night, my princess. I love you, forever and always." I place a kiss against her lips before she can answer, but she pulls away from me slightly.

"And where do you think you're going?" One of her dark, manicured brows shoot up on her forehead and desire crawls down my spine.

"You said you wanted to sleep alone tonight."

"I want to sleep alone... with you." The insinuation in her voice sends blood rushing low in my body. God, this woman is like nothing I've ever encountered in my life. She places another soft kiss against my lips before pulling away from me and going to lock the door. When she turns toward me, her hands move down to the hem of her white tank top. She removed her blazer hours ago, leaving her in a flimsy tank and dress pants.

My eyes drop to her hands as she starts to peel the material off of her body. But I don't let it get too far. I stalk towards her and before she can get it passed her ribs, I have my hands on the shirt and I'm removing it for her.

I stare down at her chest, the thin white lace just barely revealing each of her pink nipples. I bring my hands behind her back and unclasp the two hooks, letting the bra fall to the floor beneath us and taking in her perfection. My hands find the soft, supple skin and the minute I touch each of her breasts, her skin starts to glow and her head falls back.

I squeeze and grope her chest, trying to ignore the raging hard on pressing against my pants so I can savor this moment. I want to take my time with her. I want to worship her body the way it deserves.

I place a soft kiss against her shoulder, her warm skin heating up my lips. Then, I travel across her collar bone, pulling barely audible moans from her mouth. She grabs onto my shoulders to steady herself as her knees buckle. I don't want her falling, so I pick her up and move us over to the bed. Carefully, I place her on her back and then I continue my perusal of her body with my lips.

When I reach her chest, I let my tongue glide across each one of her nipples, their pebbled peaks grazing against my teeth and making her squirm underneath me. I bite down on one as my hand massages the other one and then suck on the spot, letting my tongue sooth the pain.

My lips find their way down her toned abs. The line leading down her midsection, one of my favorite parts of her. So delicate and feminine, yet strong and capable. My lips kiss their way down the line as my hands hold her waist tight. She keeps squirming underneath me, but I refuse to let her go anywhere. She's all mine tonight. Every single part of her.

When I reach the hem of her pants, I do quick work at undoing the clasp and unzipping them before lowering the thick material down her legs. Her fucking legs that go on for miles and beg to be wrapped around me as I pound into her. I groan at the image, my cock twitching in my pants.

"I'm trying to take my time with you, princess. But you're making it so fucking hard." I breathe out each word as I lower my body onto hers and rub my hard length against her almost naked body. She gasps at the feeling, and I smile to myself. Her eyes are full of lust. Her mouth lulls open and her body hums with need.

"Don... don't take your time then. P-please, ju... just fuck me now." She barely gets the sentence out, my erection rocking against her stomach.

"Oh, princess. I'm going to fuck you all night long. But first, I need to taste you. I need to taste that pretty pussy and see if it's as delicious as the rest of your skin." She moans through my dirty words but I cut it short by placing a hard, wet kiss against her panting lips.

"Stay still for me, Ren. The more you move, the longer I take. Got it?" She nods her head and her body attempts to go still as I continue thrusts my hips against her. I watch her bite her lip and wish it was my teeth biting it instead. But I have other places to put my lips right now.

Moving back down her body, I position myself right over her tiny white thong. My hands go to her legs and I hook my hands behind both of her knees before spreading her wide for me. My eyes take in the fabric covering her and I can see her wetness soaking through the white lace and glistening against her inner thighs.

"Mmm, you're dripping for me, princess." I groan out the words and then bring my face down to her center, laying my tongue flat against her thong and dragging it all the way across it. I can already taste her through the fabric and she tastes like fucking candy. Sweet and addicting.

My teeth find the edge of the thin thong at her hip and I rip the delicate lace. She stays completely still but her breathing is heavy and the sounds that escape her throat are enough to bring a man to his knees. I do the same to the other side and finally, the fabric falls to the bed, revealing her perfectly pink pussy.

"Perfection." I whisper the word with my head dipped between her legs and my hot breath against her makes her legs tremble. I bring my head up to look at her and find her staring down at me. "No moving, remember?"

She groans and I swear she's on the verge of a tantrum but it only makes me chuckle. "My princess is so impatient." I look back down and with my mouth watering in anticipation, I bend down and run the pad of it along her slit. She fucking melts into my mouth, coating my tongue with her arousal and somehow making my dick even harder.

I circle my tongue around her clit and then suck it into my mouth, desperate to pull more moans and cries out of her. And like the good girl she is, she doesn't move a muscle. I feel her tensing underneath me, her body desperate to thrash and arch off the bed as I devour her with my mouth.

I slide my tongue against her again, enjoying every lick, and then circle her entrance before pushing my tongue inside of her pussy. She's so damn tight, even around my tongue. The cry that escapes her is guttural, and involuntarily, her back arches off the bed.

"Keep your legs spread wide for me," I say as I bring one hand up between her legs and hold her stomach down. I let my other hand join my mouth, ready to push her over the edge. "I want you to scream my name as you come on my tongue, understand?" She doesn't answer me, but I know she will do exactly what I ask her to do.

I shove one finger into her, before adding another and pumping in and out of her tightness. My tongue finds its way back to her sensitive clit, circling and sucking on it in rhythm with my fingers. Her walls pulse against me as her back tries to arch again, fighting against my hand holding her down. I feel her fingers thread through my hair, holding my mouth against her and preventing me from leaving. Trust me, I'm not going anywhere.

One more flick of my tongue as I curl my fingers up against her walls and she's gone. "Noxxxx!" She draws out my name with her scream and I turn my gaze towards her face, my finger still pumping in and out of her. She's glowing. So bright, so blinding, that I almost have to look away. But I don't. Because I would rather go blind than miss a second of this.

Her mouth hangs open and her eyes squeeze shut. Her body is shaking and trembling uncontrollably and her hand rips at my hair, threatening to pull the strands from my scalp. But the pain is welcome. And any bald spots she creates will only remind me of this exact moment.

When she finally comes down from her orgasm, I don't give her any time to recover from the exertion. As her body trembles underneath mine, I remove my pants and line myself up with her soaking wet center. As much as I want to fuck her hard, I also want to take this slow and stay deep inside of her for as long as possible.

The head of my throbbing cock just barely pushes into her wetness and I can't hold back my deep, animalistic groan. She feels like heaven. Like hell. Like everything good and bad at the same time.

Her fingers dig into my shoulders as I slowly, torturously, push into her. Each glorious inch that presses against her walls is better than the last. I'm shaking by the time I finally fill her completely, my cock being squeezed like a vice inside of her.

"You're so damn tight, Ren. Fuck. I wanted to go slow with you... I wanted to take my time... but..." I don't finish my sentence, unable to control my own body as my hips pull back, my cock almost exiting her body completely, before ramming into her hard enough to make the head board shake against the wall.

"Ahh!" she screams as her fingers press into me harder, breaking through the skin. She squeezes me tighter somehow, almost painfully so, but the heat of her walls sooths the ache. I can hear her arousal coating us both as I slam into her over and over again.

"Fuck yes, princess..." I drive into her again, arching my hips to make sure I get in as deep as possible. "Feel so good..." I pull one of her legs up and stretch her as far as she can go, opening her up even more for me. "That's my good girl... Take me all the way in."

She moans when I hit a spot deep inside of her and it only drives me to fuck her harder. I feel the sweat dripping off of me and onto her. I feel our string tingling and plucking deep in my spine, threatening to snap from the overload of our connection.

Two people shouldn't be able to feel this connected. Our hearts beat as one. Our bodies move as one. Our breath leaves one of us, only to enter the other. Everything in this moment is about the two of us. Fitting together perfectly. Feeling each other perfectly.

"I love you so much," I say the words through gritted teeth, my eyes looking down between us at where we connect. I watch my length drive into her, disappearing inside of her before coming back out glistening with everything Adrienne.

"I love you more." She barely gets the four words out before her back is arching off of the bed and her second orgasm takes over. She shakes underneath me as her pussy pulses so hard around my dick that I have to hold my breath from the sensation.

The light beaming off of both of us is too much to bear, so I close my eyes as my own release threatens to spill over. I pump into her tightness two more times before burying myself as deep as I can go and letting all of me fill her completely.

I barely hear the sounds escaping both of our mouths. I know it's not quiet. I know I'm groaning like a wild animal as she screams out in bliss. My hips rock into her with each spurt of my release until finally, there's nothing left. I can feel myself coating her walls. Filling her up. Marking her forever.

"Mine," I say the one word in a growl, keeping my now twitching and exhausted dick deep inside of her. I place a kiss against her lip, our sweaty skin touching and sticking together. "Your lips are mine. Your pussy is mine. Your heart is mine. Got it?" I know I have to share her with them, but in this moment, I'd like to pretend it's just me and her.

"Yes. All of me is yours. Forever and always."

"Forever and always, my princess."

EPILOGUE

PART TWO

Two Years Later
ADRIENNE

I look down at the gown I'm wearing, before wiping away invisible dirt. The dress is gorgeous, but way over the top for my liking. By now I thought I'd be used to this extravagant lifestyle, but apparently not.

The dress is floor length and made of shimmering golden light. It hugs my curves tight and then opens up at the top, showing off parts of my midsection and chest in swirls. The many black markings of Ahriman Reaper peak through the openings until it hits the top of my chest. It reaches up to my collarbone on one side while it cups my breast on the other.

There's a golden cape draped along my shoulders and my matching crown adorned with constellations and leaves sits upon the intricate braided updo. Stella did it for me. She's my main advisor, and also my best friend. She has been with me for the last year and a half and I don't know what I would do without her.

I turn my head to look at the braided hair that twists and turns until it forms a messy, curled bun at the back of my head. Whisps of curled black tendrils tickle my face and I can already tell they are going to annoy me all night long.

My makeup is extravagant. My eyes are engulfed in a smokey black color that carries shimmering gold on top of it. My lips are a dark red and my contour makes my face look both dangerous and feminine at the same time.

Stella is talented in every way. From makeup artist, to hair stylist, to history buff, she manages to do everything better than anyone I've ever met.

As if she could read my thoughts, I hear a soft knock on my door before she walks into the room. I turn my head and smile at her, taking in her pretty features.

She's blonde and pale, like all of the other angels, but her gray eyes have a certain sparkle to them that almost make them look blue. She reminds me a little of my sister in that way. Especially with her small frame and shy demeanor.

"You look absolutely breathtaking, Ren." She calls me by my nickname after I practically beat it into her head. I hate when people call me Goddess, especially those closest to me. I want to be their friend, not their ruler.

"Look who's talking! You look hot, Stel." Her pale skin turns crimson with my words and I can't help but laugh. She does look hot though. In her white a-line dress that reaches the floor and shows off her curves.

The angels always wear white. No matter how much I beg them to stop. It's a tradition they refuse to let go of. It makes me feel like a sore thumb when I have to wear dresses like this though. I guess that's kind of the point.

"Thank you. Are you ready? All of the guests have arrived." She walks up to me and fixes the cape on my shoulders, making sure it drapes across the floor correctly. Nerves start to fill me.

They are excited nerves, but nerves none the less. Today is a big day, and I can't wait to see everyone again.

"Yes. Where are the boys? Are they with him?" I wish I was with him right now, but I was rushed away to get ready. I do spend every waking moment with him so I couldn't necessarily argue.

"Nox is with him. Ahri and Onyx are right outside the door waiting for you." I smile, excited to see them even though it's only been an hour. What can I say? Every day I fall in love with them even more.

My stomach churns again with nausea and I beg it to stop. Tonight is supposed to be a celebration. A huge day with friends and family. A day to celebrate him.

"I want everyone here. I want to walk in as a family. Can you grab them for me?" She simply gives me a smile before nodding her head and walking out of the room. When she opens the door to walk out, Onyx and Ahri walk in.

My two most opposite of husbands. Ahri keeps his black hair at his normal long length, which is tucked behind one ear. His beard is thick and unruly, even though it was just trimmed. His muscles and tattoos that match mine can't be hidden under his black suit. The golden shirt underneath lacking a bow with three buttons undone to reveal his hard chest.

And then there's my Onyx. His blonde hair is perfectly styled, the sides short with the top slightly longer. His square jaw is bare and his light skin makes his lilac eyes pop. While he's not lacking in the muscle department whatsoever, his black suit hugs his toned body in the perfect tailored way. He has a black bow tie on his golden shirt and his crown is on securely placed on top of his head.

"Ahriman Reaper, where is your crown?" I raise a brow at him as my arms cross in front of me.

"You look absolutely ravishing too, my darling, thank you." His sarcasm flows towards me as his red eyes undress me under hooded lids. I squirm in my spot and even though I'm trying to stay serious, I can't help but smirk at my familiar.

"You know you both look amazing. But you need your crown. Otherwise, no one will know you're mine. And if another angel touches you, I might have to get ugly." He chuckles low at my comment and then pulls me into him.

"You don't think the matching tattoos that cover every single inch of both of our bodies is telling enough? Or the fact that thousands of magical beings in all of the kingdoms attended our wedding?" He places a kiss against my lips and then steps away from me, before pulling his gold crown out from behind his back and placing it on his head.

"I hate this bloody thing. It pokes into my forehead." He rolls his eyes before winking at me and pulling another smile from my lips.

"That's just because your head is abnormally large." Onyx chimes up before I can respond and I snort at his comeback. He walks up to me next before places his huge hands on either side of my face and kissing my lips softly. "You're the most beautiful woman I've ever seen, Adrienne."

I open my mouth to answer but Ahri interrupts me. "That just means I have a big brain. You know what they say about having a big brain, right? The bigger the brain the bigger the—

"Innocent ears!" Nox yells from the doorway and we all turn towards him. His curly brown hair hangs low on his forehead and his violet eyes take me in with a sparkle. His stubble is the perfect length, as always, and when my eyes move down to look at the suit that covers up the intricate markings that he too has all over his body, I get distracted. Because Nox isn't the one I want to look at right now.

No, I am more focused on the main reason we are all meeting tonight. The reason so many magical beings are joining us for a night of festivities. The love of my life that sends my heart into a sputtering mess every time I lay my eyes on him.

He's wearing his own mini suit, sleeping in Nox's arms. My heart clenches when I see his innocent little face, his lashes pressed together with his closed eyelids. The way his lips form a pout, pushed up against his daddy's jacket, a line of drool escaping from his slightly open lips. His dark curls resting on top of his head, matching Nox's perfectly.

Nathaniel Alexander Blackwell. Named after Than and Nox's father. The reason we are all gathering today. It's his first birthday. A day that every world is excited to celebrate. A day that reminds me of the first time I saw him. One year ago in the infirmary wing, pushing and screaming as hard as I possibly could, trying to get the stubborn little bug out of me.

During the entire pregnancy, I had no idea who the father was. Not that any of us cared. We all agreed that our baby was exactly that. Our baby. We all love him more than life itself and our son will never go a day without feeling like the most important little boy in all of the worlds. But the minute he finally came out of me, we all knew. He had Nox's hair and his dark purple eyes. Since then, his eyes have gained a bit of red and lilac as well.

If you couldn't guess, shortly after being with Nox, I ended up sleeping with Ahri and Onyx. There was so much sex in that time of my life. Between two of us, three of us, or even all four of us. Since Nathaniel was born, we haven't been doing it as much. We are all exhausted and busy with taking care of him and running multiple worlds. The memory of our wedding night, which will never leave me, drifts through my mind and takes me away for a minute.

"*That was... a lot,*" *I say as I throw myself down on my bed, completely exhausted and ready to sleep off the last twenty-four hours. It's crazy* to think that just two months ago I found out I was a Goddess and now I'm ruling all of the worlds and married to not just one, but three men.

"It's not over yet, my darling." Ahri's deep voice makes something inside of me flutter, but the events from today still ring through my brain. Stella made sure everything ran smooth, but the amount of champagne I drank, the tight corset I am wearing, and the hundreds of people I had to dance with at the reception are sending me into a downward spiral of sleep.

"I can't breathe." I suck in a breath and try to remove my corset myself, needing to rid this obscene white dress from my body. The train is twenty feet long, the skirt is thick and puffy, and the lace sleeves are just as tight as the corset that squeezes me to death. It's a beautiful dress, but it's not me.

"Let me help you with that." Onyx walks up to me on the bed, his eyes a darker color of lilac, the way they always get when he's turned on. I can feel each one of my husbands' desire floating through the room.

I hear the click of Onyx's pocket knife before he brings it right up to my cleavage, his eyes staring straight into mine. He lets the edge of the cold metal touch my skin and I gasp, before he slices down the corset in a perfectly straight line, releasing me from its tight hold.

"As beautiful as you looked in this dress, I much prefer seeing you like this. Naked and wanting." His voice is dark and I feel chills run down my spine. The sarcastic man I always knew turns much darker in the bedroom. Something I found out the first time we were together when he started choking me while fucking me hard. I fell in love with him even more that day.

My exposed breasts pebble from the cold chill in the air, or maybe it's because I can feel Ahri and Nox approaching us from either side of the bed. They all stare at me like starving animals looking at their next meal. Something they are about to devour and destroy.

Do you want to sleep, my darling? We can behave ourselves if you're too tired. Ahri speaks through our connection and I smile when I look at him on my right. Ahri, the brute, hulking man that he is, has turned into a big friendly giant when it comes to everything me. What I expected was going to be rough, controlling sex, turned out to be the most beautiful, soul shattering love making I have ever experienced.

I'm tired but I'm sure the three of you can wake me up. I shoot my thought back to him and he growls out loud, his red eyes flashing with lust before he bends down and places a kiss against my lips. He intensifies the kiss, his tongue darting into my mouth and tasting of sparkling wine.

I feel a wet heat on my nipple as Ahri kisses me before a sharp bite pricks it. I gasp into Ahri's mouth, knowing full well my Onyx is worshipping my chest as Ahri worships my lips. I feel two sets of hands near my waist, pulling on the now loose skirt that still sits on my hips.

Nox removes the huge, bulky material and throws it to the floor, before making quick work at my white lace underwear. He removes them with his fingers and then I feel a wet kiss against my hip bone.

My body tingles and spasms from the overstimulation from three gorgeous men worshipping my body. They each have their mouths on me, tasting me in different places and sending sparks through each nerve ending they pass.

Nox spreads my legs with his rough hands, holding them up high. I then feel him pass one of my legs off to Onyx, his grip obvious compared to Nox's on my other leg. Onyx grips my thigh tight and harsh. He brings it higher, testing my limits, making sure to stretch me wide so Nox has better access.

I moan and Ahri eats it up, my mind flashing with the images of what this scenario would look like to an outsider. One girl being devoured by three beasts. It would intimidate and scare most, but it's what I live for. What I crave. Being wanted, being needed by all of them. Sending all of them into oblivion at the same time.

The first contact of Nox's lips on my pussy sends my back arching off the bed. Onyx doesn't allow that though. He presses my back down hard against the mattress and bites my nipple again. The pain hurts at first until his warm lips suck on the spot and sooth the ache.

"Make her come, Nox. And then I want her mouth next." Onyx's deep voice vibrates against my body and I whimper into Ahri's mouth. Any time we have all been together, Onyx tends to be the one that takes control. That demands what he wants. It's such a weird dynamic that works so well.

Knowing exactly what Onyx plans to do with my mouth fuels me even further and I know I'm close. Nox shoves two of his fingers inside of me as his tongue circles my clit and I can't hold back my scream. Ahri pulls away, looking into my eyes as I come undone.

I feel both Onyx and Ahri staring daggers into me as my face contorts from pleasure. My body arches and shakes uncontrollably and I can feel my walls squeezing Nox's fingers, his mouth still devouring the orgasm that is passing through me like a tsunami.

"That's it. That's our good girl." Ahri's voice is even huskier than it normally is. He puts a hand in my hair and runs his fingers through it, massaging my scalp as the last remnants of my orgasm leave me.

"Our turn," Onyx speaks up and I swallow hard, already feeling another wave of pleasure coursing through my body at what his two words mean. They move as one, all of them switching positions like it's a well-choreographed dance.

Onyx flips me over, positioning me on my hands and knees. I shake, trying to hold myself up through my excitement. I turn my head and find Ahri behind me, his clothes somehow already removed from his muscular body. His tattoos stare straight into my soul, connecting perfectly with mine.

I then turn the other way and find Nox sitting back on the bed, staring at the scene playing out before him. He loves to watch. And once they're done, he always takes me for himself. Sends me into one last wave of ecstasy and claims me as his own.

"Let me see your face, Adrienne." Onyx speaks up and his fingers graze my chin, turning my attention towards him. He's kneeling in front of me, his cock standing at attention. His clothes are off as well, giving me ample opportunity to admire the hard ridges of his abs and thick biceps. "So beautiful," he says, his hand stroking his thick length already.

I look down at it and my mouth waters. A small bead of his desire glistens at the head and I lick my lips. Ahri's hands land on my ass, where he squeezes both of my cheeks before grabbing onto my waist with his huge hands. The anticipation of him filling me up makes me dizzy.

While all three of them are huge, Ahri is the biggest. The longest and the thickest, which always hurts in the best way whenever he enters me. I look up at Onyx through my lashes and his attention is on Ahri behind me.

"*Fill her up,*" he says the three words as a command and the minute the last word leaves his lips, Ahri slams into me from behind. I cry out and hang my head down, adjusting to his size. He stays still, his cock completely inside of me, deeper than anyone else ever has been. His hands massage my back and he lets my muscles relax and get used to him. Onyx, on the other hand, doesn't.

As my cry of pleasure still flows from my lips, Onyx grips my chin and brings my head up to look at him before he forces the head of his dick into my mouth. His skin is so soft yet rock solid. He guides himself between my lips, spreading them wide with his size.

"*Take me all the way in, Adrienne. Open that perfect little throat up for me.*" I do as I'm told, lust flowing through my veins and threatening to take me down with it. Ahri groans behind me and I feel him pull out of me before thrusting back in, the pain subsiding, replaced by intense pleasure.

They both start to move in unison, filling me up on either end before pulling back out and doing it over again. "*Look at me,*" Onyx says and I turn my gaze up to his perfect features. The desire flowing from him. The hair that was once perfect and now falls in his eyes.

"*So perfect. So fucking beautiful,*" he says through clenched teeth, his hips shaking as he fills my mouth over and over again. I gag on his size and his hand comes down to my throat, holding my head up with just enough pressure so I can't move.

Ahri grunts behind me, his body slapping against mine as his cock drives deep and pushes against my walls. Each thrust is better than the last. I turn my eyes toward Nox, since I can't move my head against Onyx's hand, and find him watching with a dangerous look in his eyes. He has a serious expression but I can see the raging hard on pressing against his dress pants. He acts so calm, when on the inside, I know the inner beast is banging and pounding to be let out.

"*Eyes. On. Me.*" Onyx instructs me to look back at him and I do just that. "*Good girl. I want to stare into your eyes as I come down your throat.*" I moan around his length, his dirty words sending me closer and closer to the inevitable.

"Fuck, my darling. You're squeezing me so tight." Ahri starts to pound into me harder. He grabs my thighs with both hands and spreads them apart before pressing down on my back, making me arch for him. "Oh god, yes," he says, his voice guttural as he shoves inside of me even deeper now.

I cry out, the pain and pleasure mixing together and becoming too much as the noises of both of my men take over the room. Their groans, their bodies slamming into mine, all of it becoming too much.

"Touch yourself. Now." Onyx squeezes my throat tighter and I shakily bring my hand down to my clit. My fingers just barely graze it and my body jerks from the sensitivity. The jerk makes Onyx slip even deeper into my throat, deeper than he ever has. He throws his head back with a moan and thrusts his hips, making sure to stay in that untouched spot in my throat.

I can't breathe, his cock so deep it prevents any air from passing. His hips pump in small movements as he savors the tightness of my throat. And then he pulls back out slightly and allows me to breathe.

"I'm going to come down your throat now, beautiful. I want you to swallow me down, understood?" I whimper again, tears now falling from my eyes but I manage to nod my head. I'm about to come too. I can feel myself at the precipice, about to free fall.

He thrusts in again, at the same time as Ahri, and then his hands grab at my face, holding me hostage so I can't move. He pushes into me and I close my lips around him as the first tremble of his cock fills my mouth with his release. He thrusts softly against my lips, each thrust carrying more of his sweetness until he goes still and his groans stop.

Ahri moves behind me still, his animalistic sounds getting more and more loud. He's about to come. And when I feel him pick up his speed, it sends me off. I swallow down Onyx as my orgasm crashes through me like an explosion. I scream out, my eyes shutting as my pussy squeezes Ahri.

I feel him slam into me so hard it sends me forward on the bed until my face presses into the mattress, right in front of Onyx. He pumps into me two more times and then his groan fills my ears, sounding like a wild animal. I feel his release fill me, warming me from the inside out. His cock pulses, giving me every last drop until it drips out of me and onto the bed.

When we both come to, the room is full of heavy breathing and racing hearts. I'm spent and so sensitive it hurts to even press my legs together. Ahri places a kiss against my ass as Onyx places a kiss against my forehead and I lay completely flat on the bed, so ready for sleep.

Movement next to me has me turning my head just in time to find Nox standing at the edge of the bed. He grabs my ankles before flipping me over and picking me up in his arms. He's naked now, and he holds me close to his body, his hard dick grazing against my sensitive core and making me gasp.

"My turn, princess." He walks us to the bathroom, straight for the big walk-in shower. He turns it on and steps into the stream, letting the water massage my sensitive skin. He presses my back against the wall and with one thrust of his hips, he shoves his cock into my wetness and bites down on my shoulder.

"Mine."

"Ren?" Nox's voice pulls me from my memory and I feel my cheeks blaze. Now is not the time to be thinking such intense thoughts. I feel my body reacting to the events I just imagined and I shake it off, needing to forget all of it for now. I smile at Nox and then look down at his hands again.

"Hi, my sweet boy." I walk up to Nox, my attention solely on our little Nate. His eyes open the minute he hears my voice and instead of crying, like most babies would upon waking up from a nap, he gurgles and smiles a huge gummy smile. He has two teeth sticking out of the top of his gums and they only make him more adorable.

I reach for him and put him in my arms before placing a kiss against Nox's lips. "You look gorgeous, princess." He uses the nickname he has always uses, even though I am no longer a princess. I smile at him and then look back at our son. The best thing that has ever happened to me. My everything.

"Are you ready for tonight? You're going to see everyone! Didi, Mimi, Coco, Auntie Phia, and your Uncle Ozzy!" His eyes brighten as I list off every name. We started calling Lucifer and my mom, Didi and Mimi so he could learn them quicker. Coco is for Cole, my dad, and then, of course, Sophia and Ozul, Onyx's brother. While he doesn't see them often, the time they get to spend together is always the most cherished time.

"Mama." His sweet voice fills the room and suddenly, all three of my men are surrounding us with smiles on their faces.

"No, Nay-Nay, you're supposed to say Dada. Say it with me. Da-Da." Ahri's baby talk is both adorable and hilarious. The toughest of them all is the most sappy when it comes to our bouncing boy. From the minute Nate's little fingers wrapped around Ahri's huge thumb, he was a goner.

"Mama," Nate says again and they all groan. The only words he says are Mama and Baba for his bottle. He refuses to say Dada, which is ironic since he is surrounded by three of them.

"Maybe next time, A." I wink at Ahri and he pinches my side, making me yelp. At that moment, Stella comes back in and gives me a smile.

"You guys ready? Everyone's waiting for you." I sigh, holding Nate close to me and taking a deep breath of his intoxicating baby smell. It's my new favorite smell, and yet, my stomach still churns with nausea from the nerves.

I don't want to spend the night handing him off between family and friends. I don't want people trying to get him to walk, since he hasn't taken his first steps yet, while everyone around is drinking. I just want to curl up in bed with my baby boy and our three protectors surrounding us. God, how I've changed in two years.

"Ready as we'll ever be, I guess." Nate takes that moment to place both of his hands on my cheeks and then open his mouth wide and engulf my chin between his slobbery lips. His little teeth gnaw at my skin but instead of hurting, it comforts me.

"I love you too, sweet boy. Let's go get this party over with so we can get in our pjs, okay?" He answers with an angelic giggle and then rubs his cheek against mine. He stays there the entire walk to the huge ball room.

The room that I hate. It's the stadium that I was once humiliated in. It's the arena that Ahri, Sophia, and I almost died in. But now, it's a massive ballroom. A room big enough for thousands of magical beings, and one singular human.

We walk through the huge, thirty foot double doors and the room around us lights up with smiles and bright, happy eyes. Every last person stares straight at my family, taking us all in.

The space is decorated in magical golden and white sparkling lights that glitter around the room. Every now and then, the lights spell out, *Happy Birthday Prince Nathaniel*. There are golden balloons the size of normal houses and pictures of our family suspended on the walls.

My eyes spot the white tables around the perimeter and I find myself wanting to sit down already. I'm so tired. But, instead, I bring my attention back to the huge marble dance floor, where everyone stands.

My eyes somehow spot Sophia in the crowd first, her eyes rimmed with tears already. Just seeing her blue eyes gives me the confidence I need to speak to everyone. "Thank you all for coming to our beautiful son, Nathaniel's, first birthday. Every last one of you means something to my family and we want you to party the night away! Dance, stuff your face, and drink until the heavenly light arises again!"

The crowd erupts into loud cheers and instead of scaring Nate, he claps and screams out with them. He's my little party animal. I guess he gets that from the old me.

With Ahri on one side of me, Nox on the other, and Onyx right behind us, we make our way through the room. The crowd splits in two so we can walk through until we reach the table at the far end of the room.

Stella wanted to put our table on a pedestal, for all to see, but I refused. I wanted us all to be on the same level. I wanted my family's table to be joined with all of the other ones. We are all equal. No one gets special treatment tonight. Except for, of course, my little Nate.

Sophia blocks our path when we pass her and I know exactly what she's going for. And so, the passing of my baby begins. "Gimme! Gimme! He's such a big boy! How is he already one?" Her hands reach for him and even though I know this is the beginning of the end of hundreds of people holding Nate, I pass him over. I adore how much she loves my son.

"I missed you, Phia," I say as Nate reaches for her and then giggles as he looks up at her face.

"I missed all of you guys so much! It's so hard going back home knowing you are all here and Natey is getting bigger and bigger every day. Earth is so boring compared to this place." She nuzzles her nose up against his and then looks back at me with pouty lips.

"Boring, huh? Does that mean a certain someone still isn't in the picture?" I raise a brow at her, questioning her about Sam. After she returned home, two years ago, they spoke to each other for a few weeks before they cut off communication completely. She never told me why or who did it, but I could see the sadness in her eyes when she told me.

"Nope. And I really don't want to talk about a-holes on such a big man's special day! Isn't that right, Bubba?" She raises him up in the air and then turns away from us and starts walking off with him.

"How does she end up stealing our son within ten seconds every time she's here?" Nox leans in to whisper into my ear. I look at him and jokingly roll my eyes.

"She's lonely. Doesn't have a man in her life so she's taking our little guy. Can you blame her?" He laughs and then his pinky grabs at mine and locks onto it. We walk forward, my eyes focusing on Sophia and Nate while trying to greet everyone we walk by. They all bow when I pass even though I always tell them not to.

"Would you like a drink, my darling?" Ahri leans in on my other side, his hand pressing into the small of my back. I can feel Onyx right behind me, close enough to feel his breath against my neck.

I debate on my answer, my stomach still nauseous and churning. "Yes, please. Maybe a glass of the golden ginger wine?" The alcohol will calm my nerves while the ginger soothes my stomach. It's a win win.

"Anything for you. How about you, mates? You need a bloody drink as much as I do? I don't feel like waiting for them to bring us a round." Nox and Onyx both agree and give him their orders before he walks off toward the bar.

It's a huge open bar where anyone can order anything you could ever imagine. There are also waiters circling around the room with flutes of sweet champagne. But, my Ahri is many things, and patient is not one of them. Unless he's with Nathaniel. He has more patience with him than even I do. I have a feeling it has to do with his name, since Than meant so much to him.

We reach our seats after what feels like hours and I finally take a seat at my spot. The table is adorned with gorgeous white and golden flowers along with all kinds of exotic fruits.

Turns out, that magical waterfall back in Ombra was simply a way for Atlas to keep tabs on everyone. It was never necessary. Every world can create their own food and we can simply use the waterfalls as ways to quickly get from one place to the next without going through Earth first.

Reaching for a pink pineapple slice, which was one of the first fruits I ever tried back in Ombra, I take a small bite and hope it calms my raging stomach. It doesn't help. If anything it makes it flip faster and more intensely. I don't get what's going on. I can't remember the last time I felt this sick.

"Sweetheart, you look stunning." My mom interrupts my thoughts and I feel tears fill my eyes when I take in her beauty. Her long black hair is tied back in a long pleat and the white gown she wears is satin and long, lying tight against her curves. She smiles a real, genuinely happy smile, and I no longer see the shadows in her violet eyes.

"Hi Mom," I say through my unexplainable emotion and stand to hug her. She squeezes me tight and when I look over her shoulder, I see the devil himself staring at us with his own smile. He walks towards us and I let go of my mom to hug him. He looks so happy, which makes my heart burst. They both deserve to be happy after the lives they have lived.

"It's so good to see you guys. Thank you for coming. We all missed you so much." It's been a few months since they were able to make it back here but it feels more like years. I always love having them both around. Gossiping with my mom is like no other and Lucifer always helps me with work. He's a natural born leader and all of the angels respect him so much.

"We missed you too. Let me guess, a little blonde human stole Nate away already?" Lucifer smirks and I can't help but laugh, nodding my head yes.

"How'd you guess? She had Nate in her arms seconds after we walked through the door. Come sit down, she'll bring him over here soon and you guys can get first dibs." We all sit down at the table and start chatting about nothing and everything.

Lucifer asks me about the war on Earth that I managed to prevent. It's so hard to keep humans at bay and at peace. Unfortunately, no matter how hard I try, Atlas's corruption on all of our worlds still shines through. And even though the majority of the angels support me, there are a few stragglers that like to cause chaos and want to free Atlas from captivity.

Ahri brings over our drinks at the same time my mom and I start talking about Nate's eating. I breastfed him for as long as I could, but after eight months, my supply diminished tremendously. I cried for weeks, desperate to continue that bond and connection we shared while I breast fed. But, in the end, I had to do what was best for him and start bottle feeding.

He also eats everything in sight. We started with real food around four months and the minute he tasted his first pink pineapple, he was hooked. He shoves any and all food we give him into his mouth, which shows with the many adorable rolls that cover his arms and legs.

"Ahem, do you mind if I join you all?" I look up at the interruption and find my dad standing there with a soft smile on his face. I stand up, walking over to him and engulf him in a huge hug.

"Hi, Daddy. I missed you."

"I missed you more, Adrienne." He joins us at the table, taking the open seat on the other side of my mom and I can't help but smile at how much has changed. They greet each other with a hug as my dad shakes Lucifer's hand. There's no hatred or anger anymore. It seems, our little boy has managed to bring peace to everyone's lives. He brought us all together more than I ever thought possible.

"Oh no, I see trouble." Onyx leans over and whispers in my ear, grabbing my attention from my parents. I look at him and find him staring out into the crowd with a raised brow. I follow his gaze and my eyes fall on his brother. He's very similar to Onyx with his blonde hair color and lilac eyes. But his hair falls longer, similar to Ahri's and he has a bit of scruff covering his square jaw.

I furrow my brows, confused as to why Ozul is trouble. He's become a part of the family and treats everyone with respect, even if he's the cockiest man I've ever met. But, then I notice what Ozul is staring at. Or rather, who he is staring at.

Sophia holds Nate up in the air, both of them dancing. Her tight white dress hugs her petite frame and with her hands up in the air, the V-neck cut of the dress practically spills her breasts from the top.

"Oh God. Please tell me he's just looking at Nate." I groan, not needing any family drama. I always knew Ozul thought Sophia was pretty, but Ozul thinks most women are pretty as long as they have tits and eyes. They don't spend much time together, but he was one of the people that helped nurse Sophia back to life over two years ago.

"If I know my brother, and I do, he has his sights set on something else. Or rather two somethings that are attached to a certain someone." I swat Onyx on the shoulder and he chuckles. "I bet you head that he's going to walk over there in the next ten seconds."

I look into his eyes and see the flash of lust, which sends a shiver down my spine. I lean in, whispering in his ear, "Deal. He walks over to Sophia in the next ten seconds and I'll suck you off until you come down my throat." He grips the drink in his hand tighter as I breathe against his lobe. I notice his jaw clench tight. "If he doesn't, your head will be between my legs as I hold you down by your hair."

He turns to look at me, his face contorted and clearly trying to act normal. I love how much I can affect him, affect all of them. "You got yourself a deal, wife. But just so you know, that's a win, win for me."

"Ditto," I say with a wink and then we turn out attention back to the scene at hand. Ozul continues to stare, sipping from the champagne flute in his hand.

THE HOLLOWS

"Ten, nine, eight, seven," I start my whispered countdown, not caring if he walks or not. I want either outcome at this point. I've been horny since that memory flashed through my mind.

He turns his attention towards the crowd for a minute, his jaw clenching the same way Onyx's does when he's thinking about something. "Six, five, four, three..."

Ozul turns his attention back to Sophia and then rights the white bow tie that resides on his neck. "Two..." He takes a step in her direction and I know already that I lost the bet. There's only one person his gait is pointed at. And it's my innocent little sister.

"Ha! I win!" Onyx claps his hands and hollers louder than he means to, grabbing the tables attention. He clears his throat and then rights his black tie before leaning into me and chuckling quietly. I laugh with him before he places a kiss against my forehead.

"I mean, do either of us really win though? Now we have to deal with that." I nod towards the two of them now engrossed in a conversation. Sophia has red cheeks and Ozul has a cocky smile on his face. But after a few seconds, they both laugh and Ozul places a hand on her back.

"I can assure you, Adrienne, anytime I get to fuck that perfect little mouth of yours, I win." He whispers it into my ear and I groan, feeling my insides clench with his words. This is not the time nor the place to be thinking such thoughts.

I take a huge gulp of my drink and suddenly, my stomach sends me a warning signal that it's about to reject the sparkling ginger wine. I put my hand on my stomach and take a deep, shaky breath, trying to settle the nausea.

"Hey, are you okay, my darling?" Ahri places his hand on mine from two spots over, reaching across Onyx. I nod my head, but the movement only makes the nausea worse.

"I think... I need to use the restroom. Excuse me." My tongue feels heavy as saliva floods my mouth and when I stand up, the room starts to spin around me. I feel an arm go around me and without looking I can tell it's Ahri. He quickly walks me out of the room, following the perimeter of the large space so we don't have to walk through people, until we make it back to our room. It's not a long walk, but it feels like forever.

I hear people rushing behind us but don't look to see who it is. I don't care right now. I need a toilet before I hurl right here on the floor.

The minute we cross the threshold into the bathroom, the first gag hits me and I just barely make it to the toilet before the little amount of food and liquid in my stomach empties itself into the porcelain. I heave a few times, until my stomach is completely empty and then I sit back. My head hits Ahri's chest, since he was kneeling behind me the entire time, rubbing my back.

"You okay, darling?" His words are quiet and full of worry. I nod my head but don't say anything, trying to wrack my brain as to what is going on. When's the last time I threw up? The last time I felt this sick?

"Sweetheart, are you okay? Can I get you a warm towel?" I turn to look at my mother, who is standing next to Onyx, both of their faces covered in worry. Nox is missing, but I know he's watching over Nate. I can feel him in my spine, sending his love and worry through our connection.

A thought crosses my mind as I look between Ahri and Onyx. "Mom? When was the last time you and Lucifer were here?" I question her and she furrows her brows at the random question.

"Um, about two months ago? Why?" My heart skips a beat and tears fill my eyes. I haven't had my period since the last time my mom was here. I haven't been this nauseous or thrown up since I was pregnant with Nate.

"What's going on in that head of yours?" Ahri rubs my shoulders and places a kiss against the top of my head. I look up at Onyx and see the realization in his eyes.

"You're late, aren't you?" he says, even though he already knows the answer.

"Late? For what?" I laugh and sniffle at the same time, loving how dense my Ahri can be. My mom laughs too, her own tears now filling her eyes as she places her hands over her mouth.

I turn to look at Ahri, his red eyes shining bright as he looks at me with love. My hand reaches up and cups his cheek, admiring everything that is him. I then look at Onyx, his lilac eyes rimmed with tears as a wobbly smile covers his lips. I reach a hand out for him at the same time that Nox comes rushing through the door, Nate in his arms.

I know he felt my excitement in our connection. That's why he came running. And as my family surrounds me, all three of my men kneeling before me, my son smiling as he reaches for me, and my mom crying tears of joy behind us, I know for a fact that I'm right.

I press my hand against my stomach, looking up between their three distinctively different irises. "Well, boys, it seems our little Nate is about to be a big brother. Only question is, what color eyes will she have?"

About the Author

Gillian Strong is the author of When a Rose Falls, After the Fall, and The Shadows. She is a part time author, part time Real Estate Agent, and full time mom of a beautiful two year old girl. Living in North Eastern Pennsylvania with her daughter, she spends late nights writing, taking advantage of the peace and quiet! In her free time, she loves to read romance and horror books, cook anything and everything, and spend quality time with her family.

For more books by G.L. Strong check out her website: www.glstrongbooks.com